For Andre

MW01170125

EKATERINA

THOMAS H. BRILLAT

Enjoy~ Tom

Ekaterina
Copyright © 2023 Thomas H. Brillat

Produced and printed by Stillwater River Publications.
All rights reserved. Written and produced in the
United States of America. This book may not be reproduced
or sold in any form without the expressed, written
permission of the author and publisher.

Visit our website at
www.StillwaterPress.com
for more information.

First Stillwater River Publications Edition

ISBN: 978-1-960505-04-0

Library of Congress Control Number: 2023903404

1 2 3 4 5 6 7 8 9 10
Written by Thomas H. Brillat.
Cover illustration and interior design by Elisha Gillette.
Published by Stillwater River Publications,
Pawtucket, RI, USA.

The views and opinions expressed
in this book are solely those of the author
and do not necessarily reflect the views
and opinions of the publisher.

For those seeking peace, freedom, and a better life.

Терпе́ние и труд всё перетру́т.
Nothing is impossible to a willing mind.
Literal: Patience and work will fray through anything.
—Russian Proverb

Love is of all passions the strongest, for it attacks simultaneously the head, the heart and the senses.
—Lao Tzu

ACKNOWLEDGEMENTS

I want to thank my wife, Susan Perkins Brillat, for her love, support, and understanding as I retreated to my computer for—what proved to be—long daily stretches over several years to write this story. And, of course, deep thanks and gratitude to my colleagues—the wonderful and talented participants of the Writers' Group at the Neighborhood Guild in South Kingstown, Rhode Island for their endless encouragement, helpful feedback, and, most of all, their friendship.

EKATERINA

based on a true story

1   DECEMBER 23, 2003
New York City

The cheers from the 2,804 classical music aficionados reverberated throughout the historic building. For seventy-five minutes, they had reveled in the spectacle within the revered ambiance of Isaac Stern Hall, the focal point of Mr. Carnegie's music hall. They had just witnessed the stunning debut of a prodigal talent on the world's grandest stage. It was Christmas Season, every seat filled and Sasha Danilova of Khabarovsk, Russia, had tested the full range of William Burnett Tuthill's considerable architectural skills. Tuthill, himself an accomplished cellist, had sought to ensure his design of the main theater would have acoustics enabling everyone in the audience to feel they were part of the performance. He wanted attendees in the last row of the highest balcony to hear a stage whisper. And he succeeded. The audience had been mesmerized. On this night, the fabled auditorium's curvilinear configuration offered every listener a gift beyond measure, a new voice—and it would live with each of them forever.

Quiet and respectful throughout the evening, the lucky crowd could no longer hold back their adoration. The patrons leaped out of their plush seats before the young songstress ran out of breath on her final note. The crowd exploded with cries of *Stunning! Magnificent!*

Bravo! It was a reaction so spontaneous and tumultuous it shook the venerable building. The members of the orchestra, unable to maintain their professional decorum, joined the chaotic throng in frenzied applause. Even the world-renowned maestro knelt on his pedestal in shocking admiration. Shouts of *encore, encore!* echoed loudly. Everyone knew they had just heard one of the world's great voices—a talent so raw, a voice so overpowering, it had thrust them deep into the soft padding of their velvet seats, commanded their attention, and demanded their admiration, all while bringing tears of amazement and wonder to their eyes. Sasha was a new star for a new century.

The elegant teenage chanteuse took her bows and crossed the stage to her right as quickly as she could. Her natural beauty had been enhanced by professional stylists, a glorious gown, and exquisite jewelry. She walked with grace but held her breath. Unsteady on her new heels, she was terrified that she would trip, tear the magnificent dress, and break the clasp on the borrowed necklace securing the diamond brooch from Tiffany's. But cross the stage she did, without a hint of tension visible to the adoring throng. She was a natural. Yet, she was not fully aware of where she was going and never really heard the ceaseless roar of the crowd. Sasha's long auburn hair bounced in the dazzling lights as her slim form glided behind the ornate double doors on the famous stage. The bounce of her hair matched her nerves. She had been worried for two weeks before this evening; relief overcame her once she was off the stage, and she began to shake. Sasha just needed to sit down, drink some water, hug Mama and Papa, and find a quiet place to think. Behind the doors, she nearly fell into her father's arms.

"Oh Sasha, baby Sasha! They love you. You were magnificent!" Stepan said.

The pleasant lisp of her father's Russian words cascaded into her ears. That is what she needed and wanted to hear, her Papa. He looked so strange in the tailored tuxedo, but she loved his face. And as the tears streamed down his angular and rugged visage, she let him hug her tightly until she began to gasp for air.

"Stepan—let her go! She can't breathe." Isabel hovered next to her husband and pried him away from their daughter. She grabbed Sasha's arms and guided her toward her dressing room.

Inside the room, Sasha immediately sank into the couch, drank a cup of water, and let her mind race. *How could this be?* she wondered. Was it really happening? *Did I just perform in front of all those people? In NEW YORK?! The United States?!* She was exhilarated and scared. She had been in the United States for only two weeks. Two weeks, 8,000 miles and light-years away from her life in a small Siberian village. She felt so…different. Her life was completely new. Nothing was familiar. Not bad, but uncertain, different. Back home, she had hoped to continue singing in the local youth choir and attend the university for more training. Now? Now she was being treated like a princess.

Clothes, food, cars, hotels—all new, all wonderful, yet it seemed make-believe, and it was most certainly *foreign*. She wore an evening gown made especially for her. A man whose name was embossed on cosmetic packaging in salons worldwide applied her makeup. Someone other than her mother coiffed her hair for the first time in her life. Sasha felt like she was living a dream come true. And it was all because of Ekaterina, the mysterious great-grandmother who had left Russia and China many decades before.

The precocious, nervous, and gifted opera phenom wondered how her great-grandmother could have given her this dream? As Sasha lay down on her couch, with her head in Mama's lap, she closed her eyes and smelled the stuffed cabbage as it warmed on the stove in the kitchen in Khabarovsk, where they ate it five times a week. She slowly began to regain her normal breathing, and just before drifting into a restful sleep, she quietly whispered, "Thank you, Great-Grandma Ekaterina. Thank you. Thank you for surviving. Thank you for my freedom…and I hope you heard my singing."

And she stopped shaking.

2 1916

Valday, Russian Empire

Compared to the rest of Europe, Valday, Russia was a backwater forgotten by time. Visitors often commented that the small village came to rest a century earlier, if not more. Were it not for the old Iversky Monastery sitting on a little island in the lake, Valday might have been ignored entirely by the outside world. Although the clean air invigorated the body and soul of the few thousand scattered residents, the harsh and dangerous life of harvesting lumber from the forests lowered the lifespan of most of Valday's inhabitants.

Located halfway between Moscow and St. Petersburg (many folks still couldn't call it Petrograd), Valday was a place battered by winds that raced down from the Urals. The endless blasts rattled through the vast woodlands of Scots pine, Norway spruce, mixed birch, and aspen, and then scoured the grasslands of northwest Russia. In winter, it was hard to imagine a colder place. Frozen from November through March, the land matched the character of the people who lived in the region. Hard. Resilient. Survivors.

Nikolai Palutov was one of those who knew how to survive Russian winters. He had been doing so his entire life and accepted the frigid season as a routine test of his faith in God. *I thank God for the winter,* he would tell his friends. *Are we not stronger and more grateful when the first flowers bloom in spring?*

At first blush, Nikolai's average height, bulky waist, tortured hands, and long, ragged, curly hair gave him the appearance of a middle-aged miner. And, if you didn't know him, a simple glance from his cavernous dark eyes could make the hair stand up on the back of your neck. The large orbs sat buried so deeply in his head that the village children called him *the skull.* In contrast, his arms and shoulders appeared perfectly honed by a great artist, and his easy movements and pleasant voice offered a more accurate measure of his time on earth. Those who did know him loved him.

Nikolai thrived in the winter. He could feel the movement of blood through his veins slow down. The subtle change happened to him every year as the colors brightened on the trees. He believed it happened to everyone. A natural process preserved the heavenly soul in an inner core of peace while the body adjusted to meet life's harsh demands without God's warming touch. However, he would remark that some people didn't know how to defend the warmth of their souls. These unfortunates would shiver away each winter, cursing their lives, damning their Maker for want of heat, and often became sick and died. Nikolai always looked for the positive, rarely complained, and figured his upbeat approach to life had enabled him to keep his soul warm and safe each of his thirty-two years.

Since he was twelve, Kolya, the name he used interchangeably with Nikolai, had worked the timber. Generations of his family had been loggers, and he would train his sons to do the same. Lately, with Anna's pregnancy, he daydreamed about instructing his future children in the vast woods.

"Nikolai, what are you doing standing there looking into the forest?" Anna shouted at him. "What do you see?"

A large smile spread across his face. "My dear Anna, I see the future. Can't you?"

"What does it show?" she quipped back.

"Our boy and his brothers, using the saws and axes to cut the great logs and harness the skidding teams to move them."

"You silly man. What if our baby is a little girl?" she asked with an amused look.

"No. Not possible. Only boys, for generations of Palutovs. You know that. I will take the oldest to his first logging camp and sing the lumber songs to him. He will carry on our great tradition. It is the heart of Valday."

Anna shook her head. For the most part, she agreed. After all, Valday was in that vast region of western Russia containing lush forests, fields, and great rivers. The area produced the best forest products in the world. At least that's what every Valday logger would tell you. And Anna knew this. So, when Nikolai said he would raise another generation of expert lumberjacks and loggers, he had reason to believe it to be true. But his sweet wife Anna had thoughts of her own.

"What about the bells?" she would quiz him. "Our child may want to play the bells."

"Oh, Anna, please," he would tell her. "The bells are nice, but our boys will be Palutovs. Lumbermen."

He could say whatever he wanted, but Anna would never let him forget the bells. She came from a family of bell makers. To be a Valday bell maker was a distinction of high honor and much respect, on a par with loggers, but…well…different. Valday bell makers produced bells modeled after the traditional large Russian bells that beckoned worshipers across Christian Russia for many generations. However, Valday bell makers became especially well-known for manufacturing the small bells attached to horse harnesses and carriages. These bells made a delightful and instantly recognizable melodic jingle, yet also served as a warning to *stay clear* as a carriage approached. Everyone who could afford them owned a set of Valday horse bells, even if they didn't own a horse or carriage.

When Anna was a young girl, her mother gave her half a dozen

horse bells made by her great-grandfather. They were family possessions of great value. During religious holy days and special events,
the bells rang constantly. Other than her mother's lullabies, it was
the first music Anna had ever heard, and she quickly became adept
at making lovely sounds of her own with the bells.

"Kolya," she would accost him, using his nickname, "we must
teach our child, boy or girl, the *gift of the bells*."

Nikolai would squirm at her suggestion. "A son of mine shall be
a woodsman," he would counter. He could not see any son of his as
a bell maker, no less a bell ringer. If it was music she was interested
in, his boys would learn to play stringed instruments, like the balalaika or the gusli. Those were the music makers every male Palutov
attempted to master. But Anna was always quick with a retort.

"What about Vlad Gritkov? And Yar Lenkov? Or Matvey Ange-
loff? Or—"

"Okay. Yes. I understand. They play the bells," Kolya yielded.

"And they are also strong men who work the timber with you,"
she added.

Upon reflection, Kolya would assure her, yes, their child could
learn the bells too. As it was, music was a large part of their life
together. Religious hymns, folk songs, and popular music heard at
the large music hall in Novgorod and occasionally at the small theater in Valday were sung and played in their small household daily.
It was part of life that kept a smile on their faces.

<hr />

In the forests, Nikolai would sing as he worked using the lumberjack skills that ran through the blood of every Palutov. Nikolai,
his father, uncles, his brothers, and grandfather worked for Inter-
Russia Lumber Products. It was an enormous private company, a
rare feat in Tsarist Russia. It controlled all the logging in the region,
and rumors abounded that the owner kept a palace in Petrograd and

a large house in Moscow. Workers in the forests also said that without many of InterRussia's rubles making their way into the pockets of Tsar Nicholas, the owner's lodgings and his private railcar would vanish as quickly as a jack could lay a tree.

Once a year, the great man who employed the Palutovs and their friends would come to Valday to thank his workers. During each visit, he hosted a huge celebration. But in recent years, things started to change. Generation after generation of cutting was taking its toll on the forests. The lumber was thinning, and prospects were dimming for the services of loggers. And, with the arrival of the huge Lombard steam log hauler from the United States, clearing a stand of trees took much less time, men, and horses.

"Vitya, how can we continue on these meager wages?"

Nikolai was sitting in one of the small restaurants in Valday where people could legally purchase vodka. Vitya, his older brother, and Misha, his youngest, were at the table with him and two other friends.

"It's not just us," said Misha. "The mill workers and even the fancy cabinet makers are not getting paid what they're worth."

"I heard Lev Duberov talking about moving his family to make money in the far east," Nikolai shared the news.

"Yes. Several men have gone on their own, and entire families as well," Vitya agreed. "But as long as we stay with the lumber company, the less likely we'll get called into the Army. One out of three men our age is being conscripted. For what? To die for pompous old Nicholas? Ah, but what do I know?" Vitya continued. "Maybe things are better in the East."

Everyone had heard that durable, robust, and hardworking men could earn a lifetime of earnings in only one year in the farthest reaches of the Russian domain, away from a war that was destroying Europe and their country. Eastern Russia—Siberia—was a land so boundless, the saying went, that even God himself could get lost in such a place. A place where the forests still ruled, man's footprints were rare, and—with God lost in such environs—the devil made do. They also heard stories of bone-chilling cold, rampant disease, and lawlessness being part and parcel of every pilgrim's life in the East, an unattractive and isolated destination to anyone bringing their family to such a place. However, like a sailor, many skilled lumbermen left their families behind and went east, under contract or independently. They hoped to find success and return home after a year or two with a sack full of rubles. Or, at worst, be able to send money home to keep their family stable until they could make their way back.

On occasion, Nikolai and his brothers talked about heading east despite the challenges. But their conversations were meaningless. As a young man, Nikolai's great-grandfather had come to the Valday region fleeing poverty in the city. He agreed to go to work logging for a large landowner. He also made arrangements to lease land and purchase timber from the landowner on which and from which he would construct his own house. It was a deal that tied his family to the land for generations. The Palutov brothers continued to work off the arrangement made decades earlier. Like most of their neighbors, they prayed they would live long enough to fulfill their obligations to their landowner or that they might save enough money to purchase their freedom from tenancy.

Raisa, Anna's mother, lived with Nikolai and Anna in the same small cottage built by Nikolai's great-grandfather. It was a compact, solid structure that had sustained many difficult years of Russian weather. The drastic shifts in temperature each season cracked the mortar between the logs, and it would fall out in chunks. Nikolai always made sure he recaulked before the arrival of cold weather. When Misha was born, Kolya's father raised the roof on one part of the house to build a loft. All three boys slept there until they were grown. For now, the loft was empty and used for storage. They would have to make changes as soon as the baby was born. As it was, Raisa slept in the parlor, hidden somewhat by the log poles supporting the overhang of the loft. When she wanted privacy, she would untie the drape tacked to the low ceiling and form a comfy cocoon around her sleeping space.

Raisa had come to live with her daughter and son-in-law six months earlier, upon the death of her husband. At the start of the Great War, the Battle of Tannenberg took the lives of many Russians, including the big strong man she had married who had volunteered.

"Ha!" she had exclaimed after learning of his death. "What a dummy. Stupid man! Stupid man! Who volunteers to fight a war without a rifle? Stupid man! Dear Lord, I miss him."

He had been a good worker and had loved Raisa and the children. When he didn't come back, Raisa scraped by as a laundress, and Anna contributed money she earned singing. However, the total was insufficient for Raisa and her two teenage children. Then, in the late winter of 1916, Anna's brother developed a deep hacking cough that shook his body uncontrollably. After several weeks, he began to have difficulty breathing, and the doctor from Novgorod could not help him. He died in Raisa's arms. Soon after the burial, Kolya went alone to visit her.

"Raisa—Mother—we want you to come live with us. Me and Anna. It will be better than being alone on the other side of the village without a family," Nikolai invited her.

Raisa's eyes teared up. "Thank you, Kolya," she said. "Yes, being with you and my Anna will be good. Thank you. Thank you."

When Raisa first moved in, Nikolai offered her the bedroom, specifically his place in the large bed he shared with Anna. He volunteered to sleep in the loft. Anna said she would join Kolya in the loft so her mother could have the whole bed and not climb. Raisa laughed because she knew the bed well. She had curled up in that same bed with Anna's father for nearly twenty-five years. The bed had been a unique wedding gift from Raisa to Kolya and Anna. She said she felt lost in such a large bed without a husband and knew Anna's father would want her to have it.

When Raisa sold her house, she brought the small bed that Anna had slept in as she grew up. That is the bed she used under the loft. Raisa loved her small space, but what pleased her most was not displacing her daughter and son-in-law from the big bed.

Kolya's father, uncle, and brothers lived in two other cottages set back a short distance from the road across the dirt path from Anna and Kolya's house. The three homes included a small enclave at the end of a half-mile-long side road that extended perpendicular to the main route between Moscow and Petrograd. They were built on good land above the annual flood level of the river and protected by large trees and bushes. You could step outside of any of the doors, turn one direction, and head across fields toward the forest and river—or turn the other direction toward friends, school, church, and the town's busy life. Each were a leisurely fifteen-minute walk away.

⁂

Valday's geographic location complicated the lives of the Palutovs and every working family in the region. Situated on a major thoroughfare and within relatively easy traveling distance to Moscow and Petrograd, it was easy for the Palutovs and their neighbors to hear about the latest happenings in the two great cities of modern Russia. Many residents of Valday still found it uncomfortable to use the name Petrograd for the beautiful city, and still said St. Petersburg. The highway and trains served as perfect conduits for travelers and businessmen to share news and rumors about the political, industrial, and social activities occurring within commerce and government. The people of Valday also suffered the great anxiety of being closer to the rest of Europe than many other Russian communities. Since 1914, Valday's proximity to the killing, horrors, and battles raging across the continent caused a melancholic sense of foreboding to settle in the village. No one spoke of it, yet everyone knew the future was full of danger—especially after they witnessed the death of Raisa's husband. Be that as it may, Kolya would not let himself fall into the grip of despair on a crisp fall day in late October. He was on his way to the local theater to hear Anna sing.

Nikolai was sixteen when he first saw Anna singing in the choir at the seventeenth-century Iversky Cathedral. He sat in the last pew admiring the voice of the girl who was no more than twelve. But he knew she would be the one. In addition to her captivating voice, Anna had a natural grace and a childish beauty destined to mature. From an early age, not only was she gifted with perfect pitch, but she loved to entertain. Anna wanted to sing all kinds of songs for all sorts of audiences.

When Anna was fourteen, Nikolai introduced himself and told her he liked the choir music. She smiled and told him she loved to sing. That same year she made her debut on the local theater stage and sang in a Christmas pageant full of carols, eliciting loud cheers from the audience. Kolya sat in the first row. Not long after that performance, Anna was invited to Novgorod to perform with the city orchestra, and by the time she was sixteen, audiences in St. Petersburg knew her. During one of her trips to St. Petersburg, with an uncle serving as her chaperone, Kolya visited her parents in Valday.

"Hello Mr. Kuznetsov. I'm Nikolai Palutov…I'm here—"

"Yes, Nikolai. I know who you are, and I'm familiar with your father and your brother Vitya."

"Who is at the door, Mikel?" Raisa called from the kitchen.

"It's Nikolai Palutov. You know him. He sits in front during church and listens to Anna sing."

Mr. Kuznetsov looked at Kolya and saw him blush.

"Yes, I know the Palutovs—lumber family. Good people. What does he want?" Raisa asked as she came into the room, wiping her hands on her apron.

"Well, Nikolai, what do you want?" Mikel asked him, and both parents looked at him with knowing eyes.

Without hesitation, he answered, "I ask your permission to pay calls on Anna when she returns home?" There, he'd said it. His breathing returned to normal, and to his great delight, the Kuznetsovs said yes.

Kolya visited her once a week whenever she was home. On a spring day in 1906 that was indeed a gift from God, the cathedral at the Iversky monastery witnessed the matrimony of eighteen-year-old Anna and Kolya. It brought together a family of bellmakers and a family of loggers. A not-so-unusual occurrence in Valday.

The newlyweds had little time to relax. Kolya was busy in the forests, and Anna's performance schedule was full. The good news was they were both earning wages, and their savings were building. If things continued, they would be able to buy their way out from under Kolya's obligations to his feudal landlord years sooner than they had ever dreamed possible. When they did have time together, their physical attraction to each other was overwhelming. On many occasions, Nikolai's brothers would pound on the door of his house to get him to come into the village for a drink. Kolya would yell at them to go away, and the brothers would hear laughter and the sounds of the old bed. However, Anna didn't become pregnant, regardless of their passionate lovemaking.

After a few years, people began to talk. Rumors began to fly. Everyone who loved to hear Anna sing soon began to think her voice was her curse. *God gave her a gift but left her barren.* Anna was at a loss and didn't know how to respond. Her lovely voice took her to places where people did things good folks didn't talk about in public. She met the rich and the raunchy. Greed and lust surrounded her. Behind her back, people wondered if she was faithful to Kolya. Some people speculated that perhaps she had been *treated* at a clinic and could never have children. After all, how can you travel and entertain if you're pregnant and become a mother?

One day Kolya overheard men in the restaurant talking about her.

"What are you saying?" he demanded as he rose from his chair and confronted them.

"Nothing, Kolya, my friend," one answered for the group. "It's nothing."

"My Anna? You think my Anna is nothing?" he shouted back. "You think my Anna is, is, what? A bad woman? How dare you!" Kolya reached down, yanked the man out of his chair, and was ready to hit him when Vitya and Misha pulled him away.

"Stop, Kolya! We know Anna. They don't. Leave it," Vitya ordered his younger brother.

Nikolai knew Vitya was right and wished there was more he could do except hope and pray someday he and Anna would experience the ecstasy of having a child.

⋅⋅⋅❧❦⋅⋅⋅

Ten years of marriage came and went. Anna still traveled, but not as much. Posters of her performances in Moscow and Petrograd draped the walls of their simple cabin. She never asked for a grand residence or new things. In her late twenties, Anna was, indeed, beautiful. On the road, she was also elegant and sophisticated, and at home, everyone found her friendly, down-to-earth, and caring. She continued to sing in the cathedral choir, taught songs and rhymes to village children, and frequently led sing-alongs in her parlor. They had saved enough money to buy their freedom from serfdom but continued to be frugal to help Nikolai's father and brothers. And people around town had finally stopped talking about them having a baby.

After church on a cold autumn day, the entire Palutov clan was walking back home. They attempted to talk, but the wind was strong and in their faces, so they were mostly quiet. The women took the lead that day, allowing the smoke from the men's pipes and harsh cigarettes to trail behind them. They did not want to listen to the men trying to shout over the wind with their vitriolic talk about the war, the Tsar, and the growing interest in the exiled Bolshevik, Mr. Lenin. The women chatted about the newest grandchild in between gusts when Anna suddenly sneezed. The wind had curled around her shawl and tickled her nose. The women realized what they were talking about and checked their discussion.

However, Anna spoke up, "Oh, stop your fretting about me. Come to the house. I have news to share."

They walked on, shivering with each windy blast yet content in each other's company. Typically, one of the Palutov sisters-in-law would host the other families for dinner on Sunday afternoon. On this day, everyone brought their dinner contributions to the weekly gathering at Anna and Kolya's house. As everyone enjoyed their churchkhela, a grape and walnut candy dessert on a string—which mixed well with the strong Russian tea and vodka that flowed at the end of the meal—Anna began to hum a well-known children's song. When she ran out of verses, she told the group her news.

"The doctor tells me the baby will arrive in the spring," she said.

At first, Kolya thought she was talking about one of her pregnant friends. Then Anna said, "So, my dear Kolya, what shall we name him?"

Raisa was the first to comprehend. She quickly embraced her daughter, and the tears cascaded down her cheeks as she smiled, laughed, and cried with delight. She had given up hope about being a grandmother, a babushka. The small cabin erupted with the sounds of joy and expectation. The men slapped Kolya on the back and gave him bear hugs of congratulations. Never was there such a celebration in the old log house! Never! The Palutovs were going to have another new family member. At long last. Thank the Lord. And they did.

*   *   *

Another scream pierced the fabric of his thoughts. Her shrieks of pain and fright were making him crazy. *This has to end! It must stop soon!* Kolya almost screamed himself. *How can she continue to suffer so?* How can he listen to such sounds? Her voice had always been the essence of peace and pleasure, a sheer delight she shared throughout western Russia's cities, towns, and rural villages. It had soothed him through many crises. It is what attracted him to her in the first place. He found it impossible to comprehend how a voice that brought melodies of love and tenderness to the hard lives of farmers, blacksmiths, and factory workers could also produce such mournful wailing. She screeched notes unknown to any musician and louder than the powerful crashes of thunder that rolled across the land every summer. This cannot be the same person.

Kolya hung his head and shook it sadly from side to side. His long, ragged hair dropped over his dark eyes, and he combed it back with fingers, scarred and hardened from years of labor in the forests. He reached out and retrieved the vodka bottle, which sat nearly empty on the small table in front of him. The dull brown glass hid the clear liquid that gave him false courage. He poured another finger and swallowed quickly. The burning sensation soothed him, but only for a moment. He shuddered again, tears stinging his eyes as he listened to his lovely Anna emit another primal howl.

Behind the thin curtain, Anna lay on their ancient bed close to the edge. Her position made it easier for Raisa and Sofiya, the village midwife, to tend to her. Raisa kept wiping away the sweat from her daughter's head and the drool from her mouth. She used a frayed cloth about a foot square that she kept tucked in the waistband of her apron. Sofiya and Raisa had been best friends since they were little girls. Between their ministrations to Anna, they made small talk about playing in the fields and caring for the animals that still surrounded the village. Sofiya had delivered Raisa's two children, and now, she would assist in the birth of a grandchild.

Anna's mind raced. She knew there were people around her. She could hear herself speaking to them, but it wasn't a conversation. It was yelling, crying, and screaming in a shrill voice. *Was it her own?*

She could not believe this was happening to her. She never imagined the extent of the pain. She never realized how much fluid and blood she would lose. She felt weak beyond the point of exhaustion. *It had to stop.* She was having difficulty recognizing reality from fantasy. She thought she must be dreaming. Her mind flooded with worry for the life of her new child. *Would the baby survive? Would he—it had to be a boy—would he learn to read and write? It must be a boy! Kolya needs a son. Would the war ever end? What if the armies burn her village and take the men? What would she do? What would happen to her and the baby?* She heard the familiar words of the long-memorized prayer leave her lips, but she could not figure out who was saying them. She prayed with a deep passion for her new child to have a better future. She prayed her baby would live to grow old because, sadly, many others never lived to their first birthday.

Anna gasped again, searching for air. For strength. She clutched her sweat-soaked sheets until her fingers became numb. She heard more screams reverberating from the very core of her soul, yet she could not identify the voice as her own. She felt the pressure. Tremendous pressure! She was pushing with every ounce of energy left in her exhausted body. She shook with the force of an earthquake from her head to her toes and believed the bed was coming apart. She reached out her arms in a quest for something different to hold. She felt it. A book on the bed. Her Bible. Her fingers gripped the cover. It had been at her side since she took to the bed a week earlier. Her other hand clamped the bedpost. Her body twitched some more as she pushed again and again.

Throughout much of her ordeal, Anna's eyes had been closed. She suddenly realized she had been focusing all her attention on the sounds and voices coursing through her head. But now, she sought solace in company, and her eyes parted wide, seeking a familiar face.

A tiny crack of light penetrated the logs of the cabin wall. She wondered why Kolya had not caulked the hole. She followed the beam and saw the face she had hoped to see. Her icon of St. Michael blazed under the sun's rays. *Yes, yes. Of course.* St. Michael was with her. The leader of the Army of God would protect her and her house from evil.

Another spasm wracked her as if jolted by a bolt of lightning. She pushed, she screamed again, and her voice echoed throughout the house, and then, like the miracle it surely was, she felt relief. The tiny body slipped from her womb into Sofiya's safe hands. Instantly Anna's thoughts returned to her special child. She could see her infant silhouetted by the flickering glimmer of the candles and scattered sunlight, yet she preferred to believe he was blazing in the glory of God's brilliance. *A son, yes*, she thought, *it must be a son.*

She smiled, closed her eyes once again, and never heard the gentle words of her mother: "Anna, my Anna, you have a beautiful baby girl."

Shortly after Anna's last scream, Raisa carried the baby from behind the curtain, and Kolya took his daughter into his arms for the first time. No disappointment. Just joy. She was so tiny. He could not believe such a gift belonged to him and Anna. Ten fingers, ten toes, two good eyes squinting, and lungs—my goodness, she was loud. His smile stretched his face wide. He gave his thanks to God for his child and, as they had agreed, he named her Ekaterina—"Pure," for it was certain, without doubt, that she was. Kolya had been walking toward the curtain, hurrying with exultation to hug his beleaguered wife, when Sofiya emerged from the other side. She took his arm and began to steer him back to the parlor.

"Come, Kolya. Not now. We need to talk."

"But, but Sofiya!" he nearly shouted. "I have a daughter. A beautiful girl. Anna must see my joy. She must know how happy I am!"

Raisa joined them, took his other arm, and tried to get him to sit, but he pushed his way past them and through the curtain.

"Anna, Anna, isn't she beautiful?" Then he looked down and saw his wife's stillness. Her beautiful face, frozen for eternity.

"NOOOOOO! NOOOOOO!"

His Anna, his precious Anna, was gone.

3   1924
Valday

At eight years old, Katya already resembled her mother. Not only did she have Anna's eyes, hair color, and facial structure, she had her personality and movements, too. Katya was a perpetual reminder of Anna, and the ache in Kolya's heart never subsided. Each painful scream of that cursed yet blessed day eight years earlier was seared into his brain, as if God himself had taken the branding iron and pressed it against Nikolai's scalp. No matter what he did, who consoled him, or the delight he witnessed in the beautiful child who shared his blood, Kolya felt nothing but loss. Anna, the songbird, whispering in his ears and singing only to him, was gone, and he remained adrift without her.

As she grew, Katya slowly understood her father cherished her yet frequently had difficulty showing his love. But she was a young, free spirit who enjoyed life and knew her father's remoteness had to do with her missing mother, not herself. Despite her fragile years, Katya demonstrated a level of patience and youthful optimism that would become permanent parts of her character.

Katya especially enjoyed the company of her cousins. The oldest, a boy nearly ten years older than Katya, was Uncle Vitya's. The youngest, Yuri, was born the same year as she and was Uncle Misha's. Yuri

21

and Katya became best friends and did everything together. They did chores, climbed trees, and sat next to each other at family events, school, and church—until the communists closed them. Yuri learned to pluck notes on the balalaika while Katya hummed a tune and composed simple songs. She knew nothing about her mother's bells or Grandmama's flute, but she was happy and loved to sing. She and Yuri made music together, as children do. They were inseparable.

"You better stop, Katya. Your Papa will give you extra chores if he hears you."

It was a glorious summer day, and Yuri and Ekaterina were skimming stones across the gentle water of the lake and sharing stories. They spoke of imaginary places and people, tales of danger and bravery, of knights and castles, and maidens and dragons. Katya would occasionally turn her words into a song. But Papa did not allow singing.

Anna's death had driven music out of Nikolai's heart and ultimately out of his home. He refused to permit anything that reminded him of his lovely wife. He had folded up her sheet music and the posters with her picture and put them into the leather case where he kept his important documents. He had laid them on the bottom—hidden, so he would not see them when he opened the case, even by accident. No—there would be no more music in his life. He had taken that drastic step to ease his loneliness and find a way to continue without her.

His persistent grief interfered with his relationship with the gorgeous child Anna had left him. So, he let Babushka, Grandmother Raisa, raise Katya in most ways. The older woman had lost her husband to war, her son to illness, and her daughter to childbirth. Little Katya was all she had. Besides, Nikolai needed her help. He knew nothing about raising a child, especially a young girl. He was glad to have his mother-in-law's help. However, even Babushka had her drawbacks. She, too, was a living memory of Anna. And she was the one who had encouraged Anna to play the bells, sing, and share her music. Raisa had frequently played a homemade flute carved by

Anna's father, bringing smiles to Anna's face. Nikolai remembered the first time she took it out to play after Anna's tragic death. It had been two months, and as Raisa brought it to her lips for Vitya's birthday, the lonely widower startled everyone in the room.

"No, stop! Stop playing!" Nikolai had screamed. "There is no more music in my life."

Since that day, the flute was silent, and Katya grew up without hearing the sounds of music in her home. Kolya would scowl at his mother-in-law whenever he heard her humming or whistling. But he reserved his most vicious attacks for Katya. When he heard her, he would yell, break into tirades, and banish her to the loft. Then guilt would overcome him, and he would drag himself out of the house. He'd walk to the little church with the cemetery containing Anna's remains. He would cry as he stared at the dome and the cross over the door. The communists had it right. There was no God. For if there was, He certainly would not have taken his Anna away.

Katya knew little of the problems caused by the changing politics within her country. However, she could recall the St. Michael icon and Babushka praying in front of it. It had once hung on a wall in her home. Now, Raisa kept the icon in a trunk hidden from sight, because she feared prying eyes might report her to the revolutionaries. The day the communists arrested the priests at the Iver Cathedral in Valday, Raisa and many friends cried in the streets. The government confiscated the church for use as a school not long after. The icons vanished, the crucifix was stolen, and the Bibles were destroyed. Communist dogma, atheist pamphlets, and party rallies took over in their place.

One day, when Katya was five, she saw Grandmama's feet sticking out from beneath the curtain, giving her bed some privacy. The curtain was not fully closed, and Katya could tell that her grandmother was kneeling. She could see the St. Michael icon on the bed, and she stopped to listen, but could only hear a few words.

"Grandmama, what are you doing?"

Startled but eager to share the depths of her faith with her grand-daughter, Raisa answered, "I'm praying to St. Michael, to Jesus, and to God. They give me strength and hope."

"How do they do that, Grandmama? Can they hear you?"

How to explain the mysteries of religion and beliefs in the hereafter to someone so young? Raisa turned, sat on her bed, reached underneath, and pulled out her trunk.

"Here, let me show you some things." She opened the trunk and took out her most prized possessions: her Bible and her St. Michael icon, the only memories she had of her father.

"This big book is a Bible," she said. "The Bible," she corrected herself. "And this beautiful picture, painted on this piece of wood, is the icon of St. Michael."

"Grandmama, what is special about this book and this picture?" Katya asked with typical childhood curiosity.

"My father, your great-grandfather, took my sisters and me to church every Sunday and sometimes during the week. Church, the building where they have rallies and meetings now, was where we would pray. We would pray for my mother, who died when I was seven," Raisa said. "So, you see, Katya, I also know what it's like to be a young girl without a mother."

Katya gave her babushka a big hug, and Raisa continued. "My father would carry the Bible with dignity. It was printed in the 1750s and has been part of *our* family heritage for over one hundred years. Our ancestors helped construct the beautiful Kazan Cathedral…and the reward for all their work was this," she touched her Bible. "They called it a Bible for all ages."

Raisa let Katya open the cover to see the beautiful pages with their eloquently printed words and multicolored drawings. She told Ekaterina her father had shown her the long list of birth and death announcements written on blank pages and in the margins.

"Oh look, Grandmama, there's mother's name!" The joy of discovery was in Katya's voice.

"Yes." Raisa let her fingers caress Anna's name. Then she began to teach Katya about the Father, the Son, and the Holy Ghost.

The little girl enjoyed the time with her grandmother, although her babushka told her she must keep their discussions a secret. Grandmama said if anyone found out, it might get her father in trouble. Young Katya could never imagine deliberately causing a problem for her father, so she never spoke of their secret discussions.

<hr />

"Are you okay?" Yuri asked.

Katya realized she had been daydreaming about Papa, Grand-mama, church, religion, and getting in trouble. Ah yes, trouble—for singing at home!

"Yes, Yuri. I'm fine. I'm so good, I shall sing you another song."

It was late, and they headed home. Each had chores and homework to do. At school, Yuri favored books, solving number puzzles, and learning about history, while Katya preferred playing tag in the schoolyard and singing to her heart's content during lessons about great musicians. Teachers told her father she had a natural singing voice and said Katya enjoys *making a tune* to share with others. They suggested she participate in a children's choir and try performing on stage. Nikolai would have none of it. He would not allow Katya to turn into her mother. Kolya informed her teachers that Katya needed to read and write, not sing. He gave a similar lecture to Raisa concerning Katya's domestic skills.

"She must learn to cook, sew, care for the sick, take care of the household, tend to the animals, and so on," he would tell Raisa.

Nikolai failed to see the gap in his logic. The more work he gave Katya and the more he expected her to study, the more she found ways to make those tasks enjoyable through song. She would sing "In the Dark Forest," "Kalinka, the Little Green Tree," and many more. While singing, she finished her chores with seemingly little attention paid to what she was doing.

"I wonder what everyone is doing?" Yuri asked as they approached their houses.

They saw a small crowd gathered outside, talking excitedly but somewhat quietly.

"What's going on?" Katya asked her Uncle Vitya.

"It's nothing, my dear. We're just visiting," he said.

"But today is not a visit day. Why are all these people here?" she persisted. "Where's Papa?"

Vitya pointed to his brother, and Katya scampered to his side.

"Papa, what's going on? What is everyone doing here?"

"Shush, child. It's only business. Nothing for you."

Then Ekaterina spotted her other cousins around the side of one of the houses. She raced to them and could hear Dmitri, the oldest. Even though he was eighteen, he too had been excluded from the talk of the elders—but he had friends who told him things.

"Last night. Yes, late last night," he was saying.

"What about last night?" Katya yelled.

"Hush, or they'll hear us," Dmitri chided. "Last night, they came and took Ivan Resnikov."

"Who's Ivan Resnikov? And who came?" Katya asked again.

"Who's Ivan Resnikov? My goodness, dear girl. Do you pay attention to nothing but your silly songs? He's the foreman at the lumber company where your Papa, my Papa, and our uncle work. If they can take Resnikov, they can take anyone."

"But who took him? And why would they want the foreman? Who will lead the workers?"

"Good grief, little one! They took him because they believe he's against the government. But that's ridiculous because, without the government, he never would have become the foreman."

"What is this?" the shrill voice of Uncle Misha scattered the children. He stared hard at his oldest nephew.

Dmitri straightened up and told his uncle about the story he had heard concerning Ivan Resnikov. "Is it true, Uncle? Has Comrade Resnikov been taken away?"

"You will scare the children with such words, Dmitri. It's not good to speak of such things. People are listening everywhere." As Misha walked away, all the children saw him nod his head up and down without speaking.

*

When Nikolai stopped to think about the past ten years and what his future might hold, he always got angry. Most of Europe had been ablaze with the war for much of the second decade of the 20th century. Hundreds of thousands, ultimately millions, of young men had died ugly, brutal deaths in trenches of mud, fields of gas, and makeshift hospitals clogged with the remnants of lives withered from disease and malnutrition. While the Tsar sent poorly equipped Russian soldiers into the carnage, the Russian people had debated, talked of rebellion, and tried to survive. Inside his small, tidy home, Nikolai Palutov had never spoken about the war or politics. The tavern was the place for those topics, usually only among men. However, by 1924, everyone found it impossible to ignore the whims of politicians and generals who cast their shadows over the lives of ordinary citizens.

Valday's geographic location had complicated the lives of the Palutovs, as well as every working family in the region. They lived closer to the killing fields during the Great War and the major conflicts of the Revolution. They suffered the anxiety of familiarity with tragic experiences, and as a result, political discussions had become part of the household conversation in many families. Without Anna to keep him in check and turn the talk to music, Kolya finally yielded to the inevitable and brought the fear and angst of revolutionary upheaval into his home.

Everyone knew changes were happening to the country, and Nikolai felt compelled to discuss his thoughts with his father, brothers, neighbors, and even Raisa, but only in the most private settings. He had supported the activists who forced the end of Russia's participation in the war, but he despaired when he realized the pendulum of good tidings had rapidly swung in another direction. He had not foreseen the bitter civil war.

Nikolai could not support the new communist party under Lenin. He didn't want government bureaucrats taking credit for his hard work. He thought the concept of *one for all and all for one* hoisted by the Reds was mythical. Kolya liked the idea of equity, but recognized human nature for what it was. He never believed share-and-share-alike would provide a balanced distribution of work and income as predicted by the Soviets.

As years passed, Kolya could no longer share conversations with his friends, neighbors, and even some family members. After ten years of false promises and no noticeable change, he reversed course. He no longer accepted the dogma that there was no God. He needed to believe in something. Something that could strengthen him. He found his winter soul again, and it revived his spirit.

The restoration of his faith and commitment to unpopular ideas left Nikolai ostracized from Valday's social life. He stopped visiting the restaurant to sit, eat, and drink with colleagues. The owner no longer welcomed people with independent views, because they attracted the army or police to the establishment. His isolation caused him to lose focus at work. He had seen others collapse under the pressure and give in to the demands of the nouveau petty bureaucrats in charge of the logging, lumber, and mill operations. He viewed them as puppets who lived without purpose and did only as much as was necessary to make the boss happy.

Nikolai did not want to yield, yet he had also seen what

happened to those who questioned the system. Whenever someone complained or suggested an alternative to the official plan, they were sent east. There, they were swallowed up by the wilderness and rarely heard from again. He tried and failed to confirm reports that the government executed "troublemakers" sent to Siberia. No one knew what to believe. What he did know was he could not continue to live among hypocrites. He could not continue to be a lumberjack for depressed wages insufficient to buy his only child material for a new dress. So, on a clear, cold winter day—the kind of day in which your breath is so heavy it nearly forms words as it exits your mouth—Kolya spoke his mind in public as his work group ate lunch.

"Our situation is untenable," he started. "The company rules are ridiculous, and we get no support from the government."

Gleb Chaban, the new foreman, overheard Kolya and immediately threatened him with losing his job if he didn't retract what he said. Chaban was also scared. If he didn't report Kolya, he could find himself on the train to Siberia. Likewise, working the trees and mills was dangerous, and he couldn't allow Kolya to work in such a troubled state of mind.

"Kolya, you must take back your words. Someone who might be distracted by political ideas and not pay attention to what he should be doing is dangerous for all of us."

But Nikolai waved him off. Gleb had known Kolya since they were children. They had stood with blistered hands on opposite sides of the great saw when they felled their first giant tree.

He tried again. "Kolya, please, concentrate on your work and leave politics to politicians."

Kolya stormed his reply. "Gleb, my friend, you want me to concentrate on work by joining the party that promised a better life for the workers? What have they done? It has been nine years. We are worse off than before. The Party and our new mill leaders take our money and keep it for themselves. They're no different than the Tsar and his court!" Kolya stated what many believed. "If I work harder and produce more than someone else, will I earn more?" It was rhetorical, and everyone listening knew it. "You, my foreman and friend, I request you submit that question to your superiors." Then, rather than keeping quiet, he went on. "These revolutionary leaders have left us with too many unfulfilled promises," he roared. "They have even taken away church and God. They have stifled hope. They are useless scum not worthy to shine the boots of honest workers, and I cannot support their vision."

Tears were sliding down Chaban's fat cheeks when Kolya finished his tirade. The lonely foreman stared at Kolya through moist eyes.

"Leave, Kolya. Go now," Gleb said with despair. "I cannot allow such radical ideas to disturb the lives of everyone working under my direction and on behalf of Mother Russia. Do not come back to work. And yes, I will relay your views to the manager." He said these last words with trepidation, hoping the messenger would not be the one to get shot.

Figuring things could not get worse, he spoke quietly, less than a foot away from his quivering friend. He looked directly into Gleb's eyes as if searching for the lost soul of his country. "My questions or ideas do not threaten Mother Russia, Gleb. Little men, eager to subjugate the people who helped them gain power, stole Mother Russia for their own profit."

He turned and left.

As he walked home, Kolya berated himself for challenging his long-time friend. He knew the consequences would be dire. What he didn't know was how he would tell Raisa and Katya. Nearing his house, he could hear his daughter. She was singing, something else that riled him.

"Damn that girl. What do I have to do? There's no place for music in the life we live." Kolya slammed the door open. "Ekaterina! Ekaterina! Stop it now! No more, no more! Why do you do this? Why do you disobey me? Why must you? Mama—make her stop! Not today. I cannot listen to this, this, this…happiness. This joy. It's not right."

Katya looked at her father and bounded up the ladder into the loft. "Sorry, Papa. Sorry," she called to him. "I love the music. My friends tell me I make them smile. Singing makes me smile, Papa. I'm sorry."

Ekaterina used the tips of her fingers to pry loose one of the planks along the wall, reached inside, and pulled out the faded paper. Babushka had saved one of Anna's posters, and she had given it to Ekaterina without telling Kolya. In the loft, Katya partially unrolled it and stared at the figure of the attractive young woman standing next to a piano. The lines of the face on the poster matched her own. The hair color matched hers. Even the way Anna leaned on the piano resembled Katya's posture when she stood to answer questions at school. There was an air of confidence in the eyes that looked up from the old parchment. Every time Katya looked at her mother's poster, she smiled. It helped her remain calm. She did not understand why Papa wouldn't let her sing. She knew he wanted to be happy again, but he became sad whenever he heard her sing. As she gazed with wonder at the beautiful woman she would never meet, Katya was startled by the strident banging on the front door.

"Open! Open immediately! In the name of the people of Russia!"

She heard the demanding voice and felt the fine hairs on the back of her neck stand as a nervous tingle ran down her spine. Kolya ignored the noise at the door. He shuffled around the room in a circle, holding the vodka bottle in one hand. He briefly stopped and looked at the bottle as if it had the answers to his dilemma. He raised his head, searching for the God he had grown up with, the One who had taken his Anna. What merciful God would bring these brainwashed hooligans to his door?

"Where are You?" he demanded. "Why have You forsaken my family? What have we done?"

After his plea, he straightened up and called Raisa out of the kitchen. He handed her the bottle, walked to his chair, and sat. Before their eyes, Ekaterina and Grandmama watched Nikolai change.

He composed himself, controlled his movements, and slowed his breathing. Then he instructed Raisa to open the door.

Three large men entered. They were young. *Barely old enough to be allowed out at night,* he thought. They carried no weapons other than a piece of paper. He was surprised to see two he knew. Good, respectful boys from the village.

"Nikolai Palutov?"

"Yes, Andrei. You know it's me." He rose from his chair and stood erect. Strength and confidence shone in his bearing and his eyes. He was not afraid of the news these boys would deliver, but he could not help the deep, overwhelming sense of sadness that pecked holes in his heart like moths in wool.

Andrei took a breath, swallowed hard, and continued speaking. Never once did he look at Nikolai. "We are here to deliver a personal summons from the government, and two witnesses are present as required to verify you receive it."

Andrei cautiously extended his hand and waved the paper until Kolya took it. It had the seal of the regional Party leader and his signature at the bottom. Nikolai glanced at it. It was an order to present himself to the railroad station master-at-arms at ten o'clock the following morning. He could bring no more than two bags of personal belongings. He was being relocated to "better assist the development of glorious Mother Russia and the Union of Soviet Socialist Republics." The paper didn't say precisely where, but Nikolai knew it would be far from his beloved Valday Hills. The young Soviet agents waited without speaking.

When Nikolai finished reading, he looked up at them and said, "Andrei, Felix—you two, I know. Look at me. Look at me!" he ordered them. "Do you believe I can cause the downfall of the government? Do you think I have conspired against my very Russian soul? Of course, you don't. But I forgive you. Possibly, when you are older, you will see that the men you trust and follow now will limit your lives and control what you do and think. Their rules will confine you like the walls of a prison or the isolation of a Siberian mine may restrict me. You know me to be an honorable man. I will be on the train tomorrow. No need for a guard tonight. Now, if you will, please excuse me. I must pack and say goodbye to my family."

Kolya turned his back on them and walked behind the curtain into his bedroom. The young contingent glanced at Ekaterina in her loft and at her grandmother, bowed slightly, and left.

Nikolai's eyes flooded when he thought about leaving Ekaterina, Raisa, his brothers, their families, his father, and the land upon which five generations of Palutovs had served Russia. As a boy, Kolya had made two trips with his family to see the great cities of Moscow and St Petersburg. Otherwise, he had spent every day of his life within ten miles of Valday, but he could not change who he was. He knew his self-righteousness and glib tongue were about to send him on a journey with no better chances of returning home than entering the gates of hell.

Thankfully Ekaterina can remain, he thought. The banishment order was for him alone, and he breathed a sigh of relief. Katya would continue to learn the essential things from her babushka, aunts, uncles, and cousins. She would be safe and loved. More than he could guarantee. Maybe she would even sing, without him stopping her. The thought brought a sad smile to his lips. He thought about war, the hardships of the forest, the death of the only person ever to know his innermost secrets, and now—Siberia? Again, he asked, *why?* Why had he been given so many challenges? Why did he say those things to Gleb?

Kolya quickly set the self-pity aside and thanked God for not sending Ekaterina with him. After a time, he came out from behind the curtain and announced to Grandmama and Ekaterina he was going to see his father and his brothers, although he was sure they had already heard the news. It was likely everyone in Valday had known before he did, but he must speak to his Papa to say goodbye.

Like Nikolai, his father did not have the tall stature common among many Palutov men. Although he was not short, he seemed small in comparison. He had worked hard his entire life and remained strong as he aged. *Able to do a full day's work,* he would tell anyone. As a result, his chest was so broad and muscled that Kolya's mother had always complained it took an extra yard of material to make Papa a shirt. Frederick Palutov had lost his wife during the flu epidemic when Ekaterina was only two. He adjusted to his loneliness by inviting his older brother, also a widower, to move in with him. They had liked the idea of being boys together again.

For over twenty years, Freddie—everyone called him Freddie—was the best lumberjack in Valday. He taught his three boys everything he knew about trees, wood, operating the sawmill equipment, and the animals and other plants in the forest. Despite his fame and skills, he received little substantive recognition from the landowners for his years of commitment and service. When his joints began to ache a bit too much each morning and his eyes weakened to cause him to miss making an exact cut, the landowners pensioned him out. When he was sixty-two, they told Freddie they needed his spot for a younger man. He was entitled to visit the community store once a month to collect enough food, tobacco, and vodka to sustain him. However, the government's definition of "enough" proved considerably less than what most people needed to survive.

Regardless of his hard life and his landlord's lack of appreciation for his work, Freddie had been a consistent provider for his family. He knew history, could manage his resources effectively, understood the complexities of modern politics and economics without having completed more than six years in school, and felt privileged to harbor a Russian soul within his aging frame. The elder Palutov had always known Kolya was too rigid—stubborn, many would say—in his ways, yet he admired his son's strength of character and ability to speak his mind in the face of adversity. When the knock came on his door, Freddie knew who it was.

"Come in, Kolya."

The older man sat in the kitchen at the back of the house. He was rubbing oil into the handle of the axe his father had given him when he was fourteen and first went to work in the forest. The handle glistened under the glow of a flickering lamp. As he rubbed the handle, he turned it so the broad blade reflected the hazy light into the eyes of his second son. It was the most important and valuable possession Freddie owned. He stopped working when Kolya entered the room.

Kolya looked into the eyes of the man who had taught him everything worth knowing. "Hello, Papa. The Soviets told me to report to the train going east tomorrow morning."

"Yes, I know."

"Papa, I don't know why the Lord gave me a tongue incapable of silence in the face of disagreement. I'm sorry for such embarrassment to you and the family."

"Yes, Kolya. I understand. We all understand, and we know your commitment to the truth. We shall always love you."

"I'm not afraid of going, Papa—but I will desperately miss you, my brothers, and Ekaterina. I can't bear the thought of leaving her and her grandmother."

"We'll be here for them, Nikolai. Be strong, be faithful. I shall save you a place at the dinner table."

"Thank you, Papa. I must go. Thank you for my life and the skills you taught me. Now I must see Misha and Vitya. Goodbye, Papa."

"Kolya, Kolya." His father stood quickly and reached out to hug his stubborn but inspirational son. They clung to each other like they had that time when Nikolai was six and had come between a mother bear and her cubs. Freddie had heard his son yelling for help and ran directly toward the bear to scare her away. The mother bear and the young father stopped and stared at each other. Kolya moved slowly toward his father in a wide arc, and the bear cubs did the same to their mother. When Nikolai got close enough, Freddie scooped him off the ground and backed away. They had held each other so tightly that they knew their bond would never crack.

"Here, Kolya, you must have this." Freddie held the axe in his hands and thrust it forward.

"Oh, Papa. I cannot. It's for Vitya. He's the oldest."

"He knows, Kolya. He knows I love him no less, and I know you will cherish it."

Kolya's hands shook as the fabled tool came to rest on his calluses. A tear trickled down his cheek as he whispered, "Thank you, Papa."

Misha and Vitya had gathered their families into the large central room of their house. They were waiting when Kolya knocked. As soon as he entered, the children bombarded him with questions.

"What did you do, Uncle Nikolai? Why do they need you to go so far away? Isn't there work for you here? Will you write us letters and tell us about the wilderness?"

Kolya raised his long arms and tried to settle everyone down. He tried his best to explain why he must leave and saw quiet tears on the well-creased faces of his brothers. He told them not to worry about him. He would do well. They stood, poured him a vodka, saluted him, and gave him hugs that would have crushed the ribs of smaller men. They looked at their father's axe in Kolya's hands. Kolya blushed.

"It's okay, Kolya," Vitya said. "But please, leave it with me overnight. I want to prepare it for your journey. I shall have it ready for you before you leave the house in the morning."

Kolya handed the axe to his brother and apologized to them for bringing unnecessary hardship to their families. "I pray you will be able to continue to work and prosper, despite my public words. Some people see only the family and not the individual."

"We shall be fine," Misha answered. "We think you're the strongest and bravest, speaking what many of us also believe."

"I was foolish and selfish, Misha. And I shall never see my family again because of it. Please don't do what I have done."

Nikolai kissed everyone and went home to bed. Surprisingly he slept the most peaceful sleep he had since losing Anna. Nonetheless, he awoke very early. There were things he needed to do. As he began his chores, he realized he felt invigorated. He was tingling with excitement. Although reason and rumor dictated he should be scared, Kolya surged with confidence. Things appeared difficult, yes. Troublesome and unsavory, certainly. But he knew he was a survivor, able to adapt. He started a fire in the stove, filled every available pot with water, and placed them on top to heat. Then he stepped into the dark shelter attached to the back of the kitchen and hefted the empty half-size pickle barrel. For as long as he could remember, the barrel served as a tub for bathing. Against his own rules, he brought it into the small kitchen. Nikolai was not going to bathe in the cold shed—not today.

As he waited for the water to get hot, he set out his few belongings. While sorting his things, he heard a knock on his front door. Vitya was there with their father's axe. He had stitched a sturdy leather sheath for the large blade and secured a strap to the handle, making a sling. This would make it much easier for Kolya to carry the valuable axe. He had also meticulously carved Kolya's initials into the handle and etched them into the side of the blade. Under the soft glow of a single oil lamp, Nikolai looked at his brother's work. Without words, Vitya hugged his brother, nodded his head, and left. He didn't want Kolya to see his tears.

Nikolai returned to the kitchen and filled the barrel with hot water. He decided to treat himself to extra water, and by the time he squeezed himself into the barrel, he could sink deep enough that the water could rise to his chest. He closed his eyes and let the warmth penetrate every pore. With his body cleansed and his mind relaxed, Nikolai Palutov, son of Frederick of Valday, was ready.

Ekaterina heard Papa moving around, and then Uncle Vitya enter. She peeked over the loft's edge to see her uncle give Papa the axe. Katya also heard Kolya pumping the water and filling the tub. She knew he was getting ready to leave. Like any child her age, Katya didn't want to leave her friends, especially her cousin Yuri, but the thought of Papa going someplace without her was incomprehensible. Impossible! She would not let him go alone. *Papa alone?* She laughed to herself. *He cannot cook. He cannot sew. He knows no medicine.* It was obvious Papa would need her. Therefore, Katya decided she would go with him—but first, she would say goodbye to Babushka.

After Anna died, Kolya had given up his bed to his mother-in-law. He knew she would stay to help raise her only grandchild, and she would need to be well-rested. It was also easier for him than for Raisa to climb into the loft to sleep. When Anna was old enough to understand the priest in church and began reading and writing, Kolya and Babushka decided it was time for her to sleep in her own space. So Kolya came down from the loft, and Ekaterina moved up. Raisa insisted he move back into the big bed, and she returned to Anna's old bed.

That morning, Ekaterina very carefully climbed down the ladder and peeked behind the curtain into Raisa's sleeping space. Babushka was also awake and busy arranging things.

"Good morning, Katya. Why are you up so early?"

"Oh, Grandmama—I cannot let Papa go away by himself. He knows nothing of tending house. I need you to help me pack a bag so I can go with him."

"Ah, I see. So, Ekaterina, you are going with Papa on a great adventure?"

"Oh yes, Grandmama. It will be the most exciting time. I will miss you very much, but I have no choice. He is my Papa and my responsibility. He will need me to take care of him in his new house."

"Shh, shh. Papa is taking a bath in the kitchen. Quiet, or he will hear you," Raisa answered as she hustled about her small sleeping space. She was packing things in a cloth case she had sewn hurriedly during the night—after the police had come. She made sure her bells and flute were in the sack, a few clothes, her Bible, and her icon. Ekaterina paid no attention to Babushka's activities until her grandmother spoke again.

"Katya, you must go to Uncle Vitya and ask him for a travel case. He has several, and he will give one to you."

"Oh, yes, yes! I can go with Papa!" she burst out in a shout. "Oh good, good. But I shall surely miss Yuri, and you too, Grandmama."

"Be quiet, Katya. We must surprise Papa," Babushka shushed her, almost as loudly as she spoke. Katya dashed out the door in a flash to fetch the case.

Raisa turned, sat on the bed, and sighed. What had they done to deserve such a fate? Her children and her husband were dead, and now—her son-in-law, one of the nicest men she ever knew, was banished. Yes—she would go too. Nothing but memories to leave behind in Valday.

When Papa finished his bath, the water was still warm and soapy. He called to see if Raisa or Katya wanted to enjoy it before he dumped it. Babushka came into the kitchen when she heard him call. Raisa looked at him, standing there wrapped in a meager towel, cleared her throat, and made an announcement.

"Kolya, Ekaterina, and I have decided it is not a good idea for you to enter this new life without proper knowledge or support in domestic matters. You know you are a poor cook, cannot make food last more than one day, have little training in medicinal practices, are horrible with needle and thread, and much more. Besides, we love you and will not let you become separated from us. I am old and have little time left anyway. So, it is important to have me for the start of your new life—and Ekaterina, for when I am gone. Therefore, as soon as I finish *my* bath, we will finish packing and join you on the train. Now—out of the kitchen, and let me bathe in peace!"

"No, Raisa. I forbid it. It will be too dangerous for Katya."

"She already has no mother. You want her to grow up without a father, too? We're coming."

"But we know nothing of the East. She'll miss her uncles and cousins—and it's safer for her here."

"Stop it, Kolya. We'll have each other. She needs to be with you, her father."

Babushka shoved Kolya out to give her some privacy. He started to say something else, but she stared hard at him, and he knew she would not listen to his reasoning. However dangerous, dirty, lonesome, cold, and miserable life in Siberia was supposed to be, he knew she didn't care. And he knew Ekaterina was too young to understand.

Nikolai turned at the sound of the door as Ekaterina entered with a leather satchel in her hands. She looked at him and smiled. She could tell Grandmama had told him they were all going. He went to his daughter, picked her up as if she was a feather, and hugged her as tears ran down his face.

He was terrified for her. How could he possibly protect her, the living image of Anna? So curious and joyful and beautiful. How could he expose her to the uncertainties of what lay ahead?

He put her down, went into the bedroom, and saw Babushka's case on the bed. St. George's icon was lying on top of the case—he knelt and prayed. He asked God for the strength of St. George, who had slain the dragon and protected the king's daughter. Kolya knew he would need it.

⁕⁂⁕

At the time of Ekaterina's birth, it took the fastest trains almost two weeks to cross Russia from Europe to the Sea of Japan. She had been born into a country so vast and diverse in geography, ethnic heritage, racial make-up, and languages, that a lifetime would be insufficient to learn even a tiny amount about it. But Ekaterina was a member of the ethnic majority—a *true Russian*. She was a member of a family devoted to the motherland and imbued with great pride for the preeminence of modern Russia. *Pure stock, a natural daughter of Mother Russia*, people would say about her as she grew.

In Katya's mind, there was never any doubt the long train ride would be the ultimate adventure. She knew none of her friends had ever ridden on a train, and she was excited about being the first of them to do so. She had seen the train often enough. The engine would puff slowly into the station, billowing smoke like a giant, noisy monster followed by a long tail of railcars. She had seen the coal cars and the orderly, dignified arrangement of the sleeping cars. First-class had beds, lounge chairs, stewards, and access to the dining car. Next, the *soft seat*—second-class—cars, with their small, shared chambers and cushioned seats. Finally, the *hard seat*—third-class—cars, often crowded with people and small farm animals. She had watched as the steam-driven behemoths gobbled water from the tall reservoir. She had daydreamed of the fancy goods transported in the crates and boxes that railway workers unloaded from the freight cars, and she had pictured great cities and landscapes disappearing into the distance as the train passed. Yes, Ekaterina was ready. After all, she already knew the train.

Nikolai, Raisa, and Katya left the little cottage and never looked back. Each carried a case in their hands and another strapped to their back. Kolya also had the axe in its protective sheath. They glanced across the road to see the faces of the children looking out from Vitya's house.

When they had almost reached the bend in the road that turns towards town, Frederick Palutov opened the door to his home a crack. He looked and saw three backs. His middle son, the proud one, was sheltered on either side by an old woman—who loved Kolya as if he was her child—and the delight of the village, his precious granddaughter, Ekaterina. Oh, how he would miss her and the sweet songs she sang in private just for him. *Yes,* he thought—*they are survivors. They will make it. God be with them.* He closed the door and would weep no more.

They heard the whistle signaling the train's approach. Ekaterina sucked in her breath. Today, the whistle reminded her of a bird seeking its mate. It was a good thing, she was sure. Grandmama told her she was going to see and do things beyond the limits of her imagination. She would meet people who looked different, talked differently, and ate strange foods. She was going to be in situations where she could not complain. They would have excitement, but there could be danger. They were in God's hands and could only pray that He protect them and guide them.

Katya looked at the train with new eyes as it neared the station. The thirteen cars had changed character. It was no longer the daily and sometimes twice-a-day passenger carriers representing dreams of faraway places. Unlike the cargo trains, the passenger train had always brought wonder to her eyes. She would read the long list of destinations posted on the walls inside the station and ask herself questions.

Do the children in Chelyabinsk also eat potato dumplings?

Do babushkas in Abakan tickle the toes of their grandchildren?

Do they speak Russian in Irkutsk?

Katya didn't let a day go by without asking her family and friends a question about the stops along the route of the Trans-Siberian railway. But on that day, the day when she and her family walked to the station, the train was no longer a machine of fantasy dreams. It was real. It was as alive as she, Papa, and Grandmama, and she planned to get to know it—from the big black engine, coal car, and baggage car to the six hard-seat cars, two soft-seat cars, one sleeper car, and dining car. Where Nikolai and Raisa saw dreary hardship, Katya saw new territories to explore, and she couldn't wait.

Once inside the station, they were surprised to find they weren't the only banished people. There were three other families, four single men, and one single woman. The watchful eyes of the military police monitored all of them. The single woman was restrained by two iron bracelets containing a large lock that kept her hands clasped firmly behind her back. One of the police carried the woman's small bag of belongings.

For a brief moment, Ekaterina and Raisa thought they would be left behind. The official transport papers listed Nikolai Palutov as the only authorized traveler; if the train filled, there would be no available seats for anyone else. However, eight-year-old Ekaterina would have none of it.

"What? What?!" she demanded of them. "Look in the train—it's nearly empty. There's plenty of room for us. You're sending my Papa away to some horrible place, so I will never see him again. Are you afraid Grandmama and I will kidnap him off the train? That we will be too much weight? I will not allow my father to go away without my help. We are a family. Why would you choose to separate us?"

The young policeman didn't know what to say. He was surprised by the speech and high spirits of the pretty daughter of his prisoner. He shrugged his shoulders. He had boarded entire families before, as he was doing today. But still, he had no orders for this family. Maybe they were meant to be separated, having committed some crime that mandated separation. Or perhaps it was an administrative error. Those happened too. Frustration rippled his brow, and he searched for his superior. However, after the roll call, the man had left. *What harm could it do?* he thought. There was always room at this station, though he knew the cars would fill quickly as the train made other stops. And if he let them on without proper papers, he could get in trouble. But then he saw an easy way out.

He stared at the girl and spoke. "Do what you will. I've done my duty. Your father is here, and he has boarded the train. Now—get out of my way." He strolled purposefully out of sight behind the station building.

"Quick, Grandmama. Let's go! We can get on with Papa."

Ignoring the consequences, Ekaterina and her grandmother climbed the steps into a third-class car, walked down the aisle, and sat next to Kolya. He smiled at them and opened his arms for a big hug. They were in it together.

"I knew Katya would convince the guard," he beamed with pride.

Once seated, Katya took a moment to look around. "Oh Papa, these seats are no good. I can't see through the window. There's room on the other side of the train, and the windows are cleaner." Without waiting for his response, she grabbed her belongings, got up, and settled comfortably three rows up on the opposite side.

"Well, Mother, it looks like we need to move," Kolya chuckled as he and Raisa took their suitcases and joined his precocious daughter.

"Isn't this much better?" Katya asked.

"Oh yes. Much better," Kolya answered.

They had barely stowed their gear when Katya was ready to move again. Not to another seat, but to explore. "If this train is going to be our home for the next three or four weeks, I must know all about it and everyone on it."

"Katya, you need to wait until everyone is on board and the provodnik has counted all the heads," Kolya told her.

"Yes, Papa. I will, because our provodnik looks mean and not like a regular conductor."

Kolya knew she was right. The man counting heads also served as an informal guard. He had already confiscated Kolya's axe and stowed it in a locked cupboard. He would make sure the *passengers* to Siberia did as they were told.

4   1924

Trans-Siberian Railroad
Valday to Siberia

Stoked with impatience and curiosity, Katya sat back in her seat, sulked, and waited for everyone to finish boarding. Nikolai was a bit nervous when the conductor entered and began to check everyone's paperwork. The uniformed provodnik thrust out his hand and waited for Nikolai to hand him their documents. After a cursory glance at the papers, he mumbled. "When we fill up, and we will, the babushka and girl will have no seat. You understand?"

Kolya nodded but breathed a sigh of relief once the man moved on to the next passenger. The three could stay together and figure out seating and sleeping arrangements when the time came. The car was only half full, so maybe there would be room. At least for the first night.

Their car carried all the exiled families from Valday, the single men, the woman with manacled hands, three guards in uniform with rifles, and about a dozen soldiers heading east for duty who had been in the car when the train pulled into the station. Katya gave a delighted squeal when the train jerked forward and began to move. Underway at last, she couldn't wait a moment longer.

"Now, Papa? Can I go now?"

"Yes, Katya," he smiled at her. "You may visit one car ahead and one car behind. No farther."

She was out of her seat and headed for the rear car like a racehorse bolting from the starting gate, but returned after a few minutes.

"Back so soon?" Raisa queried.

"Oh, Grandmama, you should see the men in that car. You should *smell* the men in that car. Ugh!"

"Please, dear, tell me about them."

"They're drinking from bottles like the ones on the high shelf in the kitchen."

"Oh, I see," Raisa smiled. "And how many men are in the car?"

"I didn't count everyone, but there are lots of empty seats. One man told me they're going east to work on the railroad, and more men will join them as we go."

"Are they old men?" Kolya asked.

"I don't think so, Papa. Most looked a little older than Cousin Alexi, but some are old like you."

Kolya and Raisa laughed.

"What's so funny?"

"Well, Katya, your father is not so old. But me? Well, I'm the one who is oldest in this family."

"Of course, Grandmama. But the men have sad eyes, like Papa's."

Swallowing a lump in his throat, Kolya answered. "I am a little sad, precious one. I have many memories in Valday, but with you and Grandmama by my side, we'll make new memories, and that thought makes me happy."

"I'm going to the forward car now," Katya said. She only half-heard what her father had said. "I want to find a friend to play with."

"But Katya, I see two girls in *this* car who we know. What's wrong with them?"

"Oh, Papa, they're fine, but Izolda is a year older, and Natalya is a year younger. They will do…if I don't find a friend my age."

"Ah, yes. Of course." Kolya and Raisa laughed again, watching her bounce to the door and out.

⁘⁝⁙⁞⁘

Several families, a smattering of single men, and a dozen more soldiers in uniform inhabited the forward car. The cars appeared identical, except for one notable occupant. Sitting alone on a bench in the row farthest from Katya's coach was a man dressed all in black. He had a long, scraggly, gray beard, was reading a book, and was so still Katya thought he could be a statue. Only his eyes—behind thick glasses—and the tips of his fingers moved, as he turned a page.

Before reaching the quiet man at the far end, Katya made a delightful discovery. She met three more girls—including one her age, Darya. She also found an infant, as well as several boys who smiled and said hello to her, even though they were older. She learned everyone in the car was from Novgorod, the ancient city of the Rus people. She couldn't wait to spend time with them to learn about their city, but she was most curious about the man in the last row.

"I must keep moving to meet everyone in this car before Papa gets worried," she told the boys, and proceeded up the aisle until she stood next to the man in black.

Unlike the rest of her tour, Katya remained silent alongside the man, but she did try to see the title of the book he was reading. After a minute of patience, she began to fidget—just a bit. The man's eyes shifted, and Katya could see they matched the color of his beard and contained a twinkle. It was the same look Papa had now and then when he looked at her. Without warning, he twisted in the seat and looked at her.

"Oh my! I'm sorry!" she exclaimed.

"For what, child?"

Only three words, but a hint of mischievous fun resonated

through his deep and robust voice. She wanted to hear more of that voice, and answered, "For disturbing your reading."

"Ah, yes. My reading. Don't worry. My eyes are tired, and they need a rest."

He reached into his coat pocket and pulled out a thin sliver of varnished wood about three inches long. He placed it in the book at the open page and then closed it.

"My name is Ekaterina Palutova. I'm traveling with Grandmama and Papa. We're from Valday."

"Oh, Valday. Lovely place. Do you have any bells?"

Her eyes lit up when the man asked about bells. "Of course, silly. Everyone in Valday has some bells."

"My father had some Valday bells," the man said. "He dressed his horses with them at the holidays. Maybe I could hear your bells?"

Katya shuffled her feet. "Well, they're not really *my* bells. They're Papa's. I'm not sure he'll let me show them or ring them for you."

The warm deep voice lowered to a whisper. "I understand, Miss Palutova. Sometimes fathers can be very protective of certain things. They guard them almost like a child."

"Papa still thinks I'm a child, but I shall be nine on my next birthday."

"Yes, nine is very good. Very good indeed—but I think you should enjoy being eight, for the moment."

This made her laugh, and he joined in.

"I better get back to Grandmama and Papa. They may think I jumped off the train."

"Indeed, Ekaterina. Mind your father and babushka. It was very nice of you to visit with me."

As she turned to leave, she watched him reopen his book. She could only make out the first couple words on the leather cover— *The Communist Ma…* When it was open, he removed the thin piece of wood, but before putting it in his pocket, he pulled out another small piece. It was a little shorter, and he pressed the two pieces together to form a cross, which remained together as he slid it into his pocket.

"Well, my daughter, what did you discover in the forward car?" Kolya asked.

"Everyone is from Novgorod Papa, and I met Darya. She's my age! Isn't that wonderful?"

"If you are happy, then that makes me happy. So, is Darya traveling alone?"

"Oh, Papa, of course not. She's with her parents, two older brothers, and a younger sister. I don't remember their names, but one of the boys winked at me."

"I see. I suspect he thinks you're pretty."

"Oh, Papa. Stop," she teased back, but secretly, his comment made her happy.

"On another day, you must invite her to come and meet Grandmama and me," he suggested.

"Yes, Papa. I would like you to meet her."

"Who else did you meet?" Raisa asked. "You were gone much longer in that car than you were in the car behind us."

"I met a most interesting man. He has a long gray beard, and he's dressed in black. His voice is low, and words roll out of him like notes from a bass balalaika. If a bear could be a pet, it would have such a voice."

"This man with the wonderful voice, did you ask him his name?"

"No. I forgot. He asked me mine and where I was from. When I told him Valday, we talked about bells. He said his father had some for his horses. I told him you have Mother's bells. Oh Papa, would you ring them for the man in black?"

"We'll have to see how the trip goes," Raisa interrupted before Nikolai could find the right words to answer.

"Was there anything else about this man that attracted you?" Papa continued.

"No. Nothing special, Papa. He was reading when I stopped by his side."

"You didn't interrupt him, did you?"

"Oh no. He stopped to rest his eyes and put a thin, shiny piece of wood between the pages to keep his place before talking to me."

"You're sure you did not disturb him, Katya?" Grandmama double-checked.

"No! He seemed kind and glad to speak to me."

"Very well," Kolya said. "Now, why don't you watch the scenery go by and see how many cows you can count."

"Cows?! Oh, Papa." She turned and brought her mouth within a millimeter of the window and blew a long breath. A cloudy spot appeared on the glass, and she used her finger to write in it: T-H-E C-O-M-M-U-N-I-S-T M-A and stopped. Raisa saw it, gasped, and drew Kolya's attention.

"What's wrong?" Katya asked.

"Where did you see those words?" Papa asked in a gentle but anxious tone.

"The book the man was reading had them on the cover. I couldn't see the last one. And you know what else I saw?"

"No, my dear. Tell us," Raisa encouraged.

And Katya told them about the two-piece cross bookmark.

"Thank you, dear," Kolya said. "For the time being, I think it best for you to remain here with Grandmama and me before we let you move around. I need to see who else is on this train. I'm afraid the man in black could cause us trouble. I will talk to him."

"Oh, Papa. What's wrong with the man in black?"

"I'm sure nothing is wrong with him, Katya. And I think he's reading that book because someone told him he must read it. Be patient. We have a long way to go, and for all we know, he may get off at the next stop." Nikolai turned his back on his daughter and walked to the forward car.

The man was easy to spot, still reading and seemingly unaware Nikolai had entered the car. Kolya proceeded toward the lonely traveler, stopping when his shadow caused the man's gray beard to darken. Without looking up, the man continued to read as Kolya patiently waited. After one more page, the man withdrew his simple bookmark, inserted it into his book, and looked up with a smile at Kolya.

"I'm sorry to disturb you, Father, but…"

"For years, I responded to that simple sign of respect," the man answered, "but, as I'm sure you know, you should not do so any longer." His smile persisted as he spoke.

Looking carefully at the face hidden behind the gray beard, Nikolai realized the former clergyman could not be much older than him. Maybe Vitya's age. The man in black's eyes glistened brightly, in contrast to the deep creases that carved what could be seen of his face under his beard. But his hair? Such hair should belong to someone who possessed the wisdom of age, not someone with those eyes and that voice.

"My daughter, Ekaterina, told me she met you. She also saw the book you're reading. Father, can you…"

"Please, you may call me Viktor. I would be dressed differently if I had other clothes. Alas, I was asked to leave with what I had on and nothing more."

"My name is Nikolai, Fath…er, Viktor. I'm concerned about my daughter. Not that you would say or teach her bad things, but whoever is…watching us might think she's learning something, oh… unapproved."

"I understand. You know I was ordered to read this book. Have you read it?"

"No, but I have heard stories. Some people tell me the ideas in that book are good, and others say the opposite. But any system or book that keeps my family and me from living as we wish or speaking my mind has room for much improvement."

"Ha! Excellent, Nikolai. It is nice to know the hard workers of Valday value independence of thought. I suspect you are on this train with your beautiful child and her babushka because some people in Valday knew how much *you* like your independence."

Kolya smiled at the displaced monk and agreed. "I've always had difficulty keeping my mouth shut if I saw something that bothered me."

"Then we are alike, my new friend. For it seems there are many who prefer not to hear what I say. But worry not. I will remain aloof from your daughter so my words will not corrupt either of you."

Kolya choked a bit at Viktor's comment. "I'm not worried about her being corrupted, Viktor. I only worry that any conversation between us or one you may have with Katya would be misinterpreted by those who hold sway over us during these times."

"Yes, of course. I understand and will discourage her from spending time with me."

"Thank you. That is all I ask. Good day, uh, Viktor."

"Good day, Nikolai Palutov."

Katya and her father explored the four other third-class cars during the next few days and found nothing new. Each one carried a similar assortment of single men, families, soldiers, railroad workers, and displaced workers, with most third-class passengers heading in the same direction—the unknown—a place of great potential and one also of cold beyond description, murderous villains, horrendous living conditions and strange animals.

The big Oktyabrskaya station in Moscow, recently renamed to commemorate the October Revolution of 1917, dazzled Ekaterina.

It was considered a very eclectic design at the time of its construction in the late 1840s, but Katya loved the two-story structure with the large windows and tower in the middle. It had a simplicity and elegance, reminding her of the poster of her mother—stately, beautiful, and aesthetically powerful. But the activity on the station platform truly captured her attention. As the train slowed before every station, she—sometimes with Darya—would skip to the door and hurry down the steps before Kolya could stop her. In Moscow, she vanished into the crush of tricksters, pickpockets, derelicts, and the desperately forlorn who found the station and its expansive waiting area a prime place to secure a few rubles or scraps of food to make it through another day. Although the police were visible, hunger and thirst conquered any fear people had of taking risks, especially to survive or feed a child.

"Katya! Katya! Wait!" Kolya shouted and darted after her. By the time he was outside, she was no longer in sight. He hustled toward the second- and first-class cars. He knew she always went there first to admire the beautiful dresses of the ladies who embarked and disembarked at the different stations. Likewise, numerous vendors hawked their wares at every stop. Katya frequently tried to get one of them to give her an apple, a piece of paper, or a marble. Anything. And in a rare instance, her age, innocent face, and beauty would result in a generous donation. However, more often than not, they chased her away, assuming she was just another impoverished urchin.

Kolya turned in every direction, looking for Katya, and calling her name. He had heard stories of urban poverty and hunger, but what he saw at the Moscow station was much worse than he had imagined. So many sad, weary faces on thin, emaciated bodies, all pleading for money or food. He needed to find Katya to remove her from the threats of decay in every corner—and, on a more practical level, to avoid serious trouble if the train left the station without him. Urgency flowed at high speed through his veins.

Although she heard her father calling, Katya meandered through the activity on the busy platform. She loved the endless line of shoeshine boys, paperboys, candy vendors, cigarette girls, and fortune-tellers. They mixed with people selling food, drinks, decks of cards, pocketknives, small mirrors, and postcards. Turning down another aisle, she saw birds in cages, cardboard satchels, fancy bags made from tooled leather, and many more items which had distracted her from the ladies in first-class. A small, swarthy man with rough hands sat at a table next to a woman who looked like she could be the fat lady in a circus. The two were painting toy dolls made from pinecones and needles.

"They're beautiful," she said.

"Yes. We think so," the man answered.

"You know, we're here every day, and I don't think I've seen you before," the woman added.

"I'm on the train. I come from Valday," Katya answered as they continued to paint.

"Oh, Valday. The town of the bells. Very nice. Would you like a doll?" the man offered.

"Oh my! Yes! But I have no money."

The man put down his paintbrush and said, "Follow me. I have some in another cart on the other side of the building. Ones that didn't turn out good enough to sell, but still nice. I will let you pick one."

Katya followed him to the far side of the station, where several long, parallel lines of carts were parked away from the station entrance. People coming and going into the station paid no attention to the vendors' wagons and the burly man quickly took advantage. He suddenly turned and scooped Ekaterina up as they walked between the rows. His paint-splattered hand clamped over her mouth before she could scream, and he whispered in her ear to be quiet, or he would hurt her.

As Katya struggled, Nikolai began to worry as he scanned the frenetic platform. He asked the official from his car if he had seen her, but the functionary responded he didn't care because Katya was not on the official passenger list. The provodniks on the second- and first-class cars had the same response. Kolya began to panic.

"Five minutes!" The shout went up, announcing the train would soon be leaving.

He ran back to the third-class cars and jogged through all of them.

"Kolya! Kolya! What's the matter?" Raisa demanded.

"Not now, Mother. I'm in a hurry." And he was gone.

Back on the platform, he began asking questions among the vendors. At last, a teenage boy operating a grinding wheel said he had seen a girl who looked like Katya. He said she had gone off with a gruff-looking man to the other side of the building, where they park all the horse carts.

"Four minutes!"

Kolya sprinted as fast as he could, but when he came around the corner, he saw the long double row of carts and was terrified. He didn't have enough time to check each one. He was afraid he'd lost her.

Suddenly, there was a scream. The man holding Katya stared down at the bite marks on his hand as she bolted from his grasp. She sprinted out from between the carts and began to yell for help. She ran so fast she never saw her father, who cut off the angle and grabbed her. She was about to bite him, too, when he spoke.

"Katya! Oh, Katya! Where were you? What happened?"

"Papa! Papa!" She started to cry. "A man with fingers like steel. He tricked me."

"Two minutes!"

"What happened to *three* minutes?" Kolya mumbled. He'd been too busy looking for her and had missed it. As he hugged her, the dollmaker emerged from the carts. He had a dirty paint rag wrapped around his hand.

"That's him, Papa. That man wanted to steal me. He said he would give me a pinecone doll. But he lied."

Nikolai put Katya down. "Wait here. Don't move," he ordered and turned to walk in the man's direction.

"One minute!"

He heard the conductor shout through the bull horn, and then the train whistled. "You're lucky I don't have time to teach you a lesson, dollmaker. I shall report you. The police don't like men who chase young girls."

The man laughed as Kolya turned back to Ekaterina.

He picked her up and dashed to the train. By the time he reached the platform, the train was moving. He ran alongside the first car he came to and jumped aboard. They landed safely, but on the steps of the first-class car.

<hr/>

"You can't come in here," the first-class provodnik shouted as Nikolai and Katya caught their breath, feeling the train pick up speed.

"I had no choice," Kolya countered. "I had to rescue my daughter. A man was trying to kidnap her, and we were going to miss the train."

The conductor hesitated. Stories of stolen children were not uncommon. "You will have to remain here, between the cars," he spoke with authority. "I'll put you off at the next stop."

"But the official in our car needs to know I'm on the train," Kolya said with equal conviction, "or I'll be in trouble."

A woman in elegant travel attire opened the door to her compartment and barked at the conductor.

"Oleg, where's my coffee? I asked for it before we left the station. And what is all this noise? Who are these people?" she compressed her words into one long demanding order.

"Excuse me, Mrs. Brik. I sent the steward for your coffee and expect him back any moment. And these?" he nodded at Katya and her father. "These two jumped onto the train as we left the station, and I think they may be here without tickets."

"Is that true?" she looked at Nikolai. "Did you jump on for a free ride?"

He was about to answer her when he did a double take. "You, you're Lilya Brik. I see your picture on posters everywhere."

It was true. She was on all kinds of posters—but mostly ones spouting Soviet propaganda and supporting Lenin's Bolsheviks. The people who forced Nikolai into exile. The woman had a bizarre reputation. She was a devotee of the avant-garde and was predisposed to unusual sexual behavior. She was well-known for taking many lovers—artists, actors, poets, politicians, security people, military officers—their occupation made no difference. She was unorthodox, brazen, and beautiful, and it was well known that she maintained a long love affair with another man while remaining married to her husband. Many rejected her for such behavior, but young Katya was thrilled to meet her. She found Mrs. Brik exciting.

"Yes, but so what?" Lilya told Nikolai. "Many people are on posters. But what about you? Are you here to get a free ride?"

Kolya wanted to tell the truth, but his story was complicated, and seeing Lilya Brik had surprised him.

"Papa! I've seen her posters too!" Katya couldn't keep quiet.

"Not now, Katya," he admonished and turned to the provodnik and Mrs. Brik. "No, I have a ticket. I'm on the list for third-class from Valday. I am Nikolai Palutov, and this is my daughter, Ekaterina. We're also traveling with Raisa Kuznetsova, my mother-in-law. At the station, someone tried to steal my Katya from me. A man grabbed her and took her to the vendor carts away from the station. I found her just in time, or we would have missed the train. The only way was to jump onto this car."

"Enough!" Oleg barked at Kolya. "Mrs. Brik, is there anything else?"

"Yes, Oleg. I am curious to hear what the girl has to say. I shall take them into my compartment. Tell the steward to bring a pot of tea and more cups instead of coffee. And something to eat. And send someone to the Valday car to bring the girl's babushka to join us. And inform the official in their car of Mr. Palutov's location." She turned back into the car without another word.

"Well?" Oleg yelled at Kolya with frustration. "Follow her!"

They followed Lilya Brik into her private cabin. Inside, they found a second woman, similarly dressed and about the same age as Lilya and Nikolai. There were two long bench seats lushly furnished in the best velvet, a wooden table secured to the floor, four electric lights hanging from the walls—one at each end of both benches—and an overhead light. There were also shelves above the benches holding hat boxes and fancy, leather pieces of luggage.

"Come in, come in," Lilya ordered. "This is Miss Vasilieva, a friend."

"Nikolai Palutova, Miss Vasilieva. And my daughter, Ekaterina." Kolya gave a slight bow and poked Katya with a finger. She looked at him and then made a brief curtsey.

"It is a pleasure to meet both of you," Nikolai continued. "I am sorry to interfere with your privacy. We should be getting back to our car."

"Nonsense!" Lilya told him. "Sit." she pointed to one of the seats as she eased herself down very close to Miss Vasilieva.

They sat, and within seconds the steward returned with a pot of tea and a selection of sandwiches and sweets. Katya's eyes widened with expectation, but before she could ask what each item was, the steward left, and the conductor ushered Raisa into the compartment. Reserved and quiet by nature, Raisa was surprised to find Nikolai and Katya sitting with the two distinguished, flamboyantly dressed ladies.

"Kolya! What happened to you? I was worried sick about both of you." Then she caught herself. "Do pardon me, ladies. I was so worried when they didn't return to the car, and the train began to move. I was at my wits' end."

"That is fine, Grandmother," Lilya answered. "As you see, they are safe. I invited them in for some tea and to hear the story your granddaughter has to share about their tardy return to the train."

"Oh my, yes. Thank you. Where are my manners? I am Raisa Kuznetsova. I am honored to meet you."

"Oh, dear Grandmother, we deserve no honors, although it is delightful to get them." Lilya laughed and pointed to the bench for Raisa to sit next to Katya.

"Now, Katya," Lilya said, clearly in control, "please tell us what happened to you at the station."

Katya told them about racing off the train and not listening to her father when he yelled at her to stop. "It was Moscow, and I wanted to see as much as I could." She told the four adults about the man's offer of a free doll, and her listeners nodded in understanding. Nikolai filled in the rest of the story, and when they finished, Lilya asked for a detailed description of the man. She promised to alert the authorities and, if nothing else, make sure he could no longer sell his dolls at the station.

As Lilya talked, Katya set her eyes on the sandwiches once again. After what seemed an eternity and feeling sure she would never get a chance to try one of them, Miss Vasilieva said, "Thank you for the story, Katya. Now, you may take a sandwich and a cup of tea."

The first one to attract Katya's hand was a pretty red one—caviar spread across a star-shaped piece of rye bread. She took small bites to make it last. It was a new taste, something she couldn't quite describe.

"Please, Raisa, Nikolai, help yourself. I suspect this is better than whatever nourishment you have in third class."

Kolya wasn't sure if he should be grateful or embarrassed. In the end, the gift horse was too good to refuse. "I cannot begin to thank you enough," he said to Lilya. "This is a treat the three of us will remember for a very long time."

"Oh, Nikolai, the treat is ours. Katya is beautiful. A bit precocious, but then again, so am I."

Lilya winked at him and Raisa and then pursed her lips in the direction of Miss Vasilieva. Kolya couldn't hide the blush that rose on his face, and a giant smile grew on Lilya's.

"Enjoy the food. Eat all you like, and whatever we don't finish is yours to take when our conversation has run its course."

The four adults settled into a discourse ranging from fashion to books, religion, politics, the plight of the Palutov family, and, more importantly, the country's future. Katya interrupted periodically with a question about the food but otherwise remained quiet and listened. Nikolai and Raisa were fascinated by the depth of knowledge displayed by the two lovely women. However, they also realized Lilya and Miss Vasilieva had little understanding of the substantive differences between their lives and people like Kolya and Raisa. Regardless, when the whistle blew, and the conductor announced, "Next stop: Tula," they were all disappointed.

As the train rolled to a stop, Nikolai helped remove the ladies' luggage from the shelves and assisted the steward, who guided Lilya Brik and Miss Vasilieva off the train. On the platform, Lilya turned to Nikolai, took him in both arms, and, true to her persona, kissed him—on the lips. The public display caused the blood to adorn his face once again. It also brought forth a smile from Miss Vasilieva, a look of disbelief from Raisa, but most importantly, a delightful, heartful laugh from Lilya.

"How fortunate for me that Katya took off in haste at the Moscow station, Kolya. I can call you Kolya?" Lilya said. "If she had not, I would not have met you and your family. You made the journey so wonderful. I shall immediately send a wire to the Moscow authorities about the man who tried to abduct Ekaterina." Lilya Brik then extended her hand, palm down.

Nikolai looked at it for a moment before he bent, took her hand, and kissed it. "Thank you again for being so generous."

He motioned toward the leftover food in Raisa's hands. His deep, dark eyes gleamed as he smiled at Lilya Brik, and then she was gone.

***

For several days, Katya was not allowed to leave the train without her father or grandmother. When she was with Raisa, they always looked at the ladies coming and going from the first-class cars.

"Grandmama, aren't the dresses the ladies wear in first class wonderful?"

"Yes, dear. They are lovely," Raisa was particularly impressed, considering the "traveling" clothes the women wore were certainly not their best.

"Grandmama, someday I'm going to have beautiful dresses."

Raisa looked at her granddaughter with sad eyes but offered hope. "I pray your dreams come true, because you would look even prettier in such dresses. How lucky I am to have you for my granddaughter."

"Oh, Grandmama, I'm the lucky one, because I have you."

Tears formed in the older lady's eyes, and she bent down and hugged the eight-year-old optimist.

The train made many short stops at small stations between the more populated cities, and every seat had filled up by the time it arrived at Penza. Katya, however, had lost her seat earlier in Ryazan. An elderly man named Mikhail Popov boarded there, and the provodnik assigned him Katya's seat. Mr. Popov was returning home to Irkutsk after visiting his grandchildren. He apologized for taking her place, but Katya didn't mind.

"The provodnik told me I might lose my seat, but I'm glad it's you. You remind me of my dedulya. Besides, I don't spend too much time in the seat, anyway."

Mikhail laughed and said he was delighted to meet Katya,

and they soon became fast friends. Katya's inquisitiveness sparked Mikhail, who proved to be an excellent storyteller. He would tell stories of explorers, adventurers, scientists, farmers, and Katya's favorite—fairy tales. She especially liked the fables with Baba Yaga, but after three stories she was tired of sitting cross-legged. Katya was ready for a change.

"Papa, can I visit Darya and maybe walk all the cars?"

"Make sure you stay with Darya—and don't be a pest," Kolya said as he watched Katya scamper away.

By the time Mikhail Popov came aboard, Katya knew most third-class passengers, but she always liked to learn more about them.

"Yes, she is just like my granddaughter," Mikhail said and smiled.

Katya's natural charm made her popular with everyone she met on the train. In addition to her easy and outgoing personality, people admired her dark eyes, which sparkled as she talked, and her long, shimmering, auburn hair. Grandmama would brush out her tresses every night to work out the kinks from each day's activities, and to check for the tiny bugs that thrived in the crowded, unsanitary carriages. When her babushka finished brushing her hair, Ekaterina would search for a place to sit or stand near a window and look for the moon. With eyes fixed on the distant orb, she would whisper goodnight to the mother she never knew. Something she had done every night since she learned to talk.

In the rush before leaving Valday, Raisa only had time to pack one travel bag for each of them, not the allotted two. Each had one extra set of clothes and a few notable personal items. They also carried their heavy winter coats, boots, hats, and mittens, which came in handy. Every night after saying goodnight to her mother, Katya took her canvas satchel, formed it into a lumpy pillow, and lay down to sleep. Depending on the temperature, she would use her heavy coat as a mattress or blanket. Regardless, the slow, steady click-clack of the train over the rail ties, the long whistles—to warn animals and pedestrians—and the call for engine water, all of which formed the rhythms of life for those long days on the train, put her to sleep.

On her excursions through the train, Katya relished meeting people whose skin color and physical features differed from hers. She listened closely to them when they talked in languages foreign to her ears. She wanted to try the unusual food she smelled and admired the variety of clothing the passengers wore. She particularly liked the long sleeveless shirts that reached mid-thigh and occasionally to their knees worn by the Khakas women.

"What do you call that long jacket with no sleeves?" Katya asked one of the women.

"Si—ge- dek," came the answer as Katya reached out to touch it.

The soft brown leather was so smooth Katya emitted a faint murmur of delight when she stroked it. Black and gold material formed vertical stripes decorating the middle of the garment and moved up from the waist to the neck in a deep V pattern. The sigedek circled the shoulders at the point where sleeves are customarily attached. Complementing the ensemble was an elaborate, wide, multicolored beaded necklace that covered most of the woman's chest.

"Beautiful," Katya said.

Appreciating Katya's interest, the woman undid her necklace, pulled the sigedek over her head, and draped it over Katya's. The excess material piled up on the railcar floor, and the deepest section of the black and gold V rested upon the top of the pile. Buried underneath, Ekaterina began to giggle, but the woman wasn't fin-ished. She added the elaborate necklace, and Katya wished she had a mirror. Suddenly, a man plopped a tall, heavy hat on her head, and everyone in the car began to laugh. Taking advantage of center stage, Katya bent over and picked up as much of the sigedek as possible, like a bride hauling in her wedding train. When she could see her feet, she strode up and down the car as if she were a fashion model, attracting laughter, cheers, and applause from the entire car. Yes, Katya always seemed to find a way to bring smiles to an audience.

⁘⁘

Regardless of their occasional fun, third-class passengers faced daily challenges. Discomfort was their common bond. No matter their color, religion, clothes, food, or language, they all had to sleep, eat, and survive on the train. They shared insufficient communal toilets, breathed in each other's sour breath, raced to wash their faces and hands at station facilities, and slept on the hard wooden floor and benches. Their one *luxury* was the large, metal samovar located at the end of each car next to the provodnik's compartment. You had to provide your own tea, cups, saucers, sugar, and spoons, but your train fare included wood or charcoal to keep the water heated. There was also an accepted protocol for access to it. Soldiers were first, followed by the babushkas and children, by age—oldest first for the women and youngest first for the children, followed by the married women, single women and girls, married men, and last—single men. Somehow it worked. But not always smoothly.

Grigor Korablin was one of those travelers who took offense at everyone and was never happy with the arrangement for getting his tea water. Korablin was no taller than the average woman and as lean as a walking stick, with a pockmarked face and a perpetual sneer on his lips, which quivered when he got angry. He dressed as if he belonged in first class, exuded arrogant superiority, and found reason to criticize anything and anyone at every opportunity. He was also intelligent and clever. As a descendant of Russian nobility and a minor aristocrat, he had managed to evade the fate of his peers. He successfully navigated the dangerous political waters while many friends and family fled the country or were assassinated.

Grigor had felt confident he could sustain his businesses and

64

status without attracting attention from the fanatics determined to eliminate every member of the aristocracy. For six years, he succeeded. However, when he refused to negotiate better working conditions, his workers—his serfs, in the old lexicon—informed local Soviet political leaders. Korablin's strict policies resulted in an ultimatum; he could leave the country within two days or be sent to prison. He chose to join a cousin whose family had escaped to Harbin, China. When authorities denied his request to travel in first or second class, Grigor had to ride the hard seats in third class. Nonetheless, he had purchased three tickets, ensuring he would have an entire bench to himself. Katya met Grigor as he raged on about the samovar.

"This is most unsatisfactory," Grigor bitched as Katya and Darya opened the door to the car.

"Korablin, stop your complaining," the man in line behind him answered back. "We always get our hot water. There's no problem."

"No problem?! The fact I must wait in line is beyond all common sense. I paid for three tickets. For that reason alone, I should be at the head of the line." He turned around to confront the man behind him. "And standing in line, in such proximity to—to—to *you,* and these…others! It's an affront!"

The man and almost everyone in the car began to laugh at him. Grigor's face burned, and he clenched his fists.

"Stop it! I demand you apologize for such insubordination."

This comment did nothing except increase the intensity of the laughter.

"What's so funny?" The question penetrated the room from the opposite end of the car. Heads turned to see who could have asked such a silly question. Katya asked again, "What's so funny?"

Darya took two steps back from her inquisitive friend.

"Oh, it's only the Palutova girl," someone said. "I have no doubt she entered life already speaking and asking questions. She never stops."

"Yes, I do ask lots of questions. That's how to learn things," Katya answered innocently. "That's what Grandmama taught me."

"Well, Miss Palutova," an older man responded, "we're laughing because Mr. Korablin thinks he's better than the rest of us and should be first in line to get his tea water."

"He is certainly dressed very well. I like your clothes, Mr. Korablin, but the single men always get their tea water after the others. Everyone knows that," she told him.

"Go away, child. You have no idea what you're talking about," Korablin ordered. "These people are rude and crude. You cannot trust what they say. They come from poor families and have no idea how to behave around someone with better breeding." He straightened his back and scanned the entire car with an air of self-righteousness. "Move on," he said. "Go back to your Papa, little girl. And the rest of you: learn your place, or I'll—"

"You can't do anything, Korablin," someone reminded him. "Here, now, you're no different than the rest of us. If you want your tea water, you'll wait in line until it's your turn."

Grigor had had enough. He reached into his pocket and pulled out a knife. "Stay back! I've had it with all of you. I'll get my water whenever I want. Do you hear me? People like you have been trying to get rid of me for years. I won't stand for it."

His movements were controlled and experienced. As a child of wealth, he had learned how to defend himself with various weapons. His quickness and small size had proved beneficial more than once against larger and stronger foes. He was not afraid of anyone. When a man lunged at him, he deftly stepped aside, swung the blade, and cut a swath across the man's coat with ease. The crowd shouted, and multiple men were about to seize him as the conductor came out of his compartment.

"What's going on here?" he demanded.

"He's a menace," the man behind Grigor said. "Thinks he should be privileged in our car. Get his tea water first. He's nothing but trouble. Brandishes a knife."

"Perhaps, but that's not all I see," answered the provodnik. "Looks to me like you have *him* outnumbered by a good bit. What can one man do against all of you? Stop this shouting and complaining. If you don't, I'll remove the samovar and add your names to my list of riders requiring *special* attention. And you, Mr. Korablin, give me the knife."

Outnumbered, and seeing no way out, Grigor complied.

Everyone backed off and reorganized the line for the samovar. When things settled, the conductor returned to his compartment, and Darya and Katya greeted several passengers. As the girls were about to return to their own families, the conductor reappeared and, with a barely noticeable movement of his head, beckoned to Mr. Korablin. The former patrician followed the provodnik out of the car onto the platform. Katya, perpetually curious, hurried to the door and peeked through the window. She saw the two men arguing and watched as Grigor reached inside his jacket and withdrew a large roll of rubles. He gave several to the overseer, but the official shook his head, and Korablin gave him more. Only then did Grigor get back his knife.

The door opened, and Katya backed up in a hurry. She heard the recipient of the money say, "Always a pleasure doing business with you, Korablin. Until next time."

Grigor shoved his way past Katya and glared at her, the knife safely in his pocket out of sight. "What are you doing snooping on me?" he yelled at her. "What did you hear? What did you see?"

"Nothing. Nothing, Mr. Korablin. I was going to explore another railcar. That's all."

"If you're lying to me, you will regret it. Your father, and your babushka, too. Stay away from me. I don't need to be tripping over children."

"I'll go, Mr. Korablin, but you know what? You're not very nice. People treat you the way you treat them." She quickly turned and hurried back to her car.

Korablin watched her go with his mouth open. Finally, he spit out, "Brat!"

⁂

The train rolled on toward Kuznetsk, Samara, Ufa, Chelyabinsk, Omsk, and Barnaul, with the Palutovs and their traveling neighbors well-settled into a routine. The group that had boarded in Valday worked together gathering food, cooking it—when they could—and swapping stories during the day. The men shared tobacco, and the women shared knitting needles. Katya and her growing retinue of friends also had a set practice. To a large extent, it consisted of playing games of fantasy. One day they would be great Russian explorers sailing across the Pacific and claiming lands in North America. Another day the girls were princesses trapped in castle towers by evil bandits and beckoned the boy princes to rescue them. Katya loved these games. With a never-ending imagination, she always had ideas the group quickly adopted. She was not inherently selfish or bossy but possessed an inherent likeability and honesty, allowing her to get her way more often than not.

When the train stopped in Kuznetsk, she and Darya stepped off again into a land of sights, sounds, and smells that made Katya wonder if she was still in her own country. Mongols, Kazakhs, Tartars, and Uyghurs swarmed the station, along with ethnic Russians. Katya loved the diversity, but as they wandered along the platform looking at everything, the air was gray and dingy. A pall of coal smoke from the industrial mining city cluttered the atmosphere and filled the girl's nostrils. Before they even had time to try a small piece of Tartar chebureki, the local deep-fried pastry filled with minced meat and onions, their time was up. The conductor made the call for *three minutes*. Rushed, as always, Ekaterina continued to zip through the crowd, with Darya trailing close behind.

"Oh darn, we missed her," Katya said.

"Who?" Darya asked.

"A woman with a pretty dress."

"Come on, Katya. We have to get back. And we've seen lots of pretty dresses."

"I know. Okay."

They began to run, returning to Darya's car just as the provodnik called, "Last call, all aboard!"

"See, Darya?" Katya laughed and gasped, nearly out of breath, "I knew we'd make it."

Darya eyed her friend and shook her head. "Why do we always have to wait until the last minute?"

"Now tell me," Kolya asked, once Katya was back at their bench, "What were you and Darya up to?"

"Too much coal smoke, Papa, but I saw a woman wearing a pretty blue dress."

He smiled and thought, *Another stop, and another pretty dress.* "That's better than what happened in Moscow," he reminded her.

"Yes, Papa, but it would be good to have a little excitement."

In a remote area of plains, miscellaneous farms, scrub trees, dirt tracks, and scattered ponds, the train abruptly stopped one day before its scheduled arrival in Omsk. Without warning, gunfire erupted near the front of the train. Then a blast of shots shattered the carriage door closest to the provodnik's cabin in the Valday car. Three men burst in carrying weapons. Raisa instinctively grabbed Katya, pushed her to the floor, and covered her granddaughter's body with her own as they squirmed to hide under their bench. She had heard stories of bandits along the railway, but never imagined she would encounter them. Was there no place safe in her country? Katya, forever curious, squirmed just enough to peek out from under Raisa's coat to see the men.

"You're free!" the intruders shouted. "Free to go and do as you wish. We free you in the name of—"

Before the gunmen said any more, bullets cut them down and Katya shrieked. Raisa squeezed her tighter and covered Katya's eyes. The traveling soldiers and one of the Soviet *watchers* who kept track of the exiles had opened fire with their guns. The three strangers collapsed in bloody heaps on the floor. Nikolai, who had been in the last car visiting with a logger from a small town in the Urals, raced in a panic to his car when he heard the shots. He breathed a deep sigh of relief when he saw Raisa and Katya hiding under the bench. Later, he learned the soldiers in each hard seat car shot and killed the misguided altruists. Unfortunately, the outcomes were not the same in second and first class. The desperate men killed two passengers in the sleeping car and four more succumbed in the soft-seat cars.

After army officers restored order, Nikolai went outside and walked forward to find a group of men near the engine. They told him the engineer was dead, and one of the provodniks had been sent to the nearest town to seek assistance. The senior army officer had assumed control and told the collection of weary travelers they would have to wait two or three days for authorities to claim the bodies and for a new engineer. He said everyone was free to get off the train but warned no one should wander too far for fear of insurrectionists, thieves, and escaped criminals. Kolya smirked. He knew the warning was an excuse to ensure the exiles stayed close. Otherwise, they could be shot.

"Papa, what did you find out?" Katya demanded when Kolya returned. Raisa had Katya wrapped in her arms; they were no longer hiding under the seat.

"Yes, please, Nikolai. If you don't mind," Mikhail, their bench mate, concurred. "Who was it? What were they trying to do?"

"Katya wanted excitement, but this was too much," Nikolai began. "The best guess anyone had is that some remnants of Alexander Antonov's followers from the Socialist Revolutionary Party survived and moved east when their Tambov rebellion against the Bolsheviks collapsed."

"I thought they had been destroyed," Mikhail said.

"Yes. I thought so, too," Kolya said. "I read the Soviets arrested more than 100,000 Revolutionary Party members and killed nearly 15,000 during the uprising. Antonov, himself, was killed back in '22. I bet he'd be surprised to know people are still fighting his lost cause."

Nikolai hadn't agreed with Antonov's methods, but he understood the desire to fight for freedom.

Raisa shook her head in resignation and couldn't hold back. "Will the killing never end? They lost. No need to keep fighting." She stood up and grabbed Katya's hand. "Come, my sweet. We're going outside for some air. Clear our heads from this, this—sad story."

"But Grandmama, I have more questions for Papa," Katya insisted.

"Not now. Come along. You can ask later." She took Katya's arm, and they exited the car.

"Was there anything else?" Mikhail asked Kolya after Raisa and Katya left.

"We'll be here two or three days. The rebels killed our engineer, and we need a replacement. They also caused some havoc up front, in the fancy cars. Six dead. It appears the attackers had no idea how many soldiers were on this train. Otherwise, well, who knows?"

Mikhail leaned in close to Nikolai and whispered into his ear. "Perhaps someday, the Russian people will have a better government. One where the people control their own movements and thoughts. Someday."

Kolya didn't respond. What could he say? He was heading to Siberia because he had spoken his mind. He only hoped Ekaterina would live to see such a time.

The routine of daily life on the train droned on. A number of days after the train stopped in Omsk, there happened to be an empty seat by the man in black, Mr. Molchalin. Despite Papa's warning, Katya sat near Mr. Molchalin whenever there was an open seat, and Viktor never said anything. However, on this day, he was in a talkative mood.

"Ah, Miss Palutova. How are you today? Where is your friend Darya?"

"I am well, Mr. Molchalin. Darya went forward with her mother to talk to someone about trading some tea for some beans. I think that's a good idea. Although the train's plain water tastes horrible, we can still drink tea, but if you have no beans, eggs, or bread, you will get very hungry."

"Yes. That is true. So, tell me, Katya, how is your babushka? Has she taught you the stories of Jesus?"

"Mr. Molchalin! You will get in trouble for mentioning him!"

"I am already in trouble, little one. That is why I am on this train—but the more I think about it, the less I worry. What can happen to me? They can take my life, but you know, whenever that happens, I will join my Lord Jesus in Heaven. I will finally be free. So today, I am happy and rejoice. And so pleased I have someone as pretty as you to listen to me."

Katya smiled at his compliment, then asked, "How can you be free when you die, Mr. Molchalin?"

"Once your spirit leaves your body to reside forever with God, the rulers and officials wishing to control what you do and how you think will have one less person under their power. They become powerless over you, and therefore, you are free."

She looked at him, unsure how to interpret his remarks. As she opened her mouth to ask another question, a voice boomed from the far end of the car.

"Molchalin! You sorcerer! You purveyor of false tales. I warned you. How dare you spoil this child with your nonsensical and fallacious words. You'll be punished for this!" Vladimir Sobol roared at the startled, gentle man from Novgorod.

Every head in the car turned and watched as the tall, athletic, and handsome Soviet Peoples representative from Molchalin's hometown marched down the aisle.

"Ah, Vlad. How good it is to see you. Please, do be calm. You've scared the child," Viktor answered.

Katya, still jittery from the attack, had jumped sky-high when Sobol stormed into the railcar. She began to think Papa and Grandmama had been right and she should avoid the quiet man in black.

"Have you been on the train the entire time?" Viktor asked, and continued with a second question: "And when were you last in church, my friend?"

He spoke clearly and deliberately without malice or sarcasm. The two had grown up together and had once been friends. Things changed in 1916 when Vlad went to war, and Viktor stayed home with the women and prayed. Vlad believed all clergy were cowards.

"Quiet, you self-righteous ingrate. I don't have to tell you where I've been. And more importantly, are you corrupting this girl? What have you told her? Such actions call for discipline. Strong measures."

"Go, Katya," Viktor told her. "Go to your babushka. Be a good girl." His words remained calm but forceful.

As she walked toward the door to leave, big Vlad chastised her. "You stay away from this man. Do you hear me? He is no good. If I catch you near him again, it will be trouble for you and whoever you're traveling with."

Katya was shaking but curtsied and raced out of the car. But before leaving, she turned and said, "He's a good man." Then she scooted through the door.

As it turned out, it would be easy for her to keep her distance from Mr. Molchalin. When the train stopped in Abakan the next day, two uniformed officials boarded Viktor's car and escorted him off the train in handcuffs. Moments later, Vladimir Sobol entered the

Valday railcar and spotted Ekaterina looking out the window. When Katya turned from the window, Sobol cast a shadow across the car, reaching the Palutov bench. Nikolai noticed the look of concern on Katya's face, and he swiveled around to see what sparked the look.

"Are you this girl's father?" Sobol demanded.

"I am, and who are you?" Nikolai rose off the bench as Raisa wrapped Katya in her arms.

The background chatter ceased in the car. Even the soldiers and the provodnik made it their business to be quiet and listen. The big man stared down contemptuously at the much shorter lumberman from Valday.

"My name is Vladimir Sobol. I am the Soviet People's Representative from Novgorod. I'm here to inform you that your daughter was seen speaking with an opponent of the State. A known dispenser of religious gossip that can poison the minds of young people. You should be more careful and keep her from such a demented individual. If I find her chatting with other such travelers on this train again, your journey will become one of increased interest to the State."

Before Nikolai could respond, Sobol spun away on the heels of his spotless leather boots.

The audacity of the man is outrageous, Kolya thought. *Telling me how to parent my child and who she can talk to.* He set aside the fact that Katya had disobeyed his rules. Sobol's affront required a response. Kolya reached up and tapped the taller man's shoulder.

Caught by surprise, Sobol swiftly swung one arm out, expecting to hit or knock over anyone within reach. Fortunately, Kolya ducked out of the way, but the spectators in the car gasped. When the big man realized there were numerous witnesses, he took a breath and toned down his aggression.

"How dare you strike me!" he yelled.

"With all due respect, Representative Sobol, I did not strike you. I tapped your shoulder so I could respond to your accusations about my daughter and how I failed to control her."

"You cannot—"

Nikolai didn't let him continue. "My daughter talks to everyone on this train, and there is no way for me or her to know in advance who may have personal opinions that differ from yours or anyone else's. Before long, we will no longer be of *interest* to you or your colleagues. The child is only eight years old. What were you doing when you were eight?"

Vladimir Sobol looked around at the people in the car, and each, in turn, shifted their gaze so as not to make eye contact with him.

"Ah—good riddance to all of you. You're going to a place where you belong anyway." He stomped his foot and marched out of the carriage.

Mr. Popov was the first one to say something. "Nikolai Palutov, that was either very brave or very dumb."

"My behavior and words are why my family and I are on this train. That man can do little to change things. Yes, I was hasty, I didn't think—but I'm not concerned. There's a big meeting of Soviet reps about to take place in Irkutsk, and I suspect he'll get off there. He'll soon be no more than a bad memory."

"Oh Papa, that man was not very nice. I wanted to kick him," Katya confessed. "Papa, sometimes I say things without thinking, too. I guess I'm just like you."

Mikhail, Raisa, and anyone within hearing distance turned their heads so Nikolai couldn't see the smiles on their faces. Kolya, however, looked at his daughter and ran his fingers through her hair.

"Oh, dear Ekaterina, let's hope not too much."

⁘⧉⁘

Vladimir Sobol did exit the train at Irkutsk, as did Mikhail Popov. Although Katya suffered through Mr. Popov's sour breath every time he slept on the floor near her, she realized she would miss him. He had been her temporary dedushka. She already missed his grandfatherly stories and resigned acceptance of life in the hard seats.

"Why are you crying, my dear?" Raisa took Katya's hands.

"Oh Grandmama, I miss my dedulya so much. Mr. Popov made me think of him, and now Mr. Popov is gone. I liked his stories."

"What about my stories?" Raisa asked with a smile.

"Oh, Grandmama, I love them, but it's not the same."

Suddenly Katya stopped sniffling, and brightness returned to her dark eyes. "I know. I know just the person," she said, and she skipped away. "I'm going to see Darya and tell her my idea."

It would be several days before Nikolai and Raisa discovered who that person was.

"Kolya, have you learned what the girls have been doing, or who they've been seeing?" Raisa inquired of her son-in-law.

"No, Mother. But someone told me the girls are doing something very nice that no one else would think of doing, so I'm not worried."

As Raisa and Kolya discussed the girls, Katya and Darya chatted with one of the least likable travelers on the train, Grigor Korablin. After their initial encounter with him, when he argued about waiting in line for the samovar, both girls had steered clear of him. But with Viktor, Lily Brik, and Mikhail off the train, Katya was desperate to engage someone else who might have interesting stories to share. In her mind, Korablin was the only other person she had met who would have anecdotes to capture her attention.

The day she hurried away from Raisa after crying about missing Mr. Popov, Ekaterina sat with Darya and talked for a long time. They decided they could befriend Mr. Korablin, or at least get him to talk a little if they started doing small favors for him. They could take his place in line for tea water, get his newspapers when the train stopped, shine his shoes, and so on. They could tell him jokes about their lives and carefully ask him questions about his experiences. They began simply enough one morning.

"Good morning, Mr. Korablin."

"Ah, it's you two. I thought I told you not to bother me," he gruffed.

"I'm sorry, sir," Katya went on. "We've been thinking about how you prefer not to wait in line for your tea water, and we thought we could do that for you."

He looked at both girls and raised his eyebrows. "What is the trick? Why would you do that?"

"No trick Mr. Korablin. Grandmama taught me that if I see someone I can help, I should offer to help. We would like to do that for you. I will come in the morning, and Darya will do the afternoon."

He suspected another motive for the girls' sudden actions, but decided it didn't matter. If he could remain on his bench with his books and newspapers and not be humiliated by waiting in line for the samovar, well, that was a good thing.

"Very well, young lady. Here's my cup."

So it began, and each day, they did something extra. Then one day, Korablin was flipping through the documents he carried in his valise, and Katya saw something that made her gasp. Grigor turned around at the sound, realizing he had left the case open, and quickly closed it.

"That's no business of yours. Enough for today, and you did excellent work with my boots. See you tomorrow."

But Katya didn't budge.

"Well, go on now," he scolded her.

Ignoring his order, Katya spoke up. "I'm sorry, Mr. Korablin. Your valise was open, and well, I saw something. Did you actually get to see Anna Kuznetsova sing, Mr. Korablin?"

"Oh, so you saw the broadside with her picture? Yes, I did see her. It was a year before she died." His eyes drifted to the window. He spoke as he looked out without seeing the countryside and flashed back to that remarkable evening. "Oh my, she was amazing. So beautiful! And what a spectacular voice! She could make you cry and laugh with the emotions she put into her singing. Such a shame to lose one so talented at such a young age."

Katya quietly mumbled, "My babushka, her name is Kuznetsova too."

Grigor stopped his musing and saw Katya's reflection in the murky window. Their eyes met, and he turned around. "No! You can't be! But…wait, how old are you, Katya?"

"Eight," she answered.

He took a step back and looked at her. "Yes, of course. You're her daughter, aren't you?" His eyes moistened, and he saw Katya in a whole new way. "Would you like me to tell you about the night I saw your mother perform, and how I met her?"

"I'm not sure Papa wants me to know such things, Mr. Korablin. I saw the poster, which reminded me of one Grandmama has. I'm sorry."

Grumpy and constantly complaining, Grigor became a different person. He saw the pain in Katya's eyes and wanted to tell her about her mother. "Have your father and babushka told you much about your mother?"

"No, sir. Not very much, but I think you should talk to him before you tell me."

"Very well. I will. You've been so kind to me. And Darya too. Probably when I didn't deserve it, but I must tell you I'm not used to being in such places with people like this all around me," Grigor said, waving his arm. "They think I'm weak because I'm not very tall, so I must appear strong. Oh, why am I telling this to a young child? It's just…entirely different from the life I had."

Katya let his short soliloquy glide past and said, "Come, Mr. Korablin. I will take you to my father, but first, you must tell me why you pay the provodnik."

Grigor had no intention of telling anyone, let alone the inquisitive young Miss Palutova, about his relationship with the conductor. It was no one's business except his. Besides, it had nothing to do with his encounter with her mother.

"Katya, I thought you were interested in hearing the story about how I met your mother. If it's not important to you, that's fine. I'll go back to my papers. Thank you both for your help today." He turned away and took a step.

"Oh no, Mr. Korablin! I do want to hear the story."

"Very well then." He faced her. "Let's go see your papa. I think we have more in common than he may realize."

Katya burst into the car and ran to her family's bench. "Oh, Papa, guess what? Mr. Korablin knew Mama and has her picture. Isn't that wonderful?"

The news caught Nikolai by surprise. *Was it possible that the arrogant little man who liked to brandish his knife and threaten other passengers knew Anna? Anna had known many people. But how would Katya know?*

"Why are you seeing Mr. Korablin?" he asked her.

Before she could answer, Grigor, who had followed Katya, spoke.

"Good day, Mr. Palutov. I have been meaning to come and see you, to tell you how helpful Katya—that is, Ekaterina—and her friend have been to me. You should be very proud to have such a giving and caring child."

Kolya didn't know what to say. In a few seconds, he had been shocked twice; by Korablin's presence and then by his words.

Before he could respond, Grigor continued, "And a good day to you too, Mrs. Kuznetsova."

Raisa was equally startled and sat mutely on the bench, staring at the bizarre man who interrupted her knitting. The silence was more than Katya could stand.

"Papa, without stories from Mr. Popov and Mr. Molchalin, I decided Mr. Korablin would have some different ones to share."

Korablin smiled to himself. Now he knew the real reason for the girls' attentiveness. They liked listening to his stories, and the thought made him happy for the first time in weeks. But he was concerned.

"A good choice, Katya?" he asked. "For stories? Why would you want to make friends with someone who treats people like dogs and threatens them with knives?" he looked at Korablin as he spoke. "Mr. Korablin, your previous behavior with the knife makes me question whether I should permit my daughter to see you," Nikolai said.

"Ah, yes, of course. Let me explain. I've been attacked numerous times since the Revolution, as if I were Nicholas II, himself. I carry it for self-protection."

"From what I hear, no one was trying to attack you, Mr. Korablin," Kolya followed.

Deflecting the comment, Grigor said, "Your daughter and her friend have made an impact on me I cannot describe, Mr. Palutov. Some of my fears may have been misplaced. A paranoia, if you will. Yes, it's true," he admitted, "I've been spoiled and treated special most of my life. And, often, I believe I'm entitled to certain courtesies. But you must understand, my parents taught me to be strict or people would steal what I had. So, before you chase me away and think I'm just another arrogant, angry man of wealth, I need you to know your daughter has shown me another side of life. She's shown me that not having social status or money does not mean someone wants to steal from me. Her friendliness, outgoing manner, questions, and love for her family made me realize that I never witnessed those things in my own family. I will do as you wish, but believe me, I enjoy the company of the girls. They are more helpful to me than just getting my tea or shining my shoes."

For the third or fourth time in a couple of minutes, Nikolai swallowed hard and wrinkled his brow. He mulled over Korablin's words, all the while looking him in the eyes. Generally, he considered himself to be a good judge of a man. At last, Nikolai spoke. "Yes, she's a good girl, Mr. Korablin. Very well, I'll allow her time with you. But should I hear of one instance of anything improper…"

"Oh, Papa!" Katya burst before her father could finish. "Mr. Korablin wants to tell us about how he met Mama. Can we listen?"

"I understand, Mr. Palutov. I understand completely. As to your wife, it was my privilege to hear her sing. I was also able to meet her after a concert," Grigor said with respect.

"I-I-I'm not sure I need to know," Kolya said. "I rarely speak of Anna, and thinking of her can be…" he couldn't continue.

"Maybe tomorrow," Raisa offered. "Thank you, Mr. Korablin. We'll see."

"Yes, of course," Grigor answered. He bowed, turned, and went back to his seat.

Raisa couldn't sleep. She listened to the slow rhythmic breathing of Nikolai and Katya, but she sat staring out the window. A couple of remarkably unrelated items kept rising to the fore each time she was about to drift off. She found it hard to believe someone like Grigor Korablin had been enamored by her Anna. Aristocratically refined, but also crude and presumptuous, he had softened in her eyes. And then there was the train. It would pass around Lake Baikal's southern end at night, and this made her nervous, especially after the shootout they had already experienced. Trains had to crawl through myriad dark, twisting tunnels over a deteriorating track on this part of the route to prevent accidents. Her anxiety grew when she observed a mysterious, flickering green light moments before the train slid into each tunnel. *Was the light a signal? For what?* She rubbed her hands and prayed—to the God the communists told her did not exist—for calm.

As if justifying Raisa's concern, the silent night abruptly ended. The train wheels screeched as they stopped turning and slid along the steel rails, bringing the train to a halt. People began to stir when the steady clicking of the rails vanished, and Nikolai, woken from his own never-ending dreams of Anna, could tell Raisa was upset. Rumors about bandits in the region and numerous so-called accidents compounded her unease. Seconds later, the provodnik went forward to find out why the train stopped. He returned within five minutes.

"We'll be detained for a while," he said. "Several rails are gone, and we need to repair the track. It's nothing to worry about. You can go look for yourself, but I'm going back to sleep," he said, then disappeared into his cabin.

Katya wanted to go look but, Nikolai told her to wait with Raisa while he and several others went to see for themselves. Like the provodnik, they were back in a few minutes.

"Tell me, Papa. What happened?"

"There are several track rails missing inside one of the tunnels, exactly like the provodnik said. They are replacing them now, but it will take some time. The track walker had a lantern that signaled the engineer to stop."

"Can I go see, Papa?" she begged.

"No, Katya. It's too dark now. In the morning, after we've had tea and something to eat. Now, back to bed."

When Kolya knew Raisa and Katya had fallen back to sleep, he followed suit and lay on his spot next to his daughter. Like Raisa earlier, it took him longer to nod off. He couldn't help thinking about what might have happened if the engine had come off the track. He also couldn't stop thinking about the sudden personality change he witnessed in Korablin. Can he trust the man? Katya seemed to. But…

They still had a long way to go before arriving at their destination, the small village of Skovorodino. He just wanted them to arrive safely.

While waiting for the workers to fix the rails, Katya pestered her father so much that he finally agreed to allow Mr. Korablin to share his story about meeting Anna. It was a very ordinary encounter in which an acquaintance of Grigor's was also a longtime friend of Anna's. To Kolya's surprise, it was also someone he knew. After her show, Anna permitted Grigor and his friend to enter her dressing room for a brief chat. She signed the broadside which Katya had seen in his case, and that was all. Delighted at having found some common ground, Grigor continued the conversation.

"So, Mr. Palutov, what is your destination and your plans? Or have our leaders in Moscow established them for you?" Grigor asked.

"Back home in Valday, I heard that Siberia is in great need of lumbermen. A friend's cousin settled in an insignificant village called Skovorodino, not far from the northern border of Manchuria. He's the only firm contact I have." Nikolai shrugged his shoulders in resignation. What else could he do?

Grigor wasn't sure if he should offer an alternative, but he could not imagine anyone living in such a desolate place as tiny Skovorodino. No comforts? Still under the rule of the crazy Bolsheviks? And Ekaterina, subjected to the poisonous rhetoric of State dogma? No—he would share his thought.

"You know, Mr. Palutov…"

Kolya interrupted, "By now, you should call me Nikolai."

Grigor smiled. "Thank you. It will be a privilege. And…Nikolai, please address me as…" Grigor hesitated and swallowed hard. "As… as…"

"That is fine, Mr. Korablin. No need to change," Nikolai offered.

"No! No! You have my apologies, Nikolai." Grigor rose from the bench, stood straight, thrust out his hand, and said, "Please…call me Grigor."

Kolya shook hands with the man who represented a small, lingering remnant of the decimated Russian nobility and said, "It is indeed my honor, Grigor."

They sat down, and Grigor took a breath and made his suggestion. "You know, Nikolai, I am going to Harbin in China, a city where many Russians live beyond the reach of the Soviet government." As he said this, he lowered his voice and glanced around to ensure no one was listening before continuing. "You must have heard of this place."

Kolya noticed that Katya had heard every word.

"Katya, why don't you go find one of your friends and play a game together?"

"But Papa, I want to hear what Mr. Korablin says about Harbin. Darya's family is going there too. It must be a good place."

"Yes, well, possibly. But my conversation with Mr. Korablin is not for a child's ears. Now scoot, Katya!"

Raisa stood, took Katya by hand, and escorted her out of their carriage.

"Yes, Grigor. I know of this place, but my documents indicate travel to Skovorodino with specific instructions to stay in Russia. Besides, I have no contacts in Harbin. What would I do?"

"There are forests nearby," Grigor encouraged. "Wouldn't it be best to live with free Russians, people who still worship in churches and teach their children more than communist garbage? Let me see what I can do. I don't have much influence anymore. However, I might be able to arrange something."

"Grigor, such a move worries me. We could get sent to the prison camps if we get caught. Or shot! And, I suspect such *arrangements* would have a price tag beyond my reach."

"Stay right here. I want to show you something." Grigor hurried to his car and returned with his leather business valise. He sat down and pulled out half a dozen color postcards. "Here, look at these." He thrust the cards into Koyla's hands. They were scenes in Harbin and showed fancy hotels, broad boulevards with shops and trees, gorgeous churches, and, most importantly, a new school only for Russian children. "Doesn't this look like a place of prosperity compared to every hole-in-the-wall dirt town and rail station we've passed?" Grigor asked. "And, oh yes, I forgot. Look at this one." Grigor reached into his case and withdrew a final card. "This is the railroad station!"

The cards made a strong impression on Nikolai. "Such a place! And all this in the middle of Manchuria? Is this a trick, Grigor? Is this some other city? Are there really many Russians there?"

"Nikolai, look again at the churches in these pictures. They are Russian churches. In China! Please believe me." Then a final thought flashed through Grigor's head, and he went back into his case. "One last item. Read this."

He gave Kolya a letter addressed to Korablin from a friend. The postmark read Harbin, dated three months previously. As Nikolai read, the only thing that mattered was the handwritten note: "See the enclosed postcards of my city, Harbin."

"Grigor, I don't think you should have shown all this to me."

"Don't worry, Nikolai. We will devise a plan so you don't have to dissolve into the wilderness of Skovorodino. Now, if I don't see Katya or Darya again today, please tell them I'm looking forward to their continued assistance. Of course, in return, I shall be happy to tell stories of my pampered life, and perhaps I can discover a few kopeks in my sack to show them my true appreciation. Good day, Nikolai."

After speaking with Grigor, Kolya talked to Darya's family and learned several other riders were going to Harbin. They confirmed what Grigor told him, that Harbin was a Russian city in China and a haven for White Russians. Nikolai's plan had always been to settle in some small, remote location, such as Skovorodino. However, the allure of Harbin was hard to resist. It was a bustling and energetic refuge for Russians. New possibilities swirled in Nikolai's head. Unfortunately, by 1924, the creep of communism was also penetrating China. So, although it was a preferred sanctuary from the Bolshevik rulers in Moscow, it was not entirely a peaceful retreat. There were xenophobic Chinese Manchurians who didn't trust foreigners, as well as warlords, Japanese interests, and many other obstacles, all unknown to Nikolai Palutov.

5   1924
Trans-Siberian Railroad
Chita To Harbin

Kolya had to decide by the time the train reached the cross-road city of Chita. Some of the railcars would proceed into the deepest heart of Siberia and ultimately terminate at the Pacific port city of Vladivostok. Others would be switched to a different line and traverse Manchuria, stopping in Zabaykalsk, Manchulie, and Harbin before continuing to Vladivostok. The Russians constructed the latter route between 1897 and 1902 under a concession with the Qing dynasty of Imperial China, creating a much shorter line to the sea. The project spurred the development of Harbin as a Russian city within China. But, as the train approached Chita, Nikolai nervously paced up and down the length of the carriage.

"Kolya, come sit!" Raisa ordered him.

"Yes, Papa. Why are you walking so much?" Katya asked. "Come look out the window with me."

"The window! Child, we've been looking out the window for the past three hours. There's nothing to see. It's a horrendous dust storm. Anyone out in that would breathe nothing but desert sand. And I'm walking because I must make a choice."

Nikolai had not mentioned Harbin to Raisa or Katya, but going there sounded better every day compared to Skovorodino. Harbin was a Russian city. People like him. Schools for Ekaterina. Friends for Raisa. Hospitals. Shops. He was confident he could find work. Most significantly, they'd be free. But the specter of severe punishment and possibly death if they got caught tempered his thoughts. He wasn't sure what to do.

The train rolled slowly into the Chita station. Sand swirled fiercely around everything, and people disembarking to switch for Harbin wrapped their heads and faces with anything they could find.

"Nikolai, are you ready?" Grigor was carrying bags under each arm and two others in each hand. He was still a man of some substance and had more possessions than the three Palutovs combined. "Hurry. Let's go. I've arranged everything."

"What? What do you mean? I'm still not sure. The prison camps would be much worse than just trying to survive in the woods near Skovorodino."

"Mr. Korablin, what did you arrange?" Katya asked.

The men turned at her voice. They had been talking loudly to overcome the noise of the relentless sandstorm and the commotion of passengers coming and going. Too loudly, it seemed. Kolya stared at her and shifted his eyes to Raisa.

"Grab your things. We're getting off here," he said with conviction.

"Yes! Hooray, Papa! Darya is getting off here too. Are we going to Harbin like Darya?"

"We shall see. But now, my sweet, you must hurry!"

The provodnik did not see them get off the train with their luggage. If he had, he had no reason to worry. There were many spies in Chita. People of all stripes received petty payments for turning in friends, neighbors, and foreigners, often for fabricated violations of the ever-growing list of crimes against the State. No, he wasn't worried. Someone would catch them, and Kolya would either have to pay a very hefty fine or spend time in prison. Regardless, Grigor

Korablin had paid the conductor handsomely to ignore the Palutovs, although that meant little to the authorities in Chita. In the remote eastern outpost, the Bolsheviks were more interested in keeping track of foreigners than Russian citizens who'd been ostracized, sent into exile, or sent to the mines and prison camps in the Siberian wilderness. And with such a violent sandstorm, everyone was covered from head to foot. It was impossible to tell one person from another. So, Nikolai, Ekaterina, and Raisa entered Chita and the dusty world of the capital of Eastern Russia, where they would wait for another train to take them to China.

Once upon a time, Chita had been a prosperous town like many places across the vast Russian domain. Factories, manicured boulevards, and busy shops with a wide assortment of products had been commonplace. However, what the Palutovs and other visitors found in 1924 was a community that had fallen on tough times. Deserted manufacturing plants, streets with grass growing on them, and mostly empty shelves in the few shops not boarded up were all that remained. There were few accommodations. Transient passengers had to barter or beg for a place to stay while they waited for a train into China. People took up residence with local apartment dwellers, homeowners, and shopkeepers eager for added income. Many riders had nothing with which to barter or pay. They could trade their railway ticket balance for a minuscule refund, but that would leave them stranded in Chita, or they could find a place to hide. Many found respite from the storm in private garages, livery stables, and other out-buildings.

"This is horrendous, Kolya! We must find a place to get out of this storm. I can barely breathe and hardly see," Raisa pleaded with her son-in-law while keeping an iron grip on Katya.

"Yes, Mother. Of course. But we also need to avoid curious

officials. Someone mentioned there's only one hotel open in the city, but it's a government hotel. That would be very risky and expensive. Maybe we can find a room in someone's house."

"I don't care, Kolya. Just find us something!"

They bent their heads and continued walking, but avoiding the ferocious sand pellets was impossible. They felt like a million pinpricks from a sewing needle. Even Katya, typically effervescent, began to complain, but to cheer herself up, she tried to sing. It sounded more like humming, but it worked. The music buoyed her spirits. Then suddenly, fingers wrapped around her upper arm.

"I'm taking you all to the hotel," Grigor shouted in her ear. Following his lead, she pulled on Raisa's arm to get her grandmother's attention. Raisa turned and saw a figure carrying multiple pieces of monogrammed luggage and knew it was Korablin.

"Kolya! Kolya!" she yelled as loud as she could, and Nikolai finally turned.

"Grigor! How did you find us?" Kolya yelled. "We're trying to move away from the station as quickly as possible."

"Yes, I know." Grigor let go of Katya and moved next to Kolya so they could hear each other. "I'm taking you to the hotel. You will be my guests."

"But it's a government hotel! Surely they'll know we should be on the train."

"Don't worry, Nikolai. In these strange times, the truest believers in the Bolshevik cause become instant hypocrites when money is on the table. Come. Let's get out of this weather." Grigor marched off, and Nikolai and his family followed without further thought.

"Papa, when can we leave here? There's no one to talk to. Nothing for me to do," Katya mildly complained about their temporary quarters.

"We'll leave as soon as a Harbin train comes," he answered. "Until then, it's safest for us to remain inside. Besides, the sand continues to fly outside. And don't tell me there's nothing to do. You've seen Darya, Mr. Korablin, and others from home. Didn't you tell me one of the women showed you the dresses stored in one of her trunks?"

"Yes, Papa. Her name is Mrs. Alec Tweedie, from England. She writes about her travels and told me stories of America, England, India, France, and places I don't remember. I think someday I'll go see places like America. You have to cross an ocean to get there, Papa. Wouldn't that be something?"

He smiled at her and could only pray for her dreams to come true, no matter how improbable they might be. In the meantime, they spent four days and nights in the hotel. No one questioned their identification papers; more importantly, no one asked to see their ongoing train tickets. The only good thing any of them could say about the hotel was it protected them from the sandstorm. Bed bugs, little water, no restaurant, no heat, cracked windows, and worrying about being in the wrong place did not nurture happy visitors. The other hotel guests were foreigners or wealthy Russians, like Mrs. Tweedie and Grigor, and thanks to Grigor's generosity, Nikolai, Raisa, and Katya shared a room and made do. On the morning of the fourth day, they got word their train would arrive in the early evening.

"This miserable shithole of a hotel isn't worthy of a mangy dog," Korablin confided to Nikolai outside the Palutovs room. "Did you realize this building had been a prison until recently? No wonder it's such a decrepit place."

"You should keep your voice down, Grigor Korablin," Kolya scolded him. "Grandmama says there are spies everywhere, and bad comments can get us in trouble."

"How right you are!"

The two men were surprised by the voice. They turned and recognized someone from the train. He was a man in his twenties, of average height, on the plump side, with a sharp, pointed, youth-fully wispy goatee and piercing yellowish eyes. As he talked, his lips formed a smug countenance of superiority.

"And who are you?" Grigor demanded.

"I am the new regional Soviet representative for Chita. My name is Dmitri Drozdov."

Before he could say anything else, Grigor showed his contempt. "Drozdov. How appropriate, a blackbird indeed. The name suits your new title. What do you want, *Tovarishch* Drozdov? We were not speaking with you." Grigor emphasized the colloquial Russian for "comrade," which had become much more popular since the Revolution.

Nikolai made a very slight but noticeable gasp at Grigor's words. The last thing he wanted was an encounter with a Soviet agent. "Do excuse me, gentlemen. I need to tend to my family. Thank you," Kolya half-turned to open the door to his room.

"If you don't mind," Drozdov interjected, "who are *you,* and why are you here?"

"My name is Nikolai Palutov. My family and I are waiting for the train." Kolya's hands began to get clammy. If Drozdov discovered he was supposed to be heading to Skovorodino and not Harbin, all would be lost.

Uncertain if this was a benign inquiry or something sinister, Nikolai hesitated guiltily for the briefest moment, but Grigor filled in. "And inside the room, you can hear Ekaterina Palutova, Mr. Palutov's daughter. She has the voice of a choir angel, does she not, Tovarishch Drozdov?"

Dmitri ignored the comment and gave another order. "Open the door!"

Nikolai obliged, and as soon as it swung in, Katya became quiet. "Oh Papa, I'm sorry. I know you don't like me to sing, but I'm excited about getting on the train."

"You don't like your child to sing?" Drozdov accused Nikolai, wondering what could be wrong with him. "Look at her. She's beautiful and still such a child, but her voice...Ekaterina, please, sing some more," Drozdov said. "I cannot believe it was you making such wonderful sounds."

Katya looked at her father, and he nodded for her to proceed. She sang loud and strong for five minutes, attracting a small crowd to the door of their room. When she stopped, they applauded, and Dmitri Drozdov joined in.

"Bravo! Simply magnificent! Now..." he turned to Nikolai, "you must let this child sing whenever she desires. Our great Mother Russia deserves to hear her. Enjoy the rest of your journey." Drozdov turned on his heel and spun out the door, dispersing the onlookers.

Kolya bent over, lifted Katya into the air, and gave her a tremendous hug.

"Oh, Papa. Are you happy?"

"Yes, my child. Very, very happy."

"Well, Nikolai, I will see you at the station. Thank goodness your lovely Katya sings like her mother," Grigor said and smiled. "But I have one last detail to discuss with you." The two men stepped into the hallway one more time. "I don't trust our Mr. Drozdov. I ran off at the mouth and have no doubt he will not forget that."

"Oh, Grigor, I'm sure he won't..."

"No, Nikolai. He will. So listen and pay attention. I was going to do this at the station, but I better do it now in case there's...a problem. I want you to take this." Grigor thrust an enormous wad of money into Kolya's hands, along with train tickets and several papers. One had a bank account number, and another was a letter of introduction to Grigor's contacts in Harbin. "Make sure you hide these well or memorize the number if you can. That would be best.

"I...I...cannot take this, Grigor. It is too much."

"You must. For years I could have helped others, but I did nothing. Besides, it's not for you. It's for Ekaterina. She deserves every opportunity to flourish and succeed. This little bit will help. Use it wisely." Korablin winked, turned, and ran down the hall, down the stairs, and onto the street.

The Palutovs had come to the station early to ensure they wouldn't miss the train. No one wanted to remain in Chita if they didn't have to, and they were happy when it arrived. As they boarded into third class, Nikolai received a tap on his shoulder. He turned, expecting to see Grigor Korablin, but lost his breath when he looked into the face of Dmitri Drozdov.

"Hello, Tovarishch Palutov. Good to see you again."

"Ah, and you too, Tovarishch Drozdov. How can I help you?"

"Have you seen Tovarishch Korablin? It's my understanding he is also going to be on the train." His tone remained neutral, but the look in his eyes was that of an animal tracking prey.

"No. I haven't seen him since you met us earlier. I have no idea where he might be. The train is early. Perhaps he's still in his room."

Drozdov searched Nikolai's eyes for any sign of deception. To Kolya's credit, his breathing remained normal, and he maintained eye contact throughout the younger man's query. Surprising both men, Katya appeared at the top of the boarding steps.

"Papa, are you coming? Grandmama wants to know where you'd like to sit. Oh, hello, Mr. Drozdov. I'm sorry to interrupt. We're waiting for Papa."

"Hello, my singing bird. It is good to see you again. Your Papa and I were just talking, but seeing you again makes me hope you will sing for everyone on the train."

"Oh, I've already—" she began.

"Katya, get back to Grandmama and tell her I will be there momentarily." Nikolai didn't want her to mention singing on the long ride from Valday. He thought it could lead to problems.

"Yes, Papa. Goodbye, Mr. Drozdov."

"Goodbye, Ekaterina. It was a pleasure to meet you." He refocused his eyes on Nikolai and said, "I already checked his room, and he was not there. And he has not checked out. Do you know if he has any friends or relations here in Chita?"

"I don't know," Kolya said. "He never mentioned anyone, and I suspect if he did, he would have stayed with them and not in the hotel."

"Five minutes!" the provodnik's yell echoed across the platform.

"Well, Tovarishch Palutov, I shall continue to wait. In the meantime, get settled with your family and have a pleasant trip."

"Yes. And thank you, Tovarishch Drozdov. I wish you success in your new position," he said with sincerity showing no hint of sarcasm. The ruse brought a thankful smile to Dmitri's face.

"And thank you too." He moved away from the car and began to scan the platform for the missing Korablin.

After the train started to move and the station was no longer in view, Nikolai realized he had been holding his breath. At last, he eased onto his hard seat by his daughter and mother-in-law. But where was Grigor?

"Oh Papa, isn't this terrific? We're going to China. I can't wait!" Katya was exuberant.

***

Upon arriving in Harbin, Nikolai, Katya, and Raisa alighted in a city where many well-to-do White Russians had fled from persecution immediately after the Revolution. Those with fewer resources, like the Palatovs, had also made the long journey since the Bolsheviks' rise to power. Some had been ordered into exile, some to prison, and others fled before being asked. The Soviet government subsequently abandoned anyone who took up residence in China, never contemplating such a concept as *loyal opposition*. Simultaneously, the Chinese had no interest in granting these new

Russian residents citizenship. Therefore, when Ekaterina, her father, and grandmother stepped off the train in Harbin in 1924, they were people without a country.

Nonetheless, before the Revolution, the city of Harbin had expanded substantially since its early days as a small fishing village. The Palutovs found a prosperous and energetic Russian community because the Chinese had allowed the Russian government to finance and build the Chinese Eastern Railway, or CER. Constructed under a concession with the Qing dynasty of Imperial China, the project spurred the development of Harbin as a Russian city within China. Many recognized the agreement as a slick maneuver. It enabled the Russians to extend political and social influence into Manchuria by extending the reach of the Trans-Siberian Railway. Conveniently, it also eliminated the need to travel around the big northern bulge of Manchuria to reach Vladivostok and ice-free Port Arthur, leased by the Chinese to the Russian Empire.

After a few weeks in Harbin, the Palutovs realized the city was amidst major changes, like most of China. Numerous political, social, cultural, and military factions jockeyed for power. The political and military shenanigans following the construction of the CER became the elephant in the room for the people of Harbin and Manchuria. The Chinese and Manchurians did all the heavy work, while the Russians were the administrators. The Russians operated like colonial overseers, and, as is historically common, resentment grew.

It wasn't just the White Russians and local Manchurians who tried to tap dance around each other. There were Chinese Nationalists, Chinese Imperialists, and a small but expanding group of Chinese Communists. There were also the Japanese, who had designs on the numerous natural resources of the region and who had no particular love for the Russians. And, of course, the Soviets—Bolsheviks—who had literally fought wars with Japan for control of the southern spur of the CER, albeit without success up to that point.

The good news was that the Pulatovs walked into a vibrant

cosmopolitan city, just as Grigor had told them. For all intents and purposes, Harbin was a pre-Revolutionary Imperial Russian city, laid out by a Polish engineer and fine-tuned by Russian and Swiss architects and Italian city planners in the middle of Manchuria, China.

In 1924, a small war in Manchuria was also being fought between two factions of Chinese warlords. The Japanese supported one side, which had the upper hand, and a Euro-American alliance backed the other. Soon after the conflict ended, Sun Yat-sen, the widely supported Chinese Republican leader, died. Then on May 30, 1925, not even a year into the Palutovs' time in Harbin, the British Military Police in Shanghai fired on student protestors complaining of foreign interference and control throughout China. The foreign involvement was true. The event became known as the Shanghai Massacre. The shootings and protests spurred increased nationalism, distrust, and outright anger at outsiders, including long-term residents and stateless Russians.

However, when the Palutovs stepped off the train, they shared a sense of freedom, not knowing what was to come.

6   1932
Harbin, China

When the Palutovs disembarked at the Harbin train station in 1924, they were overcome with a sense of joy and relief. The city had had a welcoming feel and a Russian character. They were blissfully naïve of having landed in the middle of a stew pot, with the heat getting turned up. Through Grigor Korablin's contacts, Nikolai obtained a good deal on a modest apartment in a better part of the city, and a lumber company hired him. The job, however, took him out of town for a week at a time, leaving Raisa to care for Katya. The burden on Raisa lasted only until Kolya found a good Russian school willing to accept a new student at mid-term. With Katya in school and Nikolai away in the forests, Raisa had time to take in laundry for some wealthier White Russians to increase the household income.

Overall, things were satisfactory for several years. However, by 1932, nationalistic Chinese hooligans slowly began to threaten, disrupt, and assault poor Russians. After years of subservience, the Chinese and Manchurian people and various Chinese government officials, warlords, and internal revolutionaries were tired of Russian dominance. It didn't matter if you were a White or a Bolshevik. If you were Russian, you were a target. It was common to witness poor Russians being assaulted by Manchurian Chinese police for minor infractions, no less witness ruffians mugging a destitute Russian refugee from the Revolution. This overt anger at the Russians seemed strange to Nikolai and his exiled compatriots, because it was apparent that the Japanese, not the Russians, were the ones who were determined to take over China.

Kolya had a worried look as he gazed out the window of the small apartment he shared with his sixteen-year-old daughter and mother-in-law. He could see the onion domes of several churches, read the Russian language billboards plastered on building walls, smell the blini and borscht wafting up from nearby restaurants, and almost hear the men chattering as they took steam inside the banya down the street. Everything appeared normal and relaxed on the surface, but he knew otherwise. The Japanese were firmly in control of Harbin and most of Manchuria, having conquered the Chinese and driven away the Russian Army. And Nikolai's small family was once again living life on the edge.

"Raisa, I'm not sure how much longer we can deal with this. Eight years, and our prospects haven't gotten better. If anything, they're worse."

She understood his concern. "I know, Nikolai. Today, I spoke with Darya's babushka, who told me she heard Mr. Korablin has decided to leave. And she said her family's going to Shanghai as soon as possible. They think it's safe there since the fighting stopped more than a month ago, and the Japanese left the International Settlement. She said Grigor, his cousin, and his cousin's family purchased train tickets and will be gone by the end of the week."

"I heard the same news, Mother. I trust Korablin. Anyone who could avoid all the spies and hide inside a mail sack from Chita to Harbin…Well, his instincts have served us well since the day he told us about meeting Anna. I should try to see him before he goes."

Kolya was concerned because Grigor had been his sponsor. His supporter. Heck, he had been Kolya's protector. He had helped Kolya wade through the muck and mire of the Harbin bureaucracy, a petty system at best—belligerent, threatening, and criminal at worst.

"I don't see how we can leave," he told Raisa. "At least, not yet. It's expensive, and Katya hasn't finished school."

"Yes, of course. But I worry about Katya," Raisa argued. "The random attacks have increased, and the Japanese…well, you know. They don't like us, and Katya has…grown. She's a beautiful, talented girl. Bad things happen to pretty girls, Kolya. Even in civilized places. Shouldn't we go where it's safest?"

"And where might that be?" he responded. "Are things really better in Shanghai? We certainly can't go back to Valday. I'd be arrested as soon as I stepped off the train. Others have fled to Paris and the United States. But we don't have money for that."

"I'm sorry, Kolya. I know you'll do what's best."

"The best reason for leaving is Makuda," Nikolai said. "I don't trust him around Katya."

"Maybe you're right," Raisa consented, "but Kuniaki Makuda is handsome and has money. The fact that he's Japanese also means no one gives him any trouble."

"That's true, but have you seen the looks from our friends and neighbors when he shows up here? They make it seem like we're traitors to Mother Russia because we let a Japanese man into the house. I don't like it. And, besides, have you seen how Makuda looks at Ekaterina? She's only sixteen, and he's over thirty. He says he can make her famous. I don't believe that, but she's infatuated with him. That worries me more. As I said, he's a good reason to leave. But we still need to save more money."

"You're right, of course. But have you thought about what Mr. Makuda wants Katya to do? And how much he is willing to pay her?"

"Oh, if only she weren't so beautiful and had a voice like a sick cat," Kolya complained, like all fathers of teenage girls. "Of course, I've thought about it. It seems like a far-fetched dream, but I've asked around. Kuniaki Makuda is very successful and not a fraud. People say he has helped many young women earn decent incomes as models, and he has promoted others with talent beyond their beauty, such as Katya's singing. Some have even become household names, but it still bothers me. At times she seems to be under a spell. A spell of adolescent desire."

"You and Anna were young, Kolya," Raisa said. "And it was the two of you who gave Katya to us. We both know Katya's destiny is more than just looking pretty and singing in the church choir. And Kolya, letting her come with me to church again and sing was the best thing you could have done." She smiled at him.

He returned her smile. "Oh Raisa, Katya's voice! Yes, they like her at church. And now that she's older, she sounds like her mother. But Kuniaki? Something about him gives me pause, and I hesitate to trust him."

⚜

Kuniaki Makuda stood at his office window and looked across the busy boulevard of Central Street. He could see the spires of St. Nikolai's Church on Central Square down the block, the billboards of young women advertising the latest fashions or home appliances, and the marquees of theaters beckoning patrons inside to see and hear musicians and singers he had discovered.

He sipped his tea, smiled, and spoke. "What would father think now?"

His younger brother and Kuniaki's beautiful Russian secretary said nothing.

"He wanted me to be an engineer," Kuniaki continued. "Just like him. Ha! Never! When he sent me away, that was the best thing ever."

He turned and strolled over to where his secretary sat on the expensive leather couch in his office. He reached out a hand, and his fingers stroked the side of her face. She looked up at him and pursed her lips. His smile broadened.

"He only wanted you to take life seriously, Kuni. That's all he ever wanted. You were nothing but a wealthy playboy, and now, well—what's changed?" His brother asked as he gazed at the photos on the wall of Kuni's office.

Each was a picture of Kuniaki with a beautiful woman he had shepherded to success. True, he may have received some intimate quid pro quos to boost their careers, but they never complained.

"What's changed? You ask me, brother, what has changed? Look around. I achieved success on my own, without any of his help. He should have been proud of me. But no, he mocked me until, well, until your telegram. Even on his deathbed, when I returned home to see him, he refused. I heard his words through the door. He disowned me. Said he only had one son. What a bitter old man. Nonetheless, thank you for tending to him in his illness." Kuni moved away from the secretary to the bar, put down the tea, and poured himself something more substantial. "Now, brother, are you returning to Japan, or would you like to stay here and work for me?"

"And do what? Prey on beautiful women?" His brother looked at the secretary as he said this and didn't notice Kuniaki come up behind him.

Kuni punched his brother in the kidney, doubling him over. "Get out! Don't come back. Don't ask to see me, talk to me, anything. How dare you insult me in my own office?"

His brother slowly unbent as the pain subsided. He looked at the handsome man he adored and missed. He shook his head. "I know all about you, Kuni. How you've made your money. How you get these young women, girls, to work for you. Sure, you give them a bit more yuan in their purses. Maybe even a nice place to live, but what have they lost? What have you stolen from them? You're merely a successful pimp."

This time, Kuni's younger brother responded with lightning

reflexes and swatted away Kuni's attempt to hit him. "Not so fast anymore, brother? With all your *success,* you've gained weight. Like I said, a pimp who uses blackmail to keep scared, desperate young ladies under your control. You even convince their families it's for the best. Goodbye, Kuniaki. Father was right. Enjoy your fancy but disgraceful life."

Kuniaki downed his drink with one swallow and watched his brother walk out of the office. His secretary said nothing and kept her head down.

"Damn! He gave me a headache. Fix me another drink, then rub my shoulders and neck," he ordered her. "You know I helped you and all of them. Don't you?"

With her head still bowed, she brought him his drink and whispered, "Of course, Mr. Makuda. It was the best day of my life when I met you, and I know all the girls feel the same way."

"Exactly. So, how do I get Mr. Palutov to feel the same about me helping Ekaterina?"

***

"Oh, Darya, I don't want you to go," Katya complained. It was early September, and she and her best friend were sitting on a park bench across from St. Sofia Church, enjoying the sunshine of an unusually warm late summer day. The two had been trying to find a time to relax together since Darya's father had decided to head south to Shanghai.

"Papa's going to buy tickets today. He finally saved enough money. I don't want to go, Katya. I want to finish school here, but Papa says it has become too dangerous."

"Did he say when you'll be leaving?"

"No. He just said as soon as he could make arrangements. Some of our friends who left went back to Russia. Papa says the Soviets think they're spies for China or Japan and arrested them. Can you imagine?"

Katya wasn't paying attention. She had news of her own, and the prospect of her best friend leaving increased her anxiousness.

"Katya? Katya, did you hear what I said?" Darya asked with concern.

Over the past few weeks, she had seen Katya change. Subtle though it was, she knew Katya had something on her mind. Ordinarily gregarious and outgoing, Katya had become more subdued. Her beauty and her voice, which some called angelic, made her self-conscious. She was nervous but also excited about being pretty and singing well. Regardless, Katya had no pretensions and rebuffed the idea that people responded to her differently than other girls her age. Darya had never felt insignificant around Katya, yet she understood her best friend was unique. As they grew, she witnessed how easily Ekaterina attracted boys—and then grown men. Even mature women seemed to defer to Katya when they were together in a group.

"Oh, Darya, I'm sorry. I *did* hear you," Katya apologized. "And yes, it is horrible to think about what might be happening to friends back in Russia. Oh, but...I have something I need to tell you. I don't know what to do. And I...I'm...scared. Darya, I'm really scared." Tears formed in her pleading eyes and slowly flowed down her cheeks.

"My goodness, Katya. What's the matter? Things can't be all that bad."

Katya wiped her cheeks and eyes with her handkerchief. She sat up and took a deep breath. "Oh, Darya...you know Kuniaki? I told you about him?"

"Yes, that good-looking Japanese man. The one with the fancy car and clothes. But that was months ago."

"Yes, he's the one. And it was six months ago. He had approached me on the street as I walked home one day after shopping for some groceries. He was so polite. He saw me struggling with my bags, and he offered to help. I let him, and the very next day, he came to our door. I never did ask him how he knew where I lived. Anyway, he called again and again during the following two weeks. Each time, Father thanked him for his interest in me but informed him I was too young to go out with him. But after Papa said no the tenth time, Kuni—that's what his friends call him—found me one day after school. And Darya, I went with him.

"He took me to a café for tea and sweets. Such a place! The decorations made me feel like I was in a museum, and the food was magnificent. It was in a Chinese neighborhood with few Russians, but he told me not to worry. He said everyone knew him, liked him, and left him alone. And that was true. Many people greeted him on the street and in the café."

"Katya, you probably shouldn't have gone, but I want to hear everything. Go on. Give me all the details." Darya's curiosity was unrestrained.

"Oh, Darya, that's not what I want to talk about. After that first trip to the café, Kuni and I set up regular meeting times. He took me to places away from our part of the city where no one would recognize me. And you know what? He wanted me to go to work for him. He asked me to be a model. It sounded so exciting—I would get to wear all those new fashions. I could dress up just like Lilya Brik, Miss Vasilieva, and Mrs. Tweedie back on the train, and the actresses we see on the billboards and in the theaters. And, most importantly, I would earn a lot of money. Money for emergencies. Like moving to Shanghai."

"So, what did you do? Oh, don't tell me. I know you. You said yes, and never told your father. But Katya, you kept all this from me, too. Your best friend. Why? Oh, never mind. I can guess."

Katya turned her head away for a moment. "Oh, Darya, I...I was afraid I'd lose you if you knew. I'm sorry." She pleaded for Darya to understand.

"Best friends should trust each other," Darya said. "You know I can keep your secrets. Anyway, continue."

"I know. Thank you. I know I can trust you. Those first two months with Kuniaki were wonderful. I wore fancy clothes, and he sent my picture to other cities for billboards and magazines that Papa and Grandmama would never see. And I began to make money. Oh, Darya, I've saved a lot of money. But then, things changed."

"What happened? It sounds so good." Darya sat on the edge of the bench, breathlessly waiting to hear more.

"One Sunday, maybe four months ago, Kuni sat in the back of the church and heard me sing in the choir. After that, he had all new plans for me. He said he could make me into a big star. Someone had told him my mother had been a popular singer before I was born, and he was sure I could be famous if Papa would let me go with him to Tokyo, Shanghai, Hong Kong, or Singapore."

"I would give anything to get out of here. No matter what my Papa said." Darya offered encouragement. "But I would miss you, Katya."

"Well, no need to worry, Darya. Kuni returned to my house and asked Papa—not if I could go to Tokyo or somewhere, but if I could go to a recording studio and make a record. Well, you know how Papa always felt about my singing. Even if he has allowed me to sing in the choir, he has no interest in me doing what my mother did. He wouldn't have me performing in public and traveling. Not at all!"

"Get on with it, Katya. What are you afraid of? Why is all this a problem?"

Katya began to cry again. "It's, it's just too hard to talk about."

"Come, come. Why are you crying? You never cry. Tell me. You're the one who said you had something to share." Darya reached across, took the handkerchief from Katya's hand, and dabbed her friend's cheeks. "Now stop that and keep going. You'll feel better if you do."

"Yes, of course. How childish of me. But I'm scared and don't know what to do."

"You've said that multiple times. Enough!"

Katya calmed her breathing once more and clenched her fists in her lap. "Yes, okay. After Kuni heard me in church, we met the next day after school. I was running an errand for Grandmama, delivering some laundry. Kuni drove up as I walked and called to me. This time he had a driver and sat in the backseat. He offered to drive me to make the laundry delivery. Why would I say no? I hopped in, and in no time, I was finished."

"Katya, this doesn't sound scary. I would have done the same thing."

"Yes, I was glad for the ride, but when I came out from the delivery, he was still there. He said he wanted to show me something. Said it was a picture of what my future could be. Oh, Darya, I was so excited by the prospect of singing *and* continuing to model I didn't hesitate. I went with him."

Darya raised her eyebrows but said nothing.

"Yes, I know what you're thinking, but it was daylight, and there was a driver. Anyway, he took me to different nightclubs and introduced me to the women entertainers who came in early to rehearse. They told me how wonderful their lives had been since Kuniaki Makuda became their agent and how they were earning more money than they could imagine.

"After the last stop, he drove me to his office. It's in a building with a recording studio and many small apartments."

"Katya! Get to the point. None of this sounds scary. Maybe not a good idea to go without your father's permission, but not dangerous."

Katya twisted her fingers together so tightly that she yelped when her knuckles popped, but then the words came in a rush. "Oh, Darya, he took me to one of those apartments, put on music, and gave me something to drink. Something I never had before. We sat on his couch listening to music, and he pulled me close and kissed me. I was surprised, but Darya…I liked it. It felt good to be held and kissed like that. But then—then his hands reached and, and he—grabbed my breasts. It was such a shock I didn't say anything, but he kept whispering in my ear, telling me I was the most beautiful woman he'd ever seen, and he loved me and wanted to marry me."

"Stop! Don't say anything more. I'll be right back." Darya raced to a street vendor and returned with more tea. "Here, take a sip," Darya passed a cup and sipped her own. *Her* throat had suddenly gone dry listening to Katya's tale. After they each drank half, Darya was ready to hear more.

"He caressed me all over, " Katya said. "I never felt anything like that in my life; it was wonderful, but I knew it was wrong. I tried to wriggle away from him, but he was too strong, and he began to unbutton my dress. I told him to stop. Over and over. I told him I wasn't ready. After he undid the last button, he yanked my dress down to my waist, sat back, and stared at me. His smile, the one I love so much, looked different. He seemed to be possessed. When he undid his belt and pulled down his pants, he lost his balance, and I shoved him away. I jumped up from the couch and ran to the door, trying to pull my dress back up, but he grabbed the dress, and I never made it to the door. I began to scream."

"Someone must have heard you," Darya almost shrieked.

"If they did, no one came," Katya said. "He slapped me across the face, told me to be quiet, and instantly apologized. He said he didn't mean it. It was just that I was so special, and he wanted me to have the best of everything. I told him I wanted to leave. Then, in a tone I will never forget, he said, 'Yes, Katya, my sweet. After.' That was it. He stripped off my dress and bra. I was powerless to stop him. And then he ripped off my short bloomers."

Katya had been holding it in until then but began to sob violently. Darya took her friend's hands, pulled Katya close, and hugged her. After a couple minutes, they separated, a handkerchief made its way to Katya's nose and cheeks, and her breathing was almost normal.

"I closed my eyes and held my breath, Darya. I gave up. I was so weak, and I just stopped fighting. He…he…he entered me. He raped me, Darya. Kuniaki raped me. Right there on the couch in that small apartment. And I had thought I was in love with him. How foolish."

Darya looked at her friend with tears in her own eyes. She was also attractive, and had Kuniaki spotted her, *she* might be telling the story. She shuddered briefly, realizing she had no idea what she would have done.

"You didn't tell your Papa or Grandmama, did you?"

Katya shook her head no. "What could I say, Darya? And more importantly, we needed the money. I needed to keep modeling and singing when Papa was away in the forests. It's money we need to get to Shanghai, but that will end soon."

"Why? Has Mr. Makuda let you go free? Oh, forgive me, Katya, but you haven't, well, you haven't…"

"No, Darya. It was only that once, but now things are going to change. And this is what I really wanted to tell you." This time she took Darya's hands in hers, and with a serenity that surprised her, she added, "I'm pregnant."

"You're pregnant?! Kuniaki?!"

Darya couldn't hide the mixture of jealousy, amazement, and disappointment on her face. A million things raced through her head. After listening to Katya, she had doubts about the truthfulness of what her friend told her. She knew Katya could be a flirt and exuded a natural sensuality. Additionally, Katya had a daring streak, always seeming to push the limits and stretch the rules. She wanted to shorten the hems of her dresses and wear make-up. *Who had money for make-up?* Darya wondered. And she remembered how Katya had told her that promiscuous Lilya Brik was the most fascinating woman she'd ever met.

Darya could picture her friend drinking champagne, listening to music, and doing a dance for Kuniaki. Unfortunately, she could also imagine Katya disrobing and willingly giving herself to him. Try as she might avoid it, Darya excited herself thinking about a man touching her in all *her* private places. Both girls had learned about boys and men from the older women in their lives. They had seen pictures and diagrams of naked men, and they understood. But neither had ever seen a real, live, naked man. She began to tingle, but no matter how much she yearned to have someone hold her that way, Darya knew she would wait until she was married. She had been shocked and, to a strange degree, jealous after Katya told her everything. Darya had never been kissed by a boy—well, at least nothing more than a quick peck. But Katya had always been willing to explore. Darya hated disbelieving her friend, but she suspected Katya had wanted Kuniaki as much as he wanted Katya, even if he had forced himself on her and done so without any emotional involvement.

Darya wanted to believe that Katya had no choice. But truth be told, she knew things called hormones, something adults called "teenage infatuation," and, in Katya's circumstances, necessity—the need for money—could lead people to do things they might not ordinarily do. She was old enough to know that throughout history, desperate women and men, Russian or not, yielded to outside pressures for love, sex, money, and power. It made no difference which one, or all. Regardless, Katya was pregnant, and Darya had no idea how to help her. These thoughts took seconds before Darya changed her perspective and sought to reassure her friend.

"Oh my goodness, Katya. I'll help in any way I can. What are you going to do?"

"I don't know. You're the only one I told. Kuni is so busy, and I'm terrified of what Papa may do. He'll be crushed and angry."

"Have you been to a doctor? Are you sure?"

"I've missed three months now, Darya. I'm sure. I don't need a doctor. I need advice."

"Maybe your babushka would be the best one to tell. She's a smart woman."

"I'm not sure. I think she'll just cry."

"I know. You need to talk to Mr. Korablin. I'm sure he knows people who can help, and I bet he knows a doctor who could, well, you know…make this go away."

"I've thought about that too, but *making it go away* scares me more. The more I thought about it, the more I decided I want this baby. Besides, the people Mr. Korablin might know would expect a large payment, and we need the money for other things."

"Babies are expensive too, Katya. But it sounds like you've made up your mind. Soon you'll have no choice. It's hard to hide such things. "

"You're right, of course. What do you think your parents would do if you were in my situation?"

"I don't know. Send me away, I guess, until the baby's born and make me give her up for adoption. Something like that. Papa would make up a story to tell his friends. That seems like it might be the easiest way."

"I don't want to go away alone, and I don't want to be an embarrassment either. I have no idea."

"What about Kuniaki?" Darya asked. "If you tell him, he might offer to marry you. That's a perfect solution."

"He might, but I'm not so sure. But…" The *but* hung in the air because they both knew Kuniaki *liked* many women. "Besides, I need to keep working as long as I can. We need the money. If I tell Kuni, he may not…" She stopped, not wanting to think Kuni may not care. Instead, she said, "He may stop using me to model or sing. I don't know."

"Katya, you won't be able to work much longer anyway. You said it's already been three months. I think you need to make plans right now."

The realization she probably needed to leave her family and friends, even for just a few months, gave her a chill. Despite all her bravado and carefree behavior, Katya's small family kept her grounded. To be separated from them was something that frightened her even more than telling her father she was pregnant. But what choice did she have?

The physical closeness of the two friends on the bench and the intensity of their conversation meant they failed to notice the man standing near them until he cleared his throat.

"Ahem. Good day, ladies. Pleasant weather for this time of year." Grigor Korablin's greeting was routine, and he showed no indication of having overheard any part of their conversation.

"And a good day to you, Mr. Korablin," Katya shifted gears away from her tale without a hint of hiding something from him. "Darya and I are catching up. We've been on different schedules at school and home and have had precious little time together."

"Yes," Darya added, "as Katya said, with chores and classes, we don't see each other as much as we used to."

"Well, I'm delighted to see you both. I suppose you heard I will soon be leaving Harbin. I don't see a future here for Russians. Not that Shanghai is the best option, but it is the nearest. Also, it's a major seaport, so should the need arise to depart to places even farther afield, that will be helpful. Darya, did I hear correctly your family is also considering the move?"

"Yes. Father has reached the same conclusion. He's worried about what might happen to us if we stay."

"Indeed. And what about the Palutovs, Katya? Does your father have plans?"

"Not in so many words, Mr. Korablin. I know finances are an issue, but I shouldn't discuss personal family matters. So, please tell us, how are Mrs. Korablin and your children? I haven't seen them in months."

A wide smile lit up Gregor's face. "They're the best things that ever happened to me, Katya. They've changed my perspective on life, and I bet you've seen the difference. All the things I used to think were important have become mere fragments. Children are gifts from God. I'm blessed to have two beautiful boys and a dedicated and loving wife. I can't wait for the time you both can experience such remarkable joy."

Darya began to choke, and Grigor bent over to check her. "Are you alright, Darya? Can I get you some water?"

The choking brought tears to her eyes, but she shook her head. "No…thank…you. I… will be…fine. Just swallowed a bug or something." In a moment, she was breathing normally, but the pause had been enough for Katya to reassess her situation.

"Mr. Korablin, I…I, well, I asked Darya to meet me here today, so I could give her some news and ask her for advice. It seems, however, I need more help than my dear friend can provide."

Katya hesitated before continuing, and Grigor said nothing. She looked directly into his eyes, which reminded her of the day she first met him on the train and told him he was not very nice. Yes, he had changed a lot. He had become a good man.

"Mr. Korablin, I'm pregnant."

Grigor absorbed this news without changing the expression on his face. He owed this young lady so much, and she had no idea. She had been a child when she put a crack in his surly, arrogant, and privileged approach to life. Simply by being herself, she had taught him manners and genuine self-respect while opening his eyes to the conditions of those around him. It had started slowly, but life in Harbin, even though the social classes remained stratified, awakened a sense of caring for others Grigor had never before experienced.

Spontaneously, he repeated, "As I said, children are a gift from God. I have no doubt you will be a wonderful mother."

Without further comment, he told the girls to follow him to a small restaurant where the waiter knew him. They sat in a curtained booth in the back, and soon a pot of tea and a platter of food were on their table. After a few bites, Darya returned to the business at hand.

"She's too afraid to tell her father or babushka, Mr. Korablin. She's worried—and I suspect, with good reason—to think he would send her away."

"I see." He looked at Katya with deep concern. "Your father is a proud man, Ekaterina. He values your family's reputation. He has protected you from the day you were born, but unfortunately, we live in times where society labels someone in your condition. That label gets spread among the entire family. It is even likely my friend Kolya may lose his job because of what has happened to you. Not fair, I know, but..." Mr. Korablin stopped for a second to think. "It makes no difference whether or not you are in love or if you were raped on the street by some thug. Many of the people who would brand you are hypocrites. Nonetheless, the stamp is real, and if you stay here and give birth as a single mother, you will be scorned, ridiculed, and left without the means to raise your child safely."

Tears dribbled down Katya's cheeks. "What does that mean, Mr. Korablin?"

"I'm afraid it means if you ever want to have a normal life, as much as anyone can, you cannot have a child until you have a husband."

The reality of what he said felt like hot iron stakes piercing her heart, but Katya had never been one to dwell too long on things. She was determined to be a survivor and live as normally as possible. But what was normal? Nothing seemed normal. Turmoil surrounded them. Why else would Mr. Korablin and Darya's family be leaving?

"What about the father?" Grigor asked her. "*Could* you get married? That would solve things."

A wan smile crossed her face. Yes, she could tell Kuni, as Darya suggested. But was he the solution? During the past few weeks, she wondered how many other girls he had seduced or raped. It made no difference. No, she knew he was not the man she wanted to parent her child.

"No, Mr. Korablin. I've given that idea much thought, and I don't believe the *father* is the kind who would make a good parent, even if he did agree to marry me. No, I'm not even going to tell him."

Grigor nodded slowly and began to speak but stopped again.

"What? Do you have another suggestion?" she pressed.

He shifted his eyes from one girl to the other and remarked, "There is an…no, never mind. That is not you. Forget it."

"You're right, Mr. Korablin. *That* is not an alternative. I need to find a place to go where I'll be safe. Then, I'll have to make another decision after the baby comes."

"Yes, Katya, of course. But maybe your father would not react the way you think. He may want to care for and protect you no matter what."

"That's possible," she said. "But I don't want his friends and coworkers to think less of him and less of his ability to *raise* me properly. No, even if Papa says I should stay, I wouldn't do that to him."

"If you are determined, I think I can help you," Grigor offered.

Katya saw he was serious.

"I have another cousin. You haven't met him, although he lives here in Harbin. He's from my mother's side. Married, but no children. He's an engineer with the CER and has somehow managed to dance around the politics of the railroad. He gets along with all the communists without giving up his soul."

"How can that be?!" Katya interrupted. "The only way for him to work at the CER is if he…"

"Yes, yes. Katya. You're right. He's a radish—Red on the outside, but he remains quite White on the inside. As you know, he had no choice but to register with the Soviets to keep his position with the CER. However, that works to *your* advantage."

"How?" she demanded. "What's the difference?"

"That's easy. You and the baby will have the protection of the CER. Japanese and Chinese nationals won't interfere in your life, at least not very much. And, using his name and address—which is across the city in a different neighborhood, your father will not have problems at work."

"Yes, Katya! That's the answer. You must," Darya beseeched her friend.

"Oh, I don't know."

"He's well-connected, Ekaterina," Grigor continued. "I know he would take good care of you and your baby. Particularly one who will be…different. Russian and Japanese."

"Katya, you know this is the best option. Your father will retain his job. No one will find out, *and* you'll be protected."

⁂

When she told Kolya, his first reaction was to raise his arm to strike her.

"No! Nikolai!" Raisa grabbed his arm before he could act.

He was so angry. He had never felt such fury, not even when his former friend fired him from the lumber works in Valday. *How could she? Didn't she realize the consequences? She's sixteen, and her life is ruined. And she had such promise. And that playboy, Kuniaki? If I see him, I'll strangle him.* Nikolai was breathing so hard his chest heaved in and out like a bellows. His mind raced. *What will the boss say when he learns? He will find out. And his friends? They'll badger me and won't welcome me back to their homes. Even poor Raisa will lose many of her laundry customers. It's a disaster, and it makes no difference how it happened. Everyone knew pretty young women bring such events on themselves.*

Raisa pulled Katya into another room while Kolya paced. A few minutes went by, then he concluded they would leave and go someplace where they were unknown. He would find another job and make up a story about her age and the accidental death of her husband. But where to go? He collapsed into the small settee Raisa used and closed his eyes. Noticing his pacing had stopped, the two women returned to the parlor, and Katya gave a slight cough.

"Papa, Mr. Korablin had a suggestion."

The softness and sweetness of her voice brought a tear to each of his eyes. He loved her so much, and was full of guilt at his initial reaction to the news. She was naturally forgiving and trusting, but how to proceed? It seemed helpless to think the well-connected Japanese promoter would help, even if he loved her. And bringing charges against Kuni Makuda was pointless. Kolya was also confident his daughter had not told him everything. But, no matter.

"So, you told Mr. Korablin before telling me and Grandmama? How many people do you think he will tell? Soon everyone will know." This last remark came out much harsher than he intended.

"Kolya, that's not fair!" Raisa admonished. "Grigor has been our friend for years. His contacts have been most helpful, and he adores Katya. There's no way he would betray her confidence."

The deep breath Kolya took could have filled a giant balloon. He sighed, "Yes, I'm sorry. You're right. So, Ekaterina, what is this plan of Mr. Korablin's?"

When she finished, Nikolai remained pensive. "I'll need to speak to Grigor myself before I decide." He rose, looked around for his cap, grabbed it, and left the apartment.

"Oh, Grandmama, what will become of us?" Katya broke down in sobs once again.

Nikolai agreed to Grigor's plan, and a week later, Katya moved across town until the baby was born. Less than an hour after the birth, Nikolai sat with his daughter.

"I've made arrangements for the baby," he told her.

"Arrangements?" She began to tremble in her bed. She had a private room at the hospital through the good graces of Grigor's cousin.

"Yes. It's best this way, Katya. The baby will have a good life with a good family, and you won't have the stigma of being an unwed mother," Kolya said.

"Or you, a grandfather with a wanton daughter!"

She was bitter, and the words stung him, but he said nothing. She couldn't imagine giving away her baby, yet she always knew this would happen.

"It's all set," Kolya went on. "And you can't see the baby. I'm sorry. It's for the best, Katya."

"Oh, Papa!" she wailed with the grief of every mother who loses a child.

"I've also made train reservations for us to depart in two weeks, at the beginning of March. The train will take us to Dalian, and from there, we'll go by ship to Shanghai. You can reunite with Darya, and we can personally thank Grigor for all his help during our years in Harbin. Without it, who knows where we'd be." He leaned down and kissed her on the forehead. "You're more precious to me than anything, Katya. This decision will free you so you can lead a normal life."

She said nothing as he stretched upright. She knew their departure from Harbin had been inevitable, with or without the child.

"I have to leave later today to return to the forest and the mill for one more week," Kolya continued. "When I get back, we'll pack and join friends in a place away from the Japanese and the Soviets."

She turned away from him without speaking and looked out the window into the gray world that was Harbin in winter. Realizing she was not going to respond, Kolya patted her head, turned, and left. She listened to his footsteps fade down the hall, and only then did she allow the tears to flow without interruption. However, Katya's quiet sobbing failed to prevent her from being herself. She had to see her baby, and damn the rules.

Sometime after midnight, she got out of bed, wrapped herself in a blanket, and peeked into the hallway. She tiptoed barefoot down the dimly lit corridor until she passed the empty nurses' station. She stopped, looked carefully around the next corner, and saw a nurse walking in the opposite direction. Katya waited until the nurse entered a room, then hurried to the nursery door and slowly snuck inside. She made her way between the dozen cribs containing the new babies in the faint light. Each bassinet had a name tag, but the darkness made them impossible to read.

Frustrated, Katya's desire to find her child overcame caution, and she switched on the lights. A yellowish glow flickered from the bulbs, and she scanned the name tags as quickly as possible. Not a single one had the name Palutova. How could that be? She was devastated. Had her baby already been taken? Then she realized the problem. The baby would have the name of the adoptive parents. She raced back through the aisles, and there it was, "Markova—girl." Grigor's cousin's family name. As she was about to pick up her baby, the door opened, and the nurse walked in.

"What are you doing in here? You're supposed to be in bed."

"I-I-I just wanted to see her. Watch her sleeping. She's so beautiful."

The overnight nurse smiled. She had failed to see the note about not allowing Ekaterina to see the baby. "Well, did you get a good look? They *are* adorable. That's why I love to work this shift. They mostly sleep. If not, I get to rock them." She nodded to the chair in the corner. "But the lights, you should not have turned them on." And the nurse quickly switched them off. "Now, get back to bed. You've just had a baby and need your rest."

"Yes. Yes. Thank you. Take good care of my baby."

"Don't worry. I care for them as if they were my own. Now scoot!"

Katya left her child in the excellent care of the nurse. She had seen her baby—a lovely child with a full head of hair. *How appropriate for a girl*, she thought. Then it hit her like a tsunami. That may have been the only time she would ever see her child. She crawled into bed and cried herself to sleep.

The next day was a full day of rest. Raisa visited early in the morning and talked about Nikolai's decision to allow the Markovs to adopt his granddaughter.

"They're a good couple, Katya. They will love her, and it's better than not knowing who will have her. They are well off and can do much for her."

Katya listened in silence. After Grandmama left, she rose and walked toward the newborn room. Halfway there, she was stopped by an orderly bringing around meals for the new mothers.

"If you're not in your room, you won't get anything to eat. Those are the rules."

"I'm fine. Thank you," she told him.

"I'm supposed to report any new mother who doesn't eat. Doctors' orders. What's your name?"

Katya answered, "Markova. Just going to see my baby for a few minutes. I'll be right back."

"Very well." The orderly continued his deliveries, but the day nurse spotted Katya and sent her back to her room before she made it to her daughter's crib.

She spent the afternoon reading a newspaper, staring at the horrendous weather outside, and trying to be patient until the night nurse came back on duty so she could see her baby again. It was almost time for the evening meal when Raisa burst into the room, followed by the monk from their church. Grandmama was visibly upset and dabbed a handkerchief on her watery red eyes. The hairs on Katya's neck rose when she saw the priest. She instantly understood something was wrong. Terribly wrong. Then the world, as Katya knew it, disintegrated into dust.

"Oh, Katya! My baby! I…" Raisa cried.

The holy man gently moved Raisa to the side and came to Katya's bedside.

"What is it, Father? What is it? Why are you here? Did something happen to my baby? My baby! Is my baby alright? I just saw her last night! She must be okay!"

"Your baby is fine, my dear," he said and took her hand to comfort her. "She is fine."

"Well then, why are you here? I can't think…" She stopped talking, and then she knew. "Papa! It's Papa! What happened to Papa? Please no. No! Not Papa!"

"I'm so sorry, Ekaterina. There was an accident," the priest said.

She cried with deep endless moans and shook so hard her bed rocked and bumped along the floor. "Why? How? Where is he? He just saw me yesterday. Is he safe in a hospital?"

"I'm sorry, Katya, your Papa has gone to be with your Mama. They shall rejoice together in Heaven." The monk said a short prayer, and Raisa moved back in and took his place.

"But how? He was always careful. It's my fault. It's all my fault. He wanted me to have a good life, so he risked his to earn more money. It paid well, but…the danger." She rolled to her side and sobbed into the pillow.

"It's not your fault, Ekaterina," Raisa leaned in and brushed her granddaughter's hair. "The weather…the men were trying to secure logs on a railcar, and the chain broke. And, well, your papa couldn't get out of the way in time. He…" She couldn't continue.

Katya wept with such lament Raisa couldn't bear the sound and left the room. She returned when Katya had quieted from exhaustion. The young mother looked at her grandmother and spoke with heartbreaking regret.

"I ignored him when he left yesterday. He kissed my head, Grandmama, and told me he loved me, and I ignored him. I told him he only thought about how people would look at him if his daughter had a baby but no husband. Oh, Papa. Why didn't I tell you how much I love you?" Her tears flowed hard again, but stopped as if none remained. "I know Papa's gone," she sputtered. "And I know this isn't what he wants, but I'm leaving here today. And I'm taking my baby. I don't care what anyone thinks. I'll never leave my child."

Those words brought tears back to Raisa's face. "Oh, my child, you cannot. It's impossible," she said. "The baby is already gone. Please…Kat…"

"Gone! My daughter is gone! Gone where? I saw the name on the crib. I know where she'll be. I will get her."

"No child, you will not," the monk told her. "She has been adopted, and the papers are all signed. And even though you know the family's name, they departed for several weeks. They will not be in their apartment, and you are going to Shanghai.

"Katya, it will be okay," Raisa said. "We will do as your papa arranged. We will go to Shanghai and find our old friends there. You'll see. It will be good.

Katya began to wail again, bellowing out the insufferable pain of lost love. A love she realized she'd never get to share with her daughter. Her cries of despair rang down the hospital's corridors, and soon a doctor arrived and gave her a sedative. She drifted into sleep with a blown kiss on her lips for the tiny infant she had seen asleep in the crib.

7   1933–1938
Shanghai

A week after the funeral, Katya and Raisa were packing their few belongings. Katya stopped for a moment. "At least Papa died working in the forests, but Grandmama, he was only forty-eight. I miss him dreadfully."

"I know. I miss him too," Raisa said.

When Raisa said that, Katya made a short gasp. "Oh, Grandmama, I'm sorry. You've lost so many. Forgive me."

"Nothing to forgive, my dear. Death is as much a part of life as anything. It is the way. My grieving for those I love never stops. But now, did you remember to send a note to Mr. Korablin thanking him for his help?"

"Yes, Grandmama. He was so generous to send the money for Papa's funeral, but I'm afraid I'll never be coming back to decorate his grave."

Raisa said nothing.

The next day they boarded the train and headed for Dalian, where they met their ship for Shanghai. Like their earlier exodus from Valday, Katya and Raisa took very little with them. In one large travel chest, they crammed their clothes and made space for Anna's poster, the Valday bells, the Bible, St. Michael's icon, and Nikolai's axe (which had been returned to them), and other personal items. Grigor greeted them at the busy Huangpu docks along the Bund when they arrived in Shanghai. He was helpful and comforting, but getting settled would not be as easy as Harbin. Shanghai was lightyears different from Harbin, especially regarding the Russian community's influence on the city's life. It was negligible. If you were Russian, unless you were wealthy or talented, no one paid any attention to you. You were invisible.

Shanghai was large, with more than three million residents. It was easy to be insignificant in such a place. Although Harbin was cosmopolitan and felt European, it could not compete with the diversity of the hectic and congested seaport city. Trade and commerce flowed along the Huangpu and up Suzhou Creek in numbers too great to count. Shanghai was at its early 20th century zenith when Ekaterina and her grandmother stepped ashore. It was where the famous and infamous expanded their notoriety or quickly flamed out. It had a nightlife equivalent to, if not more extensive and bohemian than, New York City. Dance halls, cafes, opium dens, US, British, and French military personnel, artists, gangsters, bureaucratic officials, writers, prostitutes, journalists, penny hustlers, and bigtime con artists mingled to form a potpourri of excitement and intrigue that captured the attention of the world. Shanghai represented the peak of modern living, mixed with the realities and tensions of regional and global conflicts.

The United Kingdom, the United States, and France held sway, operating and controlling areas known as the International Settlement and the French Concession. These portions of the city had independent police, defense forces, laws, banks, etc. Russians living in Shanghai did not have a designated domain. Despite the many social service organizations that had arisen since the first wave of White Russians arrived in the early 1920s, only limited places to live and work existed for newcomers in 1933. Many found rooms among the Chinese locals throughout the city, although most Russians had accommodations in the French Concession within a neighborhood known as Little Moscow. Even Grigor realized he would not be able to sustain any semblance of the lifestyle he cherished if he remained long in Shanghai.

Grigor, Darya, and Ekaterina had no idea what they were getting into when they left Harbin. Moving away from the imminent threat of violence against Russians in Japanese-occupied Harbin was reasonable and pragmatic. However, they had left a structured and mostly refined Russian Harbin for the much more complex Paris of the East. Shanghai in 1933 was almost the frenetic opposite of Harbin. The lives of lower and middle-class White Russians—even those better-off, like Grigor Korablin—were not protected like the Brits, Americans, and French. The growing rise of communism and the ever-present threat of expansionist Japan left the Russians easy scapegoats for various social, political, and economic problems. Ekaterina resolved to do whatever was necessary to survive.

"Oh, Katya, I can't learn it. No matter how hard I try." Darya and Katya sat chatting on a bench in French Park, just north of Rue Lafayette, in the French Concession in September 1933. The two had been getting together weekly since Katya and Raisa arrived in Shanghai in April.

"I didn't think I could either, Darya, but I'm beginning to get it."

Darya's family had been in Shanghai for more than a year, and her father insisted they must learn a second language. The Russian Emigrants Committee—REC—helped new arrivals in this regard and many others. Several dozen charitable organizations, unions of former soldiers, schools, mutual aid groups, cultural societies, and others affiliated with the REC brought a modicum of cohesiveness to the Russian community. They provided assistance with navigating life in the decidedly foreign locale. They helped Darya and Katya enroll in school to finish their education, including learning French.

"Papa says if I don't learn another language, I'll never be able to do more than the simple work I'm doing in Mrs. Plisetskaya's dress shop," Darya complained. "It's been months, and I only know a few words. Then I tell Papa there are so many Russians in our neighborhood, why do I need to learn French? Oh, Katya, it's awful."

"Dear girl, you're not alone. Grandmama thinks I need to learn some English as well. She's convinced the British and Americans will be the ones to protect Shanghai from the Japanese. Who knows? But I do know that we can't survive much longer between what she earns from her laundry work and what I make cleaning tables at Dyachenko's for a few hours each week. I need to get work singing in the Cathay Hotel, the Astor House, dancing at St. George's Café, or even in the International Settlement at the Saint Anna Ballroom. Other girls say the American Marines at Saint Anna's spend more money than the French and Chinese here in the Concession."

"Yes. I guess I should be thankful that I still have Mama and Papa and my sister and brothers," Darya conceded. "We all contribute something, so we're okay. At least for the time being. I heard even Mr. Korablin must work as a clerk for several companies and earns half of what other Europeans and Americans make. It's so unfair, Katya. Why do they despise us so?"

"It's all politics," Katya stated with authority. "At least, that's what Mr. Korablin says. But he has other money in banks someplace, and that's how he's been able to help us from time to time."

The sound of a siren abruptly pierced the ordinary drone of street noise. It was nearby, and both girls looked around and saw an emergency vehicle race past them. It hurried toward the Kelmscott Gardens neighborhood, not far from where Katya and Raisa lived in a tiny one-room apartment.

"Whenever I listen to the city's noise, I realize how quiet things were in our cabin in Valday," Katya remarked. "Let's hope the siren is nothing important."

"Of course, it isn't! How many sirens do we hear each day? Too many to count. I bet it's for some rich old French official. They usually get quick attention. Not a Russian."

Katya nodded at the truth. The Russians were last to receive assistance, except for poor Chinese.

They finished their visit and headed back to their chores and studies. They lived near each other and walked together for several blocks. At the corner where they usually parted, they encountered a large crowd.

"What's all the fuss?" Katya asked an old man looking on from the fringes.

"Accident. People grabbing things," he answered in Russian.

"Things? What kind of things?" Katya persisted.

"Mostly clothes," he mumbled between shouts of a lucky woman who pushed her way through the group, proudly displaying a lovely cotton dress.

"What kind of accident involves clothes?" Darya asked as Katya began to feel a tingle up her spine.

"I didn't see," the man answered. "Someone said a babushka with several large bundles of laundry was hit by a car. That's all I know."

"Oh my God! The siren!" Katya screamed. "Today is Grandmama's day to collect laundry from families on this road."

Katya shoved her way past everyone, losing Darya in the shuffle. She ran as fast as she could to the tiny room she shared with her grandmother. When she arrived at her building, she hurried into the small-walled courtyard where a row of three privies, two large shelters protecting wood and coal, and a bricked-off area served as a fire pit. The pit contained enormous cauldrons used for doing laundry. Several women were at the pots, but said they had not seen Raisa. Katya's panic grew so intense she thought she would faint. She sprinted back to the street and ran to the nearest hospital.

"Raisa, Raisa Kuznetsova *est-elle ici?*" she barked her few words of French.

The woman at the counter went through a list of recent patients and responded with a simple, *"Non! Je regrette."*

Katya's head was spinning. If she wasn't at home and not at the hospital…She stood on the street in front of the hospital and screamed. People walked past her and avoided eye contact. With little choice, Katya set off again—to the apartment of Grigor Korablin. It was only through good fortune that she found him at home.

"Ah, Katya! Good to see you. But…what is it? What's wrong?"

"Oh, Mr. Korablin, it's Grandmama. I can't find her."

"Come in. Come in. Let me get you some tea."

"No. No time for that. I need to find Grandmama." She began to cry and told him the story of the accident and the clothes. "I'm sure it was her. She always carries big bundles that make it hard for her to see. I'm so worried."

"Let me get my jacket, and we'll go to the police."

"Are you sure? The police?" Katya was leery. With so many petty crimes committed by desperate Russians and others, the police were not always the most helpful.

"They will know what happened," Grigor reasoned. "We must go. And some of the police come from Russia. Many former soldiers have been hired by the department. It will be fine."

"But most of them are Sikhs. From India," she countered.

He took her by the hand, ignoring the truth, and hoping to ease her anxiety. They made their way to the nearest police station.

"Yes. We know of the accident," the officer behind the counter answered in response to Grigor's question. "The old woman died, and the body went to the morgue."

"Do you have her name?" Grigor followed up.

The dark, turbaned man behind the desk appeared annoyed at the request, but he shuffled through a stack of papers and found what he wanted. "The papers she carried said her name is Raisa Kuznetsova, address…"

He didn't finish, because Katya collapsed to the floor.

"Get her out of here," the officer ordered. "We can't have such a scene at this desk."

"The dead woman was this child's grandmother, and her only family member," Grigor asserted his latent aristocratic demeanor, and the officer calmed down.

"Very well. Take her to the bench along the wall, and I'll send someone to bring her tea."

Grigor gently ushered Ekaterina to the bench and assured her he would take care of everything.

"Thank you, Mr. Korablin. You've been such a big help. But Grandmama?! OHHH!"

<hr />

Katya and Darya were back on the bench for their regular visit two weeks later. The funeral, no more than a burial ceremony with a few neighbors, Darya's family, Grigor, and two other ladies who did laundry with Raisa, was already a week past.

"How are you, my sweet?" Darya took Katya's hands and looked into her friend's eyes.

Katya didn't answer immediately as her eyes gazed into the distance.

"Katya? Katya?"

Slowly Katya refocused on her friend, and her lips formed a wan smile. "I'm fine, Darya. Really. I'm okay."

"I don't believe you, but I know that won't make a difference. Several girls and a couple teachers asked after you when you didn't return to school this week."

"That's nice, but I've made a decision. I won't be returning to school. I need to work so I can stay in the apartment."

"But Katya, you need to finish school, or you'll never get a decent job."

Katya's bemused smile grew. They both knew there were few

avenues for a stateless White Russian teenager in China, even if she did finish school.

"No, Darya. I need a place to live and food to eat. I need to earn more money. That's just the way it is. And compared to what we see on the streets, I'll be okay."

They both took a quick look around. Even in the park, beggars besieged anyone who looked like they might have money or food to spare. Across the street, they saw a woman slip and fall, dropping a bowl of rice. Three young boys rushed up and quickly swept up what they could of the few morsels scattered on the road. They tossed the dirty food into their mouths without hesitating as the woman tried to chase them away.

"I'm not going to be like her, Darya. Never!" Katya said. "I'm not going to be one of the bodies they collect off the streets every night!"

"Maybe I can help. I'll ask Papa. He…"

"No!" Katya interrupted. "I'm not your problem, Darya. Besides, I know your family has their own needs. I'll be fine. I might try and get a singing position with one of the bands on Avenue Joffre. Or maybe become a hostess at the Del Monte. I've learned a little French and English. Do you think that will be enough?"

"Ha! You're asking me? You know how miserable I am at languages. But you must be careful, Katya. The men at those places— they want you to do—how should I say—other things."

"It's okay, Darya. I know what you mean, and I'll be careful." Katya spoke earnestly with a straight face but knew her options were minimal. When push came to shove, she had no doubts she would do whatever was necessary to sustain her living conditions. *Whatever was necessary.*

Katya didn't tell Darya she had already seen managers at a dozen dance halls, cafés, and cabarets. Her boss at Dyachenko's had even arranged a tryout for her with his regular dance troupe. Although reasonably competent on a ballroom floor, Katya did not do well with choreographed routines. She knew her best talent was her voice and made a list of all the major hotels throughout the International Settlement and the French Concession that used house bands and orchestras. The day following her rendezvous with Darya, she arrived mid-afternoon at one of the smaller but popular hotels and auditioned. Sergei Lobachevsky, the band leader, hired her on the spot.

"That was delightful, Miss Palutova. I've been searching for a female singer to join us, and you have such a lovely voice. And you can sing songs in different languages. Very impressive."

"Thank you, Mr. Lobachevsky," she answered with relief. "As for the languages, I'm only fluent in Russian. Although I sing in other languages, I don't know the meaning of most of the words."

"Not to worry. You seem smart, and I'm sure you'll learn meaning over time." Not only was Lobachevsky impressed by her voice, he knew she would attract a crowd, particularly men. She had *everything*. He asked her to stay and join in rehearsals for that evening's show.

"Oh my! Thank you!" Katya was excited and nervous. "But how, how can I sing tonight? I don't know the songs, and I don't even have a radio to listen to all the new music."

"Don't worry," he implored. "This will only be rehearsals, but I can already tell you'll learn quickly." His eyes scanned her. "You possess other *features* that will help you succeed, as well." He smiled approvingly as a big brother might, unlike the men Darya told her to be wary of.

Used to men staring at her and more than willing to do what was necessary to pay her rent, Katya returned his compliment with a bright smile and added with a wink, "I will do my best," understanding more each day the impact she had on men.

"That's all I can expect," Lobachevsky said. "Now, would you like something to eat before everyone arrives for practice?"

"Does the band take a break between rehearsal and the show?" she asked. "If so, I think that would be the best time to eat. Do you have any recordings I can listen to in the meantime, and maybe some music to read with lyrics?"

"Why yes, of course," he replied. Sergei went to his desk, retrieved several sheets of music, and directed her to use a worn but well-upholstered chair in his office to review everything. "I'll leave you alone for a while until the band arrives." He walked out, pulling the door shut.

Katya had begun to study music in detail as soon as Nikolai allowed her to join the church choir in Harbin. Moreover, she had perfect pitch and could visualize the notes in her head as she looked through the music. There were jazz and popular tunes she had never heard and familiar classics her mother had performed. She realized it wouldn't be too challenging to learn most of it. After a while, she looked out the window and daydreamed about having enough money to achieve independence without depending on anyone else.

Suddenly the door burst open, and Lobachevsky hurried back in, followed by a distinguished Chinese gentleman who seemed to be threatening the bandleader in perfect English.

"You must do better. We're getting beaten out by the big fancy establishments. If your band doesn't bring in more people, I'll need to search for a new orchestra," the man shouted, and then noticed Katya. "Who's this?" he demanded from Sergei.

"Mr. Zhou, I'd like you to meet Miss Ekaterina Palutova," Sergei responded.

Hearing her name, Katya rose from the chair and bowed politely to Mr. Zhou.

"What's she doing here?" Zhou quipped.

"She's our new female singer."

Zhou became quiet, gave Katya a careful assessment, and made a circle motion with his hand instructing her to turn around. She did so.

"Tell her to sing something," he demanded.

Lobachevsky translated, and Katya complied. She repeated one of the Russian folk songs she had sung earlier, a tune often sung by the young but well-known Alla Bayanova. Zhou listened quietly without changing his expression.

When she finished, he nodded and remarked, "She might just be what we need." Then he left.

"Ah, Katya—may I call you Katya?" Sergei asked. "He loved it. You are better than Bayanova. No question. You only need to learn a few modern songs, as well. Not to worry—you can do the Russian folk tunes when we have Russian audiences."

"Who was that, Mr. Lobachevsky?" she asked.

"He is Mr. Zhou Ming Jie. He owns this place and the hotel. A gangster, I'm certain, but he also has his good points. Now, with you in the band, we'll be fine. He won't be a problem."

⁂

Katya stayed with Sergei's band for a year and earned enough money to keep her tiny room, watch an occasional movie with Darya, and buy several new dresses. However, she had nothing remaining to put into savings. For the time being, that was sufficient, because life in Shanghai remained somewhat stable, despite Japan's ongoing encroachment in Northern China and the growth of Chinese nationalism. Things were going well at work. Zhou and Lobachevsky were very happy. Katya was a draw. Business flourished, and she became a minor local celebrity, but her popularity also caused a small dilemma for her.

She was still in her teens but mature in every way—so men began seeking her attention. Afraid to encourage anyone after her experience with Kuniaki, Katya rarely consented to dance, and when customers offered to buy her a drink, she stuck to tea. Occasionally a man would ask her for a date, but she avoided starting relationships with anyone she met at Lobachevsky's.

Regardless, as her reputation spread, a growing number of men sought her attention.

By the middle of 1934, she and Darya needed to find a new place for their weekly rendezvous if they wanted privacy. The public garden where Suzhou Creek flows into the Huangpu, not far from the Garden Bridge, became their new locale. It was a busy place situated within the boundaries of the International Settlement. They could watch the vessel activity along the confluence and easily spot the German, American, and Japanese consulates on the other side of the Creek. Their location also put them a few blocks from the Cathay and Palace Hotels, the central banks, and the Sassoon House, each a symbol on the Bund, representing the strength and success of modern Shanghai. It was not far from their previous rendezvous spot in the French Concession, but was noticeably more hectic. They were, in effect, anonymous in the crowd. Nonetheless, word spread about Ekaterina, and her fortunes improved again near the year's end.

"Well, at least there's a whiff of a breeze coming down the river," Katya remarked. "That definitely helps."

The two friends sat on a bench under the shade of large catalpa and magnolia trees, devoid of their spring blossoms due to the summer heat. They each held a small fan which they periodically waved in front of their face to supplement the slight movement of river air.

"Darya, I have news. Exciting news. Three days ago, Mr. Henry Nathan was in the audience at my dance hall. He heard me sing and came to see me after the performance. I could see that Sergei, Mr. Lobachevsky, had a concerned look on his face."

"Who is Henry Nathan? Someone I should know?" Darya asked.

"Well, he is an American, but he speaks some French, some

Shanghainese, and a little Mandarin. You know my English is very weak, although I'm getting better in French, I still—"

"Yes, yes, but go on," Darya interrupted, "about Mr. Nathan."

"I needed Taras to translate. You remember Taras Aristov, don't you, Darya?"

"How can I forget him? So handsome. And such good manners." Katya blushed.

"Hmmm. Is there something else you need to tell me about Taras?" Darya probed.

"You're right. Quite good looking and ever so courteous. And yes, I will tell you. He has asked me out several times, but I said no each time."

"I know you're being careful around men, Katya, but he seems to be one of the good ones."

"He may be, but it may not matter now, anyway," she said.

"What do you mean?"

"If you let me continue about Mr. Nathan, I'll tell you."

"Oh, yes, go ahead," Darya giggled.

"Well, Mr. Nathan talked about music and what kind I liked best. He laughed when I told him my favorites were the old Russians like Tchaikovsky and Rachmaninoff or classics by Mozart and Brahms. Then he said, 'But you're singing popular music every night.' I said, 'Of course. That's what audiences want to hear. And I get paid to do it.' Our conversation continued for several minutes until the practice room was empty except for me, Taras, Mr. Nathan, and his date, a lovely woman whose name I forget. Even Sergei was gone."

"Were you getting nervous? It seems strange to me," Darya asked.

"No, of course not. Taras was with me. Not only is he handsome, but he's very strong. I've seen him hauling band equipment and heavy boxes. And besides, he likes me, so I felt fine."

"Okay, okay. Then what happened?"

"Oh, Darya, this is the best part. Mr. Nathan said something Taras hesitated to translate. So Mr. Nathan repeated it. Taras took a big swallow, then said, 'Mr. Nathan is the bandleader at the Cathay Hotel, and wants you to join his orchestra. He will pay you three times your present salary.' *The Cathay,* Darya! Can you believe it?"

Darya was stunned. She was excited for Katya, yet worried too. It was a giant leap from Sergei's band to the Cathay. Sir Victor Sassoon, the wealthiest man in Shanghai, owned the Cathay. Anyone and everyone who could afford it wanted to stay at the Cathay. It was both the place to be seen and the one where they ensured your privacy. Accepting an offer to work with Henry Nathan would result in an instant change in her living conditions. To be part of his band would open doors to contacts who could truly change her life.

"Oh, Katya, that's amazing!" The words flowed, but Darya's eyes were watering.

"What's wrong, Darya? I thought you'd be happy for me?"

"Oh, Katya, of course, I'm happy for you." She took a small handkerchief from her purse and dabbed her eyes.

"Then what is it? I'll be able to buy better food, get a decent apartment, and save more money to go to Europe or the United States."

"And that's just it. Katya, I don't want to lose you. Once you become part of the Cathay, why would you choose to keep seeing me? I'd be happy for you, but it will take you down a road that will keep us apart. And did you tell Mr. Lobachevsky about the offer?"

"Don't be silly. You're my best friend. That will never change. Stop your fussing. But no, I haven't told Sergei. I wanted to tell you first."

"Do you think he'll try to stop you?"

"No. He's a good man, but I am worried about what Mr. Zhou might do. He can be quite difficult. But I don't want to think about that now. Let's go to Great World, Dashijie, to celebrate. Everyone says it is the best arcade and amusement center in the world. My treat."

"Oh, I couldn't do that. Papa would be angry."

"So, don't tell Papa. It's a perfect place for us to have some fun. Besides, I hear they have some new jugglers and magicians, and a new ice cream parlor."

"You may be right, but Great World also has hordes of pickpockets, pimps, women with their skirts slit up to their…."

"I heard the slits go even higher…." Katya interrupted.

"Oh K…," they both laughed and headed for Great World. As they walked, they discussed the fan-fan dancers, the acrobats, the men who removed earwax for a small fee, the slot machines, the giant stuffed whale, and other strange and routine attractions that made the Great World so famous.

⚜

"You're quitting?! But you can't," Taras urged. "Things are going so well. Oh, Katya, I knew it. I knew it as soon as I heard that Mr. Nathan wanted to talk to you."

Katya and Taras sat at a little café not far from the dance hall, drinking hot Russian tea. For two months, they had been meeting there before rehearsals. Today, he held one of her hands across the table.

"It's not like I'm moving to Africa, Taras."

"Does Mr. Nathan need a trumpet player? Maybe I could go with you." His voice held the sadness he was feeling in his heart and mind. Like Darya, he was scared Katya would never return once she moved to the Cathay.

"Oh, Taras, that's sweet, but I have no idea if he needs a trumpet player. And you're worrying about nothing. I'm more concerned about having Mr. Zhou find out than telling Sergei. Like you, Sergei will understand and be disappointed, but Mr. Zhou? I'm not so sure. I've heard some bad things about him."

Taras nodded his head in agreement. "Yes, I've heard people say he never allows someone to betray him."

"Well, I'm certainly not betraying him. I'm just taking a new job."

"Everyone has their own definition of betrayal, Katya."

She looked at him and let that sink in for a moment. "Oh, Taras, you make it sound as if I had some knowledge of a crime he committed and was going to the police. That's not true."

"Ekaterina Palutova." He rarely called her by her full name. "Would you marry me?" He reached with his second hand and held both of hers. "I don't want you to leave. I love you, Katya. We could be so happy together. We love music and reading. We both took the long train ride from the west. We have much in common."

Taras's voice began to push the limits. He didn't want to plead, but he loved her, and the wobble in his words betrayed his desperation.

A tear trickled down from her eye, and she removed one of her hands to wipe it away. Memories of Kuni left her fearful of trusting men, especially with her innermost feelings. And although she liked Taras very much and possibly could even fall in love with him, she didn't see him as the answer to her growing desire for freedom and independence. She straightened up and looked at him.

"Oh my, Taras! We're going to be late for rehearsal. Let's go. We can talk about this some other time." She rose and searched her purse for a few coins to pay the bill.

He brushed her arm away and placed money on the table. The blush on his face had faded, and as they walked out, she took his arm for the short stroll to the dance hall. Rehearsal and the performance that evening proceeded as usual. At the show's end, Katya went to Mr. Lobachevsky's office and knocked on the door.

"Come in," Sergei boomed good-naturedly. "Ah, Katya, you were wonderful tonight. Like always. The audience loved you, my dear. How can I help you?"

She got right to the point. "Sergei, Mr. Henry Nathan offered me a position with his orchestra, and I accepted. I won't be leaving until the end of the month because I wanted to give you time to find a replacement."

"Ah, yes," he spoke slowly. "Of course. I've been waiting for this day ever since I heard you sing your audition. And then, when I saw Nathan in the audience and speaking with you later—no surprise. Yes, Katya, you deserve much more than our small hall can offer. How much will he pay you?"

"Oh Sergei, it's not just the money," she said, although she knew money was the overwhelming reason. "It's also the chance to meet a different group of people. Oh, I'm sorry, that didn't come out the way I meant."

"No need to apologize. I understand. Long ago, I accepted the limits of my talents and abilities. I'm happy you stayed with us as long as you have." He suddenly became more serious. "I'm not sure, however, what Mr. Zhou will think. He can be…tricky to deal with."

"Should I see him myself? Or would it be best for you to do so?" she asked.

Sergei twisted in his chair, turning his head away from her. Mr. Zhou was known to take things out on the messenger. He was weighing Zhou's potential onslaught when the man himself entered without knocking.

"Ah, you're both here. Perfect." Zhou shut the door behind him and continued speaking in a quiet but sinister tone. "Do either of you know Du Yuesheng?"

Lobachevsky blanched. He recognized the name of one of Shanghai's most notorious gangsters. Connected to everyone and everything, Yuesheng controlled a vast illegal empire that had started when he monopolized the opium trade years earlier. Sergei and Katya knew several band members were opium addicts, but Katya had no idea who was behind the dangerous enterprise, whereas Sergei did.

"I know the name," Lobachevsky admitted. "Very successful. Seems to know anyone and everyone. Fancy car and clothes. I've seen him around."

"Correct, Sergei," Zhou hissed. "A man of power and influence. He asks me to do him favors every so often. They have all been most profitable for him and for me, but that's beside the point. He was in the audience tonight. I'm surprised you didn't notice him. I gave him our best table and most beautiful hostess. But, no matter. During intermission, he came to see me. He had some information for me. Imagine that. Du Yuesheng shows up in my dance hall to give *me* information. Very strange, don't you agree?"

"Yes, Mr. Zhou. Most unusual." Sergei concurred.

Katya said nothing. She had no idea who Du Yuesheng was.

"*He* told me our Miss Palutova was leaving to go work at the Cathay. In Henry Nathan's orchestra at Victor Sassoon's hotel."

Sergei and Katya opened their mouths to speak, but Zhou kept going. "Before you say anything, no matter what it is, I need you to know keeping secrets from me—how to say—is never a good thing." He glared at them.

"We weren't keeping secrets, Mr. Zhou," Katya spoke confidently. "I only recently decided to accept Mr. Nathan's offer. Mr. Lobachevsky knew nothing about it. I'm surprised you know, because I only confirmed with Mr. Henry two days ago."

"That is still one day too many to keep such a secret. Haven't we treated you well, Ekaterina? Why do you want to leave?" The scowl on his face made her uneasy, but she responded with a strong voice and sincerity.

"Yes, I've been treated well, Mr. Zhou. Nonetheless, you surely know working at the Cathay will help my career. It isn't very complicated."

"It's not complicated for me either, Miss Palutova. If you leave, I'm sorry to say, it will be necessary for me to terminate several musicians and waitresses. For instance, three trumpets would be too expensive."

His not-too-subtle threat to fire Taras surprised her, but she regrouped. "Mr. Zhou, before Sergei hired me, your club was doing fine. Do you think I'm the only woman who can sing and look pretty in a dress?" She continued speaking without thinking. "Do you think someone like Victor Sassoon would let a small-time dance hall owner interfere with a legitimate offer made to me by his friend and close associate, Henry Nathan?"

Her statement caused Zhou's expression to change. He formed a smile but one without mirth. "Oh, you silly girl. Of course, I know Sassoon is the most influential man in the Settlement, the Concession, and probably all Shanghai. But Nathan? He's only an employee. Just like you. Nothing more. He has as much influence with Sassoon as I do with Franklin Roosevelt. So my dear, do as you wish. And, aside from the number of trumpets in the band, don't forget, I know where you live."

He chuckled, turned, and let himself out.

The two weeks before her planned move to Henry Nathan's band, Katya performed as usual, and the crowds packed Zhou's dance hall to see her. Her conversations with Mr. Lobachevsky, Darya, and even Mr. Korablin provided no valuable suggestions about what to do if Mr. Zhou followed through on his threat to fire Taras or harm her. She needed a different advocate—a defender.

Her alarm woke her at eight o'clock on Saturday morning after a typical long Friday night at the club. With only four hours of sleep, Katya remained groggy but worried about Taras. That evening would be her last day with Sergei Lobachevsky's band, and she knew she would regret it if she didn't do all she could to protect Taras's job. She cleaned quickly, had a cup of tea, and set out for the Cathay Hotel. At precisely nine, she walked into the lobby and asked the concierge for Mr. Nathan.

"I'm sorry, Miss Palutova, but Mr. Nathan rarely sees anyone before rehearsal at four o'clock. I can leave a message for him," the experienced attendant told her.

"Can someone take him a message now? It's very important," she urged.

The man behind the desk was about sixty years old, not much taller than Katya, and slightly overweight, but impeccably dressed in an exquisite tuxedo distinguishing him from the uniformed bell-hops. She had watched his eyes track her as she crossed the lobby to his station, and she recognized the classic look of most men who can't keep their eyes off a beautiful woman. She knew what to do next. Katya leaned in close to him so he could smell her perfume, then shifted the tenor of her voice, adding a slight quiver, and spoke with hesitation and fear.

"But I'm desperate. If Mr. Nathan doesn't help me now, today, I may not be alive to sing with his orchestra on Monday."

The career hotel worker responded in traditional British fashion. "Young lady, I will be happy to leave a message for Mr. Nathan. Unfortunately, I cannot tell you what time he will read it. You certainly understand we have policies to protect the privacy of our guests and staff. I respect your dilemma. However, here's a sheet of notepaper, a pencil, and an envelope. Please feel free to sit and compose your message." He pointed to the seat on the opposite side of his desk, and she sat down with a groan.

When she finished writing, Katya rose. "Please make sure he gets this. There's no one else who can help me. You think I'm not serious, but you're wrong." She handed him the sealed note and walked out.

With her head down, she walked to her and Darya's favorite bench in the nearby park as if guided like a pigeon returning home. Preoccupied with her thoughts, she was surprised to find the bench occupied but quickly moved to another. Before settling, she located a street vendor selling steamed stuffed buns. She hadn't eaten since early the previous night and was famished. The bun tasted heavenly, and the savory food helped clear her head.

She made a decision. She had to act.

Without thinking through her brainstorm, Katya rushed back to the Cathay. She entered a side door unnoticed and found a staircase to the basement. It was a busy place, and she moved through the tight hallways as if she knew where she was going. At last, she saw what she wanted: the housekeepers' changing room. She went in as if she belonged, found the racks storing clean uniforms, took one, and put it on.

"Are you new?" a girl about her age asked in English.

"Yes. Mr. Nathan from band me get job," she answered in broken English. "Need thank him."

"Russian, huh? That's okay with me. People won't bother you around here. Mr. Sassoon would never allow it. But Mr. Nathan? He's never about until the afternoon. However, I know they take a tray to his room every morning at ten thirty. He's on seven. Room 714, I think. Never been there meself. I do the fourth floor. Long story about how I wound up here, but better get going. Good luck. My name's Mary, by the way."

Mary hurried out, and Katya followed her to the service elevator, where they rode up with four other housekeepers. Two got off at three, Mary at four, two more at five, and Katya stepped off at seven into a foyer-like area with two doors, each with a small window. She peeked through one and saw the hallway with guest rooms off to either side. The second window revealed a room full of supplies. Perfect. She stepped inside, put soap bars wrapped in glossy paper in her pocket, gathered a handful of towels, took a deep breath, and left the storeroom. She pushed open the hallway door and followed the numbers until she found 714. She knocked, but there was no response. She knocked again—a little harder. Still no acknowledgment. Nervous about arousing interest from other guests or staff, Katya hesitated but decided to try a third time.

"What's the urgency?" a male voice mumbled loudly from the other side of the door. "This better be something good! You know my schedule!"

Katya heard the annoyance and sleepiness in Nathan's voice. She wondered if he was a little inebriated. She couldn't tell, but it made no difference. She didn't know where else to go. He opened the door.

"Katya? Katya Palutova? Is that you? What are you doing here? And at such an hour?" Nathan growled.

More brazen than normal, she pushed past him into his suite. Too tired and slow to prevent her, Nathan shut the door and turned to face her.

"Oh, Mr. Nathan, I help need," she said in English. "I scared. I such a thing no believe could happen. I no know what do?" Her eyes and voice expressed desperation, but a careful observer would also see and hear anger and determination.

"Whoa! Slow down. Between your accent and me being barely awake… Would you like coffee?" Before waiting for her to answer, he picked up the phone and ordered coffee and breakfast for two. "It'll be up in fifteen minutes. Now, I'm going to shower, and then we can talk." He left her in his sitting room and shut the door to his bedroom.

Katya looked around, spotted the radio, and turned it on. She found the Russian station on the dial and made herself comfortable on the couch. She closed her eyes and listened to the news and music, but the knock on the door ended her reverie.

"Room Service!"

Katya opened the door and let in the waiter without waiting for Nathan. He set his tray on the low table in front of the couch and looked at her strangely.

"Who are you?" he asked.

It was then she remembered she was in a housekeeper's uniform. Katya answered in her halting English. "Mr. Nathan, ask more towels. I leaving."

On cue, like a Hollywood actor, Henry Nathan strolled out of his bedroom and interrupted. Katya made a quick gasp. Amazing what a shower, combed hair, and a shave could do. He had also changed into an exquisite silk housecoat. It was a cerulean blue with two small, embroidered gold dragons on each side of his chest and another stitched down the length of the back. She had never seen anything like it or anyone like him in one. She stared.

"Thank you, Morris," Nathan said to the young waiter and gave him a tip.

The waiter lingered, waiting for Katya to go with him.

Nathan said, "Oh, I have some cleaning for her to do. Thank you again."

Morris bowed and left.

Nathan turned his attention to Katya. He was aware of his effect on women, just like Katya had become aware of her effect on men, but Nathan knew it was not the time. "So, Katya, what's the problem?"

She asked him if he knew French, because her French was better than her English, and she wanted to make sure he understood what she said. He said yes, and they continued in French.

"Mr. Zhou says if I come to work in your orchestra, he will fire my friend, Taras Aristov, one of the trumpet players. I'm afraid I insulted him. I said Mr. Zhou was a "small-time" dance hall owner. Then he said he knows where I live. Mr. Zhou is gangster, and he scares me, Mr. Nathan."

She stopped talking and watched as Nathan walked over and turned off the radio. He poured her a cup of coffee and offered her some of the eggs and sweet rolls room service had delivered. She hesitated, but he encouraged her, so she fixed herself a plate and cup.

"Thank you," she told him between bites and a sip of coffee. The muscles in her face and neck began to relax, and she felt more hopeful now that someone else knew her situation.

"Yes, I know Zhou's reputation. He can be difficult, but there are ways to—how should I put it…to appease him."

She knew exactly what he meant. He or someone would pay off Zhou.

"Ah, the way of the world," she whispered under her breath in Russian.

This was one of the reasons she wanted the job at the Cathay. A bigger income would give her leverage in the future to *appease* others on her own, if necessary.

"I'll make an appointment to see him today," Nathan said. "There's plenty of time, especially since I had to get up so early." He looked at her and smiled.

She looked at the floor and apologized.

"It's nothing. Besides, you'll be such a wonderful addition to the orchestra. It's the least I can do."

She coughed briefly and asked, "What about Taras?"

"Don't worry about him. I'll figure something out." He lifted a perfectly browned and buttered English muffin and took a bite.

⁂

And he did. Nathan paid off Zhou and found another predominantly Russian band needing a trumpet player. But Darya's and Taras's predictions proved accurate. Within two months, Katya's weekly visits with Darya became biweekly and, soon, monthly. After a year, the friends were lucky to get together at Christmas, Easter, and each other's birthday. As for Taras, his love and infatuation with Katya also waned. They dated a couple of times, and he went to see her at the Cathay, but they never had time alone once she joined up with the Henry Nathan Orchestra.

By 1937, however, the objective of the Japanese in China was evident to the world. They wanted to control all of it. They had been creeping south since their invasion of Manchuria six years earlier, and the Chinese Nationalists had had enough. They decided to stop retreating and fight—at Shanghai. By then, Katya had found more comfortable accommodations and used rickshaws. Using the people-powered carriages aligned her closer to the Brits, French, and Americans than the Russians and Chinese. She had settled into a comfortable lifestyle well-removed from the log home in Valday. Audiences at the Cathay loved her, and when Sir Victor opened Ciro's in 1936, Henry Nathan took his orchestra and Katya to the new venue. It was the first building designed exclusively as a nightclub, and competition with the famous Paramount only blocks away became intense.

Katya was in demand. She was vivacious, fun-loving, and riding high. Local fame also meant being invited to after-show parties with celebrities whom, not long before, she could not have imagined meeting. She was earning enough money to save some and move socially and psychologically up the ladder, including hiring personal servants.

So, when the bottom fell out, she landed hard.

The Battle of Shanghai between the Chinese Nationalists and the Japanese took place over three months—August to November 1937. The Japanese drove the Chinese military out of the city, leaving the French Concession and International Settlements as remote outposts surrounded by a siege army willing to wait out the westerners still in residence. Business declined, and people left by shiploads for Hong Kong, Singapore, Australia, India, and the United States. By mid-January 1938, many Shanghailanders and local Chinese were justifiably fearful of growing Japanese power. The senseless, bestial slaughter of tens of thousands in Nanking, a horror too terrifying for anyone to comprehend, provided all the evidence anyone needed that Japan would go to any lengths to conquer China. Shanghai—that is, British, French, American, Russian, and Jewish Shanghai—wondered if they would get the same treatment. Residents knew they were living in a declining city and were forced to adapt, including Katya.

8   FALL 1938 — JUNE 1940
Shanghai

"Oh, Darya, what am I going to do?" Katya fretted. "I barely had enough money to get a rickshaw ride to Lokawei Cemetery to visit Grandmama. What's worse, dear Darya, I haven't seen you in such a long time either. What's happened to me?"

The two attractive young ladies sat on their bench in the park, looking across Suzhou Creek. The German, American, and Japanese consulates were still on the opposite shore, but there were changes. Activity at the American consulate was now a trickle, whereas the Japanese one bustled nonstop. Life had changed dramatically for everyone in Shanghai. The International Settlement and French Concession were shut off from the rest of the city by rugged iron gates installed to prevent refugees from the interior from inundating the city. Daily night patrols run by the Buddhist Benevolent Society routinely carted away more than five hundred human cadavers. The unfortunates were mainly poor, starved Chinese, but also included a smattering of others. Although the outward appearance of Shanghai was that of storied glitter and excitement, visitors barely had to scratch the surface before discovering the city's actual condition within a block of their hotel on the Bund. Beggars, sewage, bodies, shuttered businesses, disease, and every conceivable urban blight gripped their senses. It was among that wreckage that the girls chatted.

"I sent you cards and notes, Katya. Left phone messages. Worried about you after those horrendous battles in the Zhabei district. And then bombs—on the Cathay Hotel and Great World. Stupid pilots. Did you hear that *Chinese* pilots accidentally dropped the bombs that killed everyone around the hotel and Great World? Unbelievable! And the stories from Nanking—they give me nightmares."

"Yes, I heard about the pilots and Nanking. Just awful. I was lucky. The band moved to Ciro's before the hotel was hit. And I'm sorry I never called you. When Mr. Nathan said they needed to make changes to the orchestra because of declining attendance, I never realized he meant me. I was embarrassed. I had to move again. Gave up my cook, housekeeper, and telephone and sold my nice clothes. I found another job at a small dance hall, but it's even less well known than Mr. Zhou's place." Katya shifted the conversation and asked, "Are you okay, Darya? You look good."

"Yes, thank you, Katya. With everyone in the house working, we're fine. Good news—my brother Yaromir is engaged. However, Papa thinks we may need to move again, too. Leave Shanghai. He's certain it's only a matter of time before the Japanese cross the river and take over the Settlement and Concession."

"It's funny, isn't it, Darya? Our families leave Russia and go to Harbin. Leave Harbin and come to Shanghai. And now we may need to leave again. I would give anything to have a safe, consistent home, and I don't know what I'll do when my money runs out."

"You'll be fine, Katya. You're talented and beautiful. That's a good combination anywhere—but yes, the thought of moving again is exhausting. And to who knows where? More strange customs, another language. Papa has been talking about Australia. He's worried Hong Kong and Singapore are within reach of the Japanese. I don't know. I can hardly speak French here in the Concession, and if we go to Australia—jeez, Katya, English?!"

"You can't go!" Katya cried. "You mustn't! Australia? What would I do without you?" As soon as she said it, she looked at the ground. "Oh, I'm sorry, Darya. I ignored you for months on end. How selfish of me. Can you ever forgive me?"

Darya leaned across the narrow gap between them and hugged her friend. A strong, loving hug. "Who am I to judge you? I love you. You're my best friend, and I was happy for you when you had success. Yes, I missed seeing you, but that doesn't mean I stopped being your friend. You're closer to me than my sister."

Katya put her head on Darya's shoulder and began to weep. They clung to each other, ignoring the curious eyes around them. At length, Katya sat up and wiped her eyes carelessly with the fingers of one hand. "Yes, Darya. I'll make it. What choice do I have?"

They stood and agreed to meet again in a week. As Katya walked into the throng along the Bund, Darya remained and tried to imagine what she would do if she were Katya. She shivered at the prospect.

They met regularly during the coming weeks, and as the year began to wane, Darya could see the desperation forming within Katya's eyes. Something about her friend reminded Darya of tragic historical figures who never entirely escaped the destiny of the damned. Her dark vision was reinforced at one of their meetings when she noticed the excessive amount of makeup Katya wore. It was atypical, and Darya was curious to know why.

However, before getting directly to the point, she asked, "How's the tea? I bought it from the new vendor on the corner."

"Tea is something that rejuvenates me every time I drink it," Katya answered. "Thank you, Darya. It's excellent, but...but I can't pay you. Money is...I can't afford...oh, I need to move again."

Katya took a breath and looked into the two warm brown marbles through which Darya saw the world. They were eyes that never stopped radiating care and concern.

"Katya, I shouldn't pry, but I notice you're wearing more makeup than normal. Are you hiding something? Did some band member strike you?"

To an extent, the makeup hid Katya's blush. The reason for the makeup was something she couldn't tell her dearest friend.

"Oh my!" She reached into her purse and pulled out a handkerchief to dab her lips, eyelids, and cheeks. "I didn't get home until four this morning and was too tired to clean up. Then I was late waking up today, so I hurried. It's the bandleader. He says I need to 'have a pretty face.' He says it helps men stay longer at the club and buy more drinks."

Darya was skeptical but wanted to believe her friend. "Yes, what is it with men? And why do we do all these silly things to please them?" They both laughed.

"Oh, I don't mind pleasing them," Katya admitted. "At least as far as wearing nice dresses. I had to sell most of mine, but I kept three I adore. And if a little extra rouge, eyeliner, shadow, and lipstick will keep me employed, it seems like a small price to pay. And I've never minded men looking at me. Well, most men." They laughed again. "So, tell me about Yaromir," Katya asked. "The wedding. His new wife. I want to know every detail."

Darya outlined every element, and Katya listened attentively.

"So they have a separate apartment?" Katya wanted to keep the topic off of herself.

"Yes. Small, but neat and clean. It's over on Rue Montigny, not far south of the Franco-Chinese School."

"Rue Montigny? That's a busy street. How do they sleep?"

Before Darya answered, a man approached their bench and called out, "Nadine! Nadine! So good to see you."

They looked at him and turned around to see if he was speaking to someone behind them, but no one was there. They could tell he was intoxicated as he got closer, but he was persistent.

"Nadine, it's me, Fedor. Aren't you glad to see me?"

"I think he's looking at you, Katya," Darya whispered.

"Occasionally people tell me I remind them of someone else," Katya whispered. She also hoped her friend didn't notice the sweat that instantly appeared on her brow, or the little shake in her hand.

"I'm sorry, sir," Darya answered. "No one here named Nadine. You must be mistaken."

"Don't be silly," he slurred and wobbled on his feet. "I'd know Nadine anywhere," he hiccupped.

"If you don't leave us alone," Darya persisted, "I'll call a policeman." He took two steps closer, and Darya shouted, "Police! Police!"

The man backed away when he saw the turbaned officer make his way from the street in their direction. "My apol-apolo-apologies, miss. I'll l-l-leave. But your friend's name is Nadine." He turned and weaved his way out of the park.

"Is everything satisfactory, ladies?" the officer asked in English.

The drunk's presence had rattled Katya, and she froze. She had recognized the man. Her hands suddenly became damp, she felt a flush rise in her cheeks, and she prayed she could keep from shaking.

"The man who just left here was bothering us," Darya answered in rapid Russian. "He's gone now, officer."

The officer turned away, not understanding anything she said, but seeing that both women appeared alright.

Katya rose from her seat and pulled her watch from her clutch. "I have to go, Darya. I can't be late for work."

It was an excuse, but a good one. The popularity she had attained with Henry Nathan's band had faded, and she couldn't afford to give her employer any reason to let her go. When she agreed to meet Darya again in the park, she had assumed no one would recognize her, least of all the odious Fedor. Her current audiences were well-removed from any who saw her perform at the Cathay or Ciro's. She never believed someone who knew *Nadine* would spot her in that park. She hoped her makeup concealed the panic and surprise on her face.

"Oh Katya, must you leave so soon? We don't see each other often enough. And I'm worried about you."

Darya's sincere concern embarrassed Ekaterina even more. She felt so guilty not including Darya in everything, but she thought it was best.

"Yes, my dear. I really must go, and I do need to clean up. Then there's the walk to the club. Rehearsals. Lots to do."

"Do find time to eat something," Darya encouraged. "You look a touch thin. Are you eating right?"

"Yes, of course," Katya answered too quickly. "Just adapting to a different routine. Now, come here. Give me a hug and kiss, and I'll see you next week."

They embraced, and when they parted, Katya spun on her heels and marched off, with Darya watching her vanish into the crowd.

Nadine Bebchuk walked into the vacant club about an hour before showtime. It smelled. The aroma came from lingering cigarette and cigar smoke mixed with the sour scent of spilled beer permeating the soft wooden floor, as well as the pervasive pheromones of male bodies. The presence of the sad and melancholy men who filled the seats every night never really left the room. The third-rate building had no separate practice room. No coat check room. No food service. No private place for costume changes. The hallway leading to the delivery entrance at the rear served that purpose. Cigarettes were sold as singles by preteen girls. Tables and chairs needed regular repair. As for the musicians, half of them were opium addicts, and the other half were exhausted from lack of sleep. Playing in the band was their second or third job.

Every time Katya walked into that dingy and dirty place to perform as Nadine, she envisioned herself someplace else. Most often, she conjured up long-faded memories of Lake Valday and the scent of the fresh pine forest of her youth, wishing she was still there. However, someone would soon shatter the vision, leaving her wondering if it had all been a dream.

"Ah, Nadine. You're here. Looking quite lovely today, I suspect you'll do quite well tonight." Ivan Losev smiled at her. His chipped, tobacco-stained teeth somehow shone beneath the bushy mustache drooping over his lips.

Katya actually liked Ivan. He played clarinet but was also the bandleader and club owner. Losev worked hard to manage and accommodate the vast differences between the members of his band and their hidden demons. He was a good man stuck in a life without a future because of several bad decisions. What pleased Katya about him was that he recognized her voice's uniqueness and her extensive repertoire. He knew he needed to hang on to her.

"Yes, Ivan. I'm here. On schedule. Every day."

Her monotone was typical, and her mind elsewhere, but Ivan didn't care because she sang like an angel. But Katya did mind. She had yet to reconcile her rapid and precipitous fall from the good life. She went through the motions of living but remained in shock.

To pay her bills, not only was she singing in such a downtrodden club, but she was dancing as well. From her first days at Mr. Zhou's, Katya had supplemented her salary by dancing for commissions with men who purchased dance tickets. She had always enjoyed dancing and having men hold her. The men at Mr. Zhou's and especially those at the Cathay and Giro's were gentlemen. They were well-attired, followed the house rules, and smelled good. Notably, most of them also knew how to dance. It had been a sheer delight to take to the floor with such men, and the money was just a bonus.

But under her present circumstances, it was necessary to earn as much as possible. So Katya, as Nadine, also danced at Ivan Losev's place. She used the pseudonym to separate herself from anyone who may know Ekaterina Palutova. In her mind, they needed to be two different people.

Things at Losev's Cabaret were as distinct from the Cathay as an old Model T from a Rolls Royce. Losev ran the seedy club on a very lean budget and didn't have the money to afford bouncers to keep out unruly, dirty, and vulgar men. Therefore, Katya and the other women succumbed to their dance partners' groping and foul odors. Thank heaven she had more than one dress. She would wash her clothes each night and set them out to dry the following day.

Having been spotted by that wretched Fedor at the park, she remained shaken when she arrived for work.

"Are you feeling ill, Nadine?" Ivan expressed concern.

Katya realized she was dwelling on Fedor but smiled easily and said, "No, Ivan. Just tired."

"Yes, aren't we all?"

Katya was worried that Fedor would show up and cause problems. As it was, whenever he bought her drinks, she left them untouched. He'd offered her opium, and she'd declined. When he asked to escort her home, she never consented. Nonetheless, he physically grabbed her as she left to walk home one night. Fortunately, Carl, the all-purpose janitor, bouncer-when-necessary, fix-it man, and fill-in bartender, heard Katya yell. He was a tall, brawny former sailor from Denmark who jumped ship in Shanghai and never left, and he was as strong as anyone she ever knew. Carl pulled Fedor off Katya and tossed her soused admirer into the trash pile. Then he let loose a stream of Danish—of which Fedor didn't understand a word, but he certainly caught its meaning.

Katya's kiss of thanks made Carl blush, and he'd been keeping his eye on her ever since. His protection was important because Katya's fellow dancers were plotting against her. Katya made no apologies for the fact she could sing, wore clean clothes, and possessed natural beauty. Miss Nadine Bebchuck radiated the sultry sexiness of the era and easily beguiled the habitués and one-timers. Naturally, she attracted more dance partners than the other women hustling for tickets, and their jealousy was palpable. Nadine knew she needed to stop dancing to stay safe, but she also knew once she did so, she would need to make up the income deficit.

She continued her conversation with her boss. "Ivan, do you think it would be possible for me to take Friday or Saturday nights off? I need a break. This is too much."

"Fridays or Saturdays? Nadine, you know those are our busiest nights. And many of the men come to see *you*. Impossible." He was firm.

"I need a night off, Ivan. I can't keep this up. I'm exhausted. What night can I have? Besides, many of the guys in the band take a night off. Be fair."

"Nadine, you don't understand. I can get another trumpet player or drummer, but I can't replace you or your voice. Not easily." He pleaded his case like a man in a leaky boat, fearful of going under at any moment. "We—*I*—need you. I can't."

"Very well, Ivan. I quit. I'll get work somewhere else."

As she turned, he reached out and brushed his fingers across her shoulder without gripping her. "Oh Nadine, no. Don't go. What can I do to change your mind?"

With a straight face, she said, "Double my salary and give me a share of the bar money."

He paled at the suggestion. Barely able to make the monthly rent on the club and pay his small staff, he saw no way to meet her demands. "I…I can't do that. I simply don't have the money."

"It's that or a night off, Ivan. Otherwise, I leave. Which do you choose?"

He caved. "Mondays. Take Mondays off."

Katya smiled. She knew he would give her Mondays because it was the slowest night of the week, but she felt no joy at forcing his hand. After all, reality had forced her hand as well. Now she had Mondays free to do *whatever was necessary* to earn more money.

"Very well. Mondays. Thank you, Ivan." She held her breath and kissed him on the cheek.

It had been over a month since Darya and Katya last met in the park. They sat together, enjoying each other's company in the late winter on a Monday morning.

"Sweet Darya, how are you doing? Every day I keep thinking I'll get a message telling me you're on your way to Hong Kong."

"I know, Katya. Here it is, 1939, and we're still here. But Papa has taken ill. He hasn't gotten out of bed for two weeks. We're all worried. The doctor thinks it's tuberculosis. Tuberculosis, Katya!" She started to cry.

"I'm here, Darya." Katya hugged her friend, but the news startled her, too. Darya's father had always been strong and healthy, and she knew he earned more money than the rest of the family combined.

"Momma's going crazy. The money we saved to go to Hong Kong is now paying the doctor and others." Darya's voice registered her anxiety. "Two or three more weeks like this, and we won't be able to afford tickets for everyone. Oh, Katya…"

"Is there anything I can do?" Katya offered. "I'm doing a bit better and have started saving again."

"No, no, Katya. We'll get through this. I know you need every bit you earn. No. Please. Nothing."

"If you're sure. But Darya, please ask if there is anything you need from me."

"I will. I promise. But let's change the subject."

"Of course," Katya agreed, "but the news isn't good. Last night, I heard some of the band members saying it's only a matter of time before the Japanese break down the gates, cross the bridges, and take complete control of the most valuable real estate in the city."

"Yes. I'm scared, Katya. Yaromir says the British, US, and French forces are nearly gone. And if the Japanese do come into the Settlement and Concession, the situation for people like us—you know, without passports or a country that wants us—would be very dangerous."

"Yet despite everything, life seems normal. How do we do it? And the people in the fancy hotels and at the clubs? The rich carry on like it is still 1937 with no concern."

"Ugh! Enough, Katya. Tell me about you. What you've been up to? You look better. I'm glad things are working out."

Katya had fully expected to tell her friend the complete truth, but after the sad news about Darya's father, she decided it could wait for another day. She offered the abridged version. "I'm singing and dancing, as I told you last time. It's a grind and not remotely like Ciro's, but it keeps me busy and the money coming in."

As they often did, they simply sat and watched the river activity without speaking. Their physical closeness gave them comfort, as did the knowledge they could share personal thoughts and concerns with someone willing to help in every circumstance. After a short while, Katya checked the time and stood.

"I have to go. Still can't afford to miss rehearsals or be late." She spoke with a straight face, and Darya nodded.

"I know. Status quo. I have chores to do myself and need to take my shift caring for Papa." Her face showed the strain of not knowing what would happen.

"I'll pray to Saint Panteleimon, the great healer, for your Papa."

"Thank you, Katya. We need to meet again next week, to get back into a routine."

"Yes, of course. Give my love to your mother." She kissed Darya on both cheeks, then Ekaterina turned and walked off to her destiny, as she had so many times previously.

Katya stepped away from Darya with a heavy heart. The thought of Darya losing her father brought back the memory of that awful day when Raisa brought her news of Nikolai's death. The recollection made her dizzy, and she reeled, momentarily losing her balance on the curb and about to fall into the traffic as she mumbled, "Papa, my baby." Suddenly a strange hand yanked her back to safety on the sidewalk.

"*Etes-vous bien, mademoiselle?*" the French Army officer inquired. "*Le traffic! Vous devez faire attention.*"

Startled, all Katya said was *"Merci, monsieur,"* as tears welled in her eyes and visions of Kolya and her baby cascaded through her mind. She took a cursory glance at the slender khaki-clad officer. He was noticeably taller than she, and, to her surprise, she found him intriguing. There was something about his face that attracted her. It wasn't a perfect face, but the creases were all in the right places. He sported an elegant, thin, black mustache and dark eyes hidden beneath the shadow of the bill of his cap. His voice expressed concern, and he exposed glistening teeth when he smiled. After a moment, he dropped her arm—only when he was confident she was stable.

Touching his fingers to his cap, he responded, *"A votre service. Bonjour,"* and went upon his way.

Katya stood for a long moment, following him as he merged with the crowd on the street. After gathering herself, which entailed smoothing her dress and readjusting her mind, she continued her march at full speed toward earning as much money as possible. Several blocks later, she modified her stride and bearing upon entering Rue Chu Pao San, better known as Blood Alley. She hunched over, seemed to shrivel, professed a slight limp, and mumbled like someone with a tenuous grasp of reality. She carried a frayed satchel with her *working attire* inside. Darya had once asked her why she used the old worn-out case.

"Who'd want to steal *this?*" Katya had answered. So far, it had worked.

During her stroll down Blood Alley, named for the many grisly fights on the narrow lane resulting from too much alcohol, bad drugs, stolen women, or national pride, Ninette—for that is what she called herself on that street—passed the doors to The Palais Cabaret, Frisco, Monk's Brass Rail, and many more establishments before walking into Viveka's. Each time she passed the threshold, she chuckled. In Russian, *viveka* means beautiful voice.

"If they only knew," she said aloud as the doorman and bouncer, Maksim, opened the door and let her in. Inside, the shriveled duckling became a swan.

"Good afternoon, Miss Budnik," Maksim greeted all the ladies with respect.

For this part of her life, Katya had felt the need to distance herself from Nadine Bebchuk. On Mondays in Blood Alley, she became Ninette Budnik. Same initials. She liked that. Regardless of her name, Ninette was viewed with skepticism by nearly everyone at Viveka's because she only worked one day a week. This was a rarity for Miss Wang's women.

Wang Chia-Ling owned and operated Viveka's. The first Monday after Katya had convinced Ivan to give her Mondays off, she made her way to Blood Alley. Katya realized *Ninette* was less nervous than she thought she'd be and skipped past many doors before stopping in front of Viveka's. It was Maksim's smile that lured her that first day. Handsome, outwardly gentle, and very courteous, he had noticed odd Ninette limping down the street. When she was within speaking distance, he smiled at the strange woman and asked, "Excuse me, miss, are you looking for someone?"

"Yes," she straightened, smiled back, and answered without hesitation. "But I don't know who."

He laughed and broadened his smile. "Perhaps I can help you. Do you have a moment?"

"I have until tomorrow afternoon," Katya told him. "Then, I must get back to work."

"Well, that's enough time. Let me introduce you to Madam Wang. She has helped lots of people. Perhaps it is her you are seeking." He smiled again.

"Yes. Perhaps," Katya answered. "If you are any reflection of this establishment, then, yes, she may be the one."

Maksim opened the door and led her inside. Despite the building's rough façade, Miss Wang kept the interior attractively decorated and somehow a bit removed from the noise and fumes of the street. Music played somewhere from within, and Ninette could smell coffee. She also realized the scent of tobacco was missing. For a cigarette-consuming populace, that was rare, and Ninette was delightfully surprised. Several men and women were chatting in a large room, and then, appearing from behind an embroidered silk curtain, there was Miss Wang.

Madam Wang, all four feet, six inches, took Ninette by the elbow and guided her into the office. She shut the door, pointed Ninette to a well-upholstered chair, and poured two cups of tea.

"You are a picture of feminine beauty, my dear. How may I help you?" Miss Wang spoke perfect Russian. The look on Katya's face raised an amusing response on Miss Wang's. "I know six languages," she explained. "In my business, it is most helpful."

Katya nodded and sipped her tea before saying anything. She hesitated the briefest of seconds and then stated the obvious. "I am in great need of additional income and expect I could do quite well if I had a…sponsor."

"A sponsor. Of course. What is your name?" Madam Wang asked.

"Ninette Budnik," Katya responded instantly.

"Ah, Ninette, a lovely name. French. But you are Russian, no?"

"Yes, I am. Well, ethnically. It's a long story."

"That's fine, but I'm not interested, Ninette. You are lovely, as I already mentioned. Are you married?"

"My goodness, Madam Wang—if I was, I don't think I would be here."

"You are quite mistaken, my dear. There are many in need of, what did you say—additional income. No matter, it's better that you are not. Do you have a lover?"

Katya did everything she could to suppress the blush creeping up her face at the abruptness of such a question. Not embarrassed, just caught off-guard. Miss Wang watched her and said nothing.

"There's no one special," Katya answered.

"Do you sing, Miss Budnik?" Madam Wang asked without changing the expression on her face.

The inquiry unsettled Katya. It was unexpected. What did that have to do with why Ninette had entered Viveka's?

"Sing? Oh, no. Can't carry a tune, as they say," trying to disguise the truth.

"That surprises me," Madame Wang said, "because I'm certain I saw you, Miss Palutova, singing at Ciro's maybe two years ago. It was you, yes?"

"Madam Wang, my name is Ninette Budnik! I've never been to Ciro's, although I've heard about it. You must be mistaken." Katya realized a bit late that Ninette's false outrage at the accusation came across too defensively and revealed the truth to Madam Wang.

"Yes, you're probably right. Mistaken. You know what they say, all Russian women look alike." Madam Wang laughed at her retort. "Very well, *Ninette*, I do think I can help you."

They got down to business, and Madam Wang explained the rules of her house, which included no smoking except in the designated smoking room. She also explained how the proceeds were shared, what visitors would be expected, and the limits of acceptable behavior by her ladies and guests. Each hostess also had regular medical exams, and finally, in addition to the French, Brits, and Americans, many of the patrons who came to Viveka's were Chinese. Would that be a problem for Ninette? It would not. The sticking point came when Ninette said the only day she could work each week was Monday.

"I've never allowed such an arrangement," Madam Wang countered. "It would cause chaos in the house. This is a business, and it requires continuity. The ladies of this house are always free to leave, but they're on duty six days a week while they work here. That's the rule. Ask them, and they will tell you. I'm fair, and they make lots of money."

"It does sound like you're very fair, Madam Wang, but I, too, have a schedule. If you cannot accommodate me on Mondays, then I know that the Voluptuous Vampires of Vladivostok will be happy to oblige."

Madam Wang was taken aback by Ninette's counter. The well-known Russian ladies' *residence*, filled with many attractive women who may or may not come from Vladivostock, was a major competitor. The two women stared at each other, and neither flinched. At last, Madam Wang stood, "We have an agreement, Miss Budnik. I will see you next Monday at nine in the morning. And come prepared to spend twelve to fourteen hours here. Wear what you like, but I will provide your working uniform. We will give you lunch and a place to clean up as necessary. And should you decide you *do* know how to sing, I could arrange private, in-house performances for which you will receive added compensation. Now, until next week."

⁂

By the spring of 1939, Katya and Darya were meeting weekly again at their regular location.

"Good news, Katya. Papa is fully recovered from his brutal battle with tuberculosis. I know your prayers to St. Panteleimon made the difference."

Katya didn't have the heart to tell her friend she had only prayed once, on that first day when Darya told her about her father's condition.

"I'm so glad he's better, Darya. I'm sure everyone is relieved. Have you seen the latest news on what's happening in Europe?"

"Oh my, yes. Everyone's still talking about the Nazis marching into Czechoslovakia back in March and wondering what they'll do next."

"Yes, I know," Katya followed. "I guess it's better to worry about things far away then for us to dwell on our own predicament, surrounded by the Japanese Army as if we were on an island. As for me, however, I've been focused on saving as much as I can."

That is, until a Monday night in late May, she thought.

The evening at Viveka's had been ordinary. Men came in as usual, and when called, Madam Wang's hostesses paraded in front of them like circus animals. However, while each lady desperately hoped to be chosen, she simultaneously did her best to hide her indignity. The money was good, regardless of the risks, and while fortune reigned in such a place, at least Madame Wang maintained an iron fist over the behavior of the men. Ninette had only been hit twice in nearly two months, and both assaulters received harsh and immediate punishment from Maksim and banishment from Viveka. Additionally, most establishments on Blood Alley shared the descriptions of troublemakers. The other perils were disease and pregnancy, but Madame Wang's doctors were vigilant and provided contraception devices and ointments. Regardless, Ninette found each day utterly demeaning—but it never affected Katya.

However, that Monday night, Katya, not Ninette, found herself aflutter. A group of four mildly drunk young French Army officers entered Viveka's, three of them dragging the fourth after celebrating his birthday at one of the jazz clubs in the Concession.

"I'm tired. We have lots to do tomorrow," the fourth man spoke, trying to discourage his friends. "I bet these ladies are tired as well."

"Tired?! Ha! They're here for us. It's what they do, Marcel."

Marcel Granger was not stuck-up, bashful, or sanctimonious. He was fatigued, had more to drink than usual, and doubted if he could perform anyway. However, his friends were persistent, and rather than argue, Marcel yielded. Since it was Marcel's birthday, he had the first choice. Not surprisingly, men always selected Ninette before the others, and Marcel was no exception. Ninette took his hand and led him upstairs to her room.

Once inside, with the door closed, Ninette began to remove her clothes, but Marcel stopped her. *"Non mademoiselle. Pas ce soir.* Not tonight," he repeated in English.

"But sir, already paid," Ninette responded in her awkward English.

Marcel heard her accent and immediately switched to Russian. "I'm tired. You are lovely, and the money, well, it was my friends who paid," he laughed. "I would like some coffee if possible and just some talk. My name is Marcel Granger, and I'm from a small farming town in France called Châtenay." As he talked, he looked carefully at Ninette and said, "You look familiar, but I can't remember from where."

"Oh, I doubt that," Katya replied, although she did recall him, too. She did not understand why she lied and changed the subject. "Your Russian is very good. Most of the French people I meet know very little. Where did you learn it?"

"I spent two years as attaché to the French general on the staff of our delegation in St. Petersburg. I've always had a knack for languages. And you? They said your name is Ninette, but you're not French."

She was about to answer when there was a knock on the door, and the houseboy delivered coffee and pastries. Marcel and Ninette spent a few minutes enjoying the refreshments, and then he asked again, only with a different slant.

"So, Ninette, what is your story?"

None of the men she *entertained* at Viveka's wanted to know anything about her, and she didn't know how to answer. But with Marcel, she could tell his interest was genuine.

"My story is no different from most White Russians here in Shanghai," she said at last. "Displaced. No country. For me, no family left. I do have a best friend, Darya. We meet weekly in the park. I love—"

"That's it," he said. "I saw you as you left the park and almost walked into traffic. That was you, wasn't it?"

"…Yes," Katya slowly admitted. "It was me, that day on the street after I left my Darya. I was dizzy with worry about her sick father, thinking of my dear dead Papa, and not paying attention. I really do thank you for saving me."

"I hope your friend's father is better, and anyone would have done the same to help you that day," Marcel said.

She snickered. "He did recover. Thank you. How long have you been in Shanghai, if I may ask?"

"I arrived only a few days before I saw you," he answered. "Not very long."

"Well, by now, you probably realize that, no, not just anyone would have done what you did that day. People are out for themselves, and one less person to fight for food, a place to sleep, and so on matters to no one here. With so many people, I can't believe you found me again."

Now it was his turn to be embarrassed. "My friends, I think you may have, well…*been with* one of them before. They said we need to go to Viveka's. So, here I am."

She could only smile and be embarrassed again. "Of course."

They chatted a while longer. The handsome officer told her about his two sisters, life on a French farm, and his experience in the Army. He said he was the sixth generation to serve France and loved music. He also said everyone in his unit knew there was no way to prevent a Japanese takeover of the city. When an appropriate amount of time together passed so no one would be suspicious, he rose and said goodbye. When his hand reached the doorknob, he turned back to her and spoke quietly.

"Ninette, I wonder…would you be interested in having dinner with me some evening?" When she said nothing, he continued. "I would like to know more about you."

Her heart skipped a beat. She had not felt anything quite like this since Kuniaki. Marcel was personable and kind, but her distrust of men remained. She didn't know. She hesitated, and he filled the silence.

"We don't have to go to dinner. We could just visit on a bench like you do with your friend."

"I-I-I don't know. Won't you get in trouble if you're with some-one—like me? And I, I have other obligations. Commitments. I need to work."

"I'm sure you don't work every minute," he gently pressed. "You must rest at some point. Ninette, you fascinate me. I only wish to take you out of this place," he waved his hand around the room, "and hopefully put a smile on your face for a couple hours."

Ninette looked at the floor. *It would be nice to sit and talk again with a real gentleman,* she thought. *And he is soooo good-looking. Not to mention he speaks Russian with that hypnotic French accent...*

"Very well," she told him. "I can meet you on Wednesday morning at ten. We can meet in the park where you saw me. Now you must go, before your friends come looking."

She shooed him out the door, closed it, and sat on the bed, breathing deeply and already trying to determine what she would wear to meet him on Wednesday morning.

They finally went out to eat for their fourth get-together. On Saturday, Nadine had feigned exhaustion to Ivan, and he begrudgingly gave her Sunday off. He reasoned she'd have two days rest, including Monday, and would be fresh afterward for a long stretch. Katya woke early Sunday morning, for the first time in a long time. She found a modest skirt and blouse, low shoes, and dark hose and made the walk to the blue-domed Russian Orthodox church. She knelt in a dark pew near the back, praying her long list of wishes, half-believing and half-doubting her words. She listened carefully to the priest's message but left uninspired. Nonetheless, she felt better for having gone, and a small piece of guilt evaporated from her soul.

Katya felt like a teenager most of the day. She checked and rechecked her hair and make-up in the small mirror above the tiny bureau in her room. She put a dress on, took it off, and tried another, though her choices were few. Cleaned her face and reapplied her make-up. Fixed herself some lunch but stowed it away in the small icebox after taking only one bite. She polished her shoes and giggled with delight when she discovered a pair of nylons she forgot she hid under her mattress after only one use. She had put them there to save for a special occasion. It was time.

One last look in the mirror, a double-check on the stocking seams, a peek in her purse to ensure she had her apartment key, compact, and lipstick, then Katya was out the door and walking along the street. Pretty, confident, and full of giddiness and excitement, she walked with a joyful bounce in her stride, drawing the attention of many admirers. It was a feeling, she realized, that brought back fond memories.

She had been firm with Marcel. She did not want him to know where she lived. It was embarrassing, and people might address her by her real name. He consented without prying and agreed to meet her outside the church. They would go together via taxi or rickshaw from there. She wondered where he would take her. *Where do soldier farmers dine?* she wondered. He was a junior officer. He wouldn't have money to be extravagant. Would he? She didn't care. She just wanted his company. He spotted her first, as she glided along the sidewalk toward their rendezvous.

"She's amazing," he said aloud, receiving a few strange looks from passersby. After that first encounter at Viveka's, Marcel wrestled with his conscience. It went against every moral code he lived by to date a prostitute. An occasional visit to a brothel was one thing, but not a date. What had he been thinking? Ninette was correct—there was a real chance he could get in trouble for having a relationship with someone like her—but the hypocrisy enraged him. Marcel could name at least half a dozen senior officers in the French Shanghai contingent who were married and had mistresses. At least he wasn't married. Nonetheless, the risk remained. The mere appearance or hint of an *officer* courting a regular from Blood Alley was a sure path to discipline…but their chats on the park bench changed everything.

He discovered Ninette was a woman of substance, a survivor of complex challenges beyond his own experiences. He knew she was holding back and hadn't told him everything, and he suspected she might even be fabricating some of her stories, but not all of them. She was wary and often went out of her way to offer excuses about spending time with him, and, like it or not, the logic behind her reasons made sense. After all, he was a junior officer, not a general or big-shot businessman who could rescue her from a life of never-ending struggles. But logic, fear of military punishment, and even peer rebuke were insufficient to prevent him from wanting to see her. Therefore, a smile spread across his face as she approached. He extended both arms, she took his hands, and he leaned over and kissed her on each cheek.

"Oh, my Ninette, you get lovelier every time I see you."

She blushed a little. "Marcel, you say the nicest things. Thank you."

Marcel had a taxi waiting at the curb, and they climbed in.

"I think we shall have a wonderful time tonight. Are you ready?"

"Yes. I can't wait. Thank you for the invitation." She leaned back in the seat and admired his freshly shaved face from the dim light cast by streetlights.

"Driver: Ciro's, please," he said.

At first, she thought she must have misunderstood. Then she reacted with a surprising outburst. "No! No! We *must* go someplace else. Not there!" She was almost in tears, and visibly shaking.

"Pull over, driver," Marcel ordered. Once the car stopped, Marcel grasped her hands and tried to calm her. "What's wrong, Ninette? I thought you would be pleased. I've been saving up for this occasion. I've never been there, and everyone says they have the best food and music in the city. "

"No, Marcel. Please, not there. Save your money. You, we—oh—I should never have said yes to this evening. It's all my fault. Someplace simple would be fine. Maybe a small place in the Settlement. I don't get to spend much time there, and I understand they have many fine yet modest clubs."

She stared into her lap, and he let go of one of her hands and lifted her chin so he could look into her eyes. "There's something wrong. I know it, Ninette. You don't have to tell me. When you understand how much I care about you, when you're ready, you will. Driver, can you find us a quiet, safe place for food and music in the Settlement?"

There weren't as many clubs operating successfully since the Japanese incursion two years earlier, but twenty minutes later, the taxi deposited them in front of a pleasant-looking establishment. Mick's Pub was anything but Irish, but the poster under the name advertised food from every continent and music for all occasions by José Abayan and his orchestra. Filipino band leaders and musicians were famous throughout the city.

"How does this look?" Marcel asked her.

Ninette had recovered by then and answered pleasantly. "Perfect, Marcel. Thank you."

In May 1939, French Army forces in Shanghai and their counterparts within the International Settlement put on a significant show of force. The military and political leaders hoped their maneuvers would convince the Japanese to leave the Concession and Settlement alone. However, the Japanese escalated the situation—not in Shanghai, but farther north. They set up a blockade around the British and

French Concessions in Tientsin. They searched all persons going to and from those areas and constructed an electrified fence around the foreign enclaves. The sand was running out of Shanghai's hourglass. The leaders of France, Great Britain, the United States, and other countries with forces and citizens living in the city stepped up their plans for the inevitable.

In September, the Japanese demanded the withdrawal of all French Forces in China. Many speculated Germany's brazen actions in Poland had emboldened the Japanese. Whatever the reason, Japanese behavior forced citizens of many countries to abandon the French Concession and International Settlement. The exodus from Shanghai by those who could afford it intensified.

The weather was cool when Katya and Darya met again—below average for early October, but the sky was clear, and the odors of the streets, sewers, and river had temporarily vanished overnight, having been swept away by a gentle breeze off the ocean. They were engrossed in conversation on their bench in the park.

"Papa decided," Darya said. "He's making arrangements for us to leave by the new year, and he's back to work. We're saving every yuan, franc, yen, dollar, and pound. But I don't know, Katya—I-I-I've met someone. Can you believe it?"

Katya had news of her own but kept quiet and let her best friend continue.

"Let me see, it must be five weeks now. I didn't tell you before, because I didn't think anything of it," Darya admitted. "One day, a woman about Momma's age and a young man came into the shop speaking English, and I actually understood a lot of it."

"Impressive," Katya said. "Remember when you thought you would never learn any?"

"Oh, I know! But anyway," she continued, "the woman was in the city for her niece's wedding and wanted a new dress for the occasion. Her niece is the daughter of some senior person in the British consulate, and the man with her was her consular escort. Well, when he walked through the door, I had just finished—"

"Darya! Stop this! Get to the point! I can hardly wait," Katya urged. "Tell me about him. How many times have you seen him? What does he do? Tell me everything."

Darya smiled. "Oh, you can tell I was talking about him?"

"Of course," Katya answered.

"His name is Trenton Miles." Darya laughed. "Such an English name. He's not very tall, and he's a bit stocky...or maybe 'solid' is a better word. He said he boxed at university. He has dark hair, gray eyes, and a dimple in his chin."

"I'm starting to get the picture," Katya said. "What does he do at the consulate?"

"I can't quite explain it. He has something to do with coordinating all the British government material, supplies, equipment, and stuff moving in and out of the Settlement. He's an officer and was assigned to escort the lady because of her status. While she worked with Mrs. Plisetskaya and tried on dresses, Trenton, Mr. Miles, and I had time to talk in between me dealing with other customers.

"Then, when she and Trenton were leaving the store, he asked if he could call on me. Oh, Katya, I didn't hesitate one second. Since then, we've gone out seven times, and he's wonderful."

"Darya, that's fantastic. I can't wait to meet him. But did you tell him about your father's plans?"

"Katya, this is the best part. Papa loves him. Trenton is sophisticated, educated, and comes from a successful and connected family. He has two uncles who served in Parliament. He's from a town called Bournemouth on the south coast of England." She stopped for a moment and took a deep breath. "I think I love him, Katya. If we were still in Russia, we'd be married by now. I don't want to be an old maid. I think he's going to ask me to marry him."

"Really? Are you sure he's the one, Darya? I mean, you haven't known him very long."

"I love him, Katya. And I know he loves me. Besides, if he asks me, I'll have a good excuse to stay here and not go to Hong Kong with the rest of the family. I can still be close to you."

Katya smiled and gave Darya a long hug. Tears blurred her vision. She was truly happy for her friend, yet simultaneously wrenched with mixed emotions about her situation. When they separated, Darya couldn't help but notice. "Katya, I thought you'd be happy for me. Why are you crying?"

"Of course, I'm happy. I'm…overwhelmed. It's…so unexpected. And not going to Hong Kong? Is that the safest or smartest decision? If you stay here, even with Trenton, it will likely get much more dangerous."

"The Japanese won't dare harm the foreign troops," Darya stated. "It would only lead to war."

Katya turned her head. She didn't want Darya to see her skeptical face. Anyone paying attention could see war was looming, and even if there was no war, it was only a matter of time before the Japanese took over the entire city. The remaining British, French, and American military and naval forces were mere tokens and severely outnumbered by the Japanese. To escape the threat of a Japanese takeover was the reason Katya had been doing everything she could to save money.

She spun, faced her friend, and said, "I have news too. Not quite as meaningful as yours, but still good news."

"Oh, Katya, here I've gone off blabbing about Trenton and haven't given you a chance to speak. Tell me."

"Not to fret, my dear. I did ask you to tell me everything, but my news…I also met someone. Although he's French, not English."

They laughed at the irony. The friends knew the English and French were historical enemies and often feuded. However, with Japan as the common threat to the Settlement and Concession, the countries were recently more inclined to work together.

"His name is Marcel Granger, and he's a lieutenant in the French Army. He comes from generations of farmers, who also served in the military."

"Katya, that's not enough! What does he look like?"

"Yes, let's see. He's somewhat thin. Not unhealthy thin, but svelte—a good French word, yes? There's a certain grace to his bearing. He's about this high." She raised her hand high over her head. "And Darya, what a coincidence. I met him weeks ago when you told me of your father's illness. My mind was reeling from that news, and I almost walked into the traffic. He caught my arm and saved me. I took a quick look at him and immediately forgot about him.

"He has an elegant, thin, black mustache I adore and rich brown eyes that make me think of dark chocolate. And when he smiles, my goodness Darya, his teeth sparkle. I don't think I ever met anyone with such beautiful teeth." They giggled again. "I think it's because he doesn't smoke. At first, I thought that was strange, but I like it. No ashes or butts to clean up. No tobacco breath."

"Has he seen you perform with Ivan Losev's band? That would be a strange place for a French Army officer."

"His friends were taking him…places, to celebrate his birthday. They were already a bit drunk when they came in, but his friends kept paying for his…entertainment. During my break, he said hello and reminded me about saving me from falling into the road. There was something about him I liked. When they were leaving, Marcel turned back and asked if he could call on me. I never say yes to anyone, but I agreed. We've been meeting Wednesdays in the park. On the bench. Same place you and I meet."

"Why, you little devil. Is that all?"

"No. I finally said yes when he asked me to dinner. We had a very nice meal, but I don't know what to do, Darya. I-I-I've been lying to him. And I haven't even told you everything."

"What, Katya? What could be so bad that you lied to him?"

"I was so upset, disappointed, and ashamed when I lost my job with Henry Nathan, I wanted to run away and hide. I didn't want anyone who knew me from the Cathay and Ciro's to find me. So I took the job with Ivan Losev and his pitiful band of misfits in that questionable neighborhood. I was certain no one would spot me there. And to make sure, I changed my name. I haven't told Marcel my real name. I'm afraid he, or one of his superiors, may have seen me at Ciro's. It would be hard to explain. I just don't know what to do. Like you, I think we may be falling in love."

Katya hung her head, angry and ashamed of herself, hoping Darya forgot about the incident with Fedor and for failing to tell her the truth.

"Listen to me, Katya, and pay careful attention. Do you know Olga Lashkin? What about Annika Gusin? Or Marta Kamorova? Or Lidiya Ratkevich? I could go on. And do you know where they've been spending lots of their time? Do you know the situation they're in? Marta and Olga have two children each. Their husbands can't work because of injuries. Lidiya is like you. No family left. And Annika has four younger sisters and brothers with parents too sick to work. All of them and many more do things I know you do. They do what they must to feed their families and have a place to live. So, enough of my speech. Talk to me, Katya. I'm your friend and love you like a sister. Tell me everything. It will make you feel better."

For the slimmest of moments, Katya quivered and shook her head. "I can't, Darya. I can't tell you. I can barely look at myself in the mirror. I only see someone I vaguely remember when I want to look my best for Marcel. I can't tell you."

"Yes, you can, Katya. You must. Ever since we met, you've been the brave one. The one to challenge and dare and go exploring. You're strong, and will survive after the rest of us have met our Heavenly Father. Talk to me. No secrets. What is the saying…two heads are better than one? Let me share and help. Please. That's what friends, sisters, are for."

Slowly, and then building to a torrent, Katya broke down. She cried and shook until her teeth rattled. Darya held her and waited. At last, Katya told her everything. She wiped her eyes and blew her nose when she finished, but she couldn't look into Darya's eyes. True to her word and beliefs, Darya did not judge her friend. She couldn't imagine what it must be like to be so gifted and beautiful and yet be cast aside with no family. However, she knew she would do every-thing in her power to help Katya move out of Viveka's and find a better club than Ivan's or do something entirely different. She had no idea how, but she suspected if Marcel really cared about Katya—and he must, if he was dating her despite her Monday work—he would help provide the solution.

⁂

Two weeks later, during the Wednesday midday dinner hour, Marcel and Katya sat on the park bench. It was a hot day, and she was wearing a light and breezy dress, and he had on his summer uniform. They gazed at each other with matching smiles and dabbed each other's foreheads with handkerchiefs to soak up tiny beads of sweat. They shared lemonade and the summertime sticky rice treat stuffed with pork or red beans, called zongzi. When they finished eating, they took a stroll along the Bund, and just before he had to leave to go back to work, she began.

"I have something to tell you, Marcel. Now that I shared my tales of Viveka's with Darya, the secret I've kept from you is no longer important."

"I'm glad you told her," Marcel answered. "And Ninette, don't worry about Viveka's. We'll figure out something."

She looked into his eyes and believed him. "Yes, I hope so. Before those colonels and generals find out you're spending time with a whore."

"Don't say that word. It's so degrading. The women at Madam Wang's are all going through tough times, and it's not like you're begging on the street for sex or food. Now, what do you need to tell me?"

With a hurried intake of air, Katya steeled herself and rushed into her confession. "First, Marcel…my name is not Ninette Budnik. It's Ekaterina Palutova and—"

"*You're* Katya Palutova?! The singer?" he exploded. "From Ciro's? I've heard some officers speak about 'Miss Palutova.' Why, this is wonderful news!"

She choked, trying to swallow, as he kept talking.

"*Attends que mes amis entendant ça!*" He couldn't wait to tell his friends. "They'll want to hear you sing," he said, "and they'll want a dance, too."

She gathered herself and answered, "No. You can't tell them, because I also use the name Nadine Bebchuck and work at Ivan Losev's club. It's a miserable place, but it's steady. We have French officers and regular soldiers in there all the time. Fortunately, we get very few French at Viveka's, and graciously, Madam Wang agreed not to present me to any Frenchmen. It's best for you if you don't let your friends and colleagues know who I am."

"Ninette, lis—I mean, Ekaterina, listen to me. According to the schedule, the three who were with me at Viveka's the night we met will return to France next week. Frankly, I may get sent back as well, but I don't know when. So you don't have to worry about them. And, where exactly is Ivan Losev's place?" Marcel asked. "Our general has ordered many locations off-limits. Of course, not everyone follows every order, but the punishment can be severe if you're caught, so most obey. And what is all this secrecy? I know what you've been doing, at Viveka's anyway, and I still want to be with you. I want to help you find something else."

He pulled her close and wrapped his arms around her. He kissed the salty tears off her face. He wanted to devour her, and he would have—had they not been in public.

Katya felt the weight of her secret drift away. No matter how long she had to work for Madam Wang, she reaffirmed it was not Ekaterina working there but Ninette. Something intangible about Katya allowed her to stay removed, above whatever mire and mess she was in at any time. Overwhelmingly, she went through life with her head held high, proud of the woman she was. Proud she could survive, and maybe, just maybe, she could find a club better than Ivan's.

They rose and strolled through the park until Marcel had to return to his duties, and he promised to say nothing to his colleagues. They didn't have a plan, but had set themselves on a path to find a solution.

And so, Katya had fallen in love again. Despite her social status, Marcel Granger knew Katya was exceptional from the moment they met in the upstairs room at Viveka's. He saw inside her, and this filled her heart with joy. After all the loss she had experienced, establishing a meaningful relationship with another man brought a bit of euphoria.

⚜

By Christmas 1939, Germany and Russia had divvied up Poland, the Soviets had attacked Finland, and the screw became tighter around the foreign troops and residents of Shanghai. Internationally, most people recognized reality—yet others, including many who lived in Shanghai, chose to ignore it. Scores, hundreds, *thousands* simply pretended life was the same as it was in the early thirties. Even numerous influential Shanghailanders, including Sir Victor Sassoon, did not want to face the truth. Not surprisingly, people without the wherewithal to escape recognized the inevitable usurpation by the Japanese.

Things for Katya and Marcel progressed as they had during the first two months of their burgeoning affair. By all accounts, Marcel's three Viveka friends left Shanghai, and no identifiable French military personnel spotted Katya at Madame Wang's or recognized her in Ivan Losev's band. Katya, Marcel, and Darya conducted a vigorous search for alternative jobs where Katya could earn an equivalent income. Marcel even suggested she seek employment in the French Consulate as a secretary. Katya laughed at that. She had never used a typewriter in her life.

Ultimately, nothing changed until June 1940, when the Nazis occupied Paris and the French set up the Vichy government. On the surface, Vichy was independent. In reality, it was a government forced to govern in ways that, at best, kept the Germans at bay and, at worst, was a Nazi puppet regime under a utilitarian dictatorship that rounded up Jews and communists and killed tens of thousands. The Vichy also maintained control of the French army and navy. Patriotic soldiers and sailors became conflicted about what to do. Some believed the armistice signed with Germany made sense for the overall good of their country, and others, most notably Charles de Gaulle, disagreed and fled to England in exile.

A speech de Gaulle delivered over the radio shortly after he went to England ultimately found its way to foreigners living in the Settlement and Concession. The core of what General de Gaulle told the French people was that he wouldn't give up and that France wasn't alone. He offered hope. Among other things, he said: "I, General de Gaulle, now in London, call on all French officers and men who are at present on British soil, or maybe in the future, with or without their arms; I call on all engineers and skilled workmen from the armaments factories who are at present on British soil, or maybe in the future, to get in touch with me." He ended with, "Whatever happens, the flame of the French resistance must not be extinguished and will not be extinguished."

The speech made a big impression on Marcel. Many generations of his family had been soldiers. Fighters. Sitting around in Shanghai, being directed by some authoritarian back in Vichy, and knowing there was no chance against the burgeoning Japanese, started Marcel and his compatriots' thinking.

9   JUNE 1940 — DECEMBER 8, 1941
Shanghai to Manila

The year flew by as the news from Europe moved from unsettling to devasting. By autumn, nearly every European country had aligned with Britain or Germany and was at war. The Italians even invaded British-controlled Egypt, expanding the war to Africa. And in China, by August 1940, the British found it necessary and logical to withdraw all their troops from Shanghai. The world was falling apart, and Marcel was having difficulty watching the fray in Europe from the distant Far East.

"I made a decision," he spoke quietly.

He and Katya were enjoying the late summer warmth. They sat under the shade of the trees in the park along the waterfront, and if anyone unfamiliar with world events happened to see them, they would not detect any problems. Life in the French Concession and most of the Settlement went on in blissful disregard for the coming cataclysm. Activity bustled, and boats plied their trade on the river without noticeable interference. By every observable measure, there was no apparent reason for the decision he was about to share with Katya.

"Oh? About what, Marcel?"

As she asked, she could see the lines tighten in his face, and his eyes shifted as a glistening sheen coated them. She felt her pulse quicken and anxiety rise. Contrary to appearances, *they* had been paying attention to world events. She braced herself.

"I'm going to join de Gaulle in England," he said. "I can't sit here any longer and pretend I'm helping my country." He continued without giving Katya a chance to respond. "There's an American ship, *President Coolidge,* leaving for Hong Kong in a couple days and then to San Francisco, stopping first in Hawaii. I'll take a train from California to New York and another ship across the Atlantic to England. It's something I must do, Katya."

Over the previous months, they had become close. Very close. Her work situation had not changed, and although she *amused* various men every Monday, they both accepted that *Ninette* went to work at Viveka's on Mondays, not Katya. So, keeping true to their versions of propriety, neither had pursued the profound physical and emotional connections they craved. Instead, they settled for polite hugs and kisses on the cheeks. With the future so uncertain, it seemed to make sense. Yet, on this day, this last day of certainty of being together, Marcel stood and took Katya by the hand.

"Walk with me, my dear." He said it with such a gentle voice. His love for her enveloped every syllable. She smiled and joined him.

After several blocks, they turned down a side street and stopped at the door of a small apartment building. He led her into the dull light of the lobby, and they climbed up two flights. He pulled a key from his pocket and opened one of the four doors along the hallway. She didn't speak. With the curtains drawn back, sunlight drenched the room inside, and the vacant lot next door afforded privacy. Marcel went to the small refrigerator and pulled out a tiny bottle of champagne. He found two glasses and filled them. She was about to say something, but he put his finger to her lips and handed her a glass.

He raised his glass and said, "To us. To our enduring love for one another." Then he took a sip, and she followed. A tear trickled from her eye.

They put the glasses down, and he retook her hand and walked her into the bedroom. He pulled her close, swallowed her in his embrace, and kissed her. A kiss of passion long denied and returned in kind. A kiss so revealing and embedded with the most profound feelings of their hearts, they barely separated for a breath before savoring each other again. They moved their hands in perfect symmetry, roaming across their bodies. There was a deliberate and caring method to their movements as they disrobed one another. They stood, naked, in blazing sunlight and tried to bury themselves in the other. He pulled her to the bed, and they collapsed in a frenzy. Their lovemaking was like opening the door to heaven—an experience of bliss beyond all desire. They climaxed with such delirium that the thought of separating was beyond their comprehension, even for a moment.

Drained, they slept. Bound together as one.

After waking, they cleaned and dressed without talking. Once they returned to the small parlor, he poured them another glass and reached into his pocket. He took her hand, her right hand, respecting her Russian heritage, and slid a small ring of sterling silver with a green jade stone onto her fourth finger.

"I want to marry you, Katya. Oh, so very much." He stopped for a second, took another breath, and added, "but we must wait until we're together again."

Tears cascaded down her cheeks. She stared with overwhelming joy at the spot of green on her finger. "Oh, Marcel. Yes, yes. I want to marry you too. Yes, oh yes."

"Good. Then it's settled," he said. "We shall save our money, and as soon as we have enough, we'll make arrangements for you to join me in England. Oh, you have made me so happy, Katya. I feel like I'm floating on air."

He submitted his resignation from the official Vichy French Army the following day. He liked that de Gaulle called the forces under his command the Free French, and the newspapers followed.

Yes, that suited him perfectly. *Free* French. Within two days, he consolidated his belongings into two cases and had a taxi take him to the waterfront. Katya met him, and they walked together to the launch on the Huangpu, which would take him downriver to his ship, *President Coolidge.* They kissed in public for the first time and promised to write daily. They waved and waved, until the launch rounded a bend, and then they were each alone again, among many.

When she met Darya that week, Katya expressed the delight and sadness that engulfed her. "I've never loved someone like this," she told her friend. "Every night when I come home, I put on the ring and think of him…but I wonder if I shall ever see him again. Oh, Darya."

"Of course, you shall see him again," Darya answered. "And you shall marry in one of those fancy old English cathedrals—or, better yet, at the small church near where he grew up. Or I know, even better, Katya! At the church in Valday with your cousins all around. You will have six children. Yes, that is my wish for you."

"You're so sweet, and such a good friend, Darya. I'm going to save every bit of money I can. And you? How are things in Hong Kong for your family? I was surprised but happy when your father relented and let you stay. No doubt Trenton's character, background, and prospects were sufficient. But your mother? Darya, I know she wanted to be at your wedding. You were so beautiful. Have you sent her photos?"

"How long do you think it will take to save enough to make the trip to England?" Darya ignored Katya's question.

"You first," Katya said. "How are your parents, and what is happening with Trenton's job?"

"Very well. My parents are fine, and I did send them photos. They are staying with a distant cousin. Papa says it's only temporary because he doesn't trust the Brits or the Chinese can or will defend Hong Kong. My best guess is my family will head to Australia as soon as they have enough money. Papa's older brother went there right after the Revolution.

"As for Trenton, he told me his department at the consulate will remain as long as possible. Not sure what that means, so we're taking it one day at a time. I pray they transfer him out very soon. I don't care where. Just away from here. I've had enough of Shanghai."

"Ha! Who hasn't?" Katya agreed. "I can't wait to leave, but I think it will take me at least a year to save enough to make the trip. It's far, and it's complicated. I'll need several tickets, and I'm not even sure I'll be able to buy them here. No matter. That's my plan. It hasn't changed."

"Did Marcel tell you when he thinks he will arrive in England?" Darya asked.

"He thought if all goes well, it will take nearly a month to get there—first to Hong Kong, next across the Pacific by ship, across America by train, then another ship across the Atlantic. And that doesn't include rest days or waiting for space."

"Sounds exhausting. And you plan to do this by yourself, later? I'll worry about you constantly."

"Nothing to worry about yet," she smiled at Darya. "Can't go until I have enough money. Speaking of which, I better go."

They said their goodbyes and headed off in opposite directions—Katya to work as Nadine and Ninette, and Darya across the bridge into the Settlement, and her new life with Trenton.

With the Spring of 1941 in full bloom, Katya made a significant decision. The few letters she'd received from Marcel increased her desperation to depart China. She needed more money if she ever planned to have enough to leave Shanghai and get to England.

"That's it, Ivan. I can give you Thursdays and Sundays. No more than that."

"I can't do that, Nadine. You already have Mondays off. If you're only here twice a week, I may as well get someone else."

"Do what you must, Ivan. That's all I can do." She was curt.

"Where are you going that you can afford not to be here? I've heard nothing about openings for someone like you from any other bandleaders," he responded.

"Where I go is none of your business, Ivan. If you can increase my pay by five times, I can continue. If not, I'm sorry."

"Nadine, please. At least give me a reason. Something so I understand. I'm worried about you. Tell me something."

She was staring through the grime on Ivan's tiny office window into the nighttime blackness outside. It had been a reasonably busy evening, and Ivan had been in a good mood. She hadn't told anyone what she'd been doing on Mondays or anything about Marcel. It was best that way. But now, what difference did it make if they knew she was engaged and had a fiancé?

"It's very simple, Ivan. I'm engaged to a French Army officer and need a lot of money to join him in England. I need to get out of here soon before the Japanese take over the whole damn city. What you pay me is not enough to do that."

She saw the hurt in his eyes. She knew he had a crush on her and always treated her with dignity and kindness. On rare occasions, there would be flowers for her at the club signed by "an admirer." No one suspected they were from Ivan, but she knew. Carl had seen him sign for them one day and watched him write the card.

"Just thought you should know," Carl had told her.

"Ah. A gentleman," Ivan affirmed. "And he's gone now. To join that general—what's his name?"

"Charles de Gaulle."

"I understand the French are now divided. Much like the Nationalists and Communists here in China. Who knows who is right, eh?"

She appreciated that he didn't ask for Marcel's name. Wanting to conclude, Katya forced the issue. "Ivan, can I have the two days, or do you want me gone?"

His heart ached at not having tried to court her properly, but he consented. "You're too good, Nadine. Come when you can. We'll make it work."

She kissed him on the cheek, thanked him, and left. Ivan shut the door after her, sat in his scratched and wobbly chair, and let tears trickle down his face.

The next day Ninette sat in Madam Wang's fancy office and spelled it out for her. "I need to work more nights. Most nights—except Thursdays and Sundays," she told her diminutive boss.

"Ninette, why the sudden urge to spend more time here? It's not like anything new happened between last week and today."

Madam Wang placed a cigarette in a long holder and lit it. She blew a cloud of smoke at the ceiling and smiled at the lovely woman in front of her, acknowledging her cigarette's hypocrisy. It had taken her mere moments to verify what she knew during that first interview. Ninette Budnik was Ekaterina Palutova. She also knew when she was not at Viveka's, Ninette worked at Ivan Losev's cabaret under the name of Nadine Bebchuk. Clever girl. Motivated. Willing to do what was necessary to achieve her goals, but Madam Wang had also missed something, and she knew it was probably why Ninette wanted to spend more time at Viveka's.

It had been months since Katya stopped kidding herself that Madam Wang did not know her real identity. They never spoke openly about it, and it had been kind of the old woman not to make waves for her. Madam Wang had also arranged several *private* singing performances by Ninette for a selection of Viveka's best new clients—people who never heard of Ekaterina Palutova at Ciro's or the Cathay.

"Why the sudden interest in more time here?" Madam Wang probed for that missing "something."

"It's very simple, Madam Wang. I'm engaged to a French Army officer who has returned to England and joined the Free French forces. I want to join him before the Japanese take over the city. I've seen what they can do, and I don't intend to be here."

Madam Wang herself had made plans for a speedy departure once the Japanese took control of the Concession and Settlement. She also had grave misgivings about the agenda of the Chinese Communists. The country was a mess. Fortunately, she had relatives in Peru, and she believed, like Katya, that things would soon change for the worse.

"My dear Ninette, you are welcome here any day and any time. We shall ensure you have your own room and all the accoutrements—a good French word—you need to make your time here as pleasurable as possible. And I'm not talking about your customers. Of course, it is selfish of me, because every one of our ladies who is comfortable helps keep our customers happy."

Soon, the girl from Valday began to entertain the clientele at Viveka's more often. Because she also ate at least one good meal a day at Viveka's, Katya was able to save money on food. She hid her savings under a floorboard in her room at Viveka's, the most secure place she knew. Safer than the banks, which she suspected would be a target when the Japanese moved in.

Katya was tired but generally healthy and fit, and by the last week of November, she was ready to make the next big move of her life. She and Darya met as usual in the park.

"I'm ready, Darya. Have everything I need. I want to go as soon as possible and need to start checking with shipping companies and travel agencies, searching for the best deal. I want you to come with me."

"Trenton wants me to leave, too," Darya conceded. "He says I'll be much safer with his parents or brother in England. But Katya, the Germans have been bombing cities all over England. At least there are no bombs here."

"Not *yet*, Darya. Listen to Trenton. Come with me. It will be exciting and fun. Traveling together again. Like the two little girls on the train." Darya said nothing, allowing Katya to strengthen her case. "Even the American Marines are gone, Darya. That's a signal. *Another* signal. First, the Japanese invaded up north, and we left Harbin. Then the bombings in '37, and they surrounded the city. Then France splits in two, and Marcel leaves to join General de Gaulle. Next, the damn Jap Kenpeitai—their military police—arrest all those foreign journalists, businessmen, and local police officers. I've heard rumors of torture. Then the British Army evacuates, leaving only one pitiful gunboat in the river. What can that do against 100,000 Japanese soldiers and all their naval ships? Now the Americans are gone too. It is time to *leave*, Darya. Now! As soon as we can."

"I know. But…oh, how do I leave my husband?"

"Darya, most of the wives and families of the consulate staff are already gone. You know that. Please, come with me."

"Let me talk to Trenton. Yes, you're right. He wants me to leave. Give me a week to settle things, decide what I need to pack, and then we can go. Make the arrangements. I'll meet you tomorrow to give you money for my ticket, but don't book for a week."

"We don't *have* a week, Darya. The first ship I can get us on is the one I'm booking. You must know how hard it's going to be to find passage. See you tomorrow."

Both women were on edge and more than a little anxious. Ship traffic in and out of Shanghai had shriveled, and Katya had no idea what she would be able to find. Without waiting for Darya's money, she went immediately from their rendezvous to the offices of one of the major travel agencies along the Bund.

"I can't help you," the shipping rep told her. "Everything to

Hong Kong is booked. Same with Singapore, Manila, Jakarta, and even Honolulu. There have been numerous cancellations the past few months, and it has been worse since countries started commandeering ships for troops and other military reasons."

The booking agent was tired and disillusioned—not because he didn't want to help Katya, but because he had no options. She thanked him and walked out. Three more agencies told her the same story, pushing her frustration to the tipping point. She wanted to scream and berated herself for waiting so long. Regardless, she couldn't have gone sooner without enough money. As she leaned against a light pole, she stared into the river and watched longshoremen load lighters carrying cargo to larger ships downriver.

"That's it! Of course!" She hurried onto the docks and found someone supervising the workers. "Me excuse," she started in her broken English. "What company this cargo?"

The gruff supervisor turned toward her. He was about to tell her to keep walking until he focused on her. Men never failed to let their eyes rest on Katya for as long as possible. She couldn't decipher his accent, but he answered her in his own broken English.

"Company for ship cargo name Far East Traders. Office that way," he pointed down a side street off the Bund.

Katya thanked him and took off with long strides and a purpose. She thought she had gone too far when she finally spotted the name "Far East Traders" amidst many painted wooden signs and doors. She went in, and the beat of three ticker tape machines bombarded her ears. The room was big and smoky with rows of desks and numerous telephones; it was packed full of people of every description. A series of chairs lined one wall, and a collection of young men of mixed races and nationalities sat in them, waiting to be served. Every time one was called, the rest shifted one seat. They remained in order, and she took the end seat. After a few long, anxious minutes, the word "next" was shouted, and she walked to the man's desk who had called out.

"Oh my," he said. "My lucky day." Katya's attractive appearance and presence in the Concession prompted the clerk to speak French.

She answered him in French with her heavy Russian accent. "Sir, I hope it can be *my* lucky day."

The clerk immediately shifted to Russian, impressing her but not surprising her. He was Chinese, as were most of the men at the desks. Working such a job helped if you were fluent in several languages. "How can I help you, Miss…?"

"It is Miss Palutova," she answered. She could not afford to use a name that did not match her residency documents. "I need to get to England, and I know many cargo vessels also take passengers."

"England?!" he was startled. "Our ships stay in the far east. We have an occasional cargo ship to India or Ceylon, but that's all. I'm afraid we don't go to England. Besides, there are no berths left on any of our ships. Many people are leaving the city, as you know."

Without thinking, she answered quickly. "My husband is an officer with de Gaulle," she thought the little lie might help. After all, they were *almost* married and would be once she joined him.

"Excuse me, *Miss* Palutova. Are you 'Miss' or 'Mrs.?'"

Embarrassed but desperate, she forged ahead. "Oh, well, we are engaged. See." She showed him the ring on her finger. "And we'll get married, but we can't if I'm stuck here and he's in England. I have money for a ticket."

As they talked, one of the senior men in the office noticed her and walked over to the desk. *"Pardon, mademoiselle.* Maybe I can help you." The man was tall and hefty, but had an engaging smile. "Zhi Ming," he addressed the young clerk, "please take the next person in line."

Then he gently took Katya by the elbow and led her to his desk in the back of the room. The nameplate on the large desk read *M. Henri Laframboise, Directeur.*

"Excuse me, but I could not help overhearing…you said your betrothed is an officer with General de Gaulle. *C'est vrai?"*

"Oui monsieur," she answered. "He is descendant from many generations of French warriors. He left here to join the general and restore freedom to French peoples." She knew she was embellishing, but it wasn't far from the truth. "I'm worried it will be too late for me to leave once the Japanese take over the rest of the city. Is there any way you can help me? Please, M. Laframboise."

Laframboise lifted the phone on his desk and spoke too rapidly for Katya to understand. The only words she recognized were "Hong Kong," "Manila," "Singapore," and "Jakarta." Her hope rose as she listened. She would take tickets anywhere and deal separately with each leg of her journey.

"Bien. Bien. Merci." M. Laframboise ended his conversation and placed the phone back in its cradle. "There is a small Dutch ship, the *SS Tjipawan.* It will be uncomfortable and crowded, but I have arranged a berth for you. It includes stops in Hong Kong, Manila—"

"Yes," she interrupted. "I heard the names."

"You must pay the fare to Jakarta, but you will be free to get off anywhere you wish. Of course, the best stops to find a ship to England will be in Hong Kong or Singapore. Now, about your payment."

"I'm sorry, M. Laframboise, I should have mentioned there will be two of us."

"Deux! Merde! Alors! Un autre!" He picked the phone up and made a second call. *"Oui, oui. Je comprends. Au revoir."* He hung up and looked at her. "No more surprises, mademoiselle. You and your friend will have to share one bed *and* your meals. There are no beds or provisions for both of you. This is very risky. I don't know exactly how many evacuees will be on the ship, and if the weather is bad, it may be dangerous."

Katya contemplated her options, but the choice was obvious. "We'll take the tickets. When does it depart?"

Katya and Darya stood on the wharf, waiting to board the ship along with what appeared to be half of Shanghai's remaining Dutch population. The morning of November 30, 1941 dawned clear, chilly, and windy. They wore coats and hats and moved in small circles to stay warm or to hide their nervousness. The lighter, no more than a transfer barge with an engine, would take them down the Huangpu to the deeper Yangtze, where the larger ships swung on their anchors. Trenton waited in line with them while Darya couldn't hide her tears.

"Oh, Trenton, I don't want to leave you here. I'm so worried."

"You'll be fine," he assured her. "And as for me, they won't harm English citizens. The government back home also instructed our consular general to prepare us for departure very soon. Everything will be alright. You'll see. Besides, I will feel so much better knowing you're on your way to safety, away from this tinderbox."

She leaned into him, and he squeezed her so tight she gave a little gasp.

"Sorry, my sweet."

A shout rang out in Dutch, and people began to pick up their belongings and shuffle toward the lighter. Trenton lifted Darya's suitcase, and the three moved with the line. When they reached the short gangway, the shipping clerk verified their tickets.

Darya and Trenton kissed, and then the Englishman turned to Katya and said, "Take good care of her, Katya."

Katya said she would, and Trenton kissed her on the cheek. The women showed their tickets and carefully traversed the two, ten-inch-wide boards separating the small craft from the shore. A Chinese longshoreman assisted them with their bags, and they squirmed onto the ferry-like vessel. Most of their fellow passengers stood in quiet contemplation. They had spent years in China and only knew Shanghai as home. They felt like emigrants destined for unfamiliar places. Some hoped to return to Shanghai, but Katya and Darya had their sights on Singapore and securing ongoing passage to England.

It was not long before Trenton was no longer in view, and the reality of the separation from her husband began to worry Darya.

"Oh Katya, what is going to happen to him? No matter what he said, we know there have been many brutal attacks and false claims by the Japanese. To think they will leave the English alone is fantasy."

"Look at me, Darya," Katya said. "You've been strong and supported me for many years. Now, it's my turn to help you. Trenton is smart, creative, tough, and motivated enough to survive to be with you again. You need the same strong determination. I know you can do that." Katya spread her arms and hugged her friend. "It will be fine. Think of this as another great excursion. We're off to see more of the world than we ever imagined as children. Let's enjoy it."

Darya gave a little chuckle. "*Enjoy* might not be the best choice of words, but it is surely another adventure. Too bad my family stayed such a short while in Hong Kong. We could have seen them on our stop."

"They did the right thing, though, joining your uncle in Australia. Would you feel safer going to Jakarta and then Australia to join them?" Katya asked.

"No. My place is with my husband and his family in England. Besides, I'd miss the *adventure* with you," she smiled, and Katya returned one of her own.

They watched the busy shoreline pass as the lighter carried them downriver. Most passengers could not believe the number of Japanese naval vessels and the numerous Japanese flags attached to all the buildings along the riverfront. Closeted within the Settlement and Concession for four years had, for the most part, shut out the reality that eastern China was totally under Japanese control. In every imaginable way, it was part of Japan. Few saw the irony that for a century, much of Shanghai—the Settlement and Concession—was not a political entity of China but an adjunct of European nations and the United States.

"Is that it?" Darya wondered aloud as their temporary water-taxi approached an old, rusty ship.

"Let's hope so," Katya replied. "I need to find a toilet."

Darya laughed. "You and the rest of us. Somehow, I think there will be a long wait."

The two attractive Russian women found it easier than expected to fit in despite being surrounded by families of Dutch businessmen and bureaucrats. They were curiosities that attracted lots of attention, primarily from men but also from some women. Fortunately, Darya's English had improved rapidly under Trenton's tutelage and constant presence, making it easier to speak with Dutch passengers who understood various languages. And in less than a week with the Netherlanders, Katya learned one important Dutch phrase: *ze begrijpt het niet,* meaning, "she doesn't understand me." Those were the words she and Darya often heard when someone tried to talk with them, so Katya used it whenever anyone didn't understand her Russian. Many of her fellow passengers saw the humor, which broke the ice.

When Katya first saw the *SS Tjipawan*, she had second thoughts. While it was built the same year she was born, it appeared much older. The ship looked like a defeated relic from the Battle of Jutland, whereas Katya and Darya glowed with the natural beauty of their youth. Endless rust streaks rippled down the hull, and patches of riveted steel plastered much of the sides. Both ladies wondered how it could float. Regardless of the *Tjipawan's* navigational ability, they did learn the meaning of her name and her characteristics. "Tji" is the word used by the people of the Sunda region of Indonesia for "river." And the Pawan is one of the rivers of Borneo; both islands were part of the Dutch East Indies. The ship was 323 feet long, had a forty-eight-foot beam and a draft of twenty, and could move through the water at twelve knots—or roughly fourteen miles per hour. The schedule showed estimated arrival in Hong Kong at noon on December second, Manila on the morning of the eighth, and Singapore midday on the twelfth.

⁕

"Look at that mountain peak, Darya. I've never seen anything quite so steep. And green!"

The women stood at the ship's rails, entering Hong Kong harbor. Victoria Peak dominated the geography of the main island, and the non-stop ship and boat traffic in the enormous roadstead reminded Katya of water bugs scooting across Lake Valday during the short summer. Hong Kong seemed to contain even more vessels than Shanghai, if that were possible. However, despite the hectic appearance, British Naval forces were scarce. Rumors ran rampant among the crew and passengers that the British knew it would be impossible to defend Hong Kong against a Japanese land invasion.

"You heard the news about a land attack on Hong Kong?" a handsome Dutchman asked Katya.

"Yes." She paused, then asked, "Why are we even stopping here? Hong Kong is not a Dutch port, and neither is Manila. Why there?"

"Simple answer," he responded. "The Hague chartered the *Tjip-awan* for transporting my compatriots out of China and the entire region. There will be a few others like you and your friend, but mostly Dutch. And because the ship is so old, a day will be added at each port until we reach Jakarta for the engineers and company reps to do safety inspections before we sail."

"Well, as long as we're here, I intend to explore," Katya pronounced.

Darya spun on her heel and looked at her friend with astonishment. "You can't, Katya. What if something happens? What if the ship sails earlier than planned? Or who knows what?"

"Darya, we may never again get a chance to see this place. I want to go to the top of the peak. It will be a good hike."

"But—"

"Oh, it won't be necessary to hike, and it would take too long," the man interrupted Darya. "There's a wonderful tram that takes you up. The view is spectacular. I used to come here regularly to manage materials distribution for our consular offices."

"That sounds very similar to what my husband does for the Brits in Shanghai," Darya added.

"What's his name? Maybe I know him." Before Darya could respond, the man continued. "My apologies, ladies. Let me introduce myself. I am Johannes Meijer. There. Now, pardon my interruption. Who is your husband?"

"He is Trenton Miles," Darya said with pride.

"Yes! I do know him," Meijer said. "We occasionally had deliveries arrive on the same ships. And you and your friend, what are your names?"

Katya guessed he was about thirty-two or thirty-three, and although they were speaking in halting French, it was apparent he would have preferred Mandarin, Dutch, or English.

Darya replied in English. "I'm Darya Miles, originally Darya Smirnova. Some would say Smirnov," she answered with unexpected happiness at encountering someone who knew Trenton.

"Oh my. I think I've had some of your family's vodka! Quite excellent," Herr Meijer said.

Both women laughed at the connection. "I'm sorry, Mr. Meijer. There is no connection," Darya informed him. "The name Smirnov is quite common in Russia, but the vodka family ends in the letter 'f.' Close, but not the same."

"Oh well. No matter," he smiled. "So, back to the free time we have here in Hong Kong, I would be happy to escort both of you to the top of Victoria Peak." As he said this, Johannes had his eyes fixed on Katya, and she held his look, returning it with a corresponding enigmatic grin.

"Why, that would be lovely, Mr. Meijer. Don't you agree, Darya?"

"Oh Katya, why must you do these things? I don't think Trenton would approve of me gallivanting about Hong Kong during times like these." And before she could stop herself, Darya added, "And, well, what would Marcel say?"

The briefest shadow crossed Katya's eyes.

"Oh Katya, I-I-I'm sorry. I didn't mean to—"

Katya smiled at her friend. "It's quite alright, Darya. Marcel knows me, and he knows how I feel about him. I wouldn't have undertaken this crazy journey if I didn't love him with all my heart." She faced Johannes and said, "Marcel is my fiancé. We are to be married as soon as I reach England. My friend here is attempting to preserve my reputation, such as it is. I hope you understand."

"Most certainly, Miss Palutova. I understand completely. And let me assure you, I wish only to serve as your guide for an enjoyable day ashore."

"See, Darya?" Katya said with a twinkle in her eye. "Simply an enjoyable day away from all this." She waved her arm in a big arc to the crowded and rusted ship.

"I know when I'm beaten." Darya ended her persuasive oratory and told Mr. Meijer, "I expect you to make sure Katya is safe the entire time, and to return her to the ship before we sail."

Katya gave a short huff, then said, "Oh, Mother, stop worrying."

That lightened the mood as the ship approached its berth on the Kowloon side of the harbor. Things proceeded without complications and Katya, guided by Johannes Meijer, left the ship the next morning. Their first stop was the Star Ferry for the ride across the harbor to Hong Kong island. It proved to be a serene and calm day. The city smells were no different than Shanghai, but things changed after they stepped onto Hong Island.

Living in the French Concession, Katya had frequently enjoyed its neighborhoods, parks, and wide boulevards. The area was flat, and you could stroll, it seemed, for long distances without gaining a meter in elevation. However, things became vertical after a brief five-minute promenade into Hong Kong's interior.

"It's only one and a half kilometers to the tram. An easy walk," said the mid-level Dutch bureaucrat.

"My goodness. It's been years since I had to go up or down more than three or four flights of stairs. And people do this every day?" Katya queried.

"They grow up with it," Johannes told her.

Suddenly Katya felt a wave of guilt as she walked past a uniformed soldier on the arm of the handsome and intelligent Dutchman. But what could, what should she do? Remain onboard and hibernate like Darya? That was not her way, and Marcel knew it. Besides, it was only for one day, and they were in public.

Walking along Garden Road, Johannes pointed out interesting buildings and places, then detoured into a beautiful little park that led to Battery Path. A large church rose on one side, and off to the right, further up, was a stately, red-brick building.

"The brick building belongs to the Paris Foreign Missions Society," Johannes told her. "It's a group of secular priests and laypeople who do missionary work worldwide. And here is St. John's Cathedral. It's an Anglican church. Too bad Darya is not with us. It's typical of what she'll see in England. Would you like to look inside?" he asked.

"Only if we can take a rest and sit down." She snickered, and they went inside. Once they were settled into a pew far from the altar, Katya breathed a heavy sigh. After a few moments of contemplation, Katya asked, "Do you think there's a God, Mr. Meijer?"

"Miss Palutova, we've just met! Such a question!" he responded with a twinkle. "But the short answer is no. Look at what's happening around the world. Would God allow such behavior? No! But too many men are greedy and power-hungry. They want to control and dominate others. And regretfully, the vast masses of humanity, like you and me, allow them to do so. I don't know why, but we do."

"Oh, I don't know," Katya followed. "Somehow, I keep escaping from tenuous, even dangerous situations. I can't tell if I do so through my efforts or with the help of some greater being. I'm reserving my decision. Like my Papa did." She spoke with finality and stood. "Let's continue. Show me the views from Victoria Peak."

At the Peak, Johannes continued his narration. "There was an enormous hotel here for forty years. Opened in 1888 and appropriately called the Peak Hotel, it expanded with numerous additions over the years. But between the recent economic downturn and poor construction, it eventually closed in '36. Then it burned in '38. Too bad. It was a wonderful place for drinks and views. But no worries. We can still do both."

He took her hand and pulled her along to the vistas made famous by tourists, romantics, and travel agents.

They walked through the park-like ground, bought lunch from a street vendor, and lingered on benches, admiring the views. The entire world spread before them in the distance below. Ships in the harbor looked like flies on a broad, soft, blue-gray-green tablecloth. Steam and smoke rose from thousands of chimneys and dissipated among the clouds. And, if you followed the Pearl River's path inland, you could almost see the city of Canton, the famous trading port of the early silk traders from England and the United States. It was a magnificent scene.

"I could remain here a long time," Katya offered. "Away from all the throngs and continuous noise."

"Yes," Johannes responded. "It is a wonderful and calm place."

Their eyes signaled a desire for something more, but that's where it stopped. They understood that life creates moments of joy and nothing more.

"What time is it?" Katya asked, and without waiting for him to answer, she extended the question. "Is there enough time for us to walk down? It's so beautiful."

"I think we have time to walk the Peak Road halfway, and then take a taxi to the pier."

"Perfect," Katya said, and took his arm as they wandered into the forest below the peak.

The *SS Tjipawan* docked in Manila on December 6, 1941, with departure scheduled midday on Monday, December 8.

"Anything worth seeing during our time in Manila?" Katya asked Johannes. She, Darya, Johannes, and several other voyagers were gathered around a small table, drinking what passed for coffee as the ship made its way into one of the world's best natural harbors.

"I don't have any idea," he answered. "Although I've traveled all over the Far East, I've never been to Manila."

One of the older men standing near their table overheard Katya's question. "Pardon me, but I've been here on several occasions. It is a fine city, in the Spanish and American way, if you know what I mean. And, of course, there is a local aspect you cannot avoid, but worth a look." He went on to give them his overview of the city.

The sprawling Philippine archipelago and its capital city had been under the political, military, and commercial control of the United States since 1898. Despite the three-year war for independence ending in 1902, the relationship with its American overseer had brought some benefits. Manila was a busy, modern, and vibrant city with all the customary entertainment and services. People of means shopped along Escolta Street or Avenue Rizal and had drinks at the air-conditioned Manila Hotel, which on par with the Palace, Fairmont, and Cathay in Shanghai. Men congregated in specialty cigar stores, and women found colorful dresses in boutiques. Those with lesser resources took rides on horse-drawn carromatas and dodged the heavy traffic of the Tondo section of the city to reach the expansive Dewey Boulevard. If they remained unsatisfied, there was always a visit to Bilibid Prison to watch the prisoners march in their daily parade, accompanied by the music of the prisoners' band.

Satisfied they would find enough to do and graciously accepting Johannes's kind offer to serve as host and protector, Katya and Darya agreed to join him for, what Katya called, a "romp around Manila" the following day. The older Dutch gentleman calmed Darya by reminding her that Manila was essentially an American city. At mid-morning on Sunday, December 7, when Johannes and the ladies left the ship, the streets of Manila were quiet except for church bells calling the faithful to services.

At that exact moment, 8,500 kilometers east, it was four o'clock Saturday afternoon, December 6, in Honolulu. Families frolicked at the beach, and couples were getting ready for a night out in Waikiki.

The women had an enjoyable and tiring day with Herr Meijer generously covering all their expenses. He bought each of them a dress in one of the Escolta shops, took them for drinks and finger sandwiches on the veranda at the Manila Hotel, and concluded their *romp* with a sumptuous evening meal while listening to the music of Tirso Cruz and his orchestra. It had been a decadent day, one Katya would remember her entire life. It was the last such day she would have for many years.

⁂

"Is that the fire alarm?" Darya wondered.

The clanging bell jarred them awake before sunrise. It had been Katya's turn to sleep on the deck, and she put her hand to her head.

"Oh, whoa! My head is spinning. What time is it?" her voice was tired and hoarse.

"I told you to stop last night," Darya teased her. "I think Johannes had some other things on his mind when he kept buying drinks. And it's a little before six."

Katya forced a smile. "Perhaps he did. I think I did as well. And don't give me a nasty look. Thinking and doing are different. But oh my, I need coffee and aspirin. Help me up, please, Darya."

Darya hooked her arm under Katya's and pulled her up. "Now, let's find out what this ear-splitting alarm is all about." Darya marched into the busy passageway in her nightgown with Katya trailing behind.

No one seemed to have any official information. The ship's public address system rarely worked. It was up to the stewards and other crew to pass the word, and the word was to report to the dining hall. When they arrived, the room was overflowing. Passengers squeezed in like sardines with barely enough space to breathe, making guesses about why they were there. When the room could hold no more, the captain took the megaphone.

"We received communications a short while ago that Japanese airplanes have bombed American army and naval facilities at Honolulu in Hawaii. We're not sure what that means for us. As you know, the Philippines are linked closely with the United States. However, you may not know our ship is on lease from an American company. In times of war, the United States can terminate our charter and take custody of this ship. I need everyone to be prepared to disembark here if necessary. I suggest you remain on board and stay calm until we get more information. That is all. Thank you."

The crowded room burst into pandemonium, and the captain had to force his way out. People wanted details. Answers. When would they know if the ship could proceed? Where would they stay if they had to remain in Manila? Who would cover their expenses? Would they get a refund for the balance of the journey? Who should they see to acquire further transportation? The questions were endless, and there were no answers.

"Glad we got to see the city yesterday," Katya said, making light of their predicament.

However, the blood had drained from Darya's face, and she needed to sit before fainting.

Katya took hold of her, and they elbowed out onto the promenade, where Katya hurriedly laid claim to a deck chair for her friend.

"This can't be happening," Darya murmured. "What will we do

if we have to stay here? I wonder if we can even get word to Trenton and Marcel. Oh, Katya, this *can't be happening!*"

"We've survived much worse," Katya reminded her friend. "Things will work out, Darya. I promise. Remember, I told Trenton I'd look out for you. We're a team, a team of winners. Let's go back and get something to eat. They're setting up for breakfast, and with a little food and coffee, we'll be able to make better decisions."

Darya rose on wobbly legs, and both women returned to the dining hall. No one seemed to care that they remained in their sleeping attire. No time for nitpicking. After eating, they cleaned up and dressed in their cabin and went for a stroll on deck, where the undulating throng of passengers making loops around the ship's perimeter swept them up. They could only understand a few words among the steady drone of conversation on deck, but a sense of dread, anxiety, or annoyance was pervasive in every face. Not knowing what was coming put everyone on a razor's edge. Four hours later—ten o'clock—there was still no news. Departure for Singapore remained scheduled for noon.

"You'd think we would know something by now with all these modern radios," Darya complained.

Katya, usually the impatient one, told her friend she trusted the captain. "As soon as he knows something, he'll tell us. Nothing we can do about it until then. Let's play cards."

So they did.

At 11:30, a great sense of relief spread through the ship as stewards passed the word around that the ship would get underway on time. The crew moved toward their assigned stations, and a sense of normalcy returned.

"See, I told you," Katya bragged. "Just a few more days, Darya, and we'll be England-bound."

Darya formed a weak smile, and as the ship's bell struck eight times, dock workers cast off, and diners sat down for the midday meal. All was well on the *SS Tjipawan.*

Less than an hour from the dock, with the ship not yet out of Manila Bay, a new sound reached their ears. Airplanes. Most guests who had finished the midday meal were standing at the rails, enjoying the grandeur of the bay. They looked up. There weren't many planes, but enough. Japanese. Without warning, the reality of war was upon them. Bombs fell on scattered vessels in the vast bay. It was hard to tell which ships were hit, but one, the US steamship *Capillo*, was severely damaged and smoking.

The *Tjipawan's* captain ordered everyone into their bulky life-jackets, warning them to be ready for anything. Katya and Darya waited for further instructions near their lifeboat station. Johannes and his friends were on the opposite side of the ship. Rumors began to spread that US airbases on Luzon were also under attack. As people prayed and complained, the ship made a slow U-turn to return to Manila.

A few remaining Japanese planes raced around the skies and dropped the last of their bombs. One struck the *Tjipawan,* exploded, and tore a large hole in the superstructure. Damage to the ship was jarring enough, but the abrupt, deadly horror of war also claimed fifteen souls who had been standing along the port rail. The screams of the dying and injured fueled fear and panic throughout the ship. It wasn't until later that Katya and Darya learned Johannes and his party were among those killed.

Instead of frightening her, the bombing strengthened Katya's will to live. If the communists, the perverted man at the Moscow train station, the Mongols, the Japanese Army, Kuniaki, the jealous women of Shanghai's nightclubs, and the loss of her family couldn't destroy her, certainly a few random bombs were not going to claim her. A sense of fatalism settled onto her psyche. What will be, will be, she reasoned. She could only control what she did. Nothing more.

At 2:30 in the afternoon, the crew returned the *Tjipawan's* mooring lines to the dock in Manila. Shortly afterward, passengers crammed into the ship's dining hall a second time, overflowing onto the promenade deck. This time, Katya didn't go.

"Waste of time," she told Darya. "Go listen to the captain if you want, but we know what he's going to tell us. We stand a better chance if we head down the gangway before the masses."

Darya repeated her mantra from earlier: "I can't believe this is happening. Where would we go?"

"We go to the British embassy. You're married to an Englishman. They'll help you. And maybe they'll have some ideas for me. Come. Let's go, before we get stuck by some petty, bureaucratic rules."

The force of Katya's will was too much for Darya to resist. They consolidated their luggage into one bag each, although Katya found the packing difficult. Her Bible, icon, and bells were heavy, but she refused to leave them behind. In ways she couldn't put into words, the three items described who she was and where she came from, and gave her strength. Driven only by intuition and faith, the two women carried their heavy satchels toward the gangway. A member of the purser's staff blocked their exit.

"No one can leave without permission," he told them gently. "There may be more bombing."

"That is exactly why we're leaving," Katya groused. "Besides, if Japan and the United States are at war, the Americans will confiscate this ship. We're getting off now to save everyone the trouble of figuring out what to do with us then. Departing on our own initiative."

"One moment," the crewman said and lifted the gangway phone.

He spoke rapidly in Dutch to whoever answered and then returned the phone to its cradle. As he hung up, he reached under his dais and withdrew the passenger and crew list. He asked the women their names, wrote a notation next to them on the roster, and stepped aside.

"Good luck, ladies," he bade them as they carried their bags down the gangway.

Two other ships had also returned to the Manila wharves. The scene on shore was not quite chaotic, but it was not organized, either. Darya and Katya moved away from the crowd and walked several blocks into the surrounding neighborhood before stopping. The roads were busy, and people appeared to be doing their daily business without concern. Hunger drove the two travelers to a small-wheeled cart parked on a corner selling pancit. The noodles were warm and spicy and tasted almost like those they ate in Shanghai.

"This is excellent," Darya commented on the pancit. "Even better than Shanghai."

Katya licked a finger and nodded in agreement. "We could have made a fortune selling these. I wonder what the spices are?"

"I don't know, but the shredded green papaya adds a great touch. I could eat these for days." They shared a laugh and a cold Coca-Cola before getting serious once again.

"We need to find a carromata to take us to the British embassy," Katya restated her plan.

They scanned every conveyance coming down the street and hustled to one that stopped a block away. The driver climbed down from his seat, helped with their bags, and asked in Tagalog where they wanted to go.

"Do you speak Russian?" Katya said.

He looked at her with a blank stare.

"English?" Darya followed.

"A little," he answered in a heavy accent.

"Do you know the British Embassy?" Darya encouraged him.

"No embassy," he answered.

They were stunned by his response.

"No embassy?" they asked simultaneously.

"There has to be an embassy!" Darya exclaimed. "What are we

going to do?!" She was practically screaming, and tears started blurring her eyes.

The driver was so surprised at her reaction that he could only sputter. They ignored him until they heard him say, "No embassy, consul office." He repeated it twice.

"Of course, only a consulate," Katya said. "The Philippines are American, not independent. Please, take us to the British *consulate*."

His smile exposed a missing front tooth. He gave a quick command to his horse, and off they went. The driver got them as close to the consulate as possible. Activity around it was buzzing as numerous people came and went, many with faces steeped in worry. A line trailed out the door and, after more than an hour, the ladies finally reached a reception desk. A Filipina receptionist greeted them.

"How may I help you?" They were surprised by her formal London accent, and she noticed. "I was raised in London. My father worked there for many years. When he got promoted, he brought our family back to Manila. Now, may I see your passports?"

"We just got off the SS *Tjipawan*," Darya explained. "It returned to the dock and left us stranded." She knew this wasn't entirely accurate, but close. "We have no passports, but we have these."

Darya passed her document from the British consulate in Shanghai confirming her marriage status to an Englishman, along with the two papers indicating she and Ekaterina were legal White Russian residents of Shanghai. The woman raised her eyebrows when she looked at Katya.

"Give me a moment." She stood and disappeared into the heart of the building.

"Oh, Darya, I'm so impressed. Your English has gotten so good. All that time with Trenton and his friends has really helped," Katya praised.

"Unbelievable, isn't it? I was sure I could never learn such a confusing language."

"I need to learn more, too. Oh, here she comes."

The door opened, and the receptionist raised her hand and beckoned. "Mrs. Miles, please follow me. Miss Palutova, you can wait in that room," she said, pointing to a seating area in a small alcove.

The friends went in separate directions, and Darya didn't return for half an hour. Katya was gazing out the window after pretending to read the English-language newspapers in the waiting area and didn't hear Darya enter the room.

"Katya, I'm back," Darya said softly.

Katya swung around from the window. By the look on Darya's face, she could see the information Darya received was not satisfactory.

"What's wrong, Darya? Are undocumented Russians somehow a problem?" Although she had not wanted to be sarcastic, it came through. "Oh, Darya, I'm sorry. It's just that whatever you tell me, whatever you found out, it won't be a surprise to me. We have no country, at least I don't. So, no country wants to help me. Am I right?"

Darya blinked her eyes, and a tear rolled down each cheek.

"It's okay, my dear. It's not your fault," Katya consoled her. "So, tell me what you learned."

Without wiping away the tears, Darya told her the British government could put *Mrs. Trenton Miles* up in a nearby house until they made arrangements for her to continue to England, but they had no way to accommodate Katya. They suggested Katya visit the office of the Salvation Army, an American Protestant Christian organization, that aids people in need.

"They told me the Salvation Army helps place people into the homes of locals for short periods. I have the name, phone number, and address of their contact person." She passed the note to Katya. "I'm so sorry, Katya. I never imagined they wouldn't offer to help the two of us. I didn't think of the implications."

"You must not worry about me, Darya. We can swap addresses, so we know where each other will be. And there are many churches in the city. We'll find one of them and meet there regularly until we have enough money to continue our trip. If we stay positive, it will all work out. And you know me, I enjoy meeting new people. Now—if only they could speak Russian."

Darya said nothing. How could she tell Katya that the British government would cover her fare as a British dependent? No matter. For the time being, they were still together. Sort of. No ships were leaving soon anyway.

Darya gave a half-hearted laugh. They exited the building, boarded another carromata, and gave the driver the address for the Salvation Army.

10 DECEMBER 9, 1941 — JULY 4, 1946
Manila to Sagada to Manila

Ports, naval bases, and other strategic locations throughout the Philippines, including Manila, received steady bombing after December 8. On December 12, US Naval forces evacuated to Java, and not long after, MacArthur withdrew from Manila, concentrating his forces on the Bataan peninsula. The bombing also claimed the *SS Tjipawan,* and uncorroborated reports said the attack killed all hands. Unfortunately, official authorities never received the news that all passengers had disembarked before it sank.

The Salvation Army helped Katya find a place to stay with a very generous family in Manila who spoke a smattering of English. The man of the house was a senior executive with a Filipino real estate management company that owned and managed large retail properties throughout the country. He was worried about his employees as the bombing continued. Residents were anxious, and the news that Japanese troops landed on the Luzon coast in Lingayen Gulf on December 22 heightened everyone's concern. Stories of the slaughter and destruction in Nanking and Korea provided good reason. Since their departure from the ship, the constant threat of war impacted their lives. Meeting at a church each week helped Katya and Darya remain calm and stay connected.

Three weeks into their stay in Manila, they agreed to meet at Santo Domingo Church for the traditional Roman Catholic Mass on Saturday morning. It was different from their Russian service, but recognizable, and they became more familiar with it each time they attended.

***

"Katya, I'm worried," Darya blurted after the service as they sat outside and talked. "Every day, I contact the consulate, and they have no news for me. No idea when a ship will be available to take us out of here. And the bombing, it's terrifying! I heard the Japs even started bombing houses and villages. It seems so random."

Darya was a nervous wreck and gazed into the distance, where smoke from scattered fires started by bombs wafted in the air.

"I know," Katya responded with little enthusiasm. "The family I'm staying with suggests the best thing for me to do is leave the city. Go into the mountains where there are many places to hide."

Many years removed from her rural upbringing in Valday, this idea did not particularly suit Katya. She had become accustomed to city life. However, no one knew how the Japanese would deal with a single White Russian woman without a country. They might be indifferent, as authorities had treated her most of the time in Shanghai—or they could be dangerous. Fading into the mountains grew more appealing each day since the arrival of the Japanese troops on Luzon.

"The mountains?" Darya was not ready. "How would we find out if there's a ship? What would we do to earn money? And we have no idea how to speak any local language. This can't be happening. Not again! How would I get word to Trenton and my parents? And you? How would you communicate with Marcel? Goodness, Katya, we're lucky if messages sent from *here* get through, no less some small town far away."

Katya knew Darya was right about getting information. If they went to the mountains, there would be no telling how long they'd be there or how they would correspond with the outside world. But what choice did they have? Did *she* have? Prostituting herself to earn money to leave Shanghai was one thing, but the possibility of being used and abused for amusement or worse by Japanese soldiers? No! Never! Katya resolved to avoid that outcome at any cost.

"I don't see any options, Darya. It's simply too dangerous to wait here for the unknown. We know the stories. Seen all the reports. Remember Nanking? Do you want to die like that?"

As Katya let the words drift away, they heard the threatening sound of more airplanes. They knew what was coming and hustled back inside the church. They were last in line as people filed down the staircase to safety in the basement.

That's when the world came to an end.

The worshipers never heard the bomb that ravaged the fifth church built on the site since 1587. The terrified congregants, as well as the large columns of native wood, iron vault, European stained-glass windows, and four retablos, were all at the mercy of the destruction falling from the sky. No one had time to think or do anything but absorb the impacts of the explosions. Dazed from being tossed down the steps, Katya blinked through the dusty air and slowly shook her head, trying to restore her hearing. She carefully checked herself and realized she was not injured, aside from a tender spot on her shoulder from landing on the corner of one of the stone steps.

The air began to clear, as did her hearing, and she could see other parishioners. There weren't many—maybe a dozen, and they all appeared to be moving—but she didn't see Darya. Remembering Darya had been behind her, she spun. A leg protruded from under a large collapsed column near the top of the staircase. The foot had no shoe, but she recognized the color of the skirt through the thick air.

"Darya!" she screamed, and forced her legs to carry her back up the steps. "Darya!"

Several people from below, including the priest, followed her. Katya reached the top first and began to toss broken roof pieces, splintered stones, and sections of colored glass out of the way. She cut her hands, but never winced. Ignoring the blood and pain, she raced to free her friend. The work was painstakingly slow. The priest and another man helped her lift a large section of the marble column, exposing Darya, lying face down with both arms askew, one laying at a grotesque angle. Ever so gently, they turned her over.

Darya's face, the one that had given Katya joy and support for so many years, was…gone. Katya gagged and vomited without embarrassment. The priest quickly pulled her away, and someone found a scrap of cloth to lay over her friend's body.

Katya sat in a trance, eyes open, seeing nothing. She visualized Lake Valday, walking with Yuri. She saw the poster with the picture of the mother she never knew. Her uncles were waving to her. Goodbye? She saw Kuniaki and a baby girl. There was Papa and Grandmama too. Marcel stood proudly by a tractor on a farm in France, then in uniform in England with a rifle. And one more image crowded her mind: Darya. Beautiful, fun, cautious Darya. The one steady and persistent pillar in Katya's life since the train ride so long ago.

"Oh, Darya…oh, Darya…"

Katya walked to one of the pews free of debris, lay down, and stared up through the dissipating haze of dust beyond the enormous holes in the roof to the blue sky.

"Maybe the Communists are right," she whispered. "There is no God."

Then, she cried once more.

They buried Darya in the La Loma Cemetery adjacent to the Santo Domingo Church. Like Raisa, Darya received special dispensation from the priest of Santo Domingo and the bishop due to the circumstances of her death; otherwise, the cemetery was reserved exclusively for Roman Catholics. Grieving, Katya wondered what she would do without her best friend. She loved the grounds of the cemetery and prayed it would remain the same despite the war, but given how easily Darya and their friends on the *Tjipawan* were lost, she realized it was impossible to prepare for every contingency or disaster. She had to live, as best she could. After the funeral, Katya hand-delivered three messages to the British consul for forwarding: one to Marcel in England, who was with de Gaulle, the second to Darya's family in Australia, and the third to Trenton. She wanted to ensure everyone knew what had happened to her best friend.

The following day, Katya left for the mountains. She headed east toward the small fishing port of Infanta to avoid Japanese troops on the western shore. She caught an occasional ride in a car, truck, horse, or oxen cart, but mostly, she walked the ninety miles. She slept where she could, in a barn, the back of a delivery truck, or camouflaged under leaves several meters off the road. Five days later, she rode the last couple miles into town with a fisherman heading to the docks. He pointed out a boat heading north, and the skipper agreed to give her a ride.

One more day and sixty miles north, the boat stopped at the tiny village of Dingalan. From there, ancient roads led into the interior. Her hosts in Manila had told her to try to reach Sagada, a locale remote enough, they assumed, not to be of interest to the Japanese. The journey from Dingalan to Sagada was 190 miles.

Three weeks later, a young boy found Katya lying by the side of the road about half a mile outside Sagada. She was filthy, dehydrated, hungry, and suffering from spells of fever and shivers, typical of malaria. The local doctor probably saved her life. Once they revived her, communications were difficult. No one in the village spoke Russian, and Katya didn't know the local Kankanaey language. A few people spoke Spanish, and a smaller number knew a few words of English. She was stranded, isolated by cultural and language barriers, but safe within the confines and care of the people of Sagada and its Church of St. Mary the Virgin. And, as always, she remained resilient.

During her convalescence, Katya did little more than think and give thanks. Her thoughts often drifted to the question of why.

"Why am I here?" she asked her rescuers. "Why is Darya gone. Papa? Grandmama? My baby? Why is the world at war?"

At first, her gentle caregivers understood little, but soon, they slowly began to understand each other.

"There must be a reason," she would tell everyone. "And thank you, for the soup and my clean clothes," she would add.

Once healthy, Katya set aside her reflections, for the most part, and quickly ingratiated herself into the community by singing for them and learning enough of their language to explain why she was there and where she came from. She was, in short, an oddity—but a welcome one.

Although the Japanese took control of the major cities, Americans like General Donald Blackburn, who evaded capture on Bataan, joined indigenous people and did whatever was possible to disrupt the invaders' lives. Doing so required a support network and places to hide. Katya helped the people in Sagada supply guerrilla forces, but concealed herself in a secret cellar dug in the earth whenever Japanese patrols visited the area. Sometimes she spent weeks living underground, never seeing the light of day. The locals feared what might happen to a "western" woman if the Japanese found her. While she always used to be neat, tidy, and stylish, Katya gave up worrying about her appearance and resigned to live like a mole. Fortunately, the temperatures in Sagada ranged between sixty and seventy-five degrees most of the year, but rain meant her hole was perpetually damp. She battled pneumonia twice but never complained.

Japanese patrols were infrequent but resulted in short skirmishes and too many funerals. Katya had never seen anything quite like the cemetery in Sagada. The Kankanaey people secured the coffins of deceased community heroes high on a vertical stone wall to bring them closer to heaven. Katya wept when she saw so many hanging coffins with dates coinciding with her three-plus years in the village. But she knew, after those years—much of them spent underground—that she could handle anything.

Word of the atomic bombs, followed several days later by Japan's surrender, reached the small town by the third week of August 1945. However, Japanese General Yamashita—the man in charge of all Japanese forces on Luzon—continued to elude capture. No one felt safe until his army surrendered on September 3. Not long after, Katya came out of her hole, bade farewell to her saviors in Sagada, and hitchhiked the entire distance back to Manila.

Walking through the streets of Manila in September 1945 was an experience she hoped never to repeat. The destruction she had witnessed in Shanghai was like a tiny grain of sand in her shoe, a minor annoyance compared to the wholesale devastation she saw in Manila. Sometime later, Katya would read several commentaries that described what she saw better than she could herself. One was by A.V.H. Hartendorp, an American magazine publisher who operated the Philippine Magazine and spent more than three years in a Japanese internment camp:

> *Manila lay waste, stinking with the thousands of dead of massacre as well as battle. It had lost its piers, docks, and bridges, its electric light and power and gas plants, its telephone exchanges, radio stations, and newspaper plants, its factories and warehouses and office buildings, its schools and universities, libraries, museums, churches, and theaters, its hotels and apartment houses, nine-tenths of its private homes, even its parks and avenues and streets. A great city of a million inhabitants, a metropolis three hundred years in building, was gone."*

She also read something by Joaquin de Jesus, a Filipino, about the impacts of the American bombing and the Japanese abuse of the local citizenry. De Jesus said virtually everything that made Manila special, the Pearl of the Orient, had been destroyed. The cultural and historical life and structures of the city were eviscerated. The unique city that combined Spanish, American, and Asian cultures had vanished. More importantly, he went on, the loss of buildings, including most churches, eliminated the country's Catholic values, and with the loss of common values went the loss of shared sacrifice, Hispanic culture, and good manners. Gone was the willingness to work at helping others. This loss of everything—this eradication of common ground—was nothing new for Katya.

The streets were desolate. People walked like zombies. Looters scavenged whatever they could find from shattered stores, rummaging one block to the next. Katya had only one destination in mind: the home of the people who had cared for her before she fled to the mountains. She had no money, no shelter, no food, and communicating was still problematic. The Kankanaey she learned in Sagada was not the language heard on the streets of Manila. She would have to rely on her weak English and hope that would be enough.

Katya knew she was wasting time as soon as she neared the neighborhood where her host family had lived. Every building had suffered severe damage, and most were piles of rubble. Unburied bodies remained. Rotting and noxious, they induced awful memories of the poor, starving, Chinese refugees who had littered the streets in Shanghai. Nonetheless, she walked until she stood in front of the once beautiful home. She rotated slowly to see if anyone was about but only saw a couple boys sifting through detritus a block ahead.

Walking into the morass, Katya picked her way through the

remnants of the once-fashionable house. She bent down and, like the boys, began to search for anything of value, or food. Something shiny sparkled within the dusty ruins where the master bedroom had been. She moved several fallen boards and plaster pieces, stretched her arm between a collapsed wall and a heavy chest of drawers, wrapped her fingers around the object, and pulled. Slowly, she exposed a long strand of ebony and silver rosary beads with a silver cross. She smiled. She remembered her hostess holding them during the December 1941 bombings. She wished she had found something less personal. Something she could trade without feeling guilty, but she was sure the owner would understand—if she was still alive.

Katya waded deeper into the sadness of the fallen structure and surprisingly found some canned fruit, kitchen utensils, and a couple blouses and skirts inside a wardrobe. When darkness crept in, she tired of the hunt. She noticed a protected spot within the endless nooks and crannies formed by displaced beams and walls, slid down onto the lopsided floor, ate a can of pineapple chunks, and fell asleep.

She woke with a start. Dogs were barking nearby and sounded like they were fighting. She rose quickly, wrapped her few scavenged possessions in a torn pair of pants, and set course for the second place that may offer her a safe refuge: the ruins of the Santo Domingo Church. The day Darya was killed, the church suffered heavy damage, but it still stood. She hoped the priest and others were still worshiping.

The walk did nothing to raise her spirits. Many people moved in a daze with no particular destination. At times over the past few years, she, too, had vacillated in and out of a daze. But somehow, she always managed to refocus on a bright future and find a corner of her brain to hide the sadness and aches of the past. And that day, she knew exactly where she was going and felt a little relief when she saw the church spire in the distance. As she neared, minor repairs were visible, and although the marble pillars were lying where they had fallen, Katya could tell the church remained active. She found a door, opened it, and went inside. Although much of the ceiling was still missing, dedicated parishioners had installed a temporary altar and arranged lines of undamaged pews, chairs, and benches. She could hear voices coming from a side room, approached the door, and knocked.

"*¿Quien es?*" she heard someone say in Spanish first, and then, "*Sino yun?*" The same question in Tagalog. Those were words she recognized.

"It's Ekaterina Palutova. From Russia," she answered in English.

There was no immediate response, but then she heard a chair scrape the floor. The door opened, and she looked into the face of the priest who had been there on that horrible day in 1941.

"Ekaterina! Yes! I remember you. Oh, such a terrible day and—"

"That is fine, Father. No need to remind me, but it is good to see you. I've come…" she hesitated, then started again. "I've come here, to you, for help. And I'm sorry to interrupt you."

Katya shifted her eyes to the two other people in the room. They were a young man and woman. Padre Jose Aguillar introduced Humphrey Manalaysay and his new bride, Yolanda, who was several years younger than twenty-nine-year-old Katya. Father Aguillar went on to say Humphrey had spent time with American forces working with the guerillas, and both he and Yolanda could speak some English. He encouraged Katya to tell her story, and the three listened as Katya summarized the last three years, at times searching her brain for the right words in English or Kankanaey, hoping they made sense. Her tale was not uncommon, and countless others would share similar recollections of deprivation, cruelty, and survival. When she finished, no one spoke. After sitting respectfully for several moments, Humphrey restarted the conversation.

"Katya, Yolanda and I have been more fortunate than many. Our families had businesses before the war, and when things started to look bad, they transferred funds to safe places, including the United

States. The sad part is, their dedication to their families and country kept them here. They could have fled, but didn't. As a result, both Yolanda's parents and my own died at the hands of the Japanese. My two brothers died from American bombs. However, my younger sister still lives. Yolanda's youngest brother also died in the bombing, but her older brother and two sisters escaped serious injury. So, the six of us joined together and live in my parents' large house, which, amazingly, still stands. It received only minor damage to windows, the roof tiles, and things of that nature. It is a large place with plenty of room. You are welcome to join us."

The suddenness of the offer caught Katya by surprise. She had expected Father Aguillar to point her toward a church-sponsored homeless shelter or possibly offer a place similar to where she stayed in 1941.

"Please come. Don't think about it," Humphrey said.

"Oh my! Yes. Thank you. Thank you so much," she heard herself answer.

"Before you get too excited," Yolanda spoke up, "all we have is space. It's been six months since the Americans drove the Japanese out of the city, but we still have no electricity, no running water."

"I'm used to that," Katya said.

Humphrey added, "It's not quite that bleak. We have a generator, and we can buy fuel for it so we have a little light at night and can listen to the radio. We also have two surplus Army jeeps that help us get around, which we acquired through—" He stopped mid-sentence. "Ah, that's not important. All you need to know is that everyone contributes in some way."

"Of course," Katya answered. "I'll do whatever you need."

Humphrey turned to Father Aguillar, "Padre, I think we should take Katya to her new home. Thank you for your continued support."

"Likewise, Humphrey. My dear Yolanda, I wish you a pleasant day."

Yolanda took Katya by the elbow and followed Humphrey out

the door. As soon as they were outside, Yolanda chatted something quickly to her husband, which Katya didn't understand. However, observant as ever, Katya had noticed the switch in the tone from Humphrey's conversation with the priest. She had seen the subtle look on Yolanda's face when Humphrey was about to explain how they came to possess two US Army jeeps. But, for now, Ekaterina was smart enough not to ask any questions.

It took Katya a couple weeks to settle firmly into the Manalaysay household. It wasn't easy, as moments of despair occasionally swept over her. Fortunately, she had always been able to make those moments as brief as possible. Katya knew she would have died long ago if she had dwelled on bad luck and misfortune. Nonetheless, she had much to adjust to, including names to remember and yet another language to learn. She needed to figure out what chores she could do, find clothes to wear, and devise a plan to locate Marcel. Each of these issues challenged her willpower. After two weeks without leaving the house and its immediate surroundings, she was ready to explore. She wanted to see what was happening in the rest of what remained of Manila.

"Humphrey, I need to find a paying job to save money for a ticket to France. I need to see if my fiancé is still alive."

"Fiancé? You didn't tell us about a fiancé." He made it sound accusatory.

"I didn't think it would make a difference. I'm sure you don't expect me to stay here forever. You have enough to handle without me being a never-ending extra mouth to feed." Her words worked as she intended.

"No, no. Of course not. And, well, maybe I…who knows what I had in mind. It doesn't matter. I understand. My apologies."

Katya softened and added, "I suppose I should have mentioned it. But it's been years, and I don't even know if he's alive, and he probably has no idea if I am, either. At a minimum, I need to find out."

"Yes, you do," he agreed. "Tomorrow, we'll take one of the jeeps and search for whatever building, shack, or tent is now housing the French consulate. That assumes, of course, that the current French government has reopened such an office. Perhaps they can help you."

"Thank you, Humphrey. If there is a consulate, I don't think they'll help me with transportation, but they may be able to tell me about Marcel."

It took most of the day, but their persistence paid off. Humphrey and Katya visited more than a dozen business contacts he and his father had within the shipping and banking industry. Finally, Señor Esteban Ortega, the president of Philippine Traders and a family friend and business colleague, had news. He said he heard several French diplomats who the Japanese had arrested and kept in the camps had restarted consular work in the Makati section of the city. The neighborhood had been one of tree-lined boulevards and fancy homes, but it looked just like the rest of Manila—bombed out—as they drove through it. Several structures remained more or less intact, however, and they stopped to speak to a woman doing laundry in a tub of water near the ruins of one. Katya listened as Humphrey talked with the woman, and saw the woman point, obviously giving directions.

When he returned to the jeep, he said, "We're close. Only a couple blocks away, but the woman has no idea if anyone is there. She said it had been the consul general's home, but he died in the detention camp."

Despite the near-universal leveling of every building, Humphrey and Katya had difficulty seeing over and around the rubble. Enormous piles of debris and the sporadic presence of trees, unscathed by the pounding the area had received, served as visual barriers. A surprise greeted them when Humphrey turned around a three-story mountain of broken stone, boards, roof tiles, and miscellaneous remnants of former dwellings. A hundred yards up the road, a small gathering of people and several parked vehicles clustered together. Half the group was standing in line; the rest were milling about, quietly talking. They were all camped in front of the ruins of a building flying the French flag.

"That must be the place," Humphrey said.

Katya giggled. "I'd say you're right."

He parked the jeep behind the other vehicles, they got out, and Katya's impatience took over. She hadn't been this close to Europeans since the day she and Darya disembarked from the *SS Tjipawan*. It was not that she wasn't comfortable with everyone she knew in Sagada and with Humphrey's extended family; it was simply the sense of fitting in better. She felt that way until she talked to the first person she encountered.

She had forgotten most of her French, which forced her to communicate with awkward English, bad French, and a mixture of Kankanaey and Tagalog. The look the man gave her was void of understanding. He raised his arm and pointed toward a Filipino gentleman sporting a classic mustache like the one she loved seeing on Marcel's face. He was speaking with two other men. She approached them, and when one saw her, the other two turned to see who was coming. It was evident the men admired the unfamiliar young lady, regardless of her frayed dress and tired-looking eyes. She read their eyes, like she had been doing her entire life.

She started with, *"Bonjour messieurs. Je m'appelle Ekaterina Palutova,"* however, that was where her French ended. She continued in her mixed patois, but Humphrey touched her arm and took over. He introduced himself to the men, and the Filipino explained he served as a translator when necessary for the French consul. The Filipino nodded toward two people sitting behind a table fabricated from an old door draped across two sawhorses. The individual on the left was a gentleman wearing a suit just as worn as Katya's dress. Next to him sat a woman who took notes.

Humphrey said, "I heard the Consul died in the camp."

"Sadly, it's true," answered the Filipino. "The man at the table was the deputy consul. Paris appointed him acting consul. He will be in charge until the agreement with the United States is signed and we finally have our independence. I understand the French will establish a full embassy here. So, how can the Acting Consul or I assist you?"

Katya got in line, and when it was her turn, the Acting Consul listened as the Filipino translated her comments. The French official promised to make inquiries about Marcel Granger, an officer of the Free French Army under Charles de Gaulle. He said they would send cables and try to get through by phone, if possible. Katya hadn't expected more than that.

"Dear Marcel," she mumbled as she walked back to Humphrey.

Within a month after visiting the French Deputy Consul, Katya started a laundry business, as her grandmother had. There were enough families within a half-mile of the Manalaysay house who could still afford the luxury, and with Yolanda's help, she made arrangements for a weekly service. Humphrey would drive her in one of the jeeps when it was too far to walk with a heavy load. Slowly, she started to save money.

By the end of February 1946, Humphrey had installed a gasoline-operated pump to bring water to the house and found materials to repair the war damages. The household also benefited from the increased availability of good food. Katya paid little attention to the improving conditions at the Manalaysay house compared to others. However, one day a fancy car stopped at the house, and two men dressed in suits emerged. Something about them made her think of soldiers, not businessmen.

The next day a third jeep materialized, along with several cases of engine oil, wiper blades, half a dozen tires, and various other engine parts she didn't recognize. Those deliveries clarified her suspicions. The Manalaysays were dealing in black market goods. Who else had plenty of cigarettes, new clothes, fresh food, light bulbs, shoes, toilet paper, ink, and three jeeps? She had no doubt it was more than good luck and traditional business practices that produced the rare items showing up at the house.

Esteban Ortega visited Humphrey each week, and Katya concluded that Ortega's trading company must work in consort with the Manalaysays' overseas financial resources. She figured the two were opportunistic, not necessarily criminal. And if they could work together to help their families, why not? So when Señor Ortega stopped in again the day the third jeep appeared, it was no surprise. However, she was surprised when he spoke to her as she hung laundry up to dry.

"Miss Palutova, are you free to accompany my wife and me to the movies this weekend? Humphrey, Yolanda, and Hector will also be coming. Several theaters have been repaired and are showing films again. I know it's been too long since you've had any fun or relaxation."

English was their shared language, although it was still troublesome for her. Most Filipinos she met, including those in the house, spoke a bastardized version. Therefore, she was never sure if what she said was correct. No matter; she understood Ortega's invitation.

"Ah, Mr. Ortega, thank you—but I don't think I would understand the words." She kept clipping clothes to the line.

"You know Hector is too nervous to ask you out on a date. You are a lovely woman, Katya," Ortega said. "He has eyes like all men, but, well, like many, he shies away from beautiful women. Come with us. If you don't understand, so what? We'll have a good time, and you'll make Hector happy."

Yolanda's brother, Hector, was nice enough, but not Katya's type. He was hard-working, dedicated to his family, and handsome in the way many mixed-heritage Latino men were. But he was a bit goofy and went through life playing practical jokes. She thought it might be his way of coping with the war years, but still, she found the characteristic juvenile. However, she was intrigued by Ortega's invitation because she knew she would enjoy getting out and seeing what else was going on around Manila.

"Very well, Señor Ortega," she answered. "I'll join you."

"Ah, wonderful, Katya. And please, call me Esteban." He gave a slight bow and returned to the house. She was sure he would go directly to Hector to give him the news.

The movie was a typical American western with cowboys and Indians and soldiers in blue uniforms. The plot was so simple it didn't matter if she barely understood most of the dialog. She suspected most of the audience didn't either, but everyone cheered and clapped and had a good time anyway. The chance to spend a couple hours removed from the stress and alien landscape outside appealed to people of every class. Even the rebuilt balcony was full of the city's less fortunate who still managed to scrape together enough for a ticket.

As they emerged into the evening's darkness—an inky blackness indicating the staggering amount of utility work yet to be done—it was clear Hector had loosened up a bit. He had sat on Katya's left, and after two hours of relatively close contact, albeit with little discussion, he built up the courage to extend a further invitation.

"I think we should go to the Lunetta for some music and dancing," he proposed to the group. The Lunetta was one of the old hotels that had suffered only minor damage and was operating again with a live band and dancing.

"That's a wonderful idea," Señor Ortega agreed.

Swept along with the others, Katya had no chance to object.

The sound of live music brought her back to life as nothing had since leaving Shanghai. The band was good. Not great, but fun. Well-off Filipinos, clusters of US Army and Navy personnel, and a mixture of other internationals—mainly from Europe, Australia, and Hong Kong—filled the room. Katya was thrilled to put her dancing experience back to work, and she shuffled all night among the men of her party. On her second dance with Ortega, she had a question.

"Esteban, do you know anyone who works here at the hotel? Or maybe at the Army-Navy Club or the Miramar?"

"Perhaps," was his droll reply. "Why do you ask?"

Rather than beating around the bush, she told him, "Once upon a time, I sang with various bands in Shanghai. I think I might be able to do the same thing here."

"You know, Katya, I've been waiting for you to tell us. You dance lovely, and I do enjoy sharing the floor with you. But I know you can sing. I saw you when I was at Ciro's years ago. Come."

She didn't know what to say, so she smiled. He took her hand, walked up to the side of the stage, and spoke briefly with a man wearing a frayed and slightly stained out-of-style tuxedo. The man listened, and as he did so, he kept glancing at Katya with questioning eyes. Soon, the two men separated, and when the band finished, the tuxedoed gentleman walked to the microphone and made an announcement, first in English and then in Tagalog.

"Ladies and gentlemen, it has been brought to my attention that tonight we have with us one of the foremost stars of Ciro's, the famous nightclub in Shanghai. The lovely Miss Ekaterina Palutova. Please join me in a big applause for her and her friends. She is here tonight with Esteban Ortega, whom many of you know. Maybe we can persuade her to sing for us."

Katya glared at Esteban. She didn't understand everything the announcer said but knew he had asked her to sing. Esteban was encouraging her, and others followed suit.

Yolanda spoke above the applause, "Why didn't you tell us you could sing?"

"I haven't sung in years," she lied.

In Sagada, she frequently sang old Russian folk songs and

popular tunes to keep up her spirits. The villagers often asked her to sing even though they didn't understand the words. But it had been a long time since she had "performed" for a refined audience. Katya wagged her finger at the Manalaysay contingent, then tossed her head back, stood perfectly erect, and strolled to the microphone with an elegant sexiness that made everyone forget she wore an old second-hand dress. She turned to the bandleader and mentioned a particular song. He nodded in the affirmative, raised his baton, and the music began. Katya began her vocal on the mark, and it was like she had never left the stage—effortless, melodic, and beautiful. She received a standing ovation and responded to the coaxing and applause by singing two more songs.

That night Esteban chauffeured everyone in his 1941 Cadillac Fleetwood 75 series. During the war, he had shipped the luxury automobile to the island of Tinaga, 150 miles east of Manila, in the shallow waters of the west-central Philippine Sea. He stored the black beauty in a cousin's garage for the duration. Now, Esteban cruised Manila's bombed-out but slowly mending streets in one of the most exclusive vehicles in the country. That night, the noise inside the car was intense, and it wasn't from the engine. Everyone raved about Katya and her voice, but more significantly, Esteban had arranged for Katya to start singing with the Lunetta house band at a salary that brought a grateful smile to her face.

Nonetheless, the swiftness and ease of the evening's outcome caused Katya some anxiety. Esteban Ortega seemed to come and go anywhere and do whatever he wanted. He had friends—or were they *connections?*—in most government agencies, with the US Army and Navy, and, of course, among Manila's business community. From the outside looking in, he seemed to get his way with most everything. In her experience, only criminals and corrupt officials had such continuous good fortune. She didn't want to think he was a criminal. Regardless, she looked forward to setting the laundry business aside and earning a living again with her voice.

By mid-May, Katya had saved enough to move out of the Manalaysay house and take an apartment in town closer to the Lunetta. The Lunetta manager had offered her a room, but she didn't want to live where she worked, and she worried it might have been another *gift* prompted by Esteban. Also, in the weeks since her surprise ad-lib concert, Hector wooed her constantly. They would have fun together, but she never let him do more than kiss her cheek. She was happy to have her own place.

The city's rebirth seemed to blossom steadily in some areas and barely sprout in others. Specifically, the re-establishment of businesses operated by powerful men with government connections and homes in wealthy neighborhoods moved along consistently. In contrast, ordinary people who did the laundry, repaired roads, reconstructed buildings, put air in car tires, or any of the myriad mundane chores necessary for society to function continued to live in decrepit shacks. Most had no running water, toilet facilities, or fuel and were plagued by insects and rats.

Katya witnessed this sad dichotomy daily as she walked to the Lunetta from her apartment. She knew she was lucky, and without the *favors* of Esteban Ortega and the Manalaysay family, she could see herself in a similarly miserable hovel. She wondered how Esteban Ortega acquired his money and about his relationship with the Manalaysays. She wished she could be sure the good fortunes they enjoyed came from legitimate enterprises, but she had no way to find out. Be that as it may, having a private apartment meant she saw them less frequently—often only at church on Sundays.

On one Sunday in late May, she and Yolanda sat in the shade of a narra tree, which still stood in defiance of the bombs that had landed all around it. Some of its distinctive yellow blossoms remained, but they would vanish by the end of the month. Katya had news she wanted to share.

"Oh, Yolanda, I have something to tell you."

"Let me guess. You met a man."

"Is it so easy to see?"

They both laughed.

"Yes, Katya. When joy enters, most of us who have seen so much misery can't hold back. My mother used to tell me I *radiated* whenever something good happened. So—you are radiating, my friend."

"It was a week ago," Katya said. "There were many American Army officers at Lunetta. One of the waiters came and gave me a note after I finished a set, and you'll never guess what it said."

"Of course, I can guess. It asked if you would meet one of the officers for a drink or something like that when you finished. Correct?"

"Yes, yes. You're right, but that's not all I meant. Guess what language?"

"You've made this too easy, Katya. It had to be Russian. Why else would you ask me?"

"Yes, Russian! Some *American* soldier sends me a note—in Russian! Well, I just had to meet him."

"I hope he was a general or something," Yolanda said. "Someone who—what do the Americans say—someone who has clout, with money and connections."

Katya looked at Yolanda and giggled.

"What's so funny?"

"Yolanda, you and Humphrey, and your family and friends, have *money and connections*. I wouldn't be working at Lunetta or still be alive if not for your network in the city. But, no—I don't think he has clout. However, he is an officer—a captain and an engineer who worked on General MacArthur's staff."

"So, how is it that he can write Russian?" Yolanda asked.

"He also speaks it. He grew up in the Russian-controlled area of Poland, where his grandparents had moved from Germany. He's very smart. At least, he seems to be. He taught at college in the United States before the war."

"Ah. I see. What's his name, Katya? You have not told me."

"This is the funny part. His name is Charles. Charles Delacroy. A French name like my dear Marcel. But Charles is like many countries mixed into one. And he is so different than Hec—oh, Yolanda, I'm sorry. Your brother is such a nice man, but…"

"You don't have to tell me about Hector, Katya. I grew up with him."

"Please, you won't say anything to him? I will tell him," Katya said.

"Of course. But now what about *your* Marcel, and this new Captain Charles? How do you feel?"

"I cried for years about Marcel," she said. "I still get weepy and wonder. But what can I do? He could be dead. He might think I'm dead. No word from him. I can't live in limbo forever. Charles is here now, Yolanda. We like each other."

"Yes. The damn war. It destroyed so much." She took Katya's hands and squeezed them gently before changing tones. "Tell me, how often have you seen Charles, or do they call him Charlie?"

"I haven't heard anyone call him Charlie. His friends call him Charles. And I've seen him three times."

"Ah. If no one calls him Charlie, I think this might be a good match for you, Katya. Does he call you Ekaterina?"

"Why…yes. Yes, he does."

Yolanda smiled broadly. "See—that is a good sign. You each have a bit of formality, unlike dear brother Hector. I'm happy for you. But you left out the important part—what does he look like?"

"Oh, let's see. He is tall. Over six feet. He has light hair with a reddish tint to it. But it is thin. I think Americans say wispy. He's a bit older. In his forties is my guess. He has soft gray eyes and a strange walk. He kind of thrusts his feet forward, and his legs follow. Some people must tease him, but it doesn't bother me."

"Isn't forty old for an Army captain?"

"I don't know. Does it matter?" Katya asked. "Anyway, he told me he expected to be promoted to major soon."

"I guess it doesn't matter except if the Army is his career, but you said he taught school."

"Yes, in a university. We haven't learned everything about each other yet. As I discover more, I'll tell you."

"Yes. You must," Yolanda insisted.

They laughed and parted, agreeing to meet up again the following Sunday.

"Isn't she fantastic?" Captain and soon-to-be Major Charles Delacroy shared his admiration for the lovely singer with three other officers.

They were huddled over a small table, smoking cigarettes and drinking too many cocktails at Lunetta. It was Friday night, and they had a weekend pass. Each of the four men was over forty, but only one was happy to have his stay in the Philippines extended. Charles smiled a dreamy, teenage-like swoon as Katya sang her finale.

"Yeah, Charles. She's great. But the problem is, she's not much older than my oldest daughter. Y'all better be careful. And what about Harriet?" drawled his friend, Nathan Harris from Georgia.

"Now, Nate, no need for you to chastise me," Charles defended himself. "I've been as good, as most everyone else. Been away for nearly four years, and we all know some natural…uh…*needs* require periodic attention."

"Of course," a third man chimed in. "And I wonder how Harriet's been tending to *her* needs back in Jersey?"

Charles ignored the comment and focused on Nathan, his best friend in the Army. Nathan was the great-nephew and namesake of a former Confederate cavalry officer who had also been Governor of Georgia. Nathan himself was a well-respected associate professor of engineering at the Georgia School of Technology in Atlanta. He understood the realities of being far from home, but he also saw potential pitfalls for Charles. Frankly, Nathan was one of the few people who trusted Charles without hesitation. Other officers and many soldiers in the ranks were less confident. Charles's slight German accent, not strong but obvious, caused some to question his loyalties.

Charles Delacroy grew up speaking German at home. His father was a barber whose ancestors had fled persecution in France, emigrated east into Prussia, and then further to Poland. Charles grew up in the Russian-controlled city of Białystok, where he spoke and read German, Polish, and Russian before his family finally traveled west—to the United States. And after nearly thirty years in New Jersey, his English, though tinged with a hint of foreignness, was impeccable. As a result of his multilingual talents, he assumed the Army would send him to Europe. Alas, the rumors he heard of the military bureaucracy's silly decisions proved true. He had sailed to the Pacific as a member of MacArthur's staff.

However, as Charles sat with his Army buddies, his language skills presented him with a great opportunity and possible risk—his budding friendship with the beautiful and musically gifted Katya. If his relationship with Katya became serious, he might feel tempted to violate his religious convictions but, more importantly, Army regulations. And the fact that Katya was Russian—even if she was not a Soviet—created tensions. The US and Britain were at odds with Stalin's government which had failed to abide by the Yalta Agreement. In March, when Churchill espoused, an "iron curtain" divided the free west and the communist east in Europe, whatever trust had existed between most Americans and Russians vanished. So, befriending a Russian woman was not in Charles's best interest. Regardless, Katya's lure was enticing. He knew she was someone special.

Nathan told him, "She has you under a spell."

"Maybe," he answered, "but I don't care."

When she finished singing, Katya approached the men at the

crowded table and, without hesitation, sat in Charles's lap. His colleagues chuckled, and Charles flushed in embarrassment.

"Good evening, everyone," she greeted. "I hope you enjoyed the show."

"It was wonderful," one said, and they toasted her performance.

"Charles told me you will all be heading home soon. Is that true?" She directed her question at Nathan.

"Yes," he replied. "And I can't wait. It's been four years. I hope my school takes me back."

"You'll be fine, Nate," Charles assured him. "You gave the best, most comprehensive briefings of any of us. The college will be glad to have one of its best instructors back. I'm also wondering what my situation will be."

"We all are," offered the fourth man. "Who knows what to expect? I think I'll be safe because I was at an engineering design company, but still..." The comment wiped away the upbeat and carefree attitude the men shared moments earlier just as quickly as a busboy cleaning their table.

"Stop this!" Katya ordered. "You're smart, and you won a war. You'll be fine. I won't stay and listen to such, such, oh—such *chush.*"

"Chush?" Nathan asked.

"Yes, chush," she repeated. "Nonsense, drivel—or something like that."

"You're right, Katya," Charles consented. "We're speaking nothing but chush."

Infused with more than enough liquid spirits, the men giggled and babbled, "Chush, chush, chush." Their laughter made Katya laugh too.

Nathan stood and raised his glass. "A final toast—no more chushing!"

The friends stood, clinked glasses, and departed for their weekend to a rousing chorus of "No more chushing."

None were fit to drive the motor pool jeep, but fortunately, they spotted a corporal waiting for the public bus back to the barracks. He agreed to drive, but didn't tell the officers how much *he'd* had to drink. Once in the jeep, Charles relaxed and thought of Katya. Risk or not, he knew he would continue to see her.

⁂

When they met after church on the second Sunday in June, Yolanda invited Katya back to the Manalaysays' beach cottage south of the city. It was a two-hour ride to Laiya and a world away from Manila's hustle, crowds, and reconstruction. Humphrey drove, and the entire family was happy to see Katya when she arrived. Even Hector greeted her warmly, not quite satisfied at only being Katya's friend but accepting. It was hot, although a pleasant breeze provided relief while Yolanda and Katya rocked together in a large hammock beneath the palm trees.

"Tell me more about Charles," Yolanda demanded. "Do you think he's serious?"

They sipped on a cool drink while swinging in the hammock. Katya looked into the distance and shifted awkwardly to face her young hostess.

Typical of her occasional bluntness, Katya said, "He's married. Not only is he married, but he also has a teenage son. And, well…I don't know what to do."

"Oh, Katya, I'm so sorry. Have you…has he…well…you know…have you talked to the priest?"

"Heavens, Yolanda. There's so little you know about me. There were things I did to—to survive. Yes, just to stay alive in Shanghai. Things I'm not ashamed of, but things that priests, most men, and many hypocritical women would say have damned me to hell. As for Charles, well, I do want him. Badly. I need his comfort, his love, his touch, but before we…did anything…he pushed me away and told me about his family. I was too stunned to say anything and walked out. I haven't seen him or talked to him since. That was six days ago."

Tears slowly formed tracks down Katya's cheeks. Yolanda leaned over to hug her, but as she did, the hammock swung backward, and they tumbled to the ground, spilling their drinks. The unexpected flip broke the tension of their serious conversation, and they burst out laughing. Everyone who saw what happened also laughed, and Hector rushed to help them.

"Well, I needed a good laugh," Katya said, kissed Hector on the cheek, and thanked him for his assistance.

She suddenly wondered if a permanent life with him in Manila might be her only realistic option. Then guilt flashed through her head as she thought of Marcel. But she had tried to find him without success. What to do? Maybe she should try to join Darya's family in Australia. Or could she go back to Russia? At times, these thoughts overwhelmed her, but somehow they vanished as soon as her next plan or another handsome man found his way into her life.

"Changing the subject," Yolanda said, "it's time to eat."

Before they sat, Humphrey offered grace, thanking God and then his parents for their hard work, investments, and foresight, allowing them to have so much in the midst of so little for so many. Katya continued to suspect Humphrey's and Yolanda's parents had not been simple businesspeople. She also believed a close relationship with Señor Ortega required caution. In many ways, Ortega reminded her of Kuniaki, someone who manipulates others and skirts the law. So, Humphrey's grace sounded contrived to her ears, but Yolanda's sisters had prepared an excellent meal, and she enjoyed it.

Despite the temperature, they built a fire on the shore after sundown, and everyone took a turn telling a story. When it was Katya's turn, although her Tagalog was coming along, she spoke in English. She told them about her Valday bells and what winter was like in her hometown. A few minutes after everyone had their turn, she and Humphrey were heading back to the city without Yolanda, who decided to spend the night at the cottage.

"I'm happy Yolanda talked you into making the long drive today,"

Humphrey began after they had been driving for a while. "Everyone was glad to see you."

"Me too," Katya consented. "I'd almost forgotten what it's like to have a family. A real family."

"You're part of our family now, Katya."

"Thank you, Humphrey, but you know what I mean. I miss my cousins—one in particular. We were very close when I was a child, and I don't even know if he's still alive." She turned her head and looked into the dark night.

"What was his name? Your cousin?"

"Yuri. A good, fun boy. We did everything together, and he kept me from getting into even more trouble than I usually did. He loved to hear me sing, and it still gives me joy to think of him."

"You have a wonderful voice, Katya. I wouldn't be surprised if you get a recording contract. I know the word is spreading around the city about you. I think it's only a matter of time before the right promoter hears you."

"You're very kind, Humphrey. But I have no time for a promoter, and I'm sure the next disaster will come along and change my life again."

"Stop that, Katya! Look at all you've been through, yet still, you are here. You're like the great palm trees, swaying and bending during storms but continuing to grow and straighten over time. That is who you are, and you need to believe that."

Katya turned back to him and kissed him again on the cheek. "I'm glad you see me that way. Most men see something...else. It's that *something else* that has enabled me to keep going. And I don't think it has anything to do with my singing."

"What? Of course, it does," he countered.

"Well, okay. Perhaps a little," she laughed. "Now, get me home safely so I can be discovered."

On Sunday, June 30, Katya arrived early at church. She was so excited she didn't think she could remain calm. Things had happened so quickly and put her in a whirlwind. The night she returned from the Manalaysays' beach house, she found an envelope on the floor inside her apartment door. Her name was on it, and the handwriting was Charles's. She scooped it up and tossed it into the wastebasket. However, her curiosity was too great, and the letter remained in the basket for only seconds. Despite the late hour and wanting to sleep, she fixed herself a cup of tea and sat on the small old divan that filled one wall of her two-room flat. With her legs curled under her, Katya carefully unsealed the envelope and pulled out a single sheet of paper.

My Dearest Katya,

No words can express my regret for not telling you about Harriet and Albert. These years in the Army, so far away from them, often made me forget they existed. I have no excuse. However, you sparked new life in me, and I know I love you. Please don't stop reading. Something tragic and most unexpected happened after we were last together. I received a telegram from Harriet's sister informing me that Harriet had a heart attack and died. It left me stunned and full of emotions of every kind.

The Army denied my request to return home. I became very angry and informed my superiors how I felt. Nonetheless, I was told my department has a few more critical pieces to put in place before Philippine independence, and I am required to see them through. Because I could not go home, I asked my brother Bernard, and Albert, who's still in school, to take care of the funeral. As far as I can tell, they did. Not being home for Albert as he deals with the death of his mother bothers me tremendously, but the boy is strong, and I know my brothers favor him. But still...

So, now I come to the point. I repeat, I love you, Katya.

More than I have ever loved anyone. I feel the pain and guilt of Harriet's passing, yet there is a sense of freedom to express my love for you without guilt. I want to marry you, Katya. Please say yes. I will stop at Lunetta's to talk to you after work tomorrow.

With all my heart,
Charles

Katya sat without moving, flustered and overwhelmed. She stared out the window, searching for the moon, but it had not risen. She wanted to make a wish, ask her mother's advice, live a dream, honor her commitment to Marcel, and see her cousin Yuri. Yet, she also wanted to live a normal life. Was there such a thing? She wasn't sure. And Charles was older. Would the difference in their ages matter? He was fun, handsome, and educated. But he had a teenage son. What would Albert say? How could she be a mother, a stepmother, to a teenager she had never met? And so soon after Harriet's death. She knelt and prayed, just like Babushka had taught her. She stared at the sky and waited for God's guidance. Nothing came.

Sunday in church, Katya was so engrossed in praying she didn't hear or sense Yolanda enter and sit beside her. In the time she had known her, the Filipina woman had never witnessed Katya pray with such force and out loud. In Russian. Katya appealed to God to give her a sign about what to do. She was desperate for an ordinary life somewhere safe. What better way than to marry Charles and move to America? The United States! It was a dream she had never contemplated. Europe always made more sense. It was closer to home. To Russia. To her family, whatever remained of them. But the stories she'd heard about America…it was a place of wonder, wealth, and freedom. Endless freedom. Oh, how she wanted a Heavenly beacon.

She felt a gentle but sudden nudge in her side.

"Wha…what?!" Katya turned, startled, and saw Yolanda.

"Shhh, Katya. The padre has started," Yolanda whispered in Katya's ear.

"Yes, but Yolanda, I have something to tell you. I'm not sure I can wait till the end."

"I'm sure it can wait. Now be quiet. Today there's a baptism, and Padre Aguillar's homily is never long on days when he holds a baby."

"A baby? Today? A baptism? A new life? That's it. That's my signal."

"Katya! You must be quiet. It won't be long."

Katya raised her head and looked at the sky through the hole in the damaged roof and whispered, "Thank you, Lord. Thank you for such a wonderful signal."

Yolanda was right. Not forty minutes later, the mass ended, and Katya dragged her friend outside to their favorite spot under the trees.

"My goodness, Katya. What has gotten into you?"

"You'll never guess, Yolanda. Try and guess my news."

"Señor Ortega's friends agreed to pay you more for your singing."

"Oh no. Nothing like that. Something better."

"You received a letter from Yuri, and he's doing well."

"Nice try, Yolanda. And I wish that was true, but no. That's not it." Katya giggled with excitement as she let her friend continue to guess.

After several more attempts, Yolanda gave up.

"Enough!" she shouted. "Tell me this news. I won't guess any-more. I demand to know. NOW!"

"It's Charles. It's about Charles."

"Well—what about him? Come on."

"Charles left me a note under my apartment door," she blurted.

"Yes, the cad," Yolanda said. "He should have sent you flowers and candy and apologized for leading you on. Men, they only want one thing,"

"Well, yes. I suppose that's true, but, well, he did apologize. You're right about that part. But then he wrote that he loves me. And wants to marry me."

"Oh my, Katya. Many of these GIs have said the same thing to some of my friends. Who knows if they're telling the truth? They say that to get a woman into bed. And besides, Padre Aguillar would never marry you to someone already married. Even if he divorced, it would be a problem. No—you must forget him and move on." Yolanda made a strong case, but Katya kept talking.

"I know you won't believe this, but he told me his wife died suddenly of a heart attack." Katya stopped there, waiting for Yolanda's reaction.

There was skepticism written in Yolanda's large, caring eyes. "You don't believe that, do you?"

"Why would he lie about something so serious?" Katya retorted.

"Why? Are you kidding?' Yolanda rebuffed. "You can't be that naïve. He's just leading you on, so you'll sleep with him while he's still here. Then, poof! One day he'll be gone, back to his wife in America, and for all you know, you'll be pregnant. That's why." Yolanda gave Katya a stern look.

"No, Charles wouldn't make up such a story. He wasn't even allowed to go home to the funeral. His brother and Albert, his son, took care of it. Now, we're free to marry," she said with anticipation.

Yolanda softened her tone. "Oh, Katya, this is a familiar story, but…if you love him, you must find out if it's true."

"And how would I do that?" Katya asked. "If he loves me and is telling the truth, it could ruin everything if he learns I checked on him."

"Oh, I don't think so," her friend countered. "You have every reason to be uncertain and cautious. There have been too many cases, especially with the American GIs, where men lied about such things."

"Well, maybe you're right. But there's no way for me to check," Katya fretted.

"That's where you're wrong," Yolanda said. "I think Humphrey has the right connections. And if not, certainly Esteban does. I'm sure there's a way to find out."

Katya didn't want another failed relationship, thinking of Kuniaki and still uncertain about Marcel. But she also felt it was unethical and demeaning to go behind Charles's back. "No, I'll confront him myself. I'll know if he's telling the truth. And besides, I already told him yes."

And with that final word, she marched off toward her apartment, leaving Yolanda alone on the bench under the trees, shaking her head.

Later that evening, Charles called at her apartment and took her to dinner at the Army-Navy Club. He could tell she was not quite herself and began to prod.

"Katya, I can see there's something on your mind. Tell me."

She swished the swizzle stick in her drink and glanced around the room. Many couples, like her and Charles, local—or in Katya's case, a refugee and a soldier in uniform—were dining happily. Katya wondered how many soldiers and sailors were already married to someone else, and with children at home. How many of them were using their dinner dates for other reasons? She wanted to scream.

"What is it, Katya?" Charles repeated. "You can tell me."

"Yes. You're right. And if I can't, then nothing matters. Charles—did Harriet really die? Or, like so many GIs and swabbies away from home, am I just a temporary companion?"

The shock on his face told her everything she needed to know. It was a look of hurt and confusion no one could fake. Surprise and anguish cast a pall on Charles's face.

"Oh, my Katya. I never thought about the many examples right before my eyes. You're correct, of course. There are many lonely men here, and I was lonely, too. I know many of them lie, and some even have two families, one in the states and one here. That's more common among sailors who go back and forth on scheduled ship deployments. I understand why you are worried, but here—just today, I received this telegram."

He reached into the inside pocket of his uniform jacket and pulled out the yellow paper of a Western Union telegram. He opened it and passed it to her.

*CHARLES—ALL DETAILS AND PAYMENTS RE-
SOLVED RE: HARRIET BURIAL AND AL SCHOOL*
                                            BERNARD

Her English was not great, but Harriet's name and the word "burial" stood out. She looked at him and blushed with embarrassment.

"Charles. I'm so sorry. It's just that, well…I've been disappointed in the past. And marrying an American soldier and moving again, to another culture, meeting new people, I…I just had to be sure."

He took her hands and said, "I think we should have the wedding on July Fourth. The Philippines will gain its independence that day, the same as we celebrate in the United States, and we shall commit to each other for all eternity."

"Yes. July Fourth. So very American, for this Russian girl. I like it." They stretched across the table and kissed.

Other couples in the room noticed, and several single men clapped. When they did, Charles stood and clinked his glass with a spoon. The dining room became quiet.

"Thank you for your attention. I would like to make an announcement."

Katya tugged on his jacket to pull him back into his seat, but he resisted.

He boomed, "She said, yes! I'm inviting everyone to our wedding on July Fourth. We'll celebrate the Philippines, the United States, and our love for each other."

The room exploded in cheers, and arms raised glasses to toast the happy couple.

The *Daily Pacifican,* the Army's newspaper for the troops in the Philippines, reported pertinent international, US, and local news, as well as information on sports, out-of-town visitors, and other social activities of interest, like birth announcements, obituaries, and weddings. On Monday, July 7, in a small notice on its society page, the paper reported the following, with an accompanying photograph:

"July 4 was a grand day. Our country celebrated peace and 170 years of freedom, and the people of the Philippines cheered their independence. On a smaller scale but equally significant to its participants was the wedding of Captain Charles Delacroy and Miss Ekaterina Palutova. Captain Delacroy served with distinction on General MacArthur's engineering staff throughout the war, and Miss Palutova, now Mrs. Delacroy, is a talented singer of Russian heritage. Many also know her from her days with Henry Nathan's Orchestra at the Cathay Hotel and Ciro's in Shanghai. Señor Esteban Ortega gave the bride away, and a small group of family and friends enjoyed a fine meal at the recently reopened Manila Hotel. The beautiful bride says she couldn't be happier and is looking forward to the time when Captain Delacroy completes his duty in the Philippines and returns to the States. The groom merely smiled and said he was the luckiest man in the world. From the photograph, you may understand why."

The article provided no information about the origin of the bride's gown, leading several of Katya's acquaintances to suspect she borrowed it from Yolanda or it was a gift from Señor Ortega. Regardless, the Army sent copies of the article and photo to Charles's brothers in New Jersey. Something Charles never considered at the time.

11 MAY 1947 — SEPTEMBER 1947

New Jersey

Katya and Charles remained in Manila for nearly a year after the wedding. "Needs of the service" is what Charles told his family in New Jersey. He had received only two letters since the news of his marriage reached the streets of Weehawken and the halls of Stevens Tech in Hoboken. One was from the Dean at Stevens, who assured him his position still awaited him. The second was from his father, which arrived shortly before Christmas 1946. Charles hadn't received one letter from his father during his four years away, although his mother had written weekly until the previous June. The letter from his father was brief.

How could you? And to a Russian! No one wants you to come back.

Charles wasn't an overly emotional person, but the feeling of being cast aside by his family stung, and he wasn't sure what he could do to change their minds. Likewise, he didn't want to worry Katya, and decided not to tell her about the letter. It wouldn't change anything. His time on active duty was over and they were heading to the States.

When their ship docked overnight for fuel and replenishments in

Hawaii, Katya had declared her name would now be Kathy. She told Charles that, as a prospective American, she needed an American name. He smiled, hugged her, and hoped he would remember her new name.

"My father said the same thing when our family processed through Ellis Island," Charles told her. "He wanted an American name, and the immigration officials obliged. His birth name was— Herve Delacroix. But they pronounced it, Harvey Delacroy. So, his first name and the spelling of our family name changed, which suited my new American father just fine."

"I like your father already," she said.

He gave her a wan smile.

After two weeks at sea, two days in San Francisco, and five days on two different trains, they were coming into Pennsylvania Station in New York City.

"Oh Charles, I'm so excited," Kathy said. "This entire trip has brought back so many memories of when I was a little girl crossing Russia. And now, I've crossed an ocean *and* the United States. I can't believe I've come so far."

"And I'm so happy I could be the one to share *this* journey with you." He gave her a kiss as the train came to a halt.

It was spring in New York as they gathered their luggage. Rather than go directly to Charles's house across the Hudson, they took a hotel room.

"Charles, I'm surprised no one was at the station to greet you after four years," Katya said. "It looks like committees and friends welcomed the other soldiers and sailors."

None of Charles's brothers greeted them, and certainly not any of Harriet's family. Almost two years had gone by since the surrender of Japan, yet men still trickled home from Europe and Asia. Many, like Charles, had duties that lingered beyond the surrender or had "re-upped" their commitment.

"I'm not surprised, Kathy," he answered. "My brothers have busy lives and go to work early. We'll see them soon."

Kathy listened politely but was not satisfied with his response about the lack of a welcome home. "There's something you're not telling me, Charles. I can see it in your eyes. What is it? I can guess, but I want to hear you say it."

"Nothing. Really. Look, it's still early. Let's freshen up, and I'll take you to a great New York restaurant," he diverted again.

"You're beating bushes in circles," she answered.

He laughed. "It's not 'beating bushes in circles,' it's 'beating around the bush,' or 'you're going in circles.' Two different sayings."

They laughed. After more than a year together and lots of time spent with Americans, Kathy had greatly improved her English, but some idioms were still new or confusing. Regardless, through her giggles, she persisted.

"So, tell me, what's going on? No more hiding, or no fancy restaurant."

He took her hand and they sat on the edge of the bed. "Very well. My brothers are good friends with Harriet's parents and siblings. My family and theirs have been neighbors, living within blocks of each other for more than twenty-five years, and I've become the black sheep of the family."

"Black sheep? What is the problem with black sheep?" she asked him.

"Ah, yes. Well, black sheep are rare. They're not like the others; therefore, they're not welcomed by the rest."

She saw the pain in his eyes. "It's because of me, isn't it?"

He didn't answer.

"Because we married so soon after Harriet's death. They think I stole you away from her, and this is reason she died? Yes?"

"Yes," he conceded. "They don't understand. At the beginning of the war, I wrote Harriet frequently, but she hardly ever answered. Near the end, I wrote maybe once a month. In four years, I received only six letters from her. Is that how a loving wife treats a husband at war? As time went on…well, I don't need to explain to you how I feel. Neither family is happy I found someone else. No one will ever understand what it was like to be ignored by your wife while so far away." He lowered his head and added, "I never told Al, and I don't think anyone else did either."

"He'll understand. Don't worry."

She leaned in and kissed him—a long, lingering, I-love-you-like-I-never-loved-anyone-in-my-life kiss. He yielded, and soon any thought of an early restaurant dinner slipped their minds. Clothes splattered on the floor. Their lips and hands found sensitive body parts, and they responded in a perfect ballet of synchronicity that left them satisfied, on the edge of Nirvana.

When they finished and caught their breath, she looked in his eyes and said, "They will welcome me, or they won't. They will take you back, or they won't. I did not know them before, and you prospered without them while you were away. We have each other, Charles. We will be fine."

"Kathy…Oh, I do love you," he said.

They kissed again and found they had plenty of energy for another round. Their lovemaking was passionate and tender, and when they finished the second time, they gave up all thoughts of a restaurant and ordered room service.

The following day they awoke early. Kathy was eager to be a tourist with an American soldier husband in New York City. All the years in Shanghai, she had heard comparisons between the two cities. Now, she wanted to see for herself.

First, they went to Battery Park and the Statue of Liberty. Kathy cried more than almost any time she could remember. *I lift my lamp beside the golden door.* She kept repeating the words—Emma Lazarus's words—at the statue's base. She had *yearned to breathe free* ever since leaving Valday. She felt tingling throughout her body as she read the famous poem. She finally had her freedom. Charles had opened the golden door for her. How she wished Papa was with her.

After the Statue of Liberty, they went to mid-town and the top of the Empire State Building. She felt like she could see forever and remembered climbing trees when she was a girl and the view from Victoria Peak in Hong Kong. Lunch was at a Horn and Hardart Automat, where the food waiting to be *released* from behind the little windows captivated her. They were at the Museum of Natural History by two o'clock, and at five, they took a tea break at Tavern on the Green. Back to the hotel for a shower and change of clothes, then to the Imperial Theater on West 45th Street. They watched a performance of *Annie Get Your Gun* starring Ethel Merman as Annie Oakley and concluded the evening with a late dinner and dancing at the Copacabana. Exhausted, they tumbled into bed just before four in the morning. After two more busy days in New York, Kathy was ready to move on.

"Charles, this has been wonderful. You've shown me so much, but I'm ready to get to your house. Take me to New Jersey. Take me home to Weehawken."

"Yes, of course. It's time to face the music," he agreed.

"How do you face music?" she inquired. "I listen to music or make music, but face it?"

"It's another expression that means dealing with an unpleasant situation without waiting any longer."

"I think you are worrying too much, Charles. Like I said, either your family and friends will accept us, or they won't. I love you, and we can always find someplace else to live."

"I know. But my teaching position is here. My obligation with the Army Reserves is here. It will be an inconvenience to move. I'd have to sell the house. Where would Al live? My house is the only home he has known. It wouldn't be right."

"Oh, you stubborn man. We can put up with anything for a short while. And inconvenience? You make joke, yes? I have nothing but inconvenience since I was child. This is nothing. Your house, it has electricity?"

"Yes."

"It has running water?"

"Yes."

"It has indoor toilet?"

"Yes?"

"It has kitchen, bedroom, telephone?"

"Yes, yes, yes. Stop, I get it. Very well. Let's pack and go to New Jersey."

They checked out and grabbed a cab that took them through the new Lincoln Tunnel under the Hudson River to Weehawken. On the Jersey side, they found themselves at the top of the palisades. A couple of minutes later, the taxi stopped in front of a modest three-story home.

"This is it," he said.

They opened the car doors and stepped onto the sidewalk as the driver retrieved their suitcases from the trunk. They had only two. Charles had shipped home the souvenirs he collected and their other personal effects on a cargo ship. Those items were not due in New York for another two weeks. He paid the driver, and suddenly they were alone in front of the house. The street was quiet, and trees provided early-season shade.

"Oh, Charles. I love it. It's wonderful."

He smiled at her. "Thank you, my dear. But, as you shall see, it is quite ordinary. My oldest brother still lives here, and my parents and other brothers are within easy walking distance."

"Why is Bernard with you and not your parents?" she asked.

It seemed strange to Kathy that none of Charles's siblings lived with his parents as they aged. Especially an unmarried brother.

"Ha! The four of us have incredible independent streaks. That is, up to a point. It was Bernard who came first to America. He worked hard and saved his money. Although my father is very proud of him, Bernard disappointed him. Bernard had no interest in attending college to become a doctor or something else where he could earn lots of money. He likes being a machinist, but he and my father argued about it one day, and Bernard moved out. Oh, don't get me wrong, they still love each other. My mother cooks for him twice a week and does his laundry, but…he enjoys his room in this house. And for me, he helps with the mortgage. He's been a wonderful big brother. It, it…it's just that…."

He couldn't go on. He had every reason to believe Bernard would ignore him. Charles knew some traditions should never be broken. That's how the brothers had been raised. Since his wedding, he had wrestled with himself about what to do once he returned home. And now that he was on the threshold, he felt like a child again. Afraid of the unknown. Afraid of disappointing his parents and siblings. Fearful of being ostracized from those he loved.

"Stop sputtering," she demanded. "I married a soldier who fought the Japanese. A brave man. Stop fretting!"

He smiled again. Yes, he had been in real peril several times, had fired his rifle at the enemy, and had been in a plane that got shot down. But he had been quickly rescued and spent most of his war years in an office helping solve practical engineering problems. He did not consider himself battle-hardened like frontline troops and had seen little of the ravages of war except for the horrendous destruction in Manila. But Kathy forced him to look at his current situation through a different lens, which only aimed toward the future. A future with a beautiful and talented wife, no matter where they lived.

Charles took both bags, and they walked up the front steps. He put one down and searched his pockets until he came up with a key; moments later, they were inside. It was a house similar to millions of others throughout the country, yet its finishing touches made it home. Kathy admired family photos in the entrance hall, gazed up the staircase to quiet rooms above, and nodded approvingly at the décor of the parlor. He left the suitcases near the front door and led her down the narrow hall, past the coat closet, to the kitchen and a tiny half-bathroom. There was a refrigerator, a gas range with an oven, a sink, a table for four, and a backdoor leading out to a post-age-stamp-size backyard. She opened and looked out and noticed a vegetable garden took up most of the space. All in all, it was a lovely and comfortable home.

"I'll take our bags upstairs. We'll be in the room on the left," Charles said. "Bernard lives on the third floor, and Al's room is on the right. We all share the second-floor bathroom with a tub and shower."

⁂

Within an hour of entering the house, Kathy sat on the living room couch, flipping through old magazines while Charles went to buy groceries. He went alone because he anticipated judgmental eyes demanding an explanation for his new wife, and Kathy didn't deserve a rude welcome. He chose the long route to the grocery store, avoiding the likelihood of encountering his brothers and parents.

Several neighbors did see him and waved. Happy waves, he thought. And in the shop, he was greeted with a hearty, "Welcome Home, Mr. Delacroy!" from Josef Dulachoski. Charles had to do a double take, because when he left home in 1942, Josef was twelve. Now, at seventeen, he was as big as most men and had the shadow of a beard.

"Thank you, Josef. You've certainly grown, and it is nice to be home."

"Let me know what you need, Mr. Delacroy. Father put me in charge when he's not around."

"I will. However, I hope you're still in school."

"Yes, of course. School ended about forty-five minutes ago, and I help after. Just like always."

Before heading home, Charles made sure to buy some of Bernard's favorite items as a small gesture to thank his brother for helping with Harriet's funeral and caring for Al.

Shortly after six p.m., Bernard arrived home from work. As he entered the house, he shifted his eyes between Charles and Kathy when they rose to meet him. After the briefest eye contact, he deliberately lifted the photo of Charles and Harriet from the end table next to the easy chair. He said nothing, put the picture down, and walked to the kitchen. Charles followed him, with Kathy one step behind.

"You need to stay here," Charles turned and told her. "Let me talk to him." She was about to say something, but he put his finger to her lips. "No. Not yet. Please, Kathy. Stay here."

She returned to her seat, and Charles walked to the kitchen. She strained her ears to hear but could only make out an occasional word from Charles. As far as she could tell, Bernard said nothing. After a very few minutes, Charles returned.

"I thanked him for all his help, but he said nothing. Wouldn't even look at me. I asked about my parents, other brothers—not even a grunt."

"I'm sorry, Charles. Had I known…"

"It's not you. Well, not exactly you," he confessed. "It's like I told you. I didn't grieve for the required amount of time. It makes no difference that Harriet lost interest and didn't even write. But I can't tell them that. Harriet was a good person, Kathy, but…jeez, there's nothing I can tell my family to change things."

"Did you tell him about the food for dinner?"

A cynical smile crept onto Charles's lips. "Yes. His answer was a single, slightly raised eyebrow. I'll cook it anyway and leave it for him in the refrigerator. He'll eat it when we're not around."

They spent the next hour in the kitchen, cooking, eating, and cleaning up. The meal was delicious, and they stored the leftovers neatly and visibly for Bernard's easy access.

"Let's go upstairs and turn on the radio," Charles said as he dried his hands. "Listen to some music. Do some reading and go to bed. Tomorrow I'll go to my parents' house, check in with the others, and report at Stevens. Let them know I'm home."

Kathy saw his eyes brighten when he mentioned Stevens. She knew he was anxious to return to his academic responsibilities.

Thomas H. Brillat

"What do you suggest I do while you're out?" she asked.

"The most pleasant thing I can think of is walking along the palisades. The views along the river are impressive. Or you can take the streetcar to Stevens and meet me for lunch. I want to show you the campus."

"I can't wait to see Stevens," she replied sincerely. "In the morning, I'll tend to the house and meet you at noon for lunch. All settled."

They read, talked some more, and listened to a Mr. & Mrs. North mystery, followed by a Bert Lahr comedy, and concluded with music by Frank Sinatra.

"I can't believe there are so many stations," Kathy told him. "It's almost impossible to choose."

"Yes, I love the radio, but I'm ready to sleep," Charles said. "Want to have my wits for tomorrow." He clicked off the light on the nightstand, and she did likewise. Kathy was asleep within a few minutes, but he stared at the dark ceiling and wondered what the next day would bring.

They didn't get up late, but they weren't up with the birds either. The house was quiet, and Kathy guessed Bernard had left early to avoid her. However, she noticed the stack of leftovers in the refrigerator was not as large as when they went to bed.

"Well, at least he still likes my cooking," Charles quipped, and they laughed.

She cooked eggs and toast, and he made the coffee. After eating, Charles showered, dressed, and was off to work in minutes. Kathy was sweeping the kitchen floor a little before nine when she heard several thuds on the front of the house. She opened the front door in time to see three teenage boys sprinting down the block and broken eggs flowing down the door. The last boy turned back and saw her.

"Homewrecker!" he yelled and kept going.

258

Kathy closed the door and realized she was shaking. Many instances in her life should have caused her worry, but they hadn't. Yet here, in a comfortable, safe home in Weehawken, New Jersey, United States of America, with the Statue of Liberty almost visible from the upstairs windows, her heart raced, and she felt the hairs on her neck stand. A sudden wave of dizziness overcame her, causing her to reach for balance. The motion knocked the picture of Charles and Harriet off the table and shattered the glazing into pieces. Never superstitious, Kathy still wondered if the broken glass was a bad sign.

She sat on the couch, caught her breath, and tried to rationalize what had happened. She suspected the boys were Charles's two nephews and a friend, or maybe Harriet's relations. She had no idea, but the incident demanded immediate attention as soon as she washed away the egg mess and replaced the glass in the picture frame.

With clean-up complete, she ventured out for the glass and to track down the boys before lunch. Most of the streets ran perpendicular to one another, and compared to the warrens of Shanghai, she felt confident about not getting lost. Kathy carried her purse on a strap over her shoulder and put the picture frame in a paper bag she found in the kitchen. She walked in the direction the boys had taken off running, turned left at the first corner—north—and found a small hardware store within two blocks. Paint on the store's sign camouflaged some of its original words. Looking carefully, she saw they had been written in German. Inside, a man old enough to be her grandfather was behind the counter. He smiled and greeted her.

"Good morning. How can I help such a lovely lady?" He spoke with a thick accent. "I haven't seen you before. Are you new in the neighborhood?"

"Yes, I'm new here, and I need a pane of glass for this frame." Kathy didn't mention her name as she took the frame out of the bag and showed it to the elderly proprietor.

He smiled and nodded. "This is simple problem. It should not take me very long."

"Oh, thank you. I'm going to take a short walk and return in fifteen or twenty minutes. Will that be enough time?"

"Yeah, yeah. No busy."

She thanked him, stepped out to the sidewalk, and continued her walk north. Three blocks farther, she heard laughter off to her right and followed the sounds another block. The cliffs of the palisades were only two blocks ahead, and the voices grew louder. The noise came from the driveway alongside the next house on her right. There they were, three boys tossing a rubber ball against the brick wall of the house. She stopped on the sidewalk, and one of the boys turned his head and saw her. He caught the ball, and they got quiet.

"Good morning, boys," she called in her accented English. She guessed they were between twelve and fourteen years old. "A little while ago, someone threw eggs at the front door and windows of my house. I'm new in the neighborhood," she said, "and it surprised me someone would do that. I haven't even met any neighbors yet. You don't know who did it, do you? It was a nuisance to clean up."

They listened attentively, and then the biggest boy, but maybe not the oldest, said, "You speak funny. Not like people 'round here. Well, most of 'em anyways."

"Yes, people tell me I have an accent."

A second boy chimed in, "Yeah, my gramp talks funny too. He's from Poland."

"Well, I grew up in Russia and China. That must be the reason for my funny talk," she continued. "So, do you know who tossed eggs at my house?"

The boys shrugged and remained quiet.

"Well, if you're ever on Elm Street, between Park and Palisades," she said, "I bake cookies and could use good taste-testers." She waved, turned, and headed back to *her* house.

None of the boys ever came by for a cookie, but no more eggs were thrown at the house.

Kathy returned home in time to freshen up, check her purse for streetcar money, and head out to meet Charles for lunch and a campus tour. He had provided detailed travel instructions and was waiting for her when she arrived.

"So, my dear, how was your morning?" he asked. Before she could answer, he added, "Did you miss me?"

"Of course, I missed you. Now, give me the tour."

"First, I must show you off at the faculty dining room. Come along."

She took his arm, and he pointed out Humphreys Hall, Palmer Hall, the library, and more. The campus had a prominent location on Castle Point overlooking the Hudson River and exuded the feel of a modern but established institute of higher learning. Kathy sensed it was where serious research occurred and prepared young men and a few women to meet the world's technical challenges. She felt special walking with Charles, and more than a few heads turned as they entered the dining room. They joined a table with four others, and Charles made the introductions. He began with a man wearing a Navy uniform.

"Kathy, I'd like you to meet Lieutenant Commander Joshua Fleshman."

Fleshman stood, as had the others, and welcomed her. "It's a rare treat when such a lovely lady enters this humble dining hall," he noted.

"Oh, come now, Commander. I see at least half a dozen women at other tables," she answered.

"Yes. That's true, but none as lovely as the new Mrs. Delacroy," Fleshman continued. "Men want and expect their ladies to be desirable and beautiful. Isn't that right, gentlemen?" he goaded his colleagues. Slightly embarrassed, they agreed. Kathy saw Charles cringe the tiniest bit, but frankly, the attention was familiar, and she had always loved it. As for Fleshman's chauvinism, nothing new there either. It reinforced her opinion that he, and probably the entire Navy, had a long way to go before women would ever serve on ships.

"Thank you for the compliment," she said and slipped into her chair.

During the meal, Fleshman mentioned that Frank Sinatra had grown up a few blocks away. "He even does a show now and then on this side of the river. We should all go together," he suggested.

"That would be great fun," Kathy offered.

"Sure would," the man named Gary added. "Just don't know how to do it on an associate professor's salary."

"Me too," another said. "I'm in the same boat. Heck, why else would I be teaching the summer session again? But Charles— summer session's a perfect way to get you back up to speed."

"We've got family obligations," Gary responded to Josh. "Something you never think about. What's a single guy like you doing with us married folks anyway?"

"You know Gary, I ask myself that every day," Fleshman answered. "I'm waiting for Uncle Sam to make me an offer to work at the Navy Research Lab in DC. I've applied, and I'd be perfect for them."

"Good luck with that," Gary said. "My experience with the Navy bureaucracy tells me you could be waiting a very long time."

Charles had heard enough. He rose. "I promised Kathy I would show her the campus and my office. Please excuse us."

"Office?!" LCDR Fleshman laughed. "You're in a space no bigger than a closet like the rest of us."

"It may be small, but it's mine," Charles said.

He wanted to say that he had *earned* his office, unlike the often-brash naval officer. The story around Stevens was that Fleshman had been assigned to the tech school by the Navy to oversee a joint tow tank project at the beginning of the war. According to rumors, the Navy brought in a new director to replace Fleshman because he had done such a poor job. The Navy reassigned him as the project

Administrative Officer rather than give him a billet back in the fleet. All he did now was shuffle papers, and everyone at the table knew it. Regardless of his borderline comments, LCDR Joshua Fleshman tended to be easy-going; that is, when he wasn't sarcastic or caustic. Somehow people liked him, so Charles bit his lip, and he and Kathy bade everyone a good day.

Charles's office was tiny, but it was spic-and-span and orderly. More importantly, it was in the main engineering building, not the annex. The location put him close to his talented colleagues and their exciting research and inventiveness. Kathy felt a sense of pride walking the halls at his side. When they accidentally bumped into Alice Davis, wife of the long-standing president of the institute, the two women had an instantaneous connection. The brief meeting left a great impression on Kathy; she knew life as the wife of a Stevens faculty member would be a good one. As Charles escorted her back to the streetcar stop, Josh Fleshman saw them and gave a wave. He also yelled to them across the distance.

"I hope to see more of you, Mrs. Delacroy." Then he added with emphasis, "A lot more!"

During the next two weeks, neither Charles nor Kathy saw Bernard. They heard him come and go, but that was all. Charles called and knocked on his door multiple times and got no response. Food vanished from the kitchen, so they knew Bernard was eating at home, at least some of the time. It was an uncomfortable arrangement. Charles also went to see his parents and other brothers. He caught a quick glimpse of his mother through a curtained window, but no one opened the door or acknowledged him. He had never felt so rejected in his entire life. He garnered a little amelioration from the shopkeepers, barber, mailman, and casual acquaintances who remained cordial, but he felt more and more like an outsider.

For Kathy, the first two weeks at the house in Weehawken also included more campus visits for lunch, but they came with increased attention by LCDR Joshua Fleshman. After their third encounter, Kathy told Charles about Josh's more-than-informal attention.

"Oh, he's just enamored with you," Charles answered. "You should be flattered. I'm the lucky one, and he's jealous."

"I am flattered, Charles, but it's more than that. Wednesday, he told me I could have any man I wanted, and then he asked me why I chose you?"

"What did you say? Where was I?" Charles asked in rapid-fire succession.

"It was at the end of lunch. You went to get me correct change for the streetcar."

"Oh yes. So, what did you do?" he repeated.

"I wanted to hit him, Charles. It was crude and none of his business, but I told him the truth. I love you. Reason enough."

As Kathy said this, her voice faltered. She thought she had loved Kuniaki, and she was sure she had loved Marcel. Why did her voice quiver when she talked about loving Charles? Then she thought of Marcel and felt embarrassed and shocked. Charles didn't notice and went back to his paper.

"Charles, please," she urged, "talk to Joshua and ask him to stop speaking to me like that. I'm married, and he needs to look for someone else."

"Of course, dear. I'll speak to him," he said without raising his head from the newspaper and switched topics to his dilemma. "The bigger issue is, what can we do about Bernard, Louis, Normand, and my parents? It's eating away at me."

Rolling her eyes and wondering if he'd speak to Fleshman, she said, "Let me go see them." She offered her help for the hundredth time. "What do we have to lose? Once they get to know me, they'll see we didn't do anything wrong. And why don't you tell them about Harriet's lack of interest while you were gone?"

"They'll never believe anything bad about Harriet. They're too closely involved with her family."

He had been adamantly against Kathy's involvement with his family. Yet, maybe Kathy had a point. After all, what did they have to lose?

"Oh, I don't know, but what the hell. Why don't you try with Bernard when he comes home tonight? *If* he comes home tonight and doesn't go to Normand's."

Normand was the youngest and most successful of the four Delacroy boys. He owned a sizable home with great views of the Hudson and New York City but within walking distance of his siblings and parents. He had more than enough room for Bernard, yet despite all the space at Normand's, Bernard loved his third-floor aerie at the Elm Street house.

Here, Bernard had an attractive bedroom, a sitting space for reading and listening to the radio, a small table he used as a writing desk and for eating, a large closet, and a view of the river. It was his retreat. Yes, it got hot in the summer, but it was personal and quiet. So, although he was spending more time elsewhere since Charles returned from the Pacific *with that…that woman*, Bernard came home. He returned later than usual, hoping his brother and new sister-in-law had eaten and were upstairs listening to the radio. It surprised him when he found Kathy sitting at the table in the kitchen.

"Hello Bernard," she said. "Hope you had a good day. Can I fix you something? I made a pot of sausage, potato, and sauerkraut soup. To go with it, I also made an onion tart, and for dessert, there's apple cake."

Bernard, who had adored his mother's and grandmother's German-influenced meals, felt his stomach rumble as she told him the menu. He was starving. He'd stayed late at work and didn't stop to eat on the way home. He assumed he'd finish what remained of the brown bread and beans he'd eaten at five a.m. His mouth salivated, and he realized he must have run his tongue across his lips. He saw her smile.

Oh, dear lord, she's beautiful. He saw how Charles had been smitten. *But, but to deny your wife. Sweet Harriet. To disregard her death. To never write. It was unconscionable.*

And Harriet's family? They had treated all the Delacroy brothers like sons. Bernard groaned. He worked right alongside one of Harriet's brothers. What could he do? What should he do? He said nothing as Kathy prepared him a plate and spoke to him.

"You know Bernard, Charles adores you—the big brother who came early to America. The one who prepared the way for the family. The one who learned English and taught the rest. The one who saved and saved and helped your parents and brothers come over." She placed the plate of delicious food in front of him and poured him a cup of coffee. "It was you, Bernard, who motivated Charles. He told me you were the one who encouraged him to study engineering. Now he teaches it. You must be proud of him."

Bernard continued to stare at the food. She was right, of course. He had doted on Charles. He loved Charles as only a big brother can. They had so many things in common, unlike Louis and Normand, who seemed to have entirely different interests. They were so much more American than he and Charles.

Then why has Charles shamed us by marrying you? He thought to himself. *And you? You're from a culture with strong traditions. You certainly understand.* Arguing with himself, however, was getting him nowhere.

"Look at me, Bernard. In my eyes. I'm not evil. I did not steal Charles from Harriet. Do you know she barely wrote to him? Six letters in four years. None the last eighteen months. None. What kind of a relationship was that? I'm sure they loved each other once, but before I ever met Charles, it was over. But you and your family mean everything to him."

Bernard, who had been standing, avoided looking at her most of the time. *Oh, she smelled so good. And so lovely.*

He'd never been lucky with women. His sisters-in-law teased him that he was too old-fashioned and too set in his ways. He looked at Kathy and then down at the food. He picked up the plate, walked over to the wastebasket, and dumped it in the trash.

Then he said, "If his family means that much to Charles, then he'll send you back where you belong, and life will return to normal."

Then Bernard turned, left the kitchen, and went up to bed. Kathy never saw the tears pour from his eyes.

Returning home from grocery shopping one spring afternoon, Kathy shuffled around the mail on the foyer floor where it had been deposited through the door slot. After putting everything away she came back for the mail and flipped through it until one letter caught her eye. It had been sent airmail…from France.

With a little gasp, and with her shaking hands, she looked at the postmark. It had been stamped twice in France, both dates from early spring, 1946 and then several more times. First at the main post office in Manila and then at various Army locations and finally, in Weehawken, that morning. As tears filled her eyes she read the return address on the reverse: Henri Granger, 25 La Plaine, Châtenay, France. Ever so slowly, she slit the letter open, pulled out the thin piece of onion skin paper, unfolded it, and began to read. She stopped almost immediately. It was in French and she would need help. She folded it away and decided she would head to the French consulate in New York the next day.

Charles never noticed her unease that evening. The next day, Kathy was out the door soon after he left for work. At the consulate she met a pleasant clerk who gladly translated the letter.

Dear Ekaterina,

Please forgive me for being so informal, but I feel like I know you. We're glad that you are safe in Manila and we are most sorry for the death of your friend. Things are not much better here. Marcel had told us about you and we were so hoping to see you. Now, however, whenever you get this, you need to know...our dear Marcel was killed by the Nazis as a spy while working for the Free French Army and the Underground. This happened in November, 1943. We miss him desperately.

When he discovered your ship, the one you took from Shanghai, was sunk with all hands lost, he grieved for you very much. So much so, he volunteered to work as a spy. Ultimately, he gave his life for our freedom.

If you are ever in France, please come and visit. We know Marcel would only have betrothed a very special lady.

Sincerely and with love,
Henri and Sophie

Kathy thanked the clerk and made her way home in a fog. *They received the cable,* she realized. The one she sent via the makeshift French consulate in Manila while she was living with the Manalaysays. And it took fourteen months for her to get a response.

Oh Marcel. Marcel. Dear, sweet, brave Marcel. How I loved you.

She sat on the sofa and let the tears and memories flood her consciousness. She was at once relieved, no longer having internal battles about abandoning her search for Marcel, but also saddened for the loss experienced by the potential in-laws she never had. When she heard Charles at the door, she stayed put. She told him everything. Charles took her in his arms, held her and told her he loved her. She loved him the more for it.

The next day, she wrote a long letter to Henri and Sophie Granger and told them her story.

Al got a phone call in early June, a few days before his high school graduation.

"Hi Al, it's Dad. How are you?"

Al had received occasional calls from his father, so he wasn't surprised. "Hey, Dad. I'm fine. How are you?"

"We're fine. Kathy and I made it back to Weehawken in April, and I'm calling from an office in the Pentagon. I'll be in Washington for a few days doing some work for the Army."

The news shocked Al. His father had been in the States for two months and was just calling him now. As a child, Al never talked back to his father. However, having buried his mother and survived a tough military school for years without his parents, he couldn't hold back.

"You've been home for months and are just calling me now. Why didn't you tell me?"

Charles hesitated briefly and then told the semi-truth. "No good reason. I've been busy. Kathy needed help adjusting to a new country. Wasn't sure I wanted to talk about bringing a new wife home. Maybe I was ashamed. I don't know."

That was insufficient for Al, but he didn't want to get into an argument on the phone. "So why call now, Dad?"

"Kathy and I plan to come to Fork Union for your graduation," Charles said. "Find some accommodations for us for two or three days and call me with the details." He had easily switched back to his Army-officer-giving-orders voice.

Al said nothing.

"Did you heard what I said?" Charles asked.

"Yes…I heard."

"Very well. See you then. Bye, Al."

"Yes, sir. Bye." Al hung up, stared at the phone for several minutes, and tried to recover from the shock of the call. *Dad? Kathy?*

Coming here? For graduation? The whole thing surprised and irritated him. But then, he did what he had always done—followed his father's orders—and reserved them a place to stay.

Two weeks later, Al had no idea how he was supposed to feel when he met Kathy. How was he supposed to act? His father had married her. There was no crime in that. His mother, whom he loved deeply, had written him many letters at school. He was mature enough to read between the lines and knew things had not been great between his parents, even before the war. Regardless, it didn't seem right, what his father had done…but he decided to be as nice as possible to Kathy. At least on the outside. After all, he knew he couldn't change things.

As he came out the main doors of Hatcher Hall, Al saw his father and Kathy walking toward him. When they got closer, he recorded his first impressions of Kathy. *Knockout*, he thought. *Unbelievable.* Although Al's mother had been an attractive woman, his buddies agreed Kathy was nothing like Al's mother. Al figured that was a good thing.

By the time the ceremonies ended, he sensed Kathy was sad to leave, as if she wanted to stay and get to know him better. Being honest with himself, he realized they had hit it off, at least on the surface. Kathy felt the same and was grateful. Al had genuinely enjoyed her company and was fascinated by some of the stories she shared about her life. Notably, the last thing Kathy said to him was that she was proud of him, which made him feel special. Nonetheless, there had been awkward moments, and he remained confused about how to interact with her. He was also certain it was only because of Peggy that he hadn't created a scene with his father.

Al and Louise Margaret Key, "Peggy" to her friends and a descendant of Francis Scott Key, were smitten with each other. Some months earlier, during Christmas vacation, Al had gone to a classmate's home for a few days before returning to his uncles and grandparents in New Jersey. His friend introduced him to Peggy and her parents. Al returned to see her again at Easter, and he had invited Peggy and her mother to his graduation. Fortunately, the day was a pleasant affair for everyone, and Al never stopped thanking Peggy for coming.

⁂

The summer of 1947 flew by for Charles. He immersed himself in teaching and dusted off a few research projects he had set aside before heading out to help Uncle Sam early in 1942. For the most part, he was happy and did his best to convince himself he didn't need his brothers or parents. Bernard changed work shifts to reduce the likelihood of encountering Charles or Kathy at home and food in the refrigerator and kitchen cupboards became segregated. Somehow, the garbage also vanished through some random unscripted sharing of household chores. Toilet and bath times didn't overlap, and all three residents were sound sleepers and not disturbed by anyone's comings and goings. Kathy handled laundry for herself and Charles, and they assumed Bernard took his to Normand's house. As for Al, he went to Baltimore after graduation, stayed at his roommate's house, and went to work, temporarily, in Peggy's father's trucking business. Charles assumed Al was also keeping up on his academics in the evenings in preparation for his entrance into West Point.

However, life for Kathy seemed to move at a snail's pace. Most people she met were superficially indifferent toward her, and she yearned to make friends. It took her a while, but ultimately, she discovered Saints Peter and Paul Orthodox Cathedral in Jersey City. It was at the far southern end of the streetcar service, five miles and a forty-five-minute ride from home, but when she walked into the church for the first time, she felt like she was back in Harbin. Better yet, it reminded her of the cathedral in Valday. The familiarity provided comfort, and Kathy believed things would work out. She could never have imagined how wrong she was.

As the start of the fall semester approached, Charles expected Al would visit home before he set off to attend West Point. Charles looked forward to seeing Albert and hearing how he made out during the summer.

Three days before induction day at West Point, Al arrived home. It was nearly ten at night, but as he stepped into the foyer, he shouted, "Hello! I'm home!"

"I'm right here, Albert. No need to shout," Charles answered from the comfort of his chair in the living room, hidden from Al's sight behind the short wall which helped form the house's small foyer. He rose as his son entered, and when he saw the fit young man that was his progeny, he smiled, but the smile quickly faded.

"Where's your uniform?" Charles demanded. "You're allowed to travel out of uniform?"

"And it's good to see you too, Dad." The sarcasm rolled off Al's tongue without effort. "I'm not in the Army or anything, Dad. No more uniforms. Remember? I graduated."

Al's comment caught Charles off guard. After years in the Army and having seen Al at graduation, he hadn't expected to see his son in a civilian suit. But he gathered himself and thrust out his hand. "My goodness, of course, Al. Welcome home."

Once the handshake was out of the way, there were no warm hugs. Hugging was not something the men in Charles's family did, at least not his father or grandfather, so it was not part of his interactions with Al. Cordial, professional, and somewhat aloof nonverbal communication was usually followed by an exchange of neutral words. "Hello, Father" and "Welcome home, Son"—pro forma civil expectations.

Kathy was in the kitchen when she heard the front door and Al's voice. She entered the living room with a towel in hand in time to witness the uneasy greetings, but her presence broke the spell.

"Well, Albert, nice to see you again. How handsome you are in that suit. Which reminds me, I want to repeat what I said in

Virginia: I am very proud of you, and I hardly know you. Only a few stories your father shared."

"Thank you." *Keep it simple*, Al thought to himself. He couldn't remember the last time his father told him he was proud of him, but that was not something to dwell on at the moment. He put out his hand for a handshake, but she ignored it and hugged him. He blushed, but she couldn't see his face. When she stepped back, Al sputtered.

"Yes, well, I'm...I'm pleased to see you again too. And please call me Al. Only Dad and Mom call me Albert." It just came out. He didn't mean to mention his mother. But before he could register more embarrassment, Kathy spoke up.

"And you should call me Kathy," she said with conviction, eliminating his worry about how he should address her. "I am still so sorry about your mother, Al," she continued. "I never knew my mother, and I lost my father when I was about your age. It was awful."

He stared at the floor, and then got ahold of himself and looked in her eyes. *Oh my God. She is beautiful and doesn't even look twenty-five. And she's my stepmother?!*

At last, he answered, "Thank you. Yes, it was hard. Uncle Bernard was a big help, and so were my grandparents. I can't wait to see them. Are we all getting together on Sunday as we used to, Dad?"

Charles ignored the question and said, "It's late. Let's get some sleep, and we'll catch up in the morning and discuss plans."

Al was tired too, but wanted to know why his father didn't give him an answer. Nonetheless, travel weariness won out, and he said goodnight and went to the bedroom he had rarely slept in during the past six years.

"So, what are you going to tell him?" Kathy asked after she heard Al close the door to his room.

"The truth, of course. What else can I do? I'm not going to pretend things are the same. Besides, I'm not worried about Al. You saw his reaction. He's smart and understands things. I think you two will get along just fine. I only hope his relationship stays the same with the rest of the family." And that was the last word. He put his paper down and went upstairs to bed.

Kathy, however, wasn't so sure. She remained downstairs and went back into the kitchen. In the months since she arrived in Weehawken, they had rarely seen Bernard. From the reception she had from neighbors, it was also evident Charles's brothers and Harriet's family had influence within the community. She knew Charles would be devastated if Al took the same path as the rest of the family, so, for no other reason than to help Charles, Kathy was determined to make her relationship with Al work.

The three sat around the breakfast table making chit-chat, but Al became impatient.

"So, what are the plans for the day? I'd like to see Oma and Opa."

"Sorry, Albert," Charles answered. "Uncle Norm left a note that your grandparents and Uncle Bernard have gone to see friends on Long Island for a few days. How about we do something else?" Before Al had a chance to say he'd like to see Gram and Gramp, his other grandparents, his father kept talking.

"What do you say we do something special? Like this." Charles bent down and reached under the table.

"My goodness, Charles! What are you doing?" Kathy asked.

After a brief moment, Charles sat up and produced an envelope in one hand. He had taped it to the underside of the kitchen table after everyone was asleep the previous evening.

"What's that?" Al was curious and couldn't remember his father ever doing something so unusual.

Charles passed the envelope to Kathy. Inside were four tickets to *Brigadoon* at the Ziegfeld Theater that afternoon and a reservation slip for four at the Russian Tea Room for dinner.

"A Broadway show and the Russian Tea Room? Oh Charles, how wonderful!" Kathy was excited.

Al was a bit more circumspect. "Okay. What's the deal, Dad?" he asked. "The show—sure, sounds like fun, and we've gone before, but the Russian Tea Room? Fancy, indeed."

There wasn't anyone in Weehawken, Jersey City, or Hoboken who didn't know the Russian Tea Room was one of the best food and cultural experiences in New York City.

"Not now, Albert. I'll share everything with both of you later."

"And who's the fourth ticket for?" Al asked.

"In a moment," his father answered. "I just want us to have a day to remember."

And it sure turned out that way.

⁂

"Maria Krenkel?!" The name caught Al off guard when his father told him who he had invited to be the fourth.

"What's wrong with Maria?" his father asked. "You always liked her."

"I don't think I've seen Maria more than twice in five or six years. We were both twelve, maybe thirteen, when I went off to school. People change in five years."

"If nothing else, it will be a fun reunion," Charles said. "I saw her mother two weeks ago and extended the invitation. She said Maria works part-time at Macy's on the weekends and doesn't have a steady boyfriend."

"My goodness, Dad! But what about me? Who did you think Peggy was?"

For a moment, Charles was flummoxed. He had assumed Al would want to see Maria, but more importantly, he had never considered Al might have a regular girlfriend. He had forgotten about Peggy.

"This is not a problem," Kathy joined in. "It's only for a few hours, and it will be a treat to go to a show and dinner. It's also nice to know at least one family is willing to engage with your father and allow their daughter to go with us."

"What are you talking about?" Al didn't understand.

"You need to tell him, Charles," Kathy nudged.

"Tell me what?" Al asked.

Charles gave a slight nod, swallowed, and told him. "Your aunts, uncles, grandparents—on both sides—and cousins want nothing to do with Kathy or me. They're calling Kathy a homewrecker and me a philanderer. They won't speak to me, look at me, or have anything to do with us, and many people in town seem to agree. It's awful."

Al looked at them and shook his head. "I guess I have been away a long time," he started. "You know, Dad, when you told me you remarried, I was shocked and heartbroken. I couldn't believe it. At first, I wanted to punch you in the nose. And Kathy, well, on graduation day, I prayed you would be, oh...arrogant and unlikeable. But you were the exact opposite. You treated me like a grown man, and you were very gracious. Inside, I didn't want to like you, but I could tell your condolences about my mother were genuine. So, at that moment, I decided there was nothing I could do about the marriage, and therefore, I may as well do whatever I could to get to know you and support Dad. However, I don't know what to think concerning this news about my uncles, cousins, and grandparents."

Kathy made a slight cough and got the attention of both men. "I think Al should get in touch with whoever he wants and see what they have to say. I can't imagine them holding Al responsible for the two of us falling in love."

Without waiting for his father to add anything, Al responded, "Yeah. I can deal with it."

"Of course, you can," Kathy said. "So, let's think about today?" She looked at Al, and he understood their meaning.

"Okay, about today," Al started. "It would be nice to visit with Maria," he conceded. "I'll be fine."

"There you go, Charles," Kathy gleamed. "You, Harriet, and that school where you sent Albert made him into a fine young man with manners and understanding."

Charles didn't acknowledge the compliment but said, "I told Mrs. Krenkel we'd pick Maria up an hour before showtime."

They went by taxi to retrieve Maria, and when Al rang her door-bell she opened it seconds later. To please his father, Al wore his uniform and, being a well-trained gentleman, he had also purchased a corsage for her. He nearly dropped it when he saw her. He wasn't exactly sure when he had seen Maria last, but she had most definitely *grown up*.

"Uh, hello, Maria. You-you-you…"

"It's good to see you too, Al. I can't believe we missed each other whenever you were home these past few years. I was sorry to hear about your mom."

"Uh, yeah, well, thank you, Maria. And it *is* good to see you."

"What's that in your hand, Al?"

He had to look down at his hand to remember. "Oh, it's for you. Thought you might like a corsage for tonight."

"It's lovely, Al. Thank you. Can you please pin it on my coat?"

"Oh, yeah. Sure. I mean, yes, of course." Al had to get close to Maria to pin it on, and the proximity reinforced the observation that she had, indeed, grown up. There were noticeable curves under her coat, and she smelled good, too. Any thoughts of Peggy were far from his mind. He only stabbed his finger twice before succeeding with the corsage and stepping back.

"Mom—Dad—we're leaving," Maria yelled into the house. "Al gave me a corsage, and it's beautiful."

Before he could escape, both of Maria's parents arrived at the door. Mr. and Mrs. Krenkel doted on their only daughter. They knew Al was a good boy, a hard worker, and had done well in school; they felt their daughter was safe with him. The fact that Charles and his new wife would be with the young couple, regardless of the talk around town, also put them at ease. Likewise, neither of them had paid much attention to Charles's new marriage and recognized Al had nothing to do with it.

"Good evening Albert," Mrs. Krenkel said in her thick accent.

"Good evening Mrs. Krenkel, Mr. Krenkel. It's nice to see you again."

"And you as well," Mr. Krenkel added in Polish.

"Yes, you too," Mrs. Krenkel said in English as she elbowed her husband and whispered, *"English."*

With well wishes for a good evening, the Krenkels said goodbye, and in a flash, Al escorted Maria to the taxi. The four passengers made small talk during the ride into Manhattan, and Al felt very lucky to be squeezed between Maria and Kathy while his father rode up front with the driver.

They enjoyed the show and were through the appetizer course at the Tea Room when LCDR Fleshman unexpectedly came in with someone else Charles recognized. On the Navy man's arm was Louise Litvinova, Harriet's cousin. Louise's mother had married into a family of Russian aristocrats who persisted in trying to bring back the Romanovs. Louise was every bit as lovely as Kathy but ten years older. She and Charles had gone to public school together in Weehawken, but Louise grew up with an air of superiority because of her father's pedigree. Charles found her oppressive and condescending, but he never spoke about it, and Kathy had never met her.

"My, my. What a coincidence?" Josh boomed when he saw Charles and his family across the room.

Kathy rolled her eyes when she heard the voice. She had had her fill of the pushy, arrogant naval officer decked out in his dress uniform. *Like a Christmas tree in November,* she thought to herself. *Mere decoration and way too soon.*

Ever the gentleman, Charles responded. "How nice to see you, Commander. And Louise, you look wonderful tonight."

Louise looked at Kathy, skipping the niceties, and exclaimed, "And I suppose this is the Chinese homewrecker? But she doesn't look Chinese."

Kathy leaped up to say something, but Charles stood and blocked her from reaching Louise. People at several nearby tables turned to look, while others turned away.

"We've been having a most delightful evening. Thank you for letting us continue," Charles said and showed his back to Fleshman and his cousin Louise as he and Kathy sat back down.

"I always knew you were a coward and philanderer," Louise chirped.

Charles pretended he didn't hear her as Maria watched in quiet horror. She wanted to hide under the table. Albert, however, couldn't stand by and say nothing.

"What the hell do you know, *Aunt* Louise? Where were *you* when my mom was sick? Where were *you* when the Army denied Dad permission to come home for the funeral? As a matter of fact, I don't even recall seeing you at the funeral. Leave us alone."

"Where are your manners, boy?" Josh demanded. "You don't talk to a lady like that."

Before he could stop himself, Al said, "If she were a lady, she wouldn't go out sloshed in public. No less to a nice place like this."

Al only stated the obvious. It was apparent to everyone Louise was more than a bit tipsy, and Charles knew why. Josh was a manipulator with a nasty streak. He knew Fleshman had only one objective that night: to get Louise into bed. Charles was certain the Commander had encouraged Louise to drink. It was well known that Cousin Louise had a soft spot for alcoholic refreshment.

Unfortunately, Al didn't bite his tongue—the words had come out, and LCDR Fleshman lashed out and slapped Al across the face. The hit caused Al to stumble backward into a nearby diner. Not believing what he had just witnessed and finding a paternal protective streak he didn't realize he possessed, Charles grabbed Fleshman by the shoulder, spun him around, and punched Josh with a solid right to the jaw. Charles was shaking his fist in pain when the manager and a king-sized bouncer navigated their way to the table.

Picking himself up off the floor, Fleshman responded like a child. "Delacroy, wait till the Army hears about this. And wait till Stevens hears about the lifestyle of your so-called wife. She's been making eyes at me since the first day we met."

Keeping her cool, Kathy rose and addressed the women diners in the restaurant. "Ladies, may I have your attention? Would you make a pass at a naval officer whose superiors are afraid he'd sink his own ship? Or would you rather be with a Purple Heart Army veteran from General MacArthur's staff, who is also an engineering professor at Stevens Tech? Someone like my husband." Then she turned to Fleshman. "I mean, seriously, *Lieutenant* Commander, the thought of me making eyes at you is preposterous and makes me sick." Facing the other diners again, she asked, "So, ladies?"

Most of the people in the restaurant wanted no part of the dispute, but what consensus there was tilted vocally in Kathy's favor. While Kathy was playing to her audience, Maria turned to Al and whispered if he could call a taxi for her to get a ride home.

"I'm sorry, Al. It was good to see you, but I see I'm in the middle of something."

"Yes, of course, Maria. I'm sorry too. I'll be right back." As Al began to walk away, Charles asked him where he was going, and Al told him.

Kathy overheard and immediately turned to Maria. "Please stay," she said. "They're likely to need witnesses to explain what they saw."

"Witnesses?!" Josh Fleshman cried. "Everyone saw him hit me. Unprovoked! And that deserves a rebuttal."

Josh was back on his feet quicker than expected. Embarrassed and angry, he grabbed a wine bottle from the table and took a stride toward Charles. At that point, Fleshman raised his arm to hit Charles with the bottle—but the bouncer wrapped his thick hand around Josh's wrist and gave a twist. A searing pain shot up Josh's wrist to his shoulder, his hand opened, and the bottle fell to the floor.

"Thank Heaven," the restaurant manager said as the police entered the room.

***

The situation at the precinct station wasn't much better. The only good news was Maria Krenkel was allowed to leave as soon as she finished giving her statement. Charles graciously offered to pay for a cab ride home rather than alarm her parents by having her show up in a police car. She gave Al a quick peck on the cheek and wished him well. As for Al, he felt pretty sure he'd never see Maria again.

Corralled into the precinct lieutenant's office, Fleshman and Louise continued their claims of injustice and demanded to file charges.

"Please, please," Lieutenant Molloy raised his voice, forcing Josh and Cousin Louise to get quiet and then he addressed them. "Not only did the five of you ruin your evening, but you ruined it for the other one hundred and seventy people in the main dining room. Now, one at a time, and only when I ask you, I want you to tell me what happened. Young Mr. Delacroy—Albert, is it? You may begin."

They each told their side, and Fleshman was the last to speak. "I don't care what any of them said. I'm filing assault and battery charges against *Mister* Delacroy. Where's the fucking paperwork?"

Without warning, the lieutenant slapped Josh, twice as hard as the Commander had hit Al in the restaurant.

"You know, Fleshman, you have no manners," Molloy said. "There are women present, and I won't permit you to talk like that. And you know what else? I had a jerk department head like you on my ship during the war. Always blaming somebody else for his mistakes. If I sent our military cadet here back to the restaurant, I suspect he could bring in a dozen or more witnesses. And I bet they'd all tell me that *you* struck first. So, let's skip the charges." He turned to Charles and Al and asked, "However, do either of *you* want to file charges?"

Charles immediately responded in the negative, but teenage exuberance and anger got the better of Al once again. "I want him to repay my father for our dinner tonight. And I want him to send an apology to my date, Maria Krenkel, and her parents. That's what I want."

Kathy added her own two cents. "Lieutenant, is there any way to keep this man from bothering me? From spreading untruths about me? His accusations are hurtful and likely to impact my husband's position at the college."

"Well, Mrs. Delacroy, you can file for a restraining order. However, it takes a lot of paperwork and requires evidentiary proof of harassment. If your encounters have all been without witnesses, it becomes one person's word against another's. Judges don't like that. As for the college, it has its own set of rules and standards. I'm sorry."

Kathy was ready to threaten Fleshman herself but held back. She thought the man's jealousy, arrogance, and fundamental mean streak deserved punishment. But deep down, she didn't force the issue because she feared blackmail. Kathy believed the Navy man had discovered the truth about her past in Shanghai. She didn't know for sure, but his remarks in the restaurant indicated he did.

She finally nodded her head and said, "Thank you, Lieutenant Molloy. I understand. May we leave now?"

"No, Kathy!" It was Al. "This—this poor excuse for an officer needs to pay for destroying our evening."

"Listen, kid," Josh began, "if you were my son, you'd be feeling my belt across your ass. I'm not paying zilch. Come on, Louise. Say something," he demanded. "You were part of this too."

"I…" She hiccupped. "I tol…told my side…"

"Oh, good grief. You're fu…you're useless," Fleshman complained.

"Stop!" Molloy's order was definitive. Al looked at the floor as Louise sunk into a chair, nearly asleep. The lieutenant made a decision and turned to Fleshman. "LCDR Joshua Fleshman, I'm charging you with disturbing the peace and causing a commotion. You can pay a one hundred dollar fine or fight it in court. Your choice."

"What? You're *what?!* You can't be serious. This is bullshit." Fleshman's face turned scarlet.

Another slap shut Mr. Navy up.

"You really do need some training," the lieutenant mocked him. Then he added, "and some discipline." He turned to Charles and said, "Delacroys, you are free to go. Hope tomorrow is better than this evening."

"Thank you again, Lieutenant," Kathy said with appreciation. "We wish you the same."

"Yes, Lieutenant. Thank you," Charles added, and they walked out.

As they went down the hall, they heard Fleshman bellowing, followed by a *thump* sound.

"Ha! I know that sound, Dad. Solid, right to the gut!" Al chuckled the rest of the way home.

<hr/>

Charles and Al sat in the kitchen drinking coffee while Kathy fixed a traditional Russian breakfast the following morning. Charles tended toward the serious side with most things, but all three were chuckling over what happened to LCDR Fleshman at the police station.

"He deserved it, Dad. And a lot worse." Al was still a bit gleeful. "So did Aunt Louise—always on her high horse."

"I agree," Kathy chimed in. "Mr. Fleshman is quite a cad, and frankly, he was beginning to get on my nerves."

Charles smirked but was more lenient. "When I first met Josh, the Navy had just dumped him from the action side of the project. After a while, I recognized he had some decent administrative skills and thought he would work out in that capacity. But, well…his private behavior, away from work, never did sit very well with me. I'm sorry, Kathy, for not being more forceful with him. Can you forgive me?"

"I'm fine, Charles. I don't think he'll give us any more trouble. Now, here you go." She passed out plates of syrniki and sausages.

"This is fantastic, Kathy," Al said. "Wish we had food like this at school—or, maybe not. I would have become fat. What are these pancake things? They're fantastic."

"Why, thank you, Albert. The pancake *things* are syrniki, made with farmer's cheese. You can add honey, syrup, sweetened sour cream, or whatever, depending on your preference. My grandmother used to make them for me," Kathy said with a big smile. "I wonder what you'll be eating at West Point?"

"Who knows?" Al answered quickly, wanting to change topics.

"Yes, Albert. You haven't mentioned a thing about West Point," his father chimed in. "You must be a bit anxious. Don't worry, son, I know you'll do great."

Al toyed with the food on his plate, lifted his head, straightened his back, and looked into his father's eyes. "I'm not going to go to West Point, Dad."

There, I said it, he thought and breathed a sigh of relief.

"What?! What do you mean? You did all that work, we both did, to secure you an appointment to—"

Al interrupted his father. "Yes. That's true, Dad. But I have no intention of being a soldier unless I get drafted. I gave this lots of thought. Lots. Especially since the end of the war. After the war ended, you still didn't come home…and I…I have no desire to spend my life moving from one place to another every few years. I don't want to have a family and leave them. Sorry, Dad, that's how I feel."

Charles was stunned beyond words. Every decision he had made at Stevens and in the Army, and his negotiations to get Albert into one of the finest military prep schools in the country, had been to ensure his son a future as an officer in the United States Army.

"But an appointment to West Point! It's precious," Charles argued. "It will guarantee you a good life, and people will respect you when they learn you're a United States Military Academy graduate. There's no way to describe the lifelong benefits of such an education and experience. You must go." He made it sound like an order.

In a respectful but quiet and determined voice, Al answered, "No, Dad. Thanks for all your help, but I've already had six years of army life. That's enough, unless Uncle Sam comes looking for me. Then I'll do my duty. In the meantime, I've gotten pretty good with the camera you gave me for Christmas a few years back, and I plan to become a photographer. Hopefully for a newspaper. Lots of action. Good chance to meet people."

Charles didn't know what to say. Kathy could see Charles was devastated by Al's decision. He was so proud when Al received the appointment to the Academy that he had bragged about it to everyone at Stevens and all his army friends at Reserve meetings.

Kathy filled the silence. "Al, did you give any thought to other colleges and universities? I'm sure your grades and activities are good enough to get you admitted to many of them."

"Yes. I've already applied to the New York Institute of Photography. I'll be going there part-time and working part-time."

"So, your mind is made up?" Charles asked.

"It is." Al paused, then added, "The meal was fantastic, Kathy. Thank you, I look forward to having more." He stood, left the kitchen, and climbed the stairs to his room.

Charles remained quiet. It dawned on Kathy that father and son were remarkably similar. She wondered if she was more like her father or the mother she never knew. Probably a bit of both, of course.

On Monday, Al ate a quick breakfast and departed the house early. He left a note saying he was heading to NYIP to register and would be home around dinnertime. When Charles came downstairs to eat, Kathy put out coffee for him, but before he had a chance to read the note from Al and get upset again, she brought up another topic. She told Charles she needed something to do to help contribute financially to the household. Charles, a traditionalist, balked at the idea.

"There's plenty to be done just taking care of the house," he argued. "I make a decent salary. You don't need to work."

Nonetheless, Kathy persisted. "I know we don't *need* me to work, but I've always worked and am used to it. It makes me feel worthwhile, and a little extra income means we can save for vacations or a television."

Charles listened attentively and knew she was serious.

"Besides," Kathy continued, "what I have in mind is more like project work and not a daily job."

She told Charles she wanted to see if she could get hired as a model. She had done it in Harbin and, except for Kuniaki, had enjoyed it. She had considered singing again, but working nights was no longer something she wanted to do.

"Modeling?" Charles questioned her choice.

Not only did she want to go to work, but he was positive her choice of employment would only deepen the separation between him and his family. Charles knew Kathy was attractive and would likely get hired, but modeling had a reputation. Not quite like acting, but almost—it was said that modeling was a job where photographers, magazine publishers, and others expected women to provide sexual favors if they wanted assignments. He had no idea if that was true, but it didn't matter.

"I'm not a stay-at-home housewife, Charles. You know that," Kathy stated a fact. "You knew it when we married. I need to be out and about, and this is something I can do. And like I said, wouldn't it be nice to have, what do they call it...yes, dispensable income?"

"It's *disposable*, but where'd you get this idea?" he asked. "There are many other things you could do."

"One Sunday after church, I was talking with Olga Babinova. You know Olga, she's the one whose family had the little restaurant near the Kremlin. Anyway, she told me I have *the look*."

"The look? What's that?" Charles wondered.

"She said I have natural beauty. I think many people do, but she said I have the kind other people like to look at."

Charles laughed.

"Why are you laughing?" Kathy implored. "I'm serious."

"Of course, but I'm laughing because it's true," he answered. "You attracted me, didn't you?"

"Oh, stop it, Charles. Anyway, Olga said, even if I didn't make it into the fancy magazines, so what? She was positive I could model for the department stores and catalog companies, be on calendars, and maybe even billboards. I told her I'm thirty-two and might be too old. She said Lisa Fonssagrives, one of the most sought-after models, was thirty-five when she began modeling. So that's how it started."

When she finished, Charles knew he couldn't fight her. He didn't want to cause a rift and acquiesced. Kathy wrapped her arms around him and thanked him with a kiss.

"Now, here's a note from Albert. He's off to that photography school," Kathy stated.

"I don't want to talk about that, Kath. I need to change his mind. His entire life, he'll regret not going to West Point."

Charles was stern yet despondent. He had used every contact he had and did all he could to encourage and guide Albert through his school years while being thousands of miles away. However, his efforts had not been enough, and he wondered what he could have done differently.

Kathy was about to say something else, but he raised his hand.

She stopped, and they changed topics to the news. He ate quickly, went upstairs, dressed, and left for the office in a huff. Charles had been off the campus for nearly two weeks between the summer and fall terms, and if he was honest with himself, he was glad to be back. He enjoyed teaching, interacting with the students, and working on research projects. Taking a break was anathema to his make-up, but when he arrived at his office, he found a message from the dean of the engineering department requesting to see him before he began his day. Charles walked into the dean's office, and before he could say good morning, his boss spoke.

"Hello, Delacroy. I'll make it quick. You're on probation. The college can't abide by its faculty getting into fisticuffs in public, even if you were on your own time. If no other incidents occur during the next year, no further action will be taken. That's all."

"I'm *what?!* I can't believe this." Charles was stunned. "Don't I get a hearing? Don't you even want to know what happened?"

"I know what happened. You struck Fleshman, and that's all I need to know. Now, get to work. We have a busy semester ahead."

"What about—" Charles wanted to ask what the consequences had been for Fleshman, but he caught himself. He'd heard a rumor the Navy man had paid for damages in the restaurant and left the police station without being charged with anything. Charles blamed himself for being lenient rather than filing charges. He also had no idea what action the Navy or Stevens had implemented against Fleshman. However, the only thing that really mattered was finding himself on probation, which angered him beyond belief. What would he tell Kathy? Then he realized he didn't need to tell her anything because he wouldn't get into another such incident. Regardless, he knew, at best, the probation period would delay tenure, and at worst, he would need to seek employment elsewhere. He was furious, but he kept quiet like a good soldier—or untenured faculty member.

In his office, Charles sat thinking when a voice echoed through his small cubby and the door opened without a knock.

"You should never have hit me, Charles," Fleshman gave him an arrogant smile. "What goes around comes around. Enjoy the next year."

"You never should have hit my son. And what are you talking about?"

"Come off it, Charles. You play with fire, you get burned. Don't mess with me again."

"You know my former boss General MacArthur knows all the admirals, Josh. Even lieutenant commanders can lose their stripes. Now get out!" Charles stood, took two long steps toward the door, raised his arm—and slammed the door in Fleshman's face, but not before seeing Josh flinch.

"We'll see who gets promoted and who doesn't," Fleshman yelled through the oak barrier and sauntered away, laughing.

Charles sat shaking in his chair, not believing he had eaten lunch regularly with such a jerk. Even when the flak from anti-aircraft guns sprayed all around the transport planes he rode during the war and the certainty of death seemed imminent, he had never been so outraged. He had never believed LCDR Joshua Fleshman was petty and vindictive until that very moment.

What a poor judge of character I turned out to be, he finally admitted to himself. *And it would be a miracle if General MacArthur even remembered my name.*

He considered rounding up witnesses to the incident at the restaurant but knew it would be futile. He *had* punched Fleshman. And he was glad he did.

But a year on probation? It seemed like a death blow to his academic and military careers. He supposed he could work at one of the engineering firms in New York City, but he enjoyed teaching *and* serving in the Army.

"What a fucking mess," he mumbled quietly, cursing himself for his lack of restraint.

Within a few days of discussing her modeling plans, Kathy submitted applications to New York's two largest firms, Barbizon and Powers, and added a third, a new agency called Ford Models. Unfortunately, none of them would accept her paperwork until she submitted photos, full-length and headshots. However, hiring a professional photographer was not in the Delacroy household budget.

Nonetheless, Kathy had no intentions of being deterred. A congregation member of her church took photos throughout the year for the church scrapbook. She didn't know if he was a professional, but she had seen his photographs, and they were good. The following Sunday, she approached him and made a deal. Kathy offered to pay him for his film, processing, and enlarging expenses if he agreed to let her pay it off over time from whatever work she procured. Sergei Lebedev, the photographer, eagerly agreed.

Lebedev was in his fifties, and like every man in the church since Kathy first started to attend, he had difficulty keeping his eyes off her. Fortunately for Kathy, the women at church who took the time to get to know her, especially the married ones, realized she wasn't some jezebel and discounted the rumors they had heard about her marriage. However, they were curious why Charles didn't attend church. Kathy explained he was an Episcopalian, and her friends shrugged. None of them knew any Russian Episcopalians.

Sergei chose the cliffs above the river overlooking New York City to take outdoor photos. It was a blustery but sunny day, and he used that to Kathy's advantage. The light and wind created perfect shadows, and the atmosphere allowed him to capture Kathy's alluring nature. Her face glowed, her hair swirled, and her body yielded to his direction for stunning results. Later they moved to a room inside the church hall where Sergei set up a couple of spotlights. Kathy's flair—fine-tuned from her years of performing—came across, and soon, she had a series of *almost* professional shots that she distributed to the agencies. More importantly, as far as Kathy and Charles were concerned, Sergei was a gentleman and never made her feel uncomfortable.

The day Kathy had her first modeling interview, with photos in hand, was the same day the Engineering Department Dean placed Charles on probation and the day Albert began classes at NYIP. At dinner that evening, Kathy was bubbly.

"Oh, Charles, you should see the women at these places. They're gorgeous. I can't imagine how I fit in. They are...what do Americans say—statuesask."

He heard her, smiled, and responded with, "Statuesque," but his attention was elsewhere.

"Yes, that's it," she said and continued. "The fashion coordinator had me try on different clothes, and a photographer took more photos. It was wonderful. They said they would decide within the week. Can you imagine, Charles? Charles? Oh, Charles, you're not listening, are you?"

"Oh, I'm sorry, dear. Yes, it sounds wonderful."

"Oh, Charles, for the sake of Pete…"

Al laughed and Charles corrected her.

"It's 'for Pete's sake,' dear," he said.

"I don't care who it's for," Kathy chirped back. "I can tell something's bothering you. What happened at work today? Tell me."

"Excuse me," Al interrupted. "I have coursework to get acquainted with." He left them alone to work out what they were going to do.

"Nothing. Nothing for you to worry about," Charles insisted. "Just typical university bureaucratic issues," he said and buried his head in his paperwork.

"I don't believe you, Charles. I've seen you handle *typical* things for two years now. Whatever is on your mind is not typical. Tell me." She came to him and took his hand.

He had always been stubborn and knew she was his match in that category, but if he couldn't tell Kathy, his wife, then who? He huffed and then told her. "They put me on probation for hitting Fleshman in the restaurant. Said it gives the school a bad image. They're right about the image, of course."

"You?! They put *you* on probation. What happened to that creep Fleshman? If you're on probation, I hope he got fired."

"I don't know what happened to him. Let's forget about him. I don't think he'll bother us again." He couldn't tell her about Fleshman's intrusion into his office. It was bad enough that he told her about the probation and decided to change the subject. "Now you. Tell me about your day." He rested his papers on his lap and looked at her with interest.

She rolled her eyes and laughed. "Yes, let's forget about *Mister* Fleshman. I'm sure he won't be in the Navy much longer. And of course, I'll tell you all about my day. It was most enjoyable." Kathy repeated the details of her adventurous day; this time, she knew she had his full attention. When she finished, she took his hand, and when he thought she was walking her to the kitchen, she detoured him up the stairs to the bedroom.

"I'm not hungry. Are you, Charles?"

12 SEPTEMBER 1947 — FEBRUARY 1950
Atlanta

The photos and interviews did the trick. Soon, Kathy was modeling two or three days a week.

"Just the right amount," she told Charles and her friends.

However, regardless of how happy she was with her work, Charles slipped into a mild depression. Kathy believed the confrontation with Fleshman, the ongoing isolation from his family, and the lack of support from Stevens were the causes. Of course, men didn't talk about such things, so she tried to get him to visit with the priest at her church, but Charles found excuse after excuse not to go. She also noticed his impeccable appearance began to wane.

"Want me to shine your shoes?" she would ask.

"No, I'll get to them," he would answer, but he wouldn't.

He would forgo shaving on weekends and even missed a couple bill payments. He didn't smile as much, wasn't sleeping, and gained weight. Kathy tried everything to cheer him up, but nothing seemed to work. However, in mid-October, things changed.

First, the local paper reported Joshua Fleshman and Louise Litvinova planned to marry. A Halloween wedding would be the highlight of the season for the Russian immigrant community in Hoboken, Weehawken, and Jersey City. But only a few days before the big event, Fleshman was arrested during a police raid at a New York City brothel. Outrage reverberated throughout Louise's and Harriet's extended families. A real scandal. Louise dumped him flat, and the Navy and Stevens finally cut their ties to the cavalier rascal. Not long after the unexpected notoriety and becoming unemployed, Fleshman called Charles.

"Hi, Charles. I think it's finally time I let the world know about Kathy. Everything she's done—unless you pay up. Should make interesting reading for the Dean and your Army pals. Dontcha think?"

Kathy and Charles had discussed what they would do if Fleshman tried to blackmail them again. The issue remained unresolved. Kathy didn't care what Fleshman might say. She had done what was necessary to stay alive in Shanghai and Manila, and Charles loved her anyway. He never prodded her for details, but Fleshman's threat seemed to worsen Charles's state of mind. He didn't know what to do. Should he let the ex-Navy man denigrate his wife, or should he find a way to stop him? Kathy worried Charles would do something drastic.

"Listen, asshole," Charles told Fleshman. "You better not do something stupid. I'll have you arrested for blackmail."

"Maybe, Charles, but it won't matter because everyone will know you're living with a whore. You got three days to make up your mind."

The phone line went dead.

"Well?" Kathy asked after Charles hung up.

"He gave us three days to pay up, or he'll go public with whatever he thinks he knows about you."

Kathy took Charles's hands. "Do you love me?" she asked.

"Of course. Don't be silly."

"Then that's all that matters. No matter what he says or who he tells, we can deal with it. People do what they have to do to survive. That's what I did, but that's not who I am."

He smiled at her and said, "Yeah, I know. It's just that too many people—the people in our neighborhood, where I work, where you go to church…they might prefer to believe whatever picture Fleshman paints rather than the live image of you, the person they see every day with their own eyes."

"And, I say, so what! I'm not going to fret about it. It's history." She dropped his hands and went into the kitchen.

⁂

Two days after the blackmail call and one day ahead of Fleshman's deadline, a group of young boys playing along the palisades saw something far below. It looked like a body. They were right. It was Joshua Fleshman, former lieutenant commander in the United States Navy. The authorities quickly identified him from his wallet and recent newspaper photos concerning the wedding and his arrest. Investigators learned Fleshman had been drinking heavily the day he died. A broken neck, dislocated shoulder, and twisted ankle confirmed the coroner's report that he fell off the carapace to his death. They also learned from Louise Litvinova that Charles and Fleshman had come to blows. A quick review of the whereabouts of Charles and Kathy at the time of Fleshman's accident absolved them. Surprisingly, the news about Josh Fleshman and the disproven accusation by Cousin Louise didn't cheer Charles. All it did was sadden him.

"What a waste," Kathy said as they sat in the living room.

She tuned in *Abbott and Costello* on the radio to make Charles laugh, but he didn't listen. Instead, he picked up the mail he had forgotten to check when he came in from teaching earlier. An envelope postmarked from Atlanta caught his eye. He recognized the handwriting and was eager to see how things were going with his Army friend, Nathan Harris. The letter was short, but the contents were significant.

295

Dear Charles,

I hope you and Katya are well. I have some news I hope will interest you. One of our long-time civil engineering professors is retiring. His departure will open a position, and I thought of you. It would be great to have you and Katya nearby, and I encourage you to consider applying. I think you'd be a shoo-in.

Best,
Nathan

In a postscript, Harris added that Fort McPherson was nearby and that Charles could join the Army Reserve unit operating there if he desired. Charles reread the letter twice without speaking before Kathy became impatient.

"What's it say, Charles? I can't tell by your expression if it's good news or bad."

"Nathan wants me to move to Atlanta and join the faculty at Georgia Tech. They have an opening. A professor's retiring, and he thinks I could get the position."

Their discussion was brief—Charles should apply. His CV was in the mail the next day, and he felt optimistic for the first time since the awful night in the Russian Tea Room. His boost in spirits made Kathy doubly happy, although she knew her life was about to change again.

⁂

"You're moving away?!" Al had difficulty comprehending what that meant for him.

"Yes, son. The opportunity is too good to pass up. Georgia Tech is a fine institution. We'll be able to have a very comfortable life on the salary I've been offered, along with my continuing service in the Army Reserves at the local base."

"Yeah, well, but Dad, what about me? My stuff? Where am I going to live?"

"We're not going until January, in time for the spring semester. Uncle Bernard agreed to buy my share of the house with Uncle Normand's help. They said you could continue to stay here. I expect they'll want rent, but they'll give you a great deal."

Al answered with another question. "Where are *you* going to live?"

"Nathan—my friend, Professor Harris—made arrangements for Kathy and me to stay at the home of a professor on sabbatical in Europe," Charles answered. "I need to be there no later than a week before the semester begins, around the third week in January."

"This is a real surprise," Al sputtered. "Unbelievable, in fact."

Before Charles could help himself, his frustration spilled. "Surprise?! Unbelievable?! What's unbelievable is you turning down an appointment to West Point. What a disappointment!"

"Ah, So that's it. I'm a disappointment. Now I get it," Al fired back. "You probably told everyone I was going to the Point, and now you have to backtrack. Yet, in the meantime, I'm not allowed to be surprised that someone who spent his whole life in New Jersey is leaving?"

"Let me ask you this, Albert," Charles continued. "Do you think accepting a great position at a great school is a bad decision? At least I'm smart enough to recognize a gift horse when I see one."

Al stood. The insult hurt. Kathy tried to interfere, but he gave her a vicious look, and she caught herself.

"Don't worry about me," Al said. "I've been taking care of myself since I was twelve." He remembered being sent away to school, his father going to war, and missing his mother. Yeah, he had learned how to take care of himself.

Again, Kathy broke the ice, but Al didn't stop her this time. "You're right, Albert. I'm sure you'll do fine. You have a good plan, but so does your father. He deserves his chance for continued growth by doing what he likes as much as you do. We'll write regularly, and I know you will too. Besides, it's only October, and we're not going until January. We can help you square things with Uncle Bernard if he lets us, or help you find your own place."

"Yeah. Sure." He turned and walked out.

⁂

When January 1948 arrived, Kathy began to have serious reservations about moving. She found the cold winter air of New York and New Jersey refreshing and was not in a hurry to leave, despite the treatment she and Charles sustained from his family and others. Charles, however, couldn't have been more ready. He saw no hope of improving relations with his siblings or parents and believed distance might be the stimulus he needed to get back on track.

"But what about Al, and what about my job?" Kathy said, playing devil's advocate. "Al's only eighteen, and my extra income has been fun for us," she argued. "We go to dinner and a movie once a week. And look how much we've already saved for a car."

"I know," Charles fought back. "But the looks we get from people I've known for years...Yesterday, Howard Furst and his wife crossed the street to avoid passing me on the sidewalk. Kath, that nonsense has been going on since we arrived. Then there are my brothers and parents, and the business with Stevens—it's outrageous. I'm ready for a change, and it'll be for the best. You'll see."

She didn't contest his decision. She knew Charles was unhappy, so they set their sights on Atlanta and didn't look back.

⁂

Unlike Charles, Nathan Harris had resigned his commission in the Army Reserves and resumed his full-time position at Georgia Tech. He, his wife, and their children had a small house in the

298

neighborhood just northwest of campus and only a couple blocks from where Charles and Kathy set up temporary housekeeping. The reunion with Nathan buoyed Charles's spirits, but a stretch of seventy-degree days, accompanied by unexpected January humidity, reminded Kathy of Shanghai and Manila.

"Is the weather always like this?" Kathy asked Sally Belle, Nathan's wife. "I know we moved south, but we're not in Florida, and it's January.

Mrs. Harris, the niece of the well-known mayor of Atlanta, assured her it was unusual, adding that the biggest weather problem in the winter is ice. Meteorological conditions seemed perfect to bring periodic ice storms instead of rain or snow.

"Nothing gets done during an ice storm," Sally Belle told her new friend. "You want to make sure you have lanterns, plenty of food and blankets, and a good old-fashioned chamber pot if you lose power. It can be a hassle."

Kathy laughed at the potential predicament. "Sounds like my childhood," she replied. "Guess I'll be able to handle it. In the meantime, I feel like I should be wearing a spring dress. I got used to the heat in Shanghai and Manila."

"Oh, don't worry about heat," Sally Belle told her. "It gets so hot and muggy here during the summer, all y'all will want to do is set naked in front of a fan with a glass of lemonade."

The comment made them laugh, and Kathy looked forward to getting to know Mrs. Harris much better.

Life in metro Atlanta was a noticeable shift for Kathy. As the wife of a military officer and college instructor in the American South, she found herself thrust into a new reality. Two forces were at work—their social status, based on Charles's position in the Army and at Georgia Tech, and their actual stature within those two institutions.

The war ended, and Charles never received his promotion to major, so he remained a captain in the Army Reserves. And at Georgia Tech, he was only an assistant professor, years away from becoming a full professor. As for Kathy, many locals believed she was probably a communist. After all, that's what Russians were. Right?

Nonetheless, Charles *was* an Army officer *and* a faculty member at the most respected university in Georgia, both positions of stature within Atlanta society. As such, he and Kathy were expected to participate and entertain in a particular style. Kathy thought that was silly. Only a general or possibly a colonel and a full professor could afford to host parties as if they were the Russian aristocrats of her childhood. To Kathy, many of the hoi polloi of Atlanta reminded her of her first impression of Mr. Korablin—pompous and self-absorbed. The Delacroy household income was insufficient for such a lifestyle, but where you stood on the social ladder indicated a measure of influence that could make life easy or complicated. Kathy and Charles managed to walk the tightrope between their pragmatic lives and enjoying a modicum of prestige.

After the end of the 1948 spring semester, Kathy and Charles purchased a small bungalow in a blue-collar neighborhood in southeast Atlanta near Fort McPherson. It was much farther from Georgia Tech, but its proximity to the Army base afforded many advantages. Despite the move to a modest section of the city, most of Kathy's social circles continued to accept her, albeit with mixed results. Charles never noticed.

Kathy's first significant experience with the *Old South* was an invitation to a gala hosted by the president of Georgia Tech. Despite his time at MIT, the highly respected *northern* institution, the president remained a man of the South. His father had been a leading businessman and elected to Atlanta city government for more than thirty-five years. He grew up with Black servants, including a nanny, in a culture where Whites, particularly ones with wealth and power, essentially limited opportunities for Blacks and other minorities.

This culture helped form his image of what Georgia Tech faculty members and their spouses should be. Any deviation from his vision was cause for career stagnation at best and termination at worst.

None of this was new to Kathy. She became familiar with the privileged classes during her prosperous years in Shanghai and again after her marriage in Manila. A part of her resented the poor treatment many working-class people and racial groups received at the hands of the powerful or socially connected. Yet, she had always relished being catered to by servants, friends, and family. It's not that she was afraid to work; she had *always* worked. It was more the sense of being someone special. Someone deserving of a degree of care and treatment beyond the ordinary.

Her feeling of silliness (or was it surprise?) upon finding a class culture in the United States, the land of the free, quickly wore off. Nevertheless, Kathy enjoyed the deferential treatment from the Black community, enlisted soldiers, their wives and families, and even the young faculty at Georgia Tech. She knew she would relish having others do the cooking, laundry, housecleaning, grocery shopping, and clothes mending like she had done most of her life for herself. However, segregated toilets, drinking fountains, theater seats, stores, and more made no sense to her. Why duplicate so much? She saw no reason for it. But she figured that was just the way things were. And upon reflection, she knew it was not much different than how poor Chinese were treated in Shanghai by the residents of the concessions, including, at times, herself.

Then there was employment. She wanted to continue modeling. At coffee one afternoon with Sally Belle and three other women who all lived comfortably and had been raised in so-called traditional southern homes, she put the idea to them.

"I've been thinking about going back to work," she started as the maid set another tray of tea and cookies on the table.

The women sat outside under a trellis covered with blooming wisteria. Along with Kathy and Sally Belle were Carla Rae—Sally

Belle's sister-in-law, married to a successful attorney—and Lulu Jones Aiken—wife of Professor Aiken. Both of the women had come to Atlanta from Charleston. Lulu had been voted Miss Charleston and was runner-up in the Miss South Carolina beauty pageant. Like Kathy, she was noticeably younger than her husband.

The last woman was the group's grand dame, Elsa Kate Dekalb. In her early fifties, Elsa could reel off her family ties to the Fultons, Gwinnetts, and Claytons. She had ancestors who fought in the American Revolution and against the Union in the Civil War. She occasionally bragged about hosting Clark Gable and Vivien Leigh under the same trellis where the women now sat. Elsa, however, unlike the others, was a widow.

Her husband, Avery, had been robbed and killed while heading home after departing his brokerage office several years earlier. The two young Black teenagers who were arrested, convicted, and hung for the murder, pled their innocence until the end. People in the know suspected Avery had shirked on a gambling debt and the two Black youths were convenient patsies for the New Jersey mobsters who really did the deed. It never mattered to Elsa. She had always been fearful of Black men, although she had loved her Black nanny growing up, the ones she hired for her children, and the maid who presently served everyone on the patio. But she hated Black men.

"Shiftless, arrogant killers," she called them. "They need to be put away where they can't do any harm."

When Kathy first heard Mrs. Dekalb say this, the women had been discussing the recent news about Negros playing professional baseball up north. As the newest and most junior member of the little group, Kathy said nothing.

"I agree, Elsa," Lulu Aiken concurred. "Damn nigger men are nothing but troublemakers."

Kathy watched as Sally Belle and Carla Rae looked away and pretended they didn't hear the comments. As for Kathy, she didn't know anything about baseball, but she sure knew prejudice and bigotry when she heard it. She regarded herself as open-minded and reflected on the people she had met on the long train ride, then in Harbin, Shanghai, and Manila, who came from around the world. Yes, some she didn't like, probably even hated, but not the same way as Elsa. Regardless, Kathy wanted to fit in with her new friends, so she smiled sweetly and kept quiet. The final word of the afternoon also came from Elsa.

"Kathy, my dear, you are an elegant White woman living in the South. You must put aside this foolish notion of work. Your husband can certainly provide for your wants and your....*assets* can always get you whatever you want. I'm sure you understand. See you next week."

The first year in Atlanta flew by. Kathy and Charles became regular participants within their various social and work communities, attending formal and informal gatherings at the university faculty club and the Fort McPherson Officers' Club. They got to know many neighbors on their block, including Lois Barnes and Deborah Collins, who moved into new houses on Bridgewater Street during that first year. The three women quickly became fast friends.

The Delacroy home was in a rapidly expanding section of the city. Their street and a dozen surrounding blocks epitomized a genteel yet active post-war suburban precinct. The many tidy cottages housed teachers, plumbers, bank clerks, cab drivers, secretaries, barbers, carpenters, and military personnel. If Charles's lack of a promotion bothered him, he never let it show. And living in a district of modest homes and predominantly blue-collar families also had no impact on his ego. As for Kathy, their house was the first home where she had an ownership stake and didn't pay rent. It wasn't big, but it was neat, clean, and theirs.

"So long as we make the mortgage payments," Charles would

remind her every time she got invited to one of an endless string of charity events where contributions were expected and went without saying. "But we can't go to every affair," he would chide her. "We go out at least once a week as it is."

"Yes, Charles. I know," was Kathy's standard response.

In practice, she *was* careful, and they lived within their means despite being active in numerous organizations. Although Kathy was more than content with her new life in Atlanta, she missed contributing to the household income. She lived in a conundrum. If she went to work, she was afraid her high society friends would reject her, or worse, her employment could impact Charles's at Georgia Tech and with the Army. She didn't know what to do.

After much hemming and hawing, Kathy joined the choir at the chapel on the Army base. At least she could sing, something she loved to do, even if she wouldn't be getting paid. It was at the chapel she met Milton Stillman. He was the assistant base chaplain, choirmaster, and a major in the US Army Chaplain Corps. Sunday services were nothing like her experiences in the Russian Orthodox tradition, but she said she felt close to God, Papa, and Grandmama in the chapel. She also told Charles that Reverend Stillman was one of the nicest and kindest people she had ever met. Colonel Stillman was the one who had picked her voice out from the congregation one Sunday and encouraged her to join the choir.

As the summer waned and Charles prepared for his second year at Georgia Tech, Kathy was anxious for choir rehearsals to begin again. She didn't understand why the choir took the summer off. Sure, people went on vacations, and not as many people attended church, but she believed services were incomplete without the choir. Colonel William Bull Simpson, "Billy Bull" to his friends, likewise a member of the choir and Charles's immediate superior in his Army unit, also missed the choir. As mid-August's sweltering heat baked the small contingent of worshipers, Simpson approached Kathy after one service.

"Good day, Mrs. Delacroy. It's always a delight to hear your lovely voice every Sunday." His smile dazzled almost as much as the brilliant sun.

"Thank you, Colonel. I also enjoy hearing your baritone during the hymns." She returned an equally engaging grin.

"I've been thinking that summers without the choir leave something lacking in every service."

"I agree," Kathy said, "but I'm not sure there's anything we can do about it. Besides, rehearsals for the full choir begin in three weeks, and then we'll all be back during worship a week later."

"Oh, but I think that's too long to wait. I wonder, would you be interested in working together as a duet for the next few Sundays? I'm sure Reverend Stillman won't mind, and I think Mrs. Alistair would love the company." Billy Bull referenced the organist and gave Kathy a second blinding smile.

Kathy's first thought was, *I've never seen such large teeth,* and she stifled a giggle. She had met Simpson at the first Army event she and Charles attended last summer. He was young for a colonel, only thirty-five. His courage on the battlefield, commitment to his troops, and ability to appeal to superior officers led to rapid promotions. He was also married with three children, but somehow a ring on his finger never slowed down his interest in other female companionship.

Simpson was one reason Kathy initially hesitated about joining the choir. In some ways, he reminded her of Josh Fleshman. Both men differed from the drunken sailors and soldiers she had encountered at the small clubs in Shanghai, but reminded her of Kuniaki and the lecherous men at Ivan's. But those places were memories and not in the United States. Here, she was supposed to be free—and safe. Yes, there was something about handsome Colonel Simpson she found alluring yet dangerous. And Bull Simpson knew his nickname was more than an affectation.

"Oh, Colonel, I don't know. It seems unnecessary at this point."

Kathy had taken her time before responding to his offer about working as a duet.

"Think about how much we would add to each service," Simpson countered. "It will only be for a few weeks. Come on, Kathy."

"Well…"

"It'll be fun." There was his smile again.

"I'll have to see what Charles thinks," she offered. This was a weak excuse, and she knew it. Despite her reluctance about what the Colonel's actual intentions might be, she wanted to sing. It always made her feel good.

"Charles?!" he exclaimed. "Why, Kathy, he told me how much he likes to hear you sing. I can't imagine he'd object."

"I don't have a license, so he would have to drive me to rehearsals. Between Reserve duty and his teaching, he stays very busy."

"Heavens. Is that all? I'll come and pick you up."

It never dawned on her that the Colonel might come and get her. That made her more nervous. "No, no. I'll speak to Charles. We can probably figure out a schedule."

"Fantastic," Simpson beamed. "You can't imagine how much I'm looking forward to it. I'll call you at home later, and we can set up rehearsals that will work with Charles's availability." He did an about-face and marched away with an added bounce to his stern military stride.

"Charles, have you heard the rumors about Colonel Simpson?" She had waited all day to mention her conversation with the Colonel.

Charles sat reading the *Atlanta Constitution*. The *Atlanta Journal* was on the floor next to his chair. He had read it earlier in the day after his walk while Kathy was at church. Next to his feet, on the other side of the *Journal*, was a stack of books, binders, and files so tall it appeared ready to collapse. When he finished each section of the *Constitution*, he would shift his attention to the pile and spend some time refining his plans for the fall semester before returning to the newspaper. When Kathy spoke, he allowed the newspaper to drape over both sides of his legs and looked at his wife.

"No, my dear. I pay no attention to such falderal. Rumors tend to cause nothing but trouble. I have a strictly professional relationship with Colonel Simpson, even during social gatherings. The Army requires nothing less." Satisfied he'd answered her question, Charles picked the paper back up and continued reading.

"That's all, Charles? Nothing more to say?" she responded, unsatisfied. "How can you ignore everything? I'm asking because he wants me to join him as a duet for Sunday services at the chapel before the entire choir returns. However, there's something about him that reminds me of Joshua Fleshman."

Charles let the paper flop over his legs again, giving her more attention. "Colonel Simpson has an exemplary military record. He's crisp and concise with his orders and issues discipline and praise when deserved. He's married with children and he's destined to wear stars on his shoulders. As I said, rumors mean trouble. Why would he risk giving up his career and reputation by acting poorly?"

"That's my point, Charles. I'm talking about his reputation. He has one for being a ladies' man, married or not. Do you think I should spend time with him? I told him you have a busy schedule and I'd need a ride to rehearsals. He volunteered to pick me up and bring me home. Do you think that's wise, or asking for trouble?" She desperately wanted Charles to tell her not to do it, but he did the opposite.

"Kathy, you love to sing. And you have a wonderful voice. I'm sure the two of you would make a perfect duet for the Sunday hymns and special music. I don't see any harm in it. Tuesdays are my best days to take you."

"Oh, but…I don't trust him."

"Then tell him no. It's not that hard," the frustration in Charles's voice came out in a dismissive tone.

"Aren't you concerned if I tell him 'no,' it will impact you somehow?"

"Not in the least."

He said this too fast for her to believe him, but she gave up, convinced she had no choice. The last thing she wanted was to interfere with Charles's aspirations in the Army or Georgia Tech. Simpson was his immediate superior officer and could make or break the future of officers and enlisted soldiers under his command. From the rumors Kathy *had* heard, the Colonel had stymied promotions for several officers due to some perceived slight or petty offense. All fabricated, according to the rumors. Likewise, others received promotions over more worthy candidates. The talk was they had performed personal favors for the Colonel. Kathy heard the men who got promoted had repaired Simpson's private vehicle, rebuilt a shed in his backyard, and made sure Simpson's wife was out of the house with his subordinates' wives at specific periods. And these transgressions were only part of a much longer list. Kathy did not doubt Billy Bull Simpson would get back at her through Charles if she didn't sing with him.

"Very well, if you think it's safe," Kathy resigned. "But don't you think people will talk?"

"My God, Kathy! People always talk about all kinds of nonsense. Stop fretting. If you want to sing, sing. If not, tell him no. Now, that's enough of this. Please let me finish the paper." He picked it up and hid his face from her view.

Kathy went into the short hallway and lifted the phone from its cradle on the small stand. It rang three times before being answered.

"Colonel Simpson's residence," the slow drawl of the housekeeper answered.

My goodness, Kathy thought. *Billy Bull has live-in help!* She wasn't sure why she was surprised.

"Yes, this is Mrs. Charles Delacroy calling for Colonel Simpson."

"One moment, ma'am. I'll see if he's free."

In the interlude, Kathy switched the phone half a dozen times from one hand to the next. She rarely felt nervous, but she was sure this was in Charles's best interest, although she wasn't so sure it was in hers.

"Well, hello, Kathy. So good of you to call."

She could picture his big-toothed smile. "Charles can take me on Tuesdays." She spit it out before she could stop herself.

"Oh, Tuesdays. Hmmm. Worst day of the week for me. I can get you on Wednesdays or Thursdays." He made it into a choice—no other options.

She had known he would reject whatever day Charles said. Feeling trapped, she said, "Wednesdays will have to do then," without enthusiasm, and a brief chill ran down her spine.

"Wonderful. I'll get you at nineteen hundred hours—uhh, that's seven p.m."

"I know, Colonel. I live with a soldier."

She was about to hang up when she heard him say, "I'm so looking forward to our time together, Kathy. See you Wednesday."

She squirmed and felt the hair rise on her neck. It wasn't so much what he said but how he said it. He wanted to see *her,* and she felt confident he didn't care if they did *any* singing.

As Halloween approached, Kathy settled down. The few weeks Simpson picked her up for rehearsals had proceeded without incident, and she felt happy to be singing with the full choir again. Likewise, Charles had his teaching and research routine, and the early season social gatherings had been minimal, although the weekly meeting of the ladies persisted. Most frequently, they met at the home of Mrs. Dekalb under Sally Belle Harris's careful organizational acumen.

"My, my, my. Can y'all believe how those Yellow Jacket boys are doing on the gridiron?" Lulu was gushing about Tech's football team. "That running back—think his name is Rory Meriwether if I heard correctly—he sure is one fine specimen of a man, if I do say so myself."

"Now, Lulu, how would you know such things? And to speak like that at Mrs. Dekalb's home." Carla Rae pretended outrage, and they laughed.

Over the months, Kathy realized that Lulu, seemingly in love with Professor Aiken, had a yearning to be with a younger man. Often, she pined over a man ten or more years her junior. It had become a running joke because Lulu had always been faithful to her aging academic as far as anyone knew.

"I get out, of course, Carla Rae. I go to the games. You and that lawyer husband of yours should come with me sometime."

"I thought the Professor went with you," Kathy chimed in.

"Oh, he comes on occasion. Other times, well, I have an escort," she said with a sly smile.

"My goodness dear," Elsa offered, "And who might those escorts be, Lulu? I don't want any scandal associated with me. And scandals involving friends of mine *always* affect *me*."

"Settle your sweet self down, Elsa. My escorts are exclusively the coaches' wives. And when we're together, we conduct detailed analyses of the young gladiators on the field."

Laughter resounded again as the maid refilled their glasses with more Old Fashioneds. Kathy's glass was the only one that didn't require a refill. She never had more than one drink. It was a strict rule she had followed for many years, especially after the night the man chased her after work in Shanghai. One drink was enough. Besides, she always learned much more by listening while she was sober. She noticed Mrs. Harris also rarely had more than one.

Nevertheless, with little regard for her social status, Elsa Kate Dekalb drank like a sailor, which inevitably led to her sharing some small tidbit of information. These unfiltered musings helped Kathy better understand Atlanta's society and culture.

"When I was a little girl, I remember Papa used to go out every

Monday evening for some meeting or another. He belonged to all kinds of groups. Chamber of Commerce, Georgia Bulldog Society, VFW, Church Vestry, Sons of the Confederacy, and more. It seemed he was gone most nights, but Mondays were like clockwork. He'd be gone from around six and wouldn't get home till after midnight. I know because the side door squeaked, and my bedroom was right above it. The noise always woke me up when Papa came home."

"Well, Elsa, nothing unusual in all that," said Sally Belle. "Lots of men, and women too, go to regular meetings."

"True enough, Sally Belle," Elsa agreed. "But when I was fourteen, I discovered Papa's Monday meetings were at the Kimball House, in room 534. Funny place for a weekly VFW gathering, don't y'all think?"

"No need to go on, Elsa," Carla Rae felt embarrassed for the old dame.

"Nothing to be embarrassed about, Carla Rae." Elsa read her friend's face. "It's the way of the world. Or, I should say, the way of men."

Everyone nodded in agreement but could see that pain still lingered in the older woman's eyes. It might not be all men, but it sure was plenty. At the end of Elsa's explanation of how she found out what her father was up to, Kathy reached a logical and inevitable conclusion about people in Atlanta: they were no different than people everywhere. This made her wonder whether Colonel Simpson was a good guy, or if he simply had incredible patience and persistence to get what he wanted. She couldn't help but lean toward the latter.

Thanksgiving Day was warm and sunny. Al telephoned, but Charles remained stubborn and wouldn't speak to him. This annoyed Kathy.

311

"Your parents and brothers won't talk to you, but you have a son who wants a relationship, and you ignore him. He didn't see you for years, and you're acting like a fool. Call him back," Kathy gave the order.

"You don't understand. It's hard for me to watch him throw his future away. We—Al and I—worked very hard for him to earn the appointment to West Point, and he'll regret not going his entire life."

"You're pleading, Charles. And it's been more than a year. It doesn't become you. Did you ever think perhaps what Albert told us is true? He doesn't want to be an Army officer. Besides, he's still young, and he's smart. He'll do fine. He is doing fine."

"I'm done discussing this, Kathy."

"Okay, I'll stop. At least we're having Thanksgiving dinner out," Kathy commented. "I, for one, am thankful for *everything,* which includes having Albert in my life." She turned on him and went to the bedroom to get changed.

Dinner was at the home of Colonel Simpson. It was a large, extravagant affair, with tables outside accommodating thirty guests, including Simpson's sisters-in-law and their families, his widowed mother, and his wife's parents. Kathy thought it strange no other Army personnel were present, yet Simpson was in his dress uniform. Kathy suspected it was a deliberate way for the pompous *hero* to show off. Charles wore a business suit, making him appear insignificant compared to the brash colonel. Kathy was suddenly unsure about having accepted the invitation.

"Well, I feel a bit out of place," Charles remarked to Simpson as the host made introductions.

"Oh, nonsense, Charles," Simpson answered with a huge smile. "You look fine. I made a last-minute decision because the children like my uniform. It's more about the uniform than me."

"Who are you kidding?" Kathy mumbled under her breath.

"What do you think, Kathy?" Simpson asked. "Was it worth dressing for the kids?"

"If it makes them happy, Bill, but Charles looks good in his uniform too."

She had started calling him Bill at his request not long after they first met at choir practice. Nonetheless, Charles twinged every time she called him Bill. It was too familiar, as far as he was concerned.

"Yes. Doesn't he look sharp?" Simpson's wife joined, taking her husband's arm. "And he'd look even better with a silver star on each shoulder, don't you think?"

"Of course," Kathy responded. "And gold leaves on Charles's would look good too. He's been waiting since—"

"Not now, Kathy. Please," Charles interrupted. "This is not the time or place to discuss a promotion."

"As you wish, Charles," Simpson followed. "I'm *sure* things could be done to help you along." Charles had turned away as the Colonel spoke and didn't notice Simpson's eyes lingering on Kathy's.

"Time to eat, everyone!" Simpson's wife took charge and funneled everyone to their seats.

Simpson sat at the head of the long table of adults with his mother on one side and Kathy on the other. Charles was next to Billy Bull's mother, and Simpson's beautiful younger sister-in-law sat next to Kathy. The lady of the house reigned at the other end, with her parents on either side. All the children were at smaller tables, attended to by servants just like the adults. When all the guests were seated, Colonel Simpson tapped the side of his crystal water glass to get their attention.

"It is always special to have family present on this day of Thanksgiving. We have much to be grateful for, and I'm particularly pleased to have Kathy Delacroy and her husband, Charles, join us. As you know, Charles works for me at Fort Mac, and the lovely Mrs. Delacroy sings with me in the Chapel choir. I wish I had free time in my schedule to get to know them better."

At the far end of the table, Kathy saw Mrs. Simpson roll her eyes, and Kathy rolled hers too. After all, they *had* spent lots of time together in the choir.

"But now," he continued, "let's say the Lord's Prayer together and enjoy this fantastic meal."

Everyone did as they were told and bowed their heads. The meal progressed steadily, and with each course, the waitstaff refilled everyone's wine glass. By the third glass, most of the adults began to feel the effects of the alcohol, and when dessert finally arrived, many were drinking Irish coffee, brandy, and hot buttered rum. Kathy and Charles, however, stuck to their one-glass limit and were enjoying water and coffee with their confections.

Kathy watched, amazed, as Billy Bull consumed numerous beverages. She found it amusing until she felt his hand under the table on her knee and his foot trying to pry off her shoe.

The second time she removed his hand from her knee, she leaned over to him and whispered, "Touch me again, and I'll make a scene."

He gave her that big smile and whispered back, "Oh, come on, Kathy. Have some fun. Look at the other women here. Do you think I'd invite them, their boring husbands, and their brats into my house if I wasn't getting a return on my investment?"

Kathy rose and excused herself. "Pardon me. I need to find the powder room." As she stood, she *slipped* and bumped his elbow just enough that he spilled coffee on his trousers. "Oh my, I'm so sorry," she quipped and walked off.

Simpson snickered as she left the table and wiped his pants with a napkin. Charles noticed the awkward exchange, also smiled, and wasn't surprised when she returned and told him she was tired and wanted to head home. With the meal concluded, he felt he had fulfilled his obligation to attend. Everyone had begun to move inside anyway. The men headed to the Colonel's library for more brandy, cigars, and cigarettes, while the women went to the parlor.

"I'm afraid we need to head home, Colonel," Charles said as they walked toward the house. "I want to thank you and Mrs. Simpson for a wonderful Thanksgiving dinner. I'm stuffed, and I hope we can repay your kindness over the holidays."

"No need to rush off, Charles. The boys, my brothers-in-law, have marvelous stories, and I know how much the women like to chat."

"That's very gracious, but we're tired. I have schoolwork to prepare for Monday and need to have my wits about me when I do that."

"Yes. We wouldn't want you to lose your wits." His tone was mocking, and Kathy started to say something but instead, simply stared at the stain on his pants with a gleam in her eyes.

"Thank you just the same, Colonel. I'll see you at the next reserve meeting."

"Yes. And see *you* Sunday, Mrs. Delacroy."

Kathy ignored him and turned to go.

"My apologies, Colonel. Like the rest of us, she's tired and ate too much." Charles followed his wife out the door.

"How can you tolerate that man?" she demanded as soon as they were in the car.

"What do you mean?"

"Oh, for goodness' sake, Charles. He's a lecher and a philanderer. He was squeezing my knee under the table. That's why I got up."

"He did what?" Charles couldn't believe it.

"He's also an alcoholic; for all we know, he's not even a good soldier. I bet if you tried to verify some of his medals, you couldn't. And he wore his uniform just to make you look insignificant. You know that's true," she fumed.

"No, I don't. Yes, he's got an ego and likes to show off, but to wear the uniform to one-up me? On Thanksgiving? That's hard to believe."

"You don't know him like I do," she countered. "Ever since I agreed to do the duets with him in August, he's been eyeing me. He says things with all kinds of double meanings, mostly having to do with sex."

Charles turned a little red when she said *sex,* as it was a topic of minor stress between them. They argued about having a baby, and he certainly didn't want anyone else involved in their personal affairs, especially his superior officer. But if Simpson really did squeeze her knee…They drove home in silence and went to bed the same way. The morning routine, however, was normal and life went on—but two weeks later, at the engineering department Christmas party, Charles began to wonder about Colonel Simpson. He overheard a conversation between several women.

"I slapped his hand away, and I know it made him angry," Louisa Hancock, the Dean's executive secretary, told her colleagues.

Another secretary asked the obvious. "So, what did he do after you pushed him away?"

"He leaned in and tried to kiss me on the neck. I backed off, and then he said, 'Come on, Lou. You know you want me.' Can you imagine? What a self-absorbed a-hole. And pardon me, ladies, but it's true."

"Sure sounds like it," another listener said. "Have you seen him since?"

"Oh, sure. Every time there's a social event for the enlisted men, their *great warrior leader* shows up to make sure everyone remembers who's in charge. They know who can make or break them. And it's not just me he's after. I heard he tries to tame—yes, *tame*—the wives and girlfriends of as many of the officers and senior enlisted guys as he can. He blackmails these women into doing *personal favors* to protect their husbands' army careers. If you know what I mean."

"My goodness, Louisa. Have you reported this to his boss?" the fourth member of the secretary pool finally joined in.

"I've made appointments to see the base commander about this five times. He was out twice—*skipping* the appointments as if he didn't want to talk to me. The other times he told me the same thing. 'Proof.' He said I needed a third party to corroborate things. I've had no luck. The other women are too scared to say or do anything about Billy Bullshit Simpson. Sorry, girls. So far, nothing's happened to Jeff or me, but I'm worried."

"Have you told Jeff?" one asked her.

Until Louisa mentioned a name, Charles had no idea who she had been talking about. And he had never made the connection between Louisa Hancock and Staff Sergeant Jeffrey Hancock, a member of Simpson's staff but someone with whom Charles rarely interacted.

"Are you kidding? Tell Jeffrey? No way. I'd be terrified he would do something stupid and get sent to Leavenworth. No, I need to find someone else."

Charles wasn't sure what to do with the information he overheard. See Simpson on his own? Tell Kathy what he heard, or join the conversation and tell the women he knew Billy Bull? The decision was made for him when the dean clinked his glass and began his annual holiday speech. By the time he finished, the women had separated, and the party was dispersing.

"How was the party, Charles?" Kathy asked as he settled into his favorite chair with a small glass of eggnog.

"This is excellent eggnog, Kathy. Thank you."

She plopped in his lap, wiped the small mustache of pale-yellow eggnog from his upper lip, and kissed him. "Anything for you, my dear. So, again I ask, how was the party?"

"Routine, you know. Dean made his speech, and everyone pretended to pay attention." He laughed. "Nonetheless, it was a good booster and a nice thank you to staff for a good year. The faculty contributed gifts to the secretaries and janitors, and we all received a fruit basket from the dean. The party was fine."

The way he said 'it was fine' didn't sound *fine* to Kathy. Not one little bit. "What aren't you telling me, Charles? You went to an office Christmas party, not a wake. Come on. Spit out it."

He laughed again.

"Why are you laughing?" She gave him a gentle poke on the arm.

"Okay, but sometimes you still get words in the wrong order, and it sounds funny to my ears, that's all."

"Ugh! English! It's a crazy language. But tell me, what was not *fine* at the party?"

"If you must know...well, alright." Charles repeated the conversation among the secretaries and told Kathy about his familiarity with Staff Sergeant Hancock.

"See? I told you. That man is nothing but a-a-oh...he's no good. I must meet with Mrs. Hancock. I can back up her story." Kathy seemed prepared to leave that very moment.

"Oh, no, you don't. Neither of you has any evidence. Nothing you can prove, only words, some look in his eyes, or a subtle touch. All easily explained. You need witnesses, or you have nothing."

"But Charles, what he's doing is so wrong!"

He could tell she wanted to see Billy Bull strung up, lashed, and humiliated at any price.

"Without proof, there's nothing we can do," Charles stressed.

"You're wrong," Kathy persisted. "You need to march into his office and tell him to leave these women and me alone, or he'll regret it."

"Me?! He's the one with the leverage. What do I have to use against him? Besides, if Georgia Tech doesn't offer me a tenured position, I'll need to move from the Reserves into the Regular Army. We can't afford to have something as simple as a few suggestive words ruin any prospects I may have. Remember what Fleshman's words did to me at Stevens."

Kathy was furious. "A few suggestive words? My God, Charles! He's assaulted or slept with half the wives and girlfriends of the men in his unit. And he wants to do it with me too!" She stormed out of the room, shaking her head, wondering what it was with men. She was more determined than ever to do something about Billy Bull Simpson.

13 FEBRUARY 1950—FEBRUARY 1953
Atlanta

Kathy knew Charles wasn't a coward, and Colonel Simpson didn't intimidate him, but she also knew Charles was a realist who made decisions only after careful thought. In the case of Billy Bull Simpson, Charles knew he was in no position to challenge Simpson within the Army structure; therefore, so long as Kathy was safe, his best alternative was to do his duty and not make waves. However, the do-nothing option increased Kathy's frustration. She told Charles she would take the horns of the bull and do something herself. He laughed and said it was "take the bull by the horns." Infuriated at being corrected, she stormed from the house in the middle of an ice storm. Charles found her an hour later in a coffee shop and brought her home, where she fumed in their room and decided she needed to act.

"Oh Kathy, this is a surprise! Welcome, and please come in," Colonel Simpson beamed his glistening teeth at her and told his aide that he should not be disturbed.

Kathy had waited until after the holidays. She figured the new year might be the best time to do what she had in mind. If Charles wanted proof, she would just have to get it. Before meeting with Simpson, she made several phone calls and had multiple meetings with many of the wives and girlfriends of the men under Simpson's command. What she learned was more than disturbing. Yet, there was no easy way to solve the riddle of proof. She was disheartened when none of the women agreed to assist her in her crusade. But Kathy remained hopeful some would join her once they heard her story. None did, and Kathy understood it would be up to her.

"Enough of your niceties, Bill. I'm here to talk about Christine Jones, Louisa Hancock, Pat Miller, Josephine O'Leary, Darlene Schwartz, Karen Phillips, etc. And me. You leave them and me alone, starting now, or you'll never work again. Actually, you'll find yourself locked up. The Army will only be too happy to rid itself of the likes of you. I hope you're paying attention."

For a moment, Billy Bull Simpson said nothing, then looked at her and began to laugh. It was a hearty, deep belly laugh—an honest display of mirth and delight. When he stopped, he rose, stretched to his full six-foot-three, leaned across the table, and smiled down at Kathy.

"Oh, Kathy. How little you know of life here in the US, and in the Army. I'm a war hero. I'll be a one-star by next year or the year after. And what police officer or base commander—and yes, I know all about your visits to see the General—wants to be the one to make a *hero* look bad? Besides, all those women you mentioned love the attention I give them. They sure don't get what I give them from their husbands. No doubt they didn't want you to know the truth. Just like I know how much you want me, instead of that lowly captain of yours. I bet he hasn't even figured out more than one way to stick it to you."

She reached up to slap him, but he was faster and caught her arm. He squeezed and twisted, but she refused to cry out. Water filled her eyes, but she remained stoic, and he let go.

"Now Kathy, be a good little girl and get out of here. And don't expect to see your little boy at home in the evenings during his reserve duty. He'll have all kinds of work here, or possibly at Fort Drum in New York. Perfect time of year to go to upstate New York.

Good spot for a lifelong *captain*. You know, I wouldn't be surprised if the Army calls him back to active duty this winter."

"You wouldn't! You couldn't!" she fumed at him. She never thought she was naïve, but clearly she had never considered his hero status as more than bluster.

"I would, and I can…of course, you can avoid having Charles leave town or go overseas, and you might even help him get promoted. I have Thursday evenings free. There's a wonderful little club, Ray Lee's Blue Tavern, on Ponce de Leon. I'll expect you by ten." His smile vanished, and he said, "Now get the fuck out of my office. And if you ever come in here and talk to me like that again, I'll have you arrested. Or spanked." And he chuckled.

She was scared but stood her ground. "If you go near any of those women or proposition me again, you'll be in jail." She turned and walked to the door.

As she opened it, he said loud enough for his aide to hear, "Nice to see you, Kathy. Looking forward to Sunday choir. See you there. And give my regards to *Captain* Delacroy."

Outside, Kathy walked to the far side of Simpson's building, out of sight of his windows. She was shaking and leaned against a tree so she wouldn't collapse. She had met all kinds of men in many places, but never any quite like the handsome yet arrogant, narcissistic brute, Billy Bull Simpson. She was determined to bring him down, but she would need a new tactic if she were to succeed—and she would need outside help.

"Good morning, Elsa. This is Kathy Delacroy. Thank you for taking my call."

"Yes, dear. Of course. What's on your mind?"

Kathy told her the entire story of Colonel William Bull Simpson and bluntly asked her for her thoughts about what she should do.

321

"Another damn scoundrel! And he's married, with his own family! Outrageous! He's hurting so many families. You bet I'll help. Give me a day or two, and I'll get back to you, even if you are a commie." Then she laughed. "Don't worry, darlin'. I know you're not. I'm prejudiced against all kinds, but I've come around on you. Rest easy, and I'll call back soon."

When Kathy hung up, she didn't know what to think of Elsa's "commie" comment, but she was confident Billy Bull would soon be out of the philandering and blackmail business. Two days later, as promised, Elsa called back and invited Kathy to her house the following day to meet someone who was going to help.

After Charles left for work, Kathy made the cold walk to the bus stop through spitting frozen rain and sleet. A short walk on the other end brought her to the home of Elsa Kate Dekalb. Millie, the housekeeper, answered the bell and welcomed Kathy inside.

"Miss Elsa's in the drawing room by the fireplace, Miss Kathy."

"Thank you, Millie. I know the way."

When Kathy entered the room, Elsa rose from her lounge and greeted Kathy as if she were a long-lost relative. "Oh, there you are. Let me give you a big hug. Everything's going to be just fine."

After Elsa nearly squeezed all the air out of her, Kathy noticed a small man standing behind Mrs. Dekalb. He was suppressing a laugh while watching the scene of the two women. At last, Elsa released her young friend and stood aside.

"Kathy Delacroy, I want you to meet Mr. Jeremiah June Fuller, 'JJ' to his friends. Mr. Fuller is better known around Atlanta as Detective Captain Fuller. Now retired, formerly of the Atlanta Police Department. He's a dear friend and now working in a private capacity."

"How do you do, Captain Fuller?" Kathy said.

"Please, Ma'am. I'm just JJ to most."

"Very well...JJ. And please call me Kathy."

Over the next hour, Kathy related everything she knew about Colonel William Simpson. Fuller was particularly interested in his routine off-base. Specifically, he asked where, when, and how Simpson met the other women and the types of threats he had made against them and their husbands or boyfriends. Kathy answered all his questions as best she could and provided him with a list of names, addresses, and phone numbers of the women she knew Simpson had subdued. When JJ finished his questions, Elsa called Millie to bring them lunch.

During lunch, Fuller changed topics. "Elsa tells me you spent many years in Shanghai. Before joining the Atlanta Police Department, I spent two years in China with the Marines. Was a different time back then. Glad I made it home in one piece."

"Yes, it *was* different," Kathy said softly.

"That's alright, Kathy. No need to bring up those times," Elsa consoled. "We've got enough to figure out with this bastard Simpson. Excuse my crudeness, but that's what he is."

"I don't mind, Elsa." Kathy turned to JJ and said, "I did whatever was necessary to survive, Mr. Fuller. Not proud of all of it, but there you have it."

Fuller looked at her and nodded. "None of my business. Sometimes we all have to make tough choices."

"Indeed," Kathy said.

They continued to chat, and the talk moved from politics to Hollywood, the weather, and Fuller's grandchildren. At that point, Elsa spoke her mind again. "So, Kathy, when are you and Charles going to start a family?"

Kathy almost choked on the freshly baked cookies Millie had put out for dessert. Even JJ Fuller, who's seen and heard almost everything while on the police force, turned a mild red at the question.

"Oh, do forgive me, dear?" Elsa added. "It's just that you're so beautiful, still young, and I can tell you'd make a wonderful mother. My grandchildren are in Augusta and Chattanooga, and I don't see them as often as I'd like. Well, anyway, none of my business." Elsa picked up her teacup and tried to hide behind it.

Kathy didn't know what to say. She and Charles had never really resolved the situation. He had a grown son, and although Kathy was still young, her memories of motherhood were bitter.

"No decisions yet. I've had some…uncomfortable experiences. We'll see." She let it go at that.

Retired Police Detective Captain JJ Fuller stood and thanked his hostess and said he would look into Colonel William Bull Simpson. He would also make contact, very discreetly, with the wives and girlfriends who Kathy had mentioned and see what else he could learn. He promised to report back to Elsa in a week. Kathy thanked him, and he left.

Once he was gone, Elsa said, "He's the best. Hard, smart worker. He's won awards for his police work and civic philanthropy. Caught those murderers of my Avery. He'll get your guy, Kathy. Don't you worry."

The promise of JJ Fuller's help had buoyed Kathy's spirits. The fact that Mrs. Dekalb would pay his bill was more help than she deserved, but it was greatly appreciated. However, the knowledge that Fuller was the one who brought two possibly—probably— innocent boys to the gallows was disturbing.

⁂

JJ Fuller was an excellent detective. Methodical, detail-oriented, patient, and focused on facts. The case against the boys executed for the murder of Avery Dekalb had been airtight, and JJ never lost a minute of sleep over their demise. After all, he had planted much of the evidence against them himself. Mrs. Dekalb had promised him a very handsome bonus if he brought the criminals who killed Elsa's husband to justice. He made sure *she* never doubted that those two boys did it. Based on JJ's image and record, Elsa also never considered he was anything but a good, clean cop, and Fuller knew she trusted him. So, he ensured things worked out precisely as Elsa would expect. It was not the first time he received *extra* compensation for a job well done, and Colonel Simpson's case would not be the last.

Fuller knew it would take little time to verify everything Kathy Delacroy had told him. He was sure she had told him a true story, and all he would have to do to collect payment from Elsa would be to discover the evidence—or fabricate it, if necessary. Doing so would be enough to get the man arrested, or, at minimum, embarrassed within the Army and in no position to threaten Kathy or others any longer. JJ viewed the assignment as one of the easiest of his career. The hefty sum from Mrs. Dekalb was as good as in his pocket.

After returning home from the meeting with Fuller and Elsa, Kathy sat for a long while at the kitchen table drinking tea. Something about Detective Fuller's affable yet businesslike demeanor, combined with the information concerning Avery Dekalb's assailants, left her uneasy. She knew she needed to speak to someone else and concluded Sally Belle Harris would be the best place to start. The following afternoon, both women were seated at the same kitchen table. The tea was hot, and the plate of Kathy's homemade apple-and-cherry-filled pirozhki beckoned them.

After taking a bite and licking her lips, Sally Belle rewarded Kathy by saying, "This tastes fantastic! You must give me the recipe."

"Of course," Kathy said. "I'm glad you like it. I remember my babushka would make these whenever she could get her hands on fresh fruit."

They were quiet for a moment, taking a few more bites and sips of tea. Then Sally Belle got down to business.

"So, Kathy, why this delightful invitation? I can see something's on your mind."

"No use denying that," Kathy answered. "I went to see Elsa about a problem that I, and many other women, have been having with Charles's superior officer. His name is William Bull Simpson. He is a colonel, and his nickname is Billy Bull. A Class-A jerk. I know I've mentioned him before."

"Right. The man you sang duets with at your church."

"Yes. That's him."

"I remember you were uneasy about him, but you never told me details."

Kathy proceeded to tell her the same story she had shared with Elsa and JJ Fuller.

"Wow! What is it with these men who are so full of themselves? He sounds dreadful."

"He is, but he can also be charming, and he's terribly handsome, big, and strong. I guess many people would call him a man's man, but I call him a blackmailer and a *predator*. That's a new word I learned at the library." Kathy smiled and continued. "I went to Elsa for guidance, and she generously offered to get me some help. Charles said I need evidence to prove what Billy Bull has done and continues to do, so Elsa hired a retired police detective, a man named Jeremiah June Fuller—people call him JJ—to investigate for me. I was thrilled."

"Indeed," Sally Belle agreed. "I've heard of JJ Fuller. He sounds like the exact help you could use."

"At first, I thought so too. But Sally, he's the same man who caught and testified against the boys who were hung for murdering Mr. Dekalb."

Sally's eyes grew wide at the news. "Oh. That's right. I forgot."

"You see my problem," she stated. "I haven't been here very long, and even *I've* heard all the stories about how those boys never did anything wrong. How they were set up. Some people say the police, Detective Fuller himself, and others got paid off to frame those kids. Oh, Sally, I don't know what to do. What to believe? Simpson is a bad man, and someone needs to stop him, but, well...what is the saying, two bads don't make a good?"

"Two wrongs don't make a right," Sally corrected.

"Yes. I can't have someone doing wrong things to help me. Even if it means putting a bad man in his place."

"No, you can't. When do you meet with Detective Fuller again?"

"In a few days. I can't believe I'm in this situation. I thought in America, things like this…oh, no matter."

Sally Belle reached out and took Kathy's hand. "You'll be fine. Bad things happen here, like anywhere, and I'm sorry you're in the middle of one. Maybe you could hire your own investigator?"

"I wish I could, but I could never hide it from Charles. If he became actively involved in trying to bring charges against his superior officer, it would cause a much bigger headache. The Army isn't like other workplaces."

"Yes, I suppose he's right. Don't you have other Army friends? People who know the system?"

"The only one I can think of is Reverend Dodson, the base chaplain, or his assistant, Reverend Stillman. But I think Reverend Dodson likes Billy Bull because Billy Bull sings so well, which might be how Revered Stillman feels, too. I don't know. Simpson *is* a big voice in the chapel choir."

"Still, it sounds like the chaplain might be someone worth talking to. I'd go see him."

Their chat veered off to Atlanta's wintery weather, the strength of the communists in China, rumors about a hydrogen bomb, favorite movie stars, and the next ladies' meeting. Eventually, they couldn't eat more pirozhki, and the teacups were empty.

"I better head home," Sally Belle said. "I told Nathan I'd have a pot roast for supper tonight. Call me if you need anything. And go see Reverend Dodson."

The women hugged, and Sally Belle pulled her hat down over her ears and bundled up as she stepped out into the cold.

The next day Kathy did as Sally Belle suggested. She took the bus to Fort McPherson and found Reverend Major Clark Dodson in his office adjacent to the chapel.

"Well, Kathy, this is a nice surprise. Good morning."

Clark Dodson was a man of medium height, medium build, with medium brown hair, medium brown eyes, and a medium disposition. However, what Clark lacked in first impressions, he made up with an ingratiating sense of humor and a tenor voice that deserved a broader audience. Dodson had joined the Army directly from seminary in 1917 and went to war in France with Pershing's troops. Thirty-plus years later, he was an old major, but he loved bringing the word of the Lord to soldiers and their families. He told more than one friend that God and the Army were his life, and he was grateful the higher-ups in both camps had let him stick around.

"Good morning, Reverend," Kathy responded. "I have something I could use your help with."

"Of course. Can I get you a cup of coffee?"

"No, thank you. The coffee isn't necessary," Kathy said.

"Very well. If you don't mind, I'll leave the door open in case someone else comes. If they do, I'll ask them to wait and close the door, so we can continue in private."

"Thank you. That's fine." It didn't matter to Kathy. She thought the more people who knew about Billy Bull, the better. Her goal was to get rid of him. Arrested, or at least out of the Army. It never occurred to her that spreading the word about his behavior and extortion techniques could backfire, or that a war hero like Simpson might have many allies.

Kathy told Reverend Major Dodson the complete story, including the help JJ Fuller offered and her suspicions about him. She didn't leave out any details, but she couldn't read Dodson's face. She had no idea what he was thinking. It was impossible to tell if he was sympathetic or if he felt she imagined something that didn't exist. When she finished, Dodson clasped his hands with the index fingers raised, put them under his chin as if propping his head up, and closed his eyes. He remained in that position long enough for Kathy to wonder if he had fallen asleep. She was about to say something when he opened his eyes, put his hands in his lap, and spoke.

"Most peculiar. Very peculiar."

"Peculiar?" she asked. "Seems like a strange word to use for what I just described."

"Oh, not at all, Kathy. You see, there are *things*. Things I can't share—confidential, you realize, like our conversation now. Things that give me pause."

"So, what does that mean? Can you help us or not? The man should be in jail. If not for sexual assault, at a minimum for blackmail and extortion."

"Oh, I don't know," Dodson waffled. "You have JJ Fuller's help. I see you're not sure about him, but he's a good cop. At least, so I've heard. If there's anything out there to support your case, I'm sure he'll find it."

"Or make it up," she mumbled under her breath.

"What was that?" he asked.

"Oh, nothing. It's—well—I think you could do more," she urged. "Colonel Simpson's in the choir, and he respects you. He'll listen to you."

"Oh, I don't know," Reverend Dodson repeated. "He seems to be his own man. You know, the kind who has confidence in his every move. And from what I can see, it has worked for him and for our country. But as for listening to me or following the Ten Commandments, well…I…no, I'll leave it at that. But there is another option. Have you brought this to the attention of the military police? It seems they might be able to do more than me."

"Reverend, you must be aware the officer in charge of the military police at Fort Mac, Major Vinson, served with Colonel Simpson during the war. They were in the same unit before Vinson transferred to MPs."

"I don't see how that has anything to do with it. Vinson is a fine officer. He'll do the right thing."

Kathy's frustration was beginning to bubble to the surface. Several other women had told her they'd visited Vinson, and he told them he'd look into it. However, after interviewing Simpson himself, Vinson informed the ladies he could do nothing.

"Reverend, do you know that Colonel Simpson compared himself to Frank Sinatra?" Kathy told him. "He says women are after him and not the other way around, and that they volunteer their services, of all kinds, just to please him. Don't you think that is ridiculous and unbelievable?"

"Oh, I don't know," he used his favorite phrase for the third time. "I've seen women do lots of bizarre things around men."

Kathy wanted to scream. She realized she was wasting her time and stood. "I can see you have no interest in helping. I'll be leaving." *How foolish and blind of me.*

As she turned to go, Reverend Major Clark Dodson commented, "It's been nice to see you, Kathy. I look forward to hearing you in the choir on Sunday."

She almost yielded to the temptation to turn back and let him have a piece of her mind and a five-fingered slap, but willpower kept her walking out the door.

What is it with men?

⁂

On February 13, 1950, Kathy met again with Elsa and JJ Fuller. It was Sunday afternoon, and Kathy had complete faith the retired policeman would have the "proof" needed to bring down Colonel Billy Bull Simpson. But she had little faith any of it, or most of it, would be true—or obtained legally, if true. No—she decided, before leaving home, to thank Elsa and Detective Fuller for their help and move on. No matter how badly she wanted Simpson to be accountable, she would not use whatever information Fuller gave her, and she wouldn't tell Fuller or Elsa why. She knew all JJ wanted was to be paid; likewise, she had no idea how she would repay Elsa. But she put that out of her mind as she stepped off the bus for the short, cold walk to Elsa's door. Millie opened the door at the bell.

"Welcome, Miss Kathy. Nice to see you again."

"Nice to see you too, Millie." Kathy took her coat and hat off as Millie closed the door and took them from her.

"Miss Elsa's in her favorite chair," Millie waved her into the big house.

"Thank you, Millie."

"Detective Fuller's also in the room, but he's been pacing around like a caged lion. Heard him say something about a man not to mess with."

"Oh! Well, hmmm…thank you again, Millie."

This time, Fuller saw Kathy before Elsa did; nonetheless, he nearly barreled into her as he tracked back and forth across the room.

"Ugh. Pardon me, Mrs. Delacroy. Just working out some stiff leg muscles. Not in the same shape as I used to be," JJ said.

"Of course, Detective Fuller. I can only sit so long myself." She turned to Elsa in her chair, leaned down, and kissed her cheek. "Hello, Elsa. Another cold day. Not nearly as cold as my childhood, but after so many years in warmer places, today's weather puts a chill right through me."

"Here, dear. Have some hot tea and one of Mille's wonderful turnovers." Elsa pointed to the table laden with goodies.

"They look delicious," Kathy said and helped herself to a turnover as JJ poured her a cup of tea. She thanked him, and Elsa got down to business.

"JJ told me he has what you need to take care of this snake, Colonel Simpson. Go ahead JJ, tell her what you have."

Fuller presented Kathy with three different affidavits, sworn and signed by women Kathy didn't know. He also had photos of Simpson supposedly receiving a cash payment from a fourth, photos of Simpson in bed with someone other than his wife, and the coup de grâce: testimony from a fellow Army officer who Simpson had supposedly blackmailed. In her research, Kathy had not encountered any of the people Detective Fuller mentioned. The photos looked undoctored, however, and the sworn and notarized affidavits appeared genuine.

"My goodness, JJ. This *is* exactly what I need. I can't thank you enough for your work. I should have approached Elsa months ago. I'm sure this will help. Simpson will be lucky the Army doesn't send him to the brig."

JJ beamed, and so did Elsa. "I never want you to hesitate, my dear," Elsa said. "I knew when Sally Belle brought you here the first time that a real spitfire had joined our group. Happy to help a lady with guts."

"And it was my pleasure Mrs. Delacroy," Fuller added. "These are for you, and I'll keep copies for my files in case anything happens or if we need to go to court."

"Again, thank you both. I have no idea how I can repay you."

"Oh, don't worry about that, sweetie," Elsa cooed. "Someday, I'll need a little favor, and I'll give you a call. Who knows? This was nothing."

They put all the evidence aside and finished their tea and turnovers. When Millie came in to offer refills, Kathy stood and said she needed to get home in time to fix dinner for Charles. They said their goodbyes, and Kathy walked to the foyer where Millie was waiting with her hat and coat.

"A good visit Miss Kathy?"

"Oh yes, Millie. I got everything I wanted and more. Thank you."

"Very good, ma'am. Have a pleasant evening."

"And a good evening to you, Millie."

When she walked out of Elsa Dekalb's house Sunday afternoon, Kathy knew there was little she would be able to do to stop Colonel Simpson except pray he would get transferred. She also considered talking to police officials about JJ Fuller's so-called evidence but didn't think that would be productive either. When she learned nearly twenty-five percent of the Atlanta police force were members of the Ku Klux Klan, Kathy remained convinced Fuller had set up the Black teenagers in Avery Dekalb's murder just to get paid off by a distraught Elsa.

⁂

As it was, winter turned to spring, the weather became hot, Billy Bull's physical threats never materialized, and by June, there were other things on Kathy's mind. Tensions between North and South Korea had reached dangerous levels, and on June 25, the Korean People's Army of the North invaded the South. Two days later, President Truman announced that he ordered US Forces to South Korea's aid.

Colonel Simpson quickly received a field command at the beginning of the conflict, and he selected Charles as his staff engineer. Kathy believed the selection to be a deliberate action against her for not yielding to his advances. In July 1950, Charles's reserve unit was called to active duty, and by August, before the next semester began at Georgia Tech, Charles was on a ship to the Korean peninsula.

He didn't return home again for nearly three more years.

Kathy later learned from Reverend Stillman that Billy Bull received his promotion to Brigadier General and ended his career as US Army liaison to the Navy and Air Force forces on Wake Island.

"He didn't deserve it," Kathy complained to Reverend Stillman.

The Army Chaplain ignored her and continued. "Simpson had command of exactly three people," he told her. "A male secretary, a driver, and some sort of steward. It was a humiliating assignment. The Army stationed him as far from civilization as possible."

"Big deal," Kathy said. "He still escaped. Got away with everything," she fumed.

But Reverend Stillman hadn't quite finished. "No, Kathy. He didn't. A government contractor helping reconstruct facilities after the devasting hurricane on Wake in '52, caught Simpson with his wife. He shot Billy Bull. Wounded him badly. The Army had had enough of their hero. They quietly discharged him and busted him back to Colonel. He became persona non grata to the brass.

"They did a good job keeping it secret. I never heard a word from anyone at Fort Mac," she said.

"Yes," Stillman agreed. "I only found out later when Mrs. Simpson came to me for counseling after she filed for divorce.

Kathy had only the barest twinge of guilt as she smiled.

The other major issue of the day was McCarthyism—another Red Scare. Senator Joe McCarthy and others convinced ordinary people, elected officials, businessmen, and more to believe communists were everywhere. He routinely accused freethinkers and liberal Hollywood actors of being communists. Regardless of the tacit approval Elsa Dekalb and those within her orbit gave Kathy, they couldn't help but be concerned when McCarthy, his followers, and the House Committee on Un-American Activities made their accusations. The fear of communism rapidly spread throughout the country. Mao's forces had taken over mainland China in 1949, and the Russians had implemented Churchill's Iron Curtain around most of eastern Europe at the end of WWII. The Russian and Chinese governments supported political leaders in North Korea, and the Russians exploded their first atomic bomb. It seemed like Reds and communist sympathizers were under every bed. People were paranoid, scared, and didn't know who to trust.

Kathy believed the pervasive fear within the country also impacted Charles's rank in the Army. She could never understand why Charles, who possessed excellent skills, experience, and knowledge, didn't progress past the rank of captain. Was Simpson truly vindictive, or was it their Russian heritage? Many people believed all Russians were communists. Maybe the Army did, too—to an extent. Amidst these suspicious and anxious times, with her heavy Russian accent and unique history, Kathy had to survive while her husband was away fighting the real communists and the forces they led.

1950 was notable for another reason. Charles's son, Al, married a young lady from New York City named Roberta Lynn Winstead. She worked in one of the city's department stores and met Al when he went in for lunch. The marriage stunned Charles because Al was only twenty-one years old.

"What does he know about being married?" Charles complained over his international call to Kathy. "He's too young. Why can't they wait until I come home to get married?"

"Al's a grown man," she responded. "He works hard, pays his bills—and besides, Roberta sounds lovely. You should be happy that he found someone."

Charles sighed, "Yes, she sounded nice over the phone to me too. Just hope they know what they're doing. Marriage is…can be… well…it requires effort."

Kathy laughed. "No kidding, my dear. You stay safe, and we'll plan to get together with them after you come home."

"Yes. Okay. Now—how are you doing? Is the communist paranoia fading out at home? Oh…my phone time's up. Love you. I'll call again when I can."

"I love you too."

Thankfully, the line clicked off, and she didn't have to tell him the communist purge was as strong as ever, and that only being a *former* Russian didn't matter to many folks in conservative Georgia. However, she was disappointed she didn't get to tell him how hard she worked at being the ultimate American housewife.

On a warm winter day in late February 1953, barely two weeks since Charles returned home from Korea, the doorbell rang at their small house. When Kathy opened the door, two men in dark business suits with stern faces greeted her.

"Are you Kathy Delacroy? Formerly Ekaterina Palutova?"

She hesitated before saying, "Yes...what can I do for you?"

"We need you to come downtown with us, Mrs. Delacroy," one of the men said.

"Downtown? But why? What's going on?"

"Relax, ma'am. Nothing to be concerned about," the second man said. "Just routine. That's all."

"It most certainly is not routine," Kathy answered. "Who are you, and what do you want with me?" She knew she sounded defensive.

One of the men reached into his pocket and withdrew his credentials, which identified him as working for the Georgia Attorney General's office. Kathy had no idea what that meant.

"I'm afraid that badge means nothing to me, gentlemen. What is the Attorney General's office? I'm sure you can tell I didn't grow up here."

The men looked at each other and laughed. "Obviously, Mrs. Delacroy, and that's why we're here."

"Because I didn't grow up here? That's why you want to take me into the city? For what purpose? You're not giving me answers. Perhaps I should call the police."

"That won't be necessary," the first man answered. "The police have more important things to do. Why don't you get your pocketbook and come along like a good girl? This won't take very long."

Good girl! Kathy was confused, outraged, and a little frightened. She vividly remembered the day the young Soviets came into her house and told Papa to report to the train station in Valday. The situation was not the same, but similar enough to make her shiver. She had followed all the rules, passed the exam, and was an American citizen. She knew she had rights, but she wasn't sure if refusing to go with an official from the state government was one. Flustered, she made a decision: she shut the door in their faces, hurried to the telephone, and dialed the number for the Chaplain's office at Fort McPherson. Just as she gave her name to the secretary, the front door slammed open, and the two men marched into the house. In three long strides, the taller of the two reached Kathy, removed the phone from her hand, and put it back in its cradle.

"That wasn't very sociable, Mrs. Delacroy. Closing the door in our faces like that," he said.

Kathy was shaking inside but didn't let the men see it. She put her hands on her hips and said, "I didn't invite you in. Please leave. You gave me no reason why I should accompany you *downtown*. None!"

The tall man got a nudge from his partner's elbow. "Come on, Steve. Tell her. I don't want to be here all day."

"Do you follow the news, Mrs. Delacroy? Read the papers? Listen to the radio? I see what looks like a new television. So, do you?"

"Of course," Kathy answered.

"Then you must be aware Soviet spies and communist sympathizers are running rampant all over the country," big Steve told her.

"Well, I read where some people think so. And I know about the Rosenbergs and that man, Hiss. If that's what you mean?"

"That's exactly what we mean," the shorter agent responded.

"So, what does that have to do with me?" Kathy was so angry, even though she now understood why the men were at her house. Her astonishment was genuine, and the attorney general's men believed she didn't understand.

"Oh, for Heaven's sake," Steve said. "You're Russian. Get it now? The Russians are commies. You also lived and worked in China. The Chinese are commies, too. It's easy to figure out, Mrs. Delacroy. The State of Georgia will not allow communist spies to infiltrate our communities. Now, let's go."

Steve grabbed her arm and yanked. Kathy began to yell as they dragged her out the front door. Her nextdoor neighbor, Lois Barnes, heard Kathy's shouts and stepped onto her stoop. Kathy saw Lois and screamed.

"Help, Lois! Help! They're taking me to the attorney general. They think I'm a communist spy. Help! Help!"

Lois put her hand to her mouth and froze. She watched the men bundle Kathy into the back of a car and drive off.

In a nondescript, gray government building in downtown Atlanta, Kathy sat alone at a table in a small office on the fourth floor. There was a window with an equally bland view of side streets and similar buildings. A cup of coffee sat on the table in front of her. It was untouched.

"Please wait here," Steve told her as he walked out and left the door open.

"What choice do I have?" she asked and got no answer. After five minutes, a sprite young man entered the room, leaving the door open.

"Hello, Mrs. Delacroy. I'm James Butler, assistant attorney general for the State of Georgia.

Kathy looked at him. *Barely out of college*, she guessed. Then, in her most polite voice, asked, "Why am I here, Mr. Butler? And how dare those two men drag me from my home? They're not the police, and had no warrant even if they were."

"I must apologize for the behavior of my colleagues. Sometimes they are a bit... overzealous in their duties," Butler said sincerely.

"And what, exactly, are those duties, Mr. Butler? Scaring women in their homes? Kidnapping? When I left China, I thought I'd escaped from authoritarians. Doesn't look like it. I intend to file a lawsuit against your office."

Jim Butler was caught off guard by Kathy's bravado and her

beauty. Like many men, he felt uneasy simply being in the presence of attractive and confident women. And in Kathy's experience, most men were either flustered and unsure around her—or misogynistic bullies, such as Colonel Simpson, Joshua Fleshman, and Kuniaki. As it turned out, Butler was neither. He proved to be a gentleman.

"I can see how this situation makes you angry. Please accept my apologies once again. You must understand there are people within the country who want to cause us—that is, the United States—harm, including the officials and residents of Georgia. It's my task to help identify and prosecute anyone we find who plans to do such harm."

"And for the hundredth time, Mr. Butler, where do I fit in?"

"Yes, of course. Well, I understand that while you lived in New Jersey, you had photos taken by a Mr. Sergei Lebedev. Is that correct?"

"Sergei? Sergei Lebedev? Yes. He took some beautiful photographs of me, and they helped me get a job modeling. How do you know about that? And, so what?"

"You attended church at Saints Peter and Paul *Orthodox* Cathedral in Jersey City, and you're still in touch with Mr. Lebedev?"

"Yes. Sergei's my friend, but I'm not going to answer any more questions." Kathy rose, walked to the door, and said, "How dare you spy on me? I'm leaving."

Butler pleaded, "Mrs. Delacroy, please wait. This *is* very important. It could mean life or death to any number of good people."

She glared at him with more than a skeptical eye. "Mr. Butler, so far, men broke into my house, brought me here without my permission, asked me questions about something I know nothing about, and now you bring up Sergei and the Cathedral in Jersey City. Do you know anything about Sergei? Or the people at that cathedral? Let me tell you something."

Before she could share the tragic life story of Sergei, and desperate to get something out of her, Butler blurted, "Did you know Sergei's family fought for the Reds and set up communist schools in various

Russian cities? They did such a good job indoctrinating children his family received contracts to help the East Germans set up theirs."

"Did *you* know that Sergei survived Tannenberg?" she countered. "And more than three years in a German POW camp? Then the Russian Revolution with all its craziness? He fought with the Whites— the *Whites,* Mister Butler—and got captured by the Soviets, the *real* commies, Mister Butler. So, back to prison, where he finally escaped to Shanghai. As if that was not enough, he had to flee again when the Japanese moved in.

"Next, he made his way to the Philippines and became a fisherman. He worked like a slave for six years for the boat owner. Finally, in 1939, a brother tracked him down. His brother spent a small fortune and nearly a year haggling with the US State Department before receiving permission for Sergei to immigrate. He moved to a neighborhood in New Jersey with other displaced Russians and learned to take photographs. He has done nothing but help people like me put together a portfolio and preserve memories.

"The audacity—hell, the lunacy of you or anyone else thinking Sergei Lebedev is a communist sympathizer is...is...*neveroyatnyy!* Unbelievable! And, again, it has *nothing* to do with *me!*" When she finished, Kathy caught her breath and was almost too exhausted to stand up. But she did, and headed for the door.

"That was a nice story, Mrs. Delacroy, but you know, people can change. The information we have proves his family is a big supporter of Uncle Joe. You know, Joseph Stalin." He didn't tell her that he had never heard of Tannenberg or, more importantly, he didn't care how tough Sergei's life had been.

"You know, Mr. Butler, I had to take an examination to become a US citizen. I had to read and learn a great deal about American history. Did you know in the 1860s, there was a great Civil War? Right here in the United States. And this city, Atlanta, was destroyed by the Northern Army. And did you also know the war divided many families? Some members supported the North, others the South. I see no difference with my friend Sergei. Now, get the hell out of my way. I'm leaving."

To Kathy's surprise, Butler stepped aside and let her pass. She maintained control as she walked down the hall and to the elevator. Once outside, she inhaled several deep breaths, and her heart rate slowed. She walked carefully to the corner bus stop and boarded the first bus without checking to see where it was going.

The first thing Kathy did when she got home was make sure she had something ready for dinner. If Charles walked in the door and found the stove empty or nothing warming in the oven, he would ask too many questions about her day. Whereas, if things appeared normal, he would settle into his chair for a quick smoke on his pipe, read through the mail, and come to dinner when she called without much more than kissing her and saying, *Hope you had a good day.* But she was uncertain her stamina would hold if he asked more.

As she worked in the kitchen, the doorbell rang. The hairs on the back of her neck stood on end, and she broke out in a sudden sweat. *Were they back? Would they ring the bell again or just break in?* She walked to the front door and listened but didn't hear anything. She adjusted the curtain in the living room enough to peek out and didn't see a strange car on the street. Then there was a knock, the doorbell rang a second time, and a voice rang out.

"Kathy? Kathy, are you in there? It's me, Lois."

She hurried to the door and let her neighbor in.

"Oh, Kathy, you're here, and you're okay. I'm so relieved. I saw those men take you away in that car. It looked like a kidnapping. I was getting ready to call the police…"

"The police?!" Kathy almost screeched. The look on her face was something Lois had never seen. "You didn't call, did you?" It came out as a plea of desperation.

"As a matter of fact, no. I was about to dial when my phone rang. My mother took a fall, and I had to give her a hand."

"Oh, what a relief!" Kathy exhaled, then realized what she had said. "Not that your mother fell, oh no. Is she okay?"

"Yes, she's fine, Kathy, but I'm not so sure about you. What happened?"

"It's nothing, really. Nothing."

"You're my neighbor, but more importantly, my best friend. I can tell something's wrong. What is it? Maybe I can help."

"No, Lois. Truly. The men this morning, well, they wanted to talk to me for a few minutes about some people I knew back in New Jersey who've gotten themselves into some trouble. I'm okay."

Lois's face had skepticism painted across it. "Come on, Kathy. There's something you're not telling me."

Lois and her husband had moved in a month after she and Charles. They had a toddler named Maggie, a cute little girl with glistening red hair. She was a good friend.

What am I worried about? Kathy asked herself. *Lois knows my history. Oh, what the hell?*

"Yes, you're right, Lois. Come in. You can help me get dinner ready before Charles gets here. We only have a few minutes." Kathy talked as they cut vegetables. After explaining the day's incidents in detail, Lois was also outraged.

"My God, Kathy. You need to report them. They can't do things like that to American citizens and get away with it."

"They did, and they have, Lois. Who could I report them to? I haven't lived in Russia since 1924. Almost thirty years, but they think I'm some communist spy—or in cahoots with one."

"Well, I bet Charles will know what to do," Lois offered.

"I have no intention of telling Charles what happened. Do you know he was born in an area of Poland that was part of the Russian empire? His naturalization and immigration papers list him as Russian. No, Lois. No need to make a problem for him, too."

Lois thought and added, "You know, Kathy, they may be watching him too, and he didn't want to upset *you*. I think you should tell him."

Kathy stopped her chopping. "Oh, I don't know. This can't be real, Lois," she fumed. "I'm so angry—but can handle this. I don't want to upset Charles. Thank you for listening and caring. I only ask one favor. Please don't tell anyone they took me in for questioning. I think some neighbors probably don't trust me, like those idiots from the Attorney General's office."

"You have my word, Kath. My lips are sealed."

The women turned their heads toward the front of the house when they heard the door open.

"Hi, Kathy. I'm home," Charles bellowed as he removed his winter coat and hat and hung them on the hooks in the hall. "Something smells good." He walked into the kitchen and was surprised to see Lois. "Oh! Hi, Lois! Are we having company for dinner?" he asked both women.

"No, Charles. I realized I was low on potatoes and asked Lois if I could borrow a couple. She came over, and we got to chatting and lost track of time. Thank you, Lois. With Charles home, I know your Bill won't be far behind. Sorry if you lost time getting his dinner ready."

"We'll be fine. Bye, Kathy. Charles, good to see you. Enjoy dinner." Lois picked up her coat and headed out the front door.

Charles leaned in and gave Kathy a kiss. "Good to be home, honey. I'm starved. When do we eat?"

"Ten minutes. Go wash up."

He turned to go up to the bathroom and then asked, "How was your day?"

"Okay. How about yours?"

14   SPRING 1963—SUMMER 1968
Atlanta

Charles returned home in the summer of 1953, to his and Kathy's delight.

"I feel revived. As if I was a spring flower blooming again after a long winter," Kathy told him.

"Me too," Charles said, as they shared coffee and the Sunday paper on their patio a few weeks later. "I forgot how beautiful our garden is."

"Is that all that's beautiful?" she teased.

He reached across from his lounge chair to hers, took her hand, and kissed it. "Of course not," he said. Being together again renewed their passion for each other, and he smiled, thinking of the previous evening in bed. But he also said, "And I must admit I'm looking forward to getting back into a normal routine. No military emergencies, no crises. Just you and work. It will be so dull, I'll love it."

"Me too," Kathy agreed.

Classes began for Charles. The days clicked by. Weeks. Months. Backyard picnics with neighbors, occasional visits with Al and—before long—his children, and their social commitments at Georgia Tech, church, and the Army. Life was good. It was normal. They paid careful attention to fading Red Scare and they wanted to throw a party when Senator McCarthy and his cronies were finally discredited late in 1954. They enjoyed the peace and prosperity that much of the country experienced during President Eisenhower's tenure. However, the rumblings of civil rights issues, notably the Supreme Court decision about school desegregation and the subsequent deployment of troops to Little Rock, troubled them both.

As the years progressed, Charles enjoyed his routine. His life with Kathy. Despite never receiving his Army promotion nor advancing beyond assistant professor at Georgia Tech, he never complained. He did his research, loved his students, and ushered many new, young officers through the realities of life in the Army. However, this didn't satisfy Kathy.

"You deserve a promotion, Charles. Two, in fact. One at Tech, and one from the Army. It makes me so mad. Why won't you let me go raise a rucksack?" she implored.

"Raise a ruckus, Kath. It's raise a ruckus," he giggled for the millionth time at one of her malapropisms.

"Ruckus, schmukus," she said. "Why don't you complain?"

"You remember when you were little? You had to leave home. You had to start over. Again and again. I only moved once, from Bialystok to Weehawken. I had stability from when I was born until I was fourteen and then again from fourteen until I was thirty-two. I like it. We have everything we need, and especially for me, I have you. I don't need promotions. I have all I've ever wanted."

He took her in his arms, and she said, "Me too. I won't bring it up again."

Everyone who knew Charles said he always focused on his academic and military commitments without regard to personal status. He did his duty selflessly, without ego. He never once complained about being passed over for promotions. But Kathy loved him and hated to see him work so hard without recognition and reward. Understanding Kathy's concern about his status and anticipating more time together, Charles retired from the Army in 1963. He was sixty-three years old and had served for twenty-one years, eighteen of them as a captain. He heard that he might be the senior captain in the Army at the time of his retirement, but he didn't check. It didn't matter. Kathy was only forty-seven, and from '53 to '63, she had modeled on and off and was a dedicated regular in the base chapel choir. When Charles left the Army, Kathy was, for the most part, the classic American housewife.

Well… almost.

⁂

"Who's calling?" Kathy answered the phone.

"The *Atlanta Journal,*" the pleasant male voice said.

"I'm sorry, we already have a subscription," Kathy responded. "But thank you for calling."

As she was getting ready to hang up, the voice went on. "Mrs. Delacroy? Mrs. Charles Delacroy? I'm not calling about a subscription. My name is Howard Stein, and I'm the Family Life editor at the paper. We're doing a special article for one of our Sunday editions. It's going to be about typical American housewives, and we want to include you."

"The newspaper? *You* want to put *me* in the newspaper? As a typical *American* housewife?"

"Yes, Mrs. Delacroy. That's correct."

Kathy was surprised and amused. She had worked hard during the past fifteen years to be exactly that—an ordinary suburban wife. To be recognized in the newspaper would boost her ego and improve her position within Atlanta social circles. However, she wondered how much the newspaper really knew about her.

"So, what does this mean, Mr. Stein? What do I have to do? What do you need to know?"

"We want to schedule a time for a reporter and photographer

to come to your home. The reporter will interview you, and the photographer, of course, will take some pictures."

"I see. My home is quite basic, and I'm not sure your readers will learn much from seeing it. And me, well, let's put it this way—I'm not as young as I once was."

"You see, Mrs. Delacroy, that's what we want to display. We want modern women to understand it's perfectly acceptable and possible—admirable, even—to maintain a good household and have your own life. No matter their age or neighborhood." Stein was doing his best to close the deal.

"Mr. Stein, can you tell me how *I* was selected to be one of your highlighted homemakers?"

"Well, it seems you have an admirer. Someone well-placed within the community who told us you have what we're looking for."

His last statement made Kathy break out in a hearty chuckle.

"Is something wrong, Mrs. Delacroy?"

"Oh no. Not at all, except I've heard that line before, and each time I followed up, it didn't always turn out the way I expected."

"I assure you, you have nothing to worry about. The *Atlanta Journal* can't afford to support or undertake anything that isn't above board. As a matter of fact, you'll likely gain some wonderful benefits."

Kathy doubted that, but she was intrigued by the call and replied that she would discuss the proposal with Charles before deciding. Stein said he was under a deadline and would need her response by noon the following day, or he would have to move on to someone else.

"That's fine, Mr. Stein. I'll be in touch before noon tomorrow. Thank you for considering me."

They hung up, and Kathy immediately picked the phone back up and dialed the first of several calls. "Hi, Lois? It's me, Kathy."

"Hi, Kath. What's up?"

"You're never going to believe this. And Maggie will go crazy too."

"What? What is it? Quit stalling."

"Okay. The *Atlanta Journal* just called. They want me to be one of their—what were his words—one of their *typical American housewives* for a special Sunday *Journal* supplement. Can you believe it? They want to send a reporter and a photographer to the house to interview me and take photos."

"Oh Kathy, how wonderful. I know Debby will be jealous, and your friend Sally Belle and her crew will too."

Kathy's second call was to Debby Collins. The two women had frequently talked about their modeling experiences, and although Debby was ten years younger than Kathy, they both had dealt with the loose-woman stigma that followed models. Deb's son Harry, who Charles was instructing on how to care for car engines, resulted from an ill-advised marriage. When she modeled, Debby had been infatuated with a handsome, smooth-talking account manager. But after two years, his roving eyes and antics ended the relationship. Kathy and Debby knew almost everything about each other.

"You might be right, Deb, but I'm still curious how they picked me. There are thousands of housewives around Atlanta. And most with families—you know, with kids. The more I think about it, the less I think I'm a *typical* housewife. You know what I mean?"

"I think you're fretting over a great opportunity. Don't worry about it," Debby encouraged. "The *Journal* is a responsible paper. Why would they make this up? And who would play such a hoax on you? No—I bet Sally Belle or maybe old Elsa Dekalb slipped your name to someone they know."

"Yeah. You're probably right. Thanks, Deb. Gotta go. Couple more calls to make."

"Okay, Kath. Let me know when they're coming for the photoshoot. I'd love to watch."

They said their goodbyes, and Kathy went straight to dialing another number.

"Oh, thank Heavens they called you!" exclaimed Sally Belle in her impeccable southern style. "They talked to me months ago…"

Kathy interrupted. "You're in this, too?"

"Oh, no, honey. Not me. They said because of Nathan's status, you know, as Engineering Dean, I wouldn't be considered *typical*. And they also said they wanted to add someone who might be a bit—what was the word they used—yes—exotic."

Kathy didn't know if she should laugh or feel grateful. She knew people considered her unusual, primarily because of her accent, which had never vanished, but she still had questions. "How did this all come about, Sally Belle? Who got me involved?"

"Well, I did, of course. Last fall, you know, you complained about how many hours Charles worked and how you wished he spent more time at home. Well, right around then, Nathan was interviewed because of his promotion at Tech."

"Yes, I remember. There were nice articles about Nathan in the *Journal* and *Constitution*."

"Indeed. The papers did a great job. But anyway, Nathan got to talking with a reporter about the university and newspaper stuff, and the reporter told him the *Journal* planned to do a feature on American housewives. Nathan bragged to the reporter about me, and I got a visit from this fellow—uh, Howard Stein. When he saw our new house and heard what position Nathan had, he apologized and said—oh Kathy, please don't take offense—Mr. Stein said he was looking for families, uh, less well...positioned. More middle-of-the-road. And then he said he also hoped to find an exotic American housewife. That's when I told him about you."

Kathy gave a little chuckle. "That's fine, Sally Belle. I'm not embarrassed. Our life is good. No complaints. At least now I know how come I got the phone call. I'll keep you posted. Bye, and thank you."

The last call was to Reverend Colonel Milton Stillman. He had returned wounded from Korea in 1952 and was assigned permanently to Fort McPherson as head chaplain after Dodson retired. Something about him exuded honesty and trust, combined with steadfast faith and commitment to doing the right thing. Kathy had visited him many times, discussing various topics and concerns. She always thanked him for his advice but didn't always follow it. She had a mind of her own, which she had demonstrated numerous times, and more often than not, her life experiences confirmed the wisdom of her decisions. Nevertheless, she sought out Rev. Stillman one more time.

"Reverend, this is Kathy Delacroy," she spoke into the phone.

"Hello, Kathy. How are you today? And please, why can't you call me Milton after so many years?"

"For the same reason I've told you a hundred times—my Grandmama, my Babushka Raisa, taught me that proper respect is due to clergy. That's it, and I still listen to her. And I'm fine, thank you."

"Yes. Very well. So, if you're fine, what prompts your call?"

She told him about the phone call from Howard Stein. Then asked, "Do you think I should go ahead with this?"

He answered with a question. "What do you want to do?"

"For Heaven's sake, Reverend! I'm asking your opinion. You must have some thoughts?"

"Kathy, to better assist you, I need to know why you brought this question to me. There must be some reason why you seem to be hesitating."

She looked at the floor. They had had similar conversations in the past. They all seemed to center on the roles and expectations of women in society. Many dealt with how women were treated depending on what they did. Work or stay at home. Children or no children. Cook or don't cook. And if they worked, what did they do? The list went on. As far as she was concerned, the call from Mr. Stein put her in the middle of those issues again.

"Well, is it acceptable in polite society for me to open my home as if I were some celebrity and pose for photos? What will people say? What will they think?" Her tone and questions were blunt.

"What does Charles think about the idea?" the Reverend asked.

"I haven't told him yet. He's at work, and I didn't want to bother him."

"Of course. It seems to me you may want to confer with him first."

"Oh, I know what he'll say. He'll say, 'do what you want, Kathy.'"

"If you know he won't object, then I think that's everything you need to know. He trusts you and supports your decision. It won't bother him no matter what anyone else says or thinks."

Ugh! Men, she thought. "But it matters to me!" She was frustrated and getting nowhere with the good Reverend Stillman. *Sometimes he can be as obtuse as Charles,* she thought.

"Have you told anyone else?" he asked.

"Yes. Friends…and before you say anything, they're all for it."

"So, there you are. People you care about, people you're willing to call friends, think it's a good idea."

"Oh, what's that? Oh no. I hear the front door. Look at the time. It must be Charles. Thank you, Reverend. Bye." And just like that, she hung up on him and greeted her husband.

The discussion with Charles went exactly as she thought it would. He would support her in whatever endeavor she proposed—a very liberal attitude by a conservative man in most other instances. Good thing, because Kathy always knew she would do the interview and photoshoot the minute Howard Stein made the offer. The old entertainer in her could not turn down such a proposition. And, if any backroom chatter emerged about her life during many difficult and terrible years, what could she do about it? People would say what they wanted. She didn't care—oh, yes, she did. But many of them, she had learned, were hypocrites, including her friend Elsa.

Elsa Dekalb was seventy in 1963 and remained one of the grand dames of Atlanta. She ruled at the Atlanta Women's Club, and her weekly socials with her women friends were must-attend events. Kathy was happy to be a regular and went most weeks with Sally Belle. However, Elsa, for all the help she had given Kathy over the years—particularly during the Korean Conflict with Charles away—never once consented to visit Kathy and Charles at *their* home. In a slip resulting from too many cocktails, Kathy overheard Elsa speaking to one of the women.

"Can't trust them. Either one—Russians, you know. No good, sons-a-bitches commies. And should J. Edgar and his boys think I'm colluding with them, well, he'll understand my responsibilities as a civic leader. Need to keep your friends close, but your enemies closer. Now ain't that the truth."

Although McCarthy had been gone for years, the Cold War was at its peak. Kathy decided not to mention the exchange to Sally Belle, who was very close to Elsa, but she shared it with Lois, Reverend Stillman, and Charles. The Army chaplain told her good people are often confused by *government gibberish and often fear the unknown.*

Talking to Charles that evening, he asked first what Debby and Lois thought about Elsa's comments.

"I told Lois. She's younger, and I knew she'd give me a realistic perspective. She told me not to worry. She explained with President Kennedy in office, she believes the government has moved past its fear of expatriate Russians who are US citizens."

Charles stayed true to form. "When some people get certain ideas in their head," he began, "it's nearly impossible to get rid of them. Do you like participating in the weekly teas at Elsa's?"

"Yes, I do, but it's…"

"If you like going, don't worry about it. People are always doing things behind one another's backs. It's the way of the world, my love. Just the way it is."

"I think you're wrong, Charles. It's okay to tell little white lies to children or tell me how beautiful I am right after I wake up in the morning. But when you profess to be someone's friend and instead believe that person is someone you despise, that's different."

"Look at it this way," he responded. "Even if Mrs. Dekalb thinks you're a communist, so what? She throws a fun social event each week with great food and drinks. I say you should keep going and enjoy it."

"If you say so, Charles. But it bothers me."

"Oh, come on, Kathy. She had too much to drink. In those cases, people say things they don't mean."

"Yes, that might be. But they also say what they really feel."

As they went up to bed, she couldn't help but think about Mr. Stein's offer. Here she was, inviting The *Atlanta Journal* into her home. Who knows how some people will react? Elsa's biases could turn to jealousy. She laughed at the thought. As far as she knew, Elsa Dekalb, who considered herself the epitome of a modern Atlanta woman, had never been a typical American housewife—someone worthy enough to be part of a special section in the paper. Yes— Kathy would tell Mr. Stein she would do it. If only to show Elsa how much of an American Kathy was.

The Sunday paper finally hit the newsstands and front porches in April, the week after Easter. Inside the Family Life section, the article about the *typical American Housewife* consumed three pages, including multiple column inches and half a dozen color photos. It was an impressive professional piece. Paper distribution covered all 152 counties in Georgia and neighboring counties in North and South Carolina, Tennessee, Alabama, and Florida, encompassing a potential readership of more than ten million people. However, Howard Stein hadn't told Kathy the complete truth. Although there were *comments* by other housewives, the bulk of the feature and all the photos were about Kathy Delacroy, with not a word about her *work history* in China. The phone in her house started to ring non-stop even before she left for church.

"Here she comes," one of the choir members yelled as Kathy entered the chapel for the pre-service rehearsal. Everyone applauded and cheered.

Kathy waved them off, but they kept cheering, "Our new celebrity!" or, "Way to go, Kathy!" or, "Hollywood will be calling." She smiled, took her place among them, and said, "Stop it. I had no idea it was going to be so much on me. I'll tell you the whole story later."

Her choir mates quieted down, and the service progressed until Reverend Stillman decided to make ad hoc closing comments before his benediction. "Among us today, my friends—and nearly every Sunday—is someone of strong character, determination, and, most certainly, a mind of her own. She is, by all accounts, a typical American housewife and, as such, deserves all the notoriety she can garner from taking over the Family Life section of today's paper. Three cheers for Kathy Delacroy." And the congregation did.

However, friendship and joy can be short-lived. In the most prominent *Journal* photo, Kathy wore one of her Asian silk outfits. It was reddish maroon with multicolored flowers stitched evenly across the garment. The photographer admired the gown as much as Kathy and positioned her on her old divan to highlight both. The upholstery was soft, felt-like, the color of a warm yellow sunset, and she looked spectacular on it. He had directed her to place her arms and legs in a way that many readers found alluring. "Like Cleopatra on her barge", one reader wrote. A *typical American housewife*? Not in that shot.

The sun's rays settled on Kathy through the bus window during her ride home after church, and her soft spring dress burst with colors accentuating her finer points. Her hair sparkled beneath her hat, and her moist ruby lips only heightened her appeal. Kathy hopped off at her stop and began the two-block walk to her house. The trees, shrubs, and decorative hedges that landscaped the tidy cottages had grown high since Kathy and Charles had moved in. The growth offered numerous places for neighborhood children to play hide-and-seek, cowboys and Indians, and other games. It also gave the man who followed her off the bus a place to drag her. His sudden attack caught Kathy completely unaware as he clamped a rough hand over her mouth, stifling her scream.

"I saw you, pretty bitch, in the paper. Pretending to be some fancy movie star. You ain't shit. Nothing but a pinko commie bitch. And you know what we do with commies?"

He yanked her behind a row of dense cherry laurels where no one could see them. His breath smelled of cigarettes and alcohol, but his clothes were clean and expensive. Too expensive to have been riding on the bus. He forced her face to the ground and placed one knee on her back. One hand remained over her mouth while the other held her head in the dirt.

"If I remove my hand, promise you won't scream?" he asked.

She could barely move her head but indicated yes. He slowly withdrew his hand, but as he did so, he shifted his weight just enough to give her room to roll from under him. Kathy sprang to her feet and began to run and scream. She shed her shoes in a single motion and hiked up her dress, making running more manageable, but her assaulter was fast. He caught her by the hair and pulled hard. Kathy lurched backward, spun involuntarily, and landed in the perfect position to whip her foot into her assailant's groin. He doubled over, and she took off again. Her screams brought several folks outside, and a police siren grew louder, but Kathy didn't stop. She didn't look back until she banged open her front door, nearly knocking it off its hinges.

"Charles! Charles! Oh, Charles! Help me!"

Charles rushed into the front room and found Kathy curled in a ball on the old divan, crying and seething with anger. *Stop crying,* she ordered herself, and for a long lingering moment, she began to curse her foreignness, her beauty, and—dare she say it—her sexiness. But it was natural. It was who she was. She didn't put on airs like Elsa or others she knew. She was real. And she was persecuted for it. *Damn*, she hated that.

"Damn it, Charles. I'm forty-seven, not twenty-seven. I can see my wrinkles. What is it with some men?"

"What happened? You look a mess. Are you hurt?"

"A man on the bus…" she sputtered. "He called me pretty and a pinko commie." And she told him the rest.

"You're a beautiful woman, my dear. No matter the age." He hugged her.

"It's a curse, Charles."

"If you're cursed, why am I so lucky to have you?" And he kissed her.

Charles called the police, and the patrol car dispatched earlier arrived at their house before he hung up. Two officers rang the bell, and when they came inside, Kathy was still askew. Her hair was a mess. She had lost her hat, was shoeless, and had holes in her stockings. Her face was bruised and dirty from the ground, and her dress was torn down a long seam and covered with dirt and grass stains. Regardless, her eyes were set, dried, and determined. And that's what the officers saw. Someone who escaped. A woman who could *handle it. No harm done.* Not really.

"Hey, Mrs. Delacroy, didn't I see your picture in the paper this morning?"

"Thank you for coming and taking my complaint, officers. Please try and catch this pervert. I know I gave you a good description."

"That was you, wasn't it?" the officer persisted.

"Yes, now I've had a rough time and need to clean up. Goodbye, officers."

"Officers, my wife was attacked. What are you going to do about it?" Charles demanded and red with anger.

"Yes sir. We know, but with little to go on…if you ever need any more help, please call," he said.

He walked to the door, turned, gave her a wink, and left.

"Did you see that, Charles? Did you see that asshole policeman? They aren't even going to try and find this guy. Let me tell you, I've come up against some zealous, drunken men and others who I can't even talk about, but those two policemen seem to come from the same family as the guy who chased me."

"I'll call their superiors," Charles said, but wasn't sure what anyone could do. However, from then on, he accompanied Kathy to church. The incident left her rattled. She wondered if real peace and freedom could ever be found.

The summer of 1963 was upon them before they realized it. Hot steamy weather settled in by late May, and all Kathy wanted to do was read and drink iced tea sitting in front of a fan on her shady patio. Moving around was a major effort, but not for Charles. He frequently told her that "taking a constitutional," a phrase he had learned as a boy from a teacher in Bialystok who enjoyed English idioms, was necessary. "Gets my blood going," he would say. So, nearly every day, Charles would take a walk, even on cold rainy days. He varied his route around the neighborhood and always went before breakfast when there was daylight. During the shorter daylight seasons, he walked at lunchtime. As it was, he rarely walked more than an hour, even on the loveliest days.

Wednesday morning, July 3, Charles and Kathy were at home in the middle of a vacation week. They woke just before sunrise without an alarm, as they did most mornings, and Charles was out the door by seven for his walk. It was a typical midsummer day. The outdoor thermometer on the large tree next to the patio read 83 degrees, and heavy dampness on the lounge chair cushions indicated high humidity. *Nothing new*, Kathy thought as she spread a towel on the lounge. She sat down with her iced coffee—deferring from her usual morning tea—and the newspaper Charles had tossed inside when he left. Engrossed in the newspaper, Kathy lost track of time. It wasn't until she heard the doorbell she realized it was almost 9:30. *9:30! How did I not hear Charles come in? He should be out of the shower by now—and I didn't fix breakfast! Who could be at the door on a Sunday morning?* As soon as she opened the door, she knew. She didn't know how she knew, but she knew.

"Good morning, ma'am. We're knocking on doors in the neighborhood..."

"It's Charles, isn't it?" she asked the uniformed officers. "I expected him back more than an hour ago. He's tall and thin, sixty-three, fair thinning hair with a slight red tint."

"Can you remember what he was wearing?" one of them asked.

"Yes, long khaki slacks and a lightweight gray sweatshirt over a white T-shirt."

"Ma'am, please, we'd like you to accompany us if you could get your things."

"He's gone, isn't he, officers? My Charles. My Charles is dead. Isn't he?" she said this with a sense of sadness and loss, but not one of hysterical grief.

"We're not sure the man we found is your Charles. And what is your name, ma'am?"

"Oh yes, I'm sorry. I'm Mrs. Charles Delacroy. My name is Kathy."

She invited the police officers inside while she went to change. When she returned, they were caught off-guard by her natural grace, the elegance of her appearance—although she only wore a simple dress—and her somewhat stoic, matter-of-fact attitude.

"Charles went out for one of his *vigorous* walks. He loved to 'take the air,' he would say. No matter the weather."

"Yes, ma'am."

"If you don't mind, I'd like to make a couple of calls first."

"Yes, ma'am. Go right ahead."

When she finished her calls, the officers escorted Kathy to their car and helped her into the backseat. The last time she was in the back seat of such a car, zealous bureaucrats had carted her *downtown* for questioning. *How ironic*, she thought. Now she was being ushered with courtesy by the police.

"We received a phone call from someone about six blocks from your house," the officer driving informed her. "From what you told us, the call must have been about a half-hour after Charles left home. A man walking his dog found him. When the first officer arrived, he found a man lying still on the sidewalk, not breathing. If this is your Charles, he expired before the ambulance arrived. His pockets were empty, he had no other identification, and they took him to the city morgue. I'm sorry it took so long for us to find you."

"It's not your fault, officers. No one's fault."

He could see Kathy in the rearview mirror and watched her as she absorbed the news. Her reaction was one of acceptance, with an occasional slight widening of her eyes and a gentle nod. Familiar with the twists and turns life can dish out, Kathy remained calm on the ride to the morgue. The officers took her to a basement room, where Charles was lying on a stainless steel table under bright lights. Thin wisps of his once blonde-red hair lay neatly across his head. The creases in his pants remained arrow straight. They reminded Kathy of how he fussed when he wore his uniform. He had always made sure every detail was correct, but his sweatshirt had a small tear and bloodstain at the shoulder where he had fallen on it. She ran her hand across his cheek and patted his face.

"Goodbye, Charles," she said. "Thank you, my love, for everything."

The coroner told her it looked like a heart attack, but asked if she wanted an autopsy. She declined. She said his family had a history of heart problems, and she suspected the coroner was correct. Moments later, the Reverend Colonel Stillman arrived. He had raced to meet Kathy immediately after getting her call. He led her from the room of air-conditioned, antiseptic death and took her outside into the barely breathable air of an Atlanta summer. Reverend Stillman said nothing. He had learned over many years that words are meaningless at such times.

"Tomorrow was to be our seventeenth anniversary," Kathy spoke resignedly. "We didn't have anything special planned. Probably just dinner at a favorite restaurant."

Stillman listened and continued to remain silent.

"You know, Reverend, I told him over and over to wear shorts and a T-shirt. He didn't need all those clothes in this kind of weather. And you know what he would say?" Kathy didn't wait for an answer, "He'd say, 'Kathy, grown men shouldn't dress like children when they're out in public.' Ha! He thought shorts and T-shirts were only for kids. Oh, Charles, my dear wonderful Charles."

She took Stillman's hand and asked, "Can you please take me home?"

"Of course, Kathy. Of course."

Kathy called Al with the news while he and his family were vacationing at a New England campground. Al left the family behind and took the first flight he could get to Atlanta.

"Hello, Albert," she had greeted him at the airport. "Thank you for coming. I've got everything under control. You don't have to worry."

She saw the quizzical look on his face, followed by comprehension. He was not alone, as he had been when his mother died. Sure, he could have handled it now. He was older. Experienced. But Kathy, with help from Debby, Lois, Sally Belle, and Reverend Stillman, made most of the arrangements. Al would only need to take care of a few loose ends.

The United States Government laid Captain Charles Delacroy to rest on July 8, 1963, in the National Cemetery at Marietta, Georgia. He joined 10,000 Civil War soldiers and countless other veterans from America's other conflicts. Likewise, the names of numerous spouses adorned the white marble stones. The modest headstones suited Kathy because Charles preferred simplicity. There had never been anything complex about him.

The mourners at the Fort McPherson service and the gravesite were colleagues and friends of Charles's and Kathy's, including the elderly, retired, and remorseful dean of engineering at Stevens Tech. Charles's parents and siblings had predeceased him, so there was no other family except two cousins on Al's mother's side. They sent their regrets. Nathan Harris read the eulogy for his old Army pal, and afterward, Kathy hosted a quiet reception in the shaded backyard garden of her and Charles's small house. By late afternoon, everyone had left except Reverend Stillman and Debby. Even Al was on his way back to his family. As Milton and Kathy gathered glasses, plates, and used napkins, Debby asked the question many others had asked.

"What are you going to do, Kathy?"

She looked at her kind neighbor and said, "Keep on living. That's my plan."

Although it had only been five days since Charles's heart attack, she had already shifted gears. A lifetime of sudden loss and heartache had prepared her. Growing up without a mother. Leaving her grandfather, uncles, and cousins behind. Being naïve and taken advantage of by Kuniaki. Running in fear from Chinese gangs. Losing her child through an unwanted adoption. Her father and grandmother killed in accidents. Becoming famous and then losing her job. Watching Marcel sail away and vanish from her life. The kind Dutchman Johannes and his associates blown to pieces on the *Tjipawan*. Darya, sweet Darya, bombed to death in Manila. Ignored by in-laws, challenged by government officials, brutes in the Army and more. And now, Charles. Kathy's list of sad memories was long, but she refused to feel sorry for herself. She would live. She would figure out her finances and assess her options.

"You're still young and attractive, Kathy. I know several agencies that would be happy to have you model for them," Debby offered encouragement.

"Oh, Debby, stop that. It's flattering, and I love it, but I'll be fifty soon. We both know that is way out of line for any agency."

"Well, how about singing?" Reverend Stillman joined in. "You have one of the most beautiful voices I've ever heard. How lucky we've been to have you in the choir."

"Reverend, that's a job for young people. It's mostly night work, and I'm not staying out that late anymore. I'll be fine. Don't either of you worry about me. I've got a few ideas, and when I settle on something, you'll know.

Reverend Stillman turned to look at Kathy and said, "You better."

She smiled and returned to the tasks at hand, cleaning up her garden and stacking the dishes in the kitchen sink.

"Why don't you head out, Reverend? Kathy and I will finish up here. Thanks for your help," Debby said.

"Very well, ladies. Debby, it was my pleasure, and Kathy, I'll see you Sunday."

"Yes. You will."

Once Reverend Stillman was gone, Debby remained curious. "So, come on, Kathy. Give me a clue. What are you going to do?"

"What do you think of my English?" Kathy replied with a question of her own.

"What do you mean? I understand everything you say. If that's what you're asking."

"My accent, is it a problem?"

"No. Not at all. Now and then, you still have a funny expression or get words in the wrong order, but hardly ever. What's this all about?"

"You were the one who asked me. Remember?"

Debby laughed, "Yes. Go ahead. You know what I mean."

"I'm thinking about doing some oral translation work."

"Are there many Russian speakers in Atlanta?" Debby was curious.

"I have no idea, but I'm going to find out." Kathy wiped her hands on a towel and switched on her favorite classical radio station. "We're done, Debby. Thank you. Go home to your family. Say hi to Harry for me. I'll need his help more than ever now, with the car."

"Night, Kath. Call if you need anything." And then Debby was gone, and Ekaterina Palutova Delacroy was alone—again.

It didn't take Kathy long to get on a translators' list, but it wasn't until October that she accepted her first translation job at Georgia Tech.

"They hired me," she nearly shouted to Deb Collins with excitement. "Nathan did it. He sent in a recommendation for me. It did the trick."

"That's fantastic, Kath. Come on over for dinner, and we'll celebrate."

After her first assignment, she began to receive one or two a week from various organizations. Between her translator income and her spousal pensions from the Army and Georgia Tech, she had sufficient funds to pay her bills and have a little extra. Her life had made her forever frugal, which meant she never felt deprived or in need of anything. Kathy was determined, persistent, and patient. She took oral assignments because she knew her written English was not very good; regardless, each situation was different, kept her busy, and got her out of the house.

At home, Kathy was a dedicated letter writer, corresponding with Darya's family in Australia, her long-separated cousins in Russia, Al and his children, and old church friends from New Jersey. She sang in the choir every Sunday without fail and had young Harry take her on errands in Charles's '63 Chevy Corvair. It was the only new car Charles ever owned.

Kathy also boxed away all the fancy gowns Charles had purchased for her over the years and stowed them in the attic. She gave his engineering books to Georgia Tech and sent a few more pieces of memorabilia to Al and his children, including medals, pennants, and a boomerang Charles had acquired in Australia when he was there with MacArthur. For the most part, she emptied the house of Charles's belongings, but she did keep their photo on the small table in the living room.

Watching news of the Kennedy assassination later that year deeply affected Kathy and she cried like a child. Somehow, his sudden death seemed personal. Perhaps her tears were for little Caroline and John-John, who would grow up without a parent, like she had. Or maybe…no, she couldn't go there. She had loved Charles. After all, he had brought her to freedom. Adding to her malaise, rumors about a communist connection between Lee Harvey Oswald and the Cubans felt like a bad dream. People's suspicions returned, especially members of law enforcement. Investigations of foreign nationals may have decreased after McCarthy was discredited, but they never stopped. The FBI refocused on Russian nationals, and she couldn't help but wonder if she was under surveillance. However, the trauma of losing the handsome young president was offset by joy.

In April 1965, Kathy met Peter Vasel.

"Oh, Sally Belle, I feel like a schoolgirl again. It was so unexpected. I'm tingling." Kathy showed Sally Belle the goosebumps on her arm.

"My goodness, Kathy. I've never seen you blush. Well, at least not like that."

Kathy knew she was flushed, but she was also giddy. "In many ways, he's just like Charles, but in other ways, not at all."

"So, let's hear it."

The two women occupied a small table inside Mary Mac's Tea Room, one of the original tea rooms started by women after WWII to avoid statutes permitting only men to own restaurants. It was close to Georgia Tech and had been a favorite of the Delacroys and the Harrises.

"Well, first off, he's a professor."

"You're kidding?"

"It's the truth," Kathy emphasized. "He teaches mathematics and engineering at Emory."

"That's a real coincidence, Kath." Sally Belle waited to hear more.

"And, get this: he's Russian. He was christened Dmitri Vaselyvich but uses Peter Vasel. He says it doesn't sound as foreign and has eliminated preconceived opinions about him, even after people hear his accent and find out he grew up in Russia."

"So, how'd he wind up here?" Sally Belle wasn't keen on Kathy having new Russian friends, no less a boyfriend.

"It took some prodding, but I finally pried the story out of him. He was drafted into the Russian Army and captured by the Germans during the war. He spent two years in a POW camp. Stalag VIII-F, later called Stalag 344. As the Russians advanced from the east, the Germans evacuated the camp and marched the prisoners west in January 1945. Nearly everyone died of hunger, cold, illness, whatever, but Peter was one of the survivors the Americans ultimately freed."

"That's amazing, Kathy—but it still doesn't explain how he got here."

"When he told the Americans he was an engineer and his entire family had been killed starting in WWI, through the revolution, and then by Stalin's purges, he was granted asylum and eventually permanent residency and citizenship. He went first to New York.

Spent five years there learning English, teaching math in a Russian language school for immigrants, and working part-time as a clerk for a construction firm. Then the opportunity for a teaching assistant position opened at Emory. He took it and worked his way up."

"Okay, but wait one minute," Sally Belle became more concerned. "*Where* did you meet him?"

Kathy shifted her eyes.

"Oh no, Kath! Not at those Russian expat meetings. You know that J. Edgar and his team never stopped watching, don't you? And with the FBI thinking that rabble-rouser, King, might be a communist… I hear the FBI's spending more time poking into people's lives all over metro Atlanta. They think anyone with the slightest connection to socialism or a communist country could be—what's the term they use…*subversive*. Yes, that's it. And I hear people like Dr. King make the government uneasy, no matter how religious he says he is. Some folks say King is a subversive who's trying to plot the government's downfall. You haven't forgotten your own experience, have you?" The worry was evident in Sally Belle's voice.

"Of course not," Kathy answered. "And they can track me all they want. I'm not a communist. Never was, never will be. I have nothing to do with the likes of Martin Luther King, Malcolm X, or their followers. Or Lenin or Stalin or Khrushchev or whoever. You know that. All my friends know that. And even if I did, what could I do to cause a problem for the United States? It's just ridiculous for anyone to think I could do anything." Kathy was frustrated with this topic. She'd heard it from Sally Belle, Debby, and friends at church, and she was tired of it.

"Well, that may be so, but a math professor at a school like Emory, that's a different story," Sally Belle reminded her. "Lots of professors are liberals, verging on socialists. Colleges and universities are centers for questioning the US connections to Vietnam and pushing for all kinds of rights for Black people. I think it's dangerous. And for you to ignore the potential for problems would be silly."

"Well, we agree on one thing," Kathy said, "These Black folks are causing all sorts of problems. Especially in my neighborhood. It was much more peaceful when Charles and I first came here. But since they started picketing, marching, and protesting about their rights, all around the country, well—I don't like what's happening."

"None of us like it, Kath," Sally Belle said. "Why, just the other day I could hardly walk downtown without having some group of Negros and their White friends blocking the sidewalk," she complained. "Elsa, your neighbor, Debby, and me have all told you about those college students, such as Lonnie King and Roslyn Pope, and their supporters like the Reverends William Borders and Martin Luther King, Jr. stirring the pot."

"Yes, I remember," Kathy said.

"And you've been telling us about the housebreaks, street assaults, and drug dealing in your neighborhood. And wasn't it you who told us about two fine families not three blocks away, who are moving out and who sold to Negros?" Sally Belle added.

"Yes. I said all that...but..."

"But nothing, Kathy. What are you going to do if they show up on your street?"

"I don't know, Sally Belle. Maybe you're right. I mean, I am worried. And they do seem to be creating trouble. But still, I've seen prejudice at work in other places. Even if Hoover thinks they're commies, and maybe they are, there seems to be lots of White folks siding with them. There's endless talk about how the Negros been mistreated for generations."

"Most of those White folks are self-righteous hypocrites from the North," Sally Belle said. "They wouldn't even consider having a Negro neighbor because they know the value of their property would decline. And you think they want their kids in the same school? Ha!"

"Enough, please, Sally Belle. I get it. And you're probably right. But enough. I just wanted to tell you about Peter. That's all, and you got me off on communists and Negro activists. Peter's neither one."

"Yes, I'm sorry, Kathy. Just worried about you, is all."

"Well, stop your worrying."

Kathy knew that Sally Belle was convinced the Negro population was committed to getting revenge on wealthy Whites. It was a scary concept, and one Kathy realized she couldn't ignore. The slow and steady indoctrination to the historic prejudices of the South, combined with the changing social and economic conditions throughout the country, had been wearing away at her open-mindedness since coming to Georgia. Just days earlier, she had improved the locks on her doors and added bars to the windows. She was not going to take any chances.

The women eventually ended their get-together with kisses on their cheek and promised to meet again at Elsa's. But before they went their separate ways, Sally Belle had a parting bit of advice.

"Forget him, Kath. Forget Peter. Linking up with some Russian professor will only bring you more headaches."

It was advice that Kathy let slip in one ear and out the other.

⁂

Kathy and Peter saw each other at least once a week through the spring, summer, and fall of 1965. As the holiday season approached, their relationship appeared serious. They attended social affairs together, and Peter invited his son, an officer in the Navy stationed in Hawaii, to come meet Kathy. They made a handsome couple, and everyone regularly quizzed them about wedding plans.

"A wedding?!" Kathy exclaimed to Lois Barnes. "Are you kidding? We just met."

"Oh, don't be silly, Kath. You've been together since the spring, and it's obvious you love him. Why wait?"

"Once a week for a few months does not make a long courtship," Kathy protested. "Besides, Peter is devoted to his work and doesn't seem to have the time or inclination for marriage."

"Ahem…Really?" Lois grinned. "All you have to do is look at his face when you're together. He's captivated with you, Kathy."

"Lois, let me tell you how many men have looked at me that way over the years," Kathy said. "It's been a blessing and a curse. Look at you. You're attractive. Cute. Adorable—I've heard Joe Bellows down the block say that about you."

"Joe? Better not let my Frank know," Lois joked. "He has a jealous streak. I actually like it, but it can be annoying now and then."

"That's funny," Kathy answered. "Charles was just the opposite. Never worried about any man looking at me, except Cary Grant."

"You're off topic, Kathy. Peter loves you. I know he'll ask you to marry. You need to be ready."

That was just the point. Kathy doubted she would ever be ready again. She married once, for better or worse. *Till death do we part.* Death came, sooner than she imagined it would, and she had no desire to go through it again. Yes, she loved Peter, but so what? They weren't going to have a family. Why not just enjoy their time together and let life play out without a marriage ritual?

"You're right, of course," Kathy told her. "We do love each other. But it ends there, Lois. If he asks me to marry him, I will tell him no. He has grandchildren, for goodness' sake. They take up his free time and live far away. He likes to visit them, but I've traveled enough for ten lifetimes. I'm not going anywhere. We're each set in our ways. I don't *want* to have someone else living in my house, or go to somebody else's house to live. Or, before you bring it up, find a place together. No, Lois. Marriage is out."

"People will talk, Kathy."

"I don't care. I've stopped caring. *People* have talked about me since I was little. In Valday. On the train. In Harbin. In Shanghai. In Manila. In New Jersey. And now in Atlanta. I have no regrets. Peter and I love each other, and if we spend time together without getting married, that's no one's business except ours."

"You know, there are times I wish I had half your gumption. Frank and I are, well, we're just pretty plain, I guess."

"Lois, you and Frank raised a wonderful daughter. Maggie is delightful. She's been so sweet since Charles died. Comes and listens to my music just to keep me company. I know she prefers that modern rock and roll stuff or country or whatever, but you and Frank are way more than ordinary to have a girl like that."

"Thank you, Kathy. I can't complain. Well, whatever happens, let me know."

"Of course."

Peter had an afternoon off the week before Thanksgiving and took Kathy to a matinee movie and early dinner. They waited for coffee and dessert in the restaurant and made small talk.

"I've been hesitating to bring this up, but, well…"

"Oh, Peter. Just say it. It's only me. No one's listening."

"Yes, of course." He stopped, cleared his throat, and continued. "I'd like you to come with me to Hawaii over Christmas break. You can meet Ivan's wife, Pat, and my grandchildren. They want to meet you because I told them all about you."

Kathy thought she knew what had been coming, but a trip to Hawaii was not it. She and Charles had spent a few wonderful days in Hawaii on their voyage from Manila. Kathy believed Hawaii was the one place on earth blessed with perfect weather. This kind man, Peter, now wanted her company back across the country and halfway across the Pacific to meet his daughter-in-law and grandkids. The temptation to say *yes* was real, but a weariness suddenly overcame her. The thought of unnecessary travel overwhelmed her. And the memories? Of Charles, Honolulu, the beach, just the two of them…

"Oh, Peter, what an offer," she said. "Hawaii is spectacular. Have you been there?"

"No," he said. "This will be my first trip, and the idea of you at my side would make it the ultimate voyage of my life."

She took his hands across the table. "I can't go, Peter." She looked into his eyes. She didn't waver, and she didn't get teary. "I can't go."

Peter smiled. He squeezed her hands. "I was hoping the thought of meeting my grandchildren might persuade you."

"You've shown me their pictures. It must be hard to be so far from them. I know they'll be thrilled to have Grandpa, Deduschka, with them for Christmas."

"It would also be nice for me to have a guide. Someone's who's been there to show me the highlights," Peter said, hoping for a positive sign.

"Please, Peter. Don't ask. It's just that…well…I can't go. Besides, you should save your money and spend it on the grandkids."

"Very well. I won't ask again. At least, not very soon. But you and I *are* having Thanksgiving dinner at the Top O' Peachtree. Don't forget."

"Forget? The tallest building in Atlanta with a rooftop restaurant and those views? For Thanksgiving? I won't forget. And dancing after," she stated as a fait accompli.

He groaned, "You can't wear good shoes. I'll ruin them." They laughed.

Kathy agreed with driving the Marxist Castro out of Cuba in 1961, and when Oswald was linked to Castro loyalists after JFK's assassination in '63, her vehemence toward communism grew.

By June 1968, Kathy was five years into widowhood and had re-established her routine and life. For the most part, she was content. Nonetheless, according to her friends and neighbors, during those years, her view of her surroundings began to shift. The violent deaths of JFK, Malcolm X, Martin Luther King, Jr., and Bobby Kennedy, along with the growth of the civil rights movement, riots around the country, and, most importantly, the increase in crime in her neighborhood, weighed heavy on her psyche. She trusted the Reverend Colonel Stillman and talked to him frequently about the turmoil.

"What's happening to this country, Reverend? What do those rioters know about anything?" she asked him shortly after the 1968 Democratic Convention. "I worked hard to get my freedom. To earn a dollar. Seems they just want the government to give them everything. Who are they? Oh yeah, the SDS, Students for Democracy, or some such. Democracy? Ha! *Radicals*. Every one."

"Kathy, do you need anything?" he asked in his quiet way. "Is there anything specific that makes you fearful of these groups?"

As soon the words were out of his mouth, he knew he had made a mistake. He had been talking, counseling as it were, with Kathy since Charles's death. He had watched her slow but steady migration away from the carefree, confident woman he first met in 1948 toward someone becoming afraid of invisible enemies with no interest in getting out of the house.

When she met Peter, Stillman had been hopeful Peter could bring back Kathy's easy-going demeanor. She had become more cheerful, especially when talking about Peter, but his impact on her was marginal. A weekly get-together. An occasional overnight. Not enough time for him to halt her shifting perspective. Despite best efforts by Peter and Stillman, Kathy's underlying state of normalcy remained couched in pessimism and outrage about the country and her neighborhood.

"As a matter of fact, Reverend, yes! I'm afraid. Did you see what those people did in Chicago? Have you been paying attention to all the protests around the country?

"Oh, Kathy, they just want to be treated equally."

"Equal?! I'll give you equal. They can get a job and earn their way, like I did. Dammit, Milton—" He couldn't remember her ever calling him by his given name. "—the government tried to arrest me for being a communist. ME! They need to go after *these* people. They're more communist than Stalin ever was."

Milton Stillman took a long, slow breath. When he finished exhaling, he continued. "Kathy, that was years ago. Do you personally know anyone, anyone at all, attacked by a member of these groups?"

She was flustered.

He added, "Anyone?"

"No. But that's not the point," she persisted. "Look at all the problems they're causing. And I don't want to wait until I *do know* someone who gets hurt. These kids are getting their ideas from somewhere, someone. Why not the communists? Makes perfect sense to me."

"I would like you to come to Bible study with our group on Thursday mornings," Stillman suggested. "I think it will help you get another perspective on living a calm life amid all the craziness around us. I'm sure it will make you feel more at ease. Kathy, please come."

"Oh, Reverend. You've asked me before. On Thursdays, I spend time with Elsa when she's able, or with Sally Belle, Carla Rae, and Lulu. You know that. The girls and I have been getting together since 1948, and I'm not going to stop now."

Stillman knew about the three other women and some of their stories. He was also acquainted with some of Kathy's neighbors. Each of the women was a good person. They gave to charity, went to church, helped at schools and other organizations, and never hurt or abused anyone. But he also recognized they were products of their upbringing and experiences. And each one, in her way, gave fuel to Kathy's growing phobias. None of the women trusted Negros, not even their household servants—not really. Likewise, none of them trusted foreigners, maybe not even Kathy, although they'd never tell her. None of them thought the Civil Rights Act was necessary, and each agreed communism must be stopped in its tracks in southeast Asia. He was more than troubled by the influence they had on Kathy.

"It won't hurt to miss one meeting," Stillman tried to get her to commit. "Come on Thursday. You know everyone, and you like it here anyway."

"Can't, Reverend. I can't let my friends down, but thanks for asking again. I gotta go. Getting hungry. Told Debby I'd fix dinner for her, her husband, and Harry. Harry's back from Vietnam, and he needs a good meal. He always enjoyed my beef stroganoff."

"Think about it, Kathy," he addressed her back as she left.

15 MAY 1985—MAY 2000
Atlanta To Lake Lanier

Kathy never did attend any Bible study groups, but she also never missed church. Like the years from 1953 to 1963, Kathy had another long stretch of mundane, suburban life. She and Peter spent more than twenty years in joyful camaraderie. They shared love, the ordinary, and a few adventures. From when they met in 1965 until 1985, they rarely went more than a week without being together.

In May 1972, the news of J. Edgar Hoover's death brought a wry smile to Kathy's face, but the information was anti-climactic. Kathy had ignored Sally Belle's advice back in '65 and had kept seeing Peter. Neither Kathy nor Peter cared if the FBI watched them. They were good citizens, and if they had been under surveillance, nothing ever came of it. In 1975, Peter finally convinced her to travel. She had mentioned numerous times she hoped the people in Sagada who had saved her life were doing well under martial law imposed by President Marcos. So, they went to see for themselves.

Peter had a great time and Kathy was feted by the many elders who remembered her. She was glad to find so many still alive and safe. However, when she visited Darya's grave in Manila, she collapsed with grief and Peter brought her home the next day.

Back home, the 1970s had brought more changes to Kathy and her neighborhood. Many longtime middle-class neighbors retired and moved, and new residents skewed toward lower incomes. Block after block became rundown. She frequently grumbled about "bad people" but felt reasonably safe because she had Peter. He took her mind off things she couldn't change and encouraged her outside activities. Al would later say, if not for Peter, Kathy probably would have become completely withdrawn by the late 60s. Fortunately, Kathy's work as a freelance translator persisted for years, although on occasion she would repeat something twice without realizing it. No one complained or even noticed. Her clients always preferred clarity.

Periodically, she also got hired to sing at church weddings, where she might also repeat a verse. No one noticed or cared. And Peter, who frequently accompanied her on those occasions, only offered compliments. After one reception, he told her she "radiated happiness in every song."

"You make people happy with your singing," he told her.

"Well, I like to sing, and I guess that comes across. Glad I can still do it."

"Don't ever stop. It's who you are."

She smiled and kissed him.

Kathy also modeled well into her sixties, which often made her laugh. "Who wants an old lady on a magazine cover?" she would ask Peter.

"Apparently, Atlanta Magazine and inside ads for Lady Circle. You look forty-five, Kathy. Enjoy it," he'd answer.

She would give him the quizzical eye.

"Okay, so perhaps I'm not being objective," Peter would smirk, "but you look fabulous, no matter how old you are. The magazine people think so, and I know many of your friends are jealous. And men of any age do double-takes when you walk into a room. How lucky can I get?"

Peter suspected their relationship, doing things together and in public, was the primary reason Kathy never became a real recluse who trusted no one. Regardless of her friends' and neighbors' biases and prejudices, Peter, Reverend Stillman, and Al kept Kathy from going off the deep end. They did their best to ease her concerns about the Black community and appeared to convince her she would be fine. Al was particularly helpful. From the day his father died, he was always there to care for Kathy.

Later, Peter would describe his time with Kathy as many wonderfully boring years. In 1985 he turned seventy-five and was more than ready to retire, but the opportunity to work part-time, do independent research, and teach a course he'd outlined decades earlier fell into his lap. He left Emory with good wishes and headed to Tulane University in Louisiana—but first, he had to find a way to tell Kathy.

"A picture-perfect evening," she said as they took their seats in Atlanta-Fulton County Stadium to watch the Braves play the Houston Astros.

"Yes. I heard the weatherman say sunny and low 70s. Couldn't be better," Peter agreed.

"Oh, Peter, this is exciting. I've never been to a baseball game."

"Neither have I," Peter said. "I wanted to do something special and different tonight. Do you think we'll figure it out?" he laughed.

"How hard could it be?" she asked. "They hit a ball with a stick and then run around. They need to score points."

"Sounds like you know more than I do," he said.

"Well, you know my neighbor, Debby Collins, her son Harry, and his wife? I watched Harry grow up. Oh my, I can't believe Harry Jr. is three already. But anyway, I went with Debby several times to watch Harry Sr. play Little League. So, at least, I've seen the game. I know they call the points each team scores 'runs,' but I don't know much else."

"It sounds like cricket," Peter said.

"Sounds like it, but it isn't. I watched lots of cricket, mostly through a fence but sometimes in the stands when I was in Shanghai. Both games use bats and balls and score runs, but they're different."

Peter had asked a friend where to sit, and he purchased box seats in the second row near the home team dugout. They were close to the field, could hear the players' chatter, and needed to pay attention to foul balls. When it came time for the seventh inning stretch, a ritual Peter learned about in advance, and while everyone was singing *Take Me Out to the Ballgame,* Peter leaned in close to Kathy and asked her one last time.

"Kathy, I love you. Will you marry me? Be my wife."

She wasn't sure she heard him correctly. The music and other sights and sounds had her attention. She turned to him. He repeated his question and kept talking.

"I've accepted a wonderful part-time opportunity at Tulane University in New Orleans. I'll be moving there in six weeks at the end of the academic year. Please, Kathy, come with me as my wife. We're a perfect match."

She listened as the crowd sang, *"For it's one, two, three strikes, you're out at the old ball game."*

"Strike three," she barely whispered under her breath. "You're out."

"What's that? Was it a 'yes?'"

With the tiniest of movements, her head moved left and right. Tears filled her eyes. As the crowd settled down and the players took the field, she said, "You're moving? You're going to keep working? Oh Peter, must you? Why? What more do you need to achieve? Why leave?"

They had had similar conversations multiple times about his ambitions despite his age. Moving was always possible. However, each time they talked, Kathy never explained why she couldn't or wouldn't go with him. How could she? *How would he understand?* she always asked herself. Each time he asked, she had found it easier to say *no* without explanation rather than get into some extensive discussion about *why*. But now, he was going to move. It was real. She wouldn't see him as often. Maybe, never again. She was suddenly in agony. The great time at the game became moot, and she became angry.

"How could you? How dare you spoil such a fun evening by telling me you're leaving? Going away? Oh, Peter. You can't leave. I need you. I love you."

He wrapped his arms around her, and they remained standing until people behind them yelled for them to sit.

"I needed to talk to you in a place like this. Doing something we'd never done before. I was afraid if we were alone, well...I don't know. Seemed like a good idea. And I couldn't wait any longer. You needed to know. And, if you love me, marry me, and come with me. Think of the adventures we can have."

Kathy had thought about running away with Peter for years. In quiet moments, mainly at the cemetery in Marietta, she talked to Charles about such things. She was afraid *he* wouldn't understand. Or, when she was honest with herself, the years of displacement and uncertainty—1924 until 1948—had left her yearning for a permanent base, which she finally had. She loved her little house, no matter what was happening to the neighborhood. And then there was the guilt. Charles had been her savior, but she never stopped questioning herself. Had she really loved Charles for who he was, or had she loved him because he rescued her from a life no one should ever have lived? Despite being unable to answer the question, she *did* know how to be loyal and steadfast. She had kept and preserved the only new car Charles had ever purchased and meticulously maintained the only house he had ever owned without support from his parents or siblings. She believed those acts and her decision not to remarry were necessary demonstrations of her dedication to the man who had changed her life for the better. Charles had taken her out of Hell, and she was forever grateful.

Kathy calmed, and Peter didn't pester her again. They held hands and watched the rest of the game. After lackluster years during much of the seventies, the Braves had a few good seasons in the early eighties before falling back into mediocrity. However, that night the Braves won, nine to five, putting on an offensive showing that made the game fun to watch. They ate hot dogs and drank beer. Cheered the players, booed the ump, and had a good time. To anyone watching, they appeared to be an all-American couple—because they were. Peter couldn't resist and gave it one more shot on the way to the car after the game.

"You know, New Orleans is one of the most historic and exciting cities in the States. It has spectacular cuisine, great music—music you'd love—and a vibrancy that makes me feel young again. We'd have a great time."

"Peter, you are the most wonderful man I've ever known. And I love you, but I can't go, and I can't marry you. I-I-I made a commitment, and I won't break it. Please, my dear, don't ask me again. We'll find time to be together."

He stopped walking, pulled her close, and kissed her. "I promise. I won't mention it again."

During his time in Louisiana, Peter visited Kathy's Bridgewater Street home every chance he could. He never again asked her to marry, but on those visits, their time together was heavenly. Peter remarked to his son one afternoon on the phone that he was sure most young people probably couldn't picture two old folks in intimate physical contact with each other. When there was no response, Peter laughed.

"You too? Just wait till you get to be my age," he teased his son.

In 1990, when he turned eighty, Peter admitted he was tired and permanently retired. He moved into the guest cottage behind his son's house in Hawaii. Close to his grandchildren and great-grand-children, Peter relaxed. He also realized he no longer paid attention to things with the same level of detail that he used to. He confessed to his daughter-in-law he couldn't see dirt and dust building up in places throughout his house, and he couldn't hear the TV without cranking it up. Aware of his own diminished senses, he hadn't found it unusual when Kathy repeated things or forgot where she put something, during the last few years when he visited her. Or asked the same question more than once in recent phone conversations. He figured it was normal for someone in her seventies.

But it wasn't.

"Mrs. Delacroy? Mrs. Delacroy? What are you doing outside hanging laundry on a day like this? You'll catch your death of cold," Maggie yelled from her back deck.

It was four o'clock in the afternoon, and the onset of dusk wasn't far off. Kathy wore a light bathrobe and was in the yard with her laundry basket. "Oh, hello, Lois. Are you coming over to help?" Kathy asked.

"Now, Mrs. Delacroy, you know that I'm Maggie. Momma went to live with her sister after Papa died, and I came back home here and moved in with my kids. Kept the house in the family. But enough about that. Let me help you get these things off the line and back inside. Makes no sense, you being out here at the end of December on a cold, damp, gray day trying to hang laundry. It'll never dry."

"Oh, thank you, dear. I can bring it in on my own. I wonder why it hasn't dried yet. I was sure the sun was out," she said quizzically.

Maggie helped Kathy take everything inside and get it quickly into the drier.

"When the buzzer goes off, remember to open the door and pull out your clothes. They'll be dry by then," Maggie said.

"Of course. I know that," Kathy answered. "And thank you… thank you…sorry, your name just slipped my mind. But you remind me so much of my nextdoor neighbor, Lois."

"I'm Maggie, Mrs. Delacroy. Lois is my mom. People always say we look alike. Now you take care. I've got to get back to my kids." Maggie left Kathy alone in the house.

Kathy made herself a cup of tea and put a favorite classical record on her stereo. She sat in her chair and looked through the large window into her winter brown backyard. As she sipped her tea, she checked the clock on the wall.

"Look at the time. I better fix dinner. Charles will want to eat when he gets in."

"Hi Al, thanks for calling."

"Happy New Year, Peter. I hope 1995 will be a good one for you."

"Likewise. And how's your family? Children and grandchildren?"

"They're fine, Peter. Thank you for asking. I assume all's well for yours too."

"Yes. Everyone is good. Growing and busy. I guess you're wondering why I left that message for you to call me?"

"No. I think I can guess, but go ahead and tell me," Al said.

"It has to do with Kathy. As you know, I haven't been to see her since I moved to Hawaii, but we've been corresponding regularly, and we talk once a month on the phone. It's not the same, but we stay in touch."

"Yes. I know. She tells me about your faithful writing and phone calls."

"Let me tell you, Al, she's been a bountiful letter writer. At least two or three times a week. She even sent me letters when I lived in Atlanta."

"I believe it. She writes to me as well as my children."

"Frankly, her letter writing finally made me reflect on other things."

"Go ahead," Al said.

"Her recent letters were all written in Russian. There've been random Russian words in most of her correspondence for years, but within the past few months, they're entirely in Russian. And they're overwhelmingly about her family in Valday. People I've never met, but she speaks of them as if I know them. Same way on the phone. All in Russian. At times she calls me Charles, or Papa, or Uncle Misha. Things like that. When I tell her I'm Peter, she says, 'Oh Peter, I know that. Wasn't that a fun meeting?' Referring to one of our expat get-togethers from years ago." Peter sighed heavily and became quiet.

"Yes, I've noticed the Russian too," Al broke the silence. "I don't speak Russian, but I can usually get her to switch back to English. And she talks about her babushka, Papa, and her cousin, Yuri. She talks as if she'd just seen them."

"I've heard the same stories," Peter agreed. "With me, she also talks a lot about Darya."

"Yes, Darya does come up a lot," Al agreed. "To tell you the truth, I got in touch with Reverend Stillman, talked with an attorney, and met the folks at the Georgia Office for the Aged—they call it Elderly Affairs now—and I acquired medical power of attorney for her. That should help."

"Al, has Kathy been examined by any...you know what I mean?" Peter asked.

"She recently had her annual physical," Al answered. "No major issues. She has a minor problem with her blood pressure, but you know about that. And to your question, her primary care physician recommended a memory assessment—a cognitive ability test. It will take place at her house, which, I think, is a good thing. Maggie—pretty sure you know Maggie, Kathy's neighbor—she told me Kathy has returned to the wrong house several times after taking a walk and sometimes hangs her clothes outside on cold, dreary days."

"Is she still showing signs of paranoia? It seems unusual for her to take a walk around the neighborhood if she's suspicious."

"Let me put it this way," Al answered, "there are now five locks on her doors, and she has cans of mace in various places throughout the house for easy access. However, I'm more worried about her getting into an argument on the street, not a break-in. Black families own fifty percent, maybe more, of the houses in her part of town. She's had a few, oh—let's call them *discussions* with some of the local teenagers and their parents. I know those conversations didn't leave anyone feeling kindly toward her. She thinks the kids pick flowers from her garden, but rabbits and deer are common and eat from everyone's gardens."

"She hasn't gotten into any trouble, has she?" Peter expressed concern.

"No, but I expect to hear from the memory care people at Elderly Affairs within the next couple of days with a date for her assessment."

"Please let me know what happens."

"Of course, Peter."

"Hello, Kathy? It's me—Al," he called out as he came in using his key.

"Albert? Is that you, Albert? I hear a voice. I'm out back on the patio."

Al walked through the house toward the back room. He hadn't been to see Kathy since Christmas. He found her sitting in her favorite chair, looking out across the patio into the yard. She was safe and warm inside and surrounded by several open newspapers. The TV was on in the corner, but he couldn't tell if she had been watching or not. Bob Barker returned when the commercial ended, and *The Price is Right* was about to begin. Al bent down and kissed her on the cheek. She wore a favorite evening gown pulled from the storage box she had stashed in the attic.

"Kathy, I brought someone today who would like to get to know you. Would it be okay to turn off the television for a little while?"

"The television? You know, Charles was so happy when he got that TV. He liked to watch the news. What was it, you asked?"

Rather than repeating, Al turned off the television he had purchased for her only a couple of years earlier and made an introduction.

"Kathy, this is Alexandra Cummings. She works for the State of Georgia and has a few questions for you. She won't be here very long. I'll wait in the kitchen while she speaks with you." Al went into the kitchen but left the door slightly ajar so he could listen. Alex told him that would be okay.

Kathy looked at the woman and said, "Not that Attorney General's Office, I hope?"

"Oh no, Mrs. Delacroy, I'm—" Kathy cut her off.

"Well, good. And *Alexandra!* Such a nice Russian name. What part of Russia are you from?"

"It is a pleasure to meet you, Mrs. Delacroy. Sorry to say, but I'm not from Russia. My parents liked the name, and I like it too. Is it okay if I call you Kathy?"

"Kathy? Kathy? Well, yes, I suppose so, but my Papa always called me Katya. Or, when he was serious, he would call me Ekaterina. That's my real name. But here? Charles told me Kathy would be easier, and people would accept me. Or…did I decide I wanted to be called Kathy? I can't remember."

"Would you prefer if I called you Katya, or Ekaterina? I'll do whatever you prefer."

"There are times when I only think of myself as Katya. But now? No, you better call me Kathy. Don't want J. Edgar and his cronies to think I'm a commie."

Al had briefed Alex on Kathy's background and experiences, so she wasn't surprised by the comment. "Are their people, officials, who think you're a communist?"

"Of course! Can't get away from it. Russian name. Russian accent. That's all anyone needs to know to think you're a commie."

"Well, I don't think you are. And I know Al doesn't either."

"Al? Oh yes, Albert. Charles's boy. Nice young man. Graduated from that military school. He's going to do fine at West Point. I just know it. Excuse me, uhh—oh, I'm sorry, what's your name again?"

"Alex, Kathy. My name is Alex—Alexandra."

"Oh, yes. Excuse me, Alexandra. I'm going to get some tea. Would you care for a cup?"

"Yes, that would be lovely," Alex answered.

When Kathy stood, Alex finally got a full view of the gown Kathy wore. She gasped. "Oh my goodness, Kathy. That looks just like a Pierre Balmain gown. It's gorgeous."

Kathy did a little twirl and smiled from ear to ear. "It most certainly is. His style suits me best. Elegant. Everyone tells me. Although my figure," and she ran her hands up and down her sides, "looks equally desirous in Dior and Jacques Fath. No matter. When I wear Balmain, I should be on the runway in Paris. Don't you think?"

Though in her late seventies and without help from modern surgical techniques or other devices, Kathy was easily mistaken for a woman at least twenty years younger.

"Yes, you should. But tell me, Kathy, where did you get such a special gown?"

"I have fifteen of them. All different designers. Charles bought one for me every year after we came to the United States. He stopped, though. I wonder why?"

While Kathy fussed about fixing the tea, Al filled Alex in on where the gowns came from.

"Second-hand originals?! I need to get in on this," Alex said. At thirty-seven, Alexandra was an attractive woman, and fashion design was her passionate hobby.

Once the tea was ready, Kathy and Alex returned to the other room and proceeded through the assessment. It took longer than planned because they veered off on numerous tangents about Kathy's life, loves and challenges, but that was not unusual, as Alex had explained to Al.

Alex said her goodbyes to Kathy, promising to visit again. As Alex walked toward the front door, Kathy said, "I told Charles the TV isn't working right. Look, it's off. How did that happen?"

"Not to worry, Kath. I'll get it going again," Al said and turned it back on. Bob Barker was getting ready to have the contestants bid on the two showcases.

"$23,465," Kathy said. "That'll win it."

Al left Kathy watching the show's end and stepped outside to speak with Alex.

"So, what do you think?" he asked her.

"Al, I'm sorry. You know I can't tell you anything."

"I have her medical power of attorney," he countered. "I told that to the clerk on the phone."

"They didn't tell me. And each one is different. Physically, it's clear she's not on death's door, but I'll need to see a copy of the document before I can share more details."

"I'll get one to you ASAP," Al said. "There's no one else for her. I can't abandon her. She was good to me when I was still in high school. I've looked after her since Dad died, even when Peter was around."

"Look," Alex began, "you heard the entire interview. If you want to continue to help, you should be here more often or make arrangements for someone to check on her no less than twice a week. Three to five times would be best. That's all I can say until I see the power of attorney agreement. I'm sorry, Al. I know you care. But the law is the law."

He gave her a disappointed look but nodded. "I won't let anything happen to her."

"I know you won't. Let me give you a list of licensed caregivers in the area. Maybe you can figure out a plan."

"Will she get worse?" he had to ask.

"There's no way to know," she told him. "Scientists are still searching for clues and indicators for conditions similar to Kathy's. I wish I had a better answer."

"I understand. Thank you, Alex. When will you come back to see her again, and should I be here, even if I can only listen from another room?"

"I'll see what my supervisor thinks. Best guess—about six months."

"Okay, thanks. That helps me plan."

"Bye, Al. Nice to meet you and Kathy."

"Goodbye."

Peter looked at the calendar on the wall as he reached for the phone. Saturday, October 14, 1995. It was the day before the Saints played, and he was watching ESPN's NFL show. He became a New Orleans Saints fan during his time at Tulane and wanted to hear what they had to say about the Saints game against Miami on Sunday. He wasn't optimistic, but you never know. When the phone rang, he turned the volume down on the TV.

"Hi Peter, it's Al." His voice was subdued. "It's Kathy. She's in the hospital. She fell at home, and Harry Collins, Jr. discovered her. He had come over to take her to the hairdresser because Sally Belle's dog became ill that morning, and Sally Belle had to go to the vet. Anyway, Sally Belle got in touch with Harry, and he agreed to take Kathy. What a great young man.

"Anyway," Al continued, "when Harry knocked on Kathy's door, she didn't answer. He knocked several more times, then went around back to look inside the sliding doors. He saw Kathy sitting on the floor next to her chair and noticed the small table lamp and magazines scattered across the floor. Fortunately, the slider was unlocked, and he went in. The poor dear began to swing her arms and yell at him. She shouted at him in Russian until she recognized him. Harry noticed she was bleeding from a cut on her head, and he called 911."

"My goodness, Al. How is she? What else do you know?"

"Well, Harry told the EMTs about me and that I lived in Florida, but that's all he knew. A bit of good luck surfaced because, sure enough—in her old personal phone book, they found my number and called me."

"What about the cut on her head?" Peter asked.

"Doctor says she has a concussion, and the cut needed three stitches. EMTs said there was blood on the corner of the end table, so it looks like she slipped and fell into it. All this leads up to the real purpose of my call. She spent the night in the hospital, but her behavior and failure to communicate in English prompted a visit by the Elderly Affairs person on duty.

"In short, the consensus is that Kathy requires regular care. They informed me she shouldn't be home alone and that the State of Georgia would step in unless I did something, so I conferred with Alexandra."

"Yes, good, Al. Go ahead."

"I gave Alex a destination—Lakeside Manor on Lake Lanier. It's the best senior living facility specializing in memory care I could find."

Al had been searching for the perfect spot for Kathy since Alexandra first met with Kathy in January. He discovered several he liked, but two criteria made the search more difficult. First, he wanted Kathy to be in a peaceful setting within reach of her friends and the Atlanta airport so he could visit without too much hassle. Secondly—and here was the real problem—he wanted a facility with at least one, preferably more, Russian speakers. As it turned out, the week before Kathy went to the hospital, Al located the right place.

"I think you'd like this place, Peter. Lakeside Manor is at the northern end of Lake Lanier. It's reachable from the Atlanta airport and for her friends by car. It's small, somewhat exclusive, has great views of the lake, and experienced and dedicated staff, including a man and woman who speak Russian. The woman happens to be a janitor, and the man is a nurse. After visiting more than a dozen different places, I knew it was the right one as soon as I drove onto the property."

"Wow! Thank you for doing so much. Sorry I'm not closer, but not sure what I could have done anyway," Peter conceded.

"I promised I'd keep you posted. And I will. I gotta go. Take care, Peter. Talk to you soon."

"Sure, bye Al."

·⁓⁓⁓·

"It is so wonderful to go for a drive. Thank you, Charles," Kathy said as Al drove.

"You're right, Kathy. It is a lovely day." He no longer tried to correct her. After all, she got names right about sixty percent of the time. *No big deal*, he thought.

On the phone with Alexandra, he had changed his mind and told Alex he would come to Atlanta and drive Kathy to Lakeside Manor. He didn't want strangers—even if Alexandra was no longer a stranger—or Kathy's neighbors, to be the ones who took her from her home. No—he would do it. He felt guilty about not telling her where they were going, but when he pulled through the gate into the long driveway, the views of the lake were easy to spot through the trees, and joy seemed to overcome her.

"Lake Valday! Lake Valday! Oh Charles, isn't it beautiful? Just like I remember."

"It is a beautiful lake, Kathy. Very lovely. I'm so glad you like it. I've made arrangements so you can stay here by the lake for a while. I was hoping you'd be excited."

As Al pulled into a parking space outside the main office, Kathy turned and looked at him. Her face was a mixture of sadness, anger, melancholy, and resignation. "Albert Delacroy, what *are* we doing here? The sign says Lakeside Manor, not Lake Valday. Is it a motel?"

"No, Kathy. It's not a motel. You know Alexandra Cummings, the woman who has been visiting you regularly the past few months?"

"Yes. She's a delight. Liked my Balmain gown."

"Yes, I know. Alexandra works with many people who live alone in changing neighborhoods. She helps them find places to...how does she phrase it...take a break from doing housekeeping and dealing with small annoyances. Lakeside Manor is one of those places. We made a reservation for you, and I think you'll love it here." Al held his breath as he finished his white lie. He could no longer guess when Kathy understood things or not.

"Hmmm. I don't know. I think I'd rather be home."

"Well, let's take a quick look. Okay? It's a special place. And doesn't the lake look so peaceful?"

"I think I'll sit right here if you don't mind. Whenever you're ready, you can drive me home."

Al was not going to leave Kathy alone while he went inside the office. However, true to their word, the alert staff at Lakeside saw him park, and a woman attendant came out to greet them.

"Who's that?" Kathy demanded as the woman came to the driver's side.

"I think she's part of the welcoming committee," he answered. "I told you, this is a friendly place. Let's see what she says."

Al had his window down, and the woman leaned over to talk. "Hello! Welcome to Lakeside Manor. You must be Albert and Kathy Delacroy. My name is Letisha James, the Administrative Assistant to Mr. Patel, our President. We're so glad you're here. Alexandra arrived about twenty minutes ago. Why don't you come inside? It's hard to chat like this."

"You aren't going to get me anywhere near *that* girl, Al. I don't trust her at all."

Al was kicking himself for failing to warn Lakeside about Kathy's prejudices. Especially against Blacks. Letisha overheard Kathy's comment. She was used to it. Had heard it all before, but at twenty-eight, she knew things used to be much worse for women like her. After four years of working with dementia and Alzheimer's patients, Kathy's slight didn't fluster her. Nothing anyone said surprised her, particularly people who had grown up steeped in the ways of the *old south*. And even those transplanted from up north—or—like Kathy, from overseas.

"I'm sorry, Ms. James. Kathy says things, well…"

"I'll say whatever the hell I want to say!" Kathy made sure Al and Letisha heard her.

"Not to worry, Mr. Delacroy. I think I know who can help. I'll be right back."

"That wasn't very nice," Al told Kathy. "You made her feel bad."

"I don't give a crap how she feels. Them people have caused me nothing but problems."

Al shook his head. *Them* people had never done anything to her. *Ugh! Wonder what I'll be like when I'm in my seventies?* he thought.

It was only a couple minutes before a second woman came outside. She was about sixty, wore white coveralls, and wiped her hands on a rag. When she got close to the car, she shouted, *"Dobro pozhalovat*—Welcome! *Menya zovut Polina.* My name's Polina. Everyone calls me Polly. Polly Fedorova Willis. Please, come inside."

Kathy's eyes grew wide when she heard the Russian words. "Who said that? Where are we, Albert? Is that Valday Lake? Did you bring me home?"

"Isn't it beautiful, Kathy? And isn't Polina helpful? She wants us to go inside."

"I heard her, I'm not deaf. Maybe a bit forgetful at times, but not deaf. Alright, let's go."

Al hustled out his side of the car and ran around to Kathy's door, but Polly was there, and she and Kathy were already chatting in Russian. He decided not to ask any questions but found out later that Polina grew up in St. Petersburg, where she had worked on the cleaning staff in one of the large hotels. There, she met Jacob Rose, who worked for an import company based in Atlanta and frequently traveled to the city. They hit it off and married. After twelve years, however, they split amicably. Two years later, she remarried, moved to the Gainesville, Georgia region with her new husband, where she secured a position at Lakeside Manor. As Polina, Kathy, and Al walked inside, Kathy found a new bounce in her step.

Shivansh Patel stood as the three entered his office. He was medium height, with a dark complexion and aquiline features common to many people from India. He wore a stylish suit that fit him as if it was tailor-made, but simultaneously gave him an air of being ordinary.

"Oh, welcome, welcome. Mrs. Delacroy, I am so happy to meet you. And Mr. Delacroy, nice to meet you too." He spoke with the trace of a British accent, and his brilliant white teeth shone clearly through a gracious smile.

Alexandra was also in the room, and behind her stood Fyodor Volkov, the Russian-speaking nurse. He was short, squat, rugged looking, and about forty. He bared a crooked smile uncovering several nicotine-stained teeth, reeled off some rapid Russian, and Kathy laughed. Afterward, Al discovered that Fyodor grew up in Brighton Beach, Brooklyn, New York. When he was eighteen, he left home and tried several jobs before working as a nurse's aide in Charlotte. He did such good work that the homecare company that employed him helped pay his way through nursing school. After graduating, he worked two years for them, but when the position opened at Lakeside Manor, he took it, fell in love with Lakeside and its residents, and stayed.

"Well," said Mr. Patel, "it looks like Kathy, Fyodor, and Polly will be quite the trio.

"Do you know what Fyodor said?" Alexandra asked Mr. Patel in a low voice as the three Russian speakers conversed as if the others were not there.

"Not at all. But, as you know, being happy and able to laugh goes a long way toward achieving contentment for folks like Kathy."

Alex agreed, and soon everyone sat down to enjoy a cup of tea and gab away in English and Russian. Eventually, Al got around to the *white lie* he had shared with Kathy.

"So Kathy, what do you think? Polly and Fyodor are glad you're here and eager to show you to your room."

Kathy rose, looked at everyone, and issued an order in Russian. Fyodor stood and extended his arm. Kathy took it as if he was one of her long-ago dance partners, and he led her out of the room. Fyodor looked back over his shoulder and winked at the others. He raised his other arm, extended it, and gave the thumbs-up sign. A collective sigh of relief coursed through the room.

⁂

Peter called Kathy about once a month, and they continued to send letters. In the company of Polly and Fyodor, Kathy's Russian reemerged, along with her childhood accent and stories of her cousins, uncles, Papa, and, of course, Raisa. When asked about her time in Harbin, Shanghai, and the Philippines, she mainly talked in English. Even the doctors and clinicians couldn't explain precisely why. Around 1998, Al also slowed a touch and received a pacemaker. A year later, he dealt with prostate cancer but recovered without complications and remained vigilant in his care for Kathy. He checked in weekly with Lakeside and visited Kathy three or four times a year, even as *he* aged.

Kathy had settled down quickly after her first day at Lakeside Manor but still had her share of run-ins with staff—mostly with racial and Latino minorities, who soon figured out they could get on her good side by learning a few words of Russian.

"She loves to teach Russian to the staff," Mr. Patel told Al on one of his visits.

"That's great. I could tell she's more like her old self."

"Yes, it was like night and day. One moment she was browbeating everyone, but as soon as they took an interest in learning Russian, she became a sweet old lady. People began to get to know her," he said.

"Apparently, that's not all that has cheered her up," Al added.

"You're right, Mr. Delacroy. A piano player came to entertain during one of our special guest days. He took requests, and Kathy asked for a popular tune from the 1930s. The man knew it and played it. And you know what Kathy did? She sang along."

"Of course, she did," Al said. "She always loved to sing."

"And the residents loved it. Staff too. From that day, Kathy offered to sing as often as we could get an accompanist. And in between her singing…"

"Stop, Mr. Patel. I know—I was here. Remember? She taught people to dance," Al remarked.

"Oh yes, I forgot. You were here when our retired Broadway performer, about Kathy's age, joined her for dancing. They made a great team."

"Yes, glad I had the chance to see them together," Al said. "It was a shame when he died. Late in '99, if I recall."

"Yes, Kathy took a turn for the worse after his passing. Then Polly's husband got a new job, and she moved away in February this year. I'm sorry to tell you, Mr. Delacroy, but Kathy's mood steadily deteriorated after Polly's departure. Fyodor tried to boost her spirits, but with marginal success."

"I know. And thank you again for all you and your entire staff do."

After Al's subsequent visit at Easter 2000, he called Peter. "She's declining, Peter," he said. "Fast," he added. "Fyodor and the doctors can't figure it out. They say it appears Kathy has lost interest in most things. She keeps repeating the same stories about her cousin Yuri, her father and Raisa, and even Kuniaki and Marcel. One night when the staff was doing bed checks, she started talking in her sleep about a beautiful lost child."

"Appreciate the call," Peter said. "What do you think?"

"I think you need to talk to her. And soon," Al told him. Peter called Kathy the next day. She wasn't sure who he was.

Then, it was May again. Wonderful May. A lovely month in Hawaii. And another phone call.

"Hi, Peter," Al began. "I had a call last night around dinner time. An aide found Kathy in her room, sitting in her chair. She had finished eating about an hour earlier and was dressed in the fanciest outfit she could put together. Someone had done her hair up nice, helped her put on her favorite ruby red lipstick, and polished her nails. They sure took good care of her. Classical music played on one of those iPod things, but I have no idea where she got it. On her lap was the Atlanta newspaper feature article about the All-American Housewife. And that's it, Peter. She was gone. They told me she passed while sleeping in her chair. I saw no reason for them to do an autopsy. She was ready."

"Yes, I agree." Sadness wrapped Peter's words. "So, what's next?"

"I'll give you a call. I know she prepared a will, and I know the attorney who has it. Shouldn't take too long to arrange things. My father made sure Kathy would have a spot at the National Cemetery next to him, and she never asked me or suggested that she'd like to be elsewhere. Maybe Valday. But, realistically, that's out."

"Okay, Al. Thanks. I loved her, you know. She would have loved Hawaii. But she kept her word. To your dad, to her neighbors in Atlanta. Did you speak to Milt Stillman?"

"Not yet. He's up there in age too, like you. I'll call him next."

"Good. Good."

"I'm going to miss her, Peter. She was the last connection to my small family, even if she wasn't old enough to be my mother."

"And just the right age to have been my wife," Peter responded with heartache and sorrow.

"Yes, Peter. I know. I'll be in touch," Al said.

"Thank you," Peter answered and hung up as tears reached his chin.

16 JULY 2000
Atlanta

Peter was back in Atlanta. He sat in a room sanitized from the world outside as air conditioners hummed in the background with the quiet drone of hummingbird wings. The furniture—specialty teak, custom-made by expert artisans in Malaysia—added a soothing touch to the false environment. Nonetheless, as cool air trickled across his cheeks, perspiration began to bead on his forehead and down his spine. He had never been a superstitious man, nor was he clairvoyant. Yet the inner voice that had guided him for ninety years triggered a sense of apprehension.

Peter Vasel had returned to Atlanta for the reading of Kathy's will. He knew he had to attend, regardless of the distance and his age. His love for her drew him back this one last time.

He was not alone in the room. There was Jacob Rabinowitz, the Russian Jew who had escaped to Atlanta in the early 1950s. Jacob patiently gazed through the tinted windows to the busy streets below. Long retired, the feisty lawyer still held an emeritus position with the Emory University School of Law and maintained a worldwide clientele as a legal consultant. He had the connections to make arrangements for the use of the room.

Off in a corner was the Reverend Colonel Milton Stillman, US

Army. He was sitting on one of the elegant handmade executive chairs. He leaned forward at an odd angle so his feet could reach the floor. "Short" was too long a word to describe the reverend. He was tiny. He, too, was retired, having completed a successful career as a military chaplain. Peter had always been impressed by Stillman's path to the clergy. Young Staff Sergeant Stillman scaled the vertical cliffs at Pointe du Hoc on the Normandy coast of France in June 1944, and of the nine men in his squad, four were killed, two were crippled for life, and three, including Stillman, survived, physically unscathed. Like most people in combat, the experience changed his life. The battlefield promotion he received to Second Lieutenant was insufficient to keep him in the infantry. Stillman requested a transfer to the Chaplaincy Corps. In an uncharacteristic move, the Army granted his request immediately. He never knew why and would always explain it as a divine miracle. After the war, Stillman returned home, went to seminary, rejoined the Army in time for the Korean conflict, and eventually ended his service as Chaplain at Fort McPherson in Atlanta.

Four others were in the room. Kathy's next-door neighbor, Margaret—Maggie—Waycross, now in her early fifties with one grown son and two teenagers still at home. She was hard to miss. Margaret's tremendous girth was sufficient to stress her oversized chair to the breaking point. Her every move made the chair groan and attracted casual glances from the other attendees. Maggie knew what everyone was thinking but was comfortable in her skin. She laughed while talking with Deborah Collins in the seat next to her.

Debby kept dabbing a tissue at her eyes. No matter what Maggie said to lift her spirits, tears flowed down Deb's face, accompanied by an occasional sob. She was still as slender as when she modeled as a teenager somewhere in the Midwest. An unplanned pregnancy resulted in a youthful marriage that shortened her promising career. She and her husband struggled for a while but never gave up on each other. Deborah's husband took a supervisory position with an air freight company, received a promotion, and they moved to Atlanta. A few years previously, a local TV station was looking for a *put-together, mature* woman for some commercials. She auditioned and had steady work ever since.

Accompanying Debby was her grandson, Harry Jr. At eighteen, Harry resembled his father more than his mother. He was stocky, had bushy brown hair, chocolate eyes, and a mouthful of teeth large enough to scare a dinosaur. Gifted in the ways of mechanical things, Harry had recently received a scholarship from Ford Motor Company to attend college and become an engineer. When Peter moved to Louisiana, he had asked Harry Jr. to mow Kathy's lawn and do other odd jobs as needed. Young Harry had always been happy to help Kathy with most anything and had appreciated the monthly check from Peter.

Then there was Albert Delacroy. Albert had turned seventy in 1999 and currently sported large, round, dark-framed eyeglasses set just a bit too low on his large nose. They magnified the charcoal depths of his eyes so that you thought you were looking into a pair of binoculars. At five feet, seven inches and 135 pounds, he, nonetheless, commanded the room. Energy exuded from Al wherever he went like it had his entire life. Peter was happy to see him. As always, Al attired himself in stylish clothes, yet a good tailor would be hard-pressed to realize his raiment was not custom-made but local thrift shop specials. On this occasion, he wore a silk suit of deep ocean blue with a starched, light pink shirt, muted lavender tie—secured with a gleaming silver eagle tie tack—and a pair of black Italian suede loafers. He stood behind his chair at the table, breathing at a steady pace as he scanned the papers in his hands.

After a lengthy delay, Senior Partner Aloysious Lincoln King of Pembert, King, Oglethorpe, Lee, and Carter, Attorneys-At-Law, entered the room, accompanied by two assistants. Everyone sat down, and without prelude or apologies, King began right in.

"We're here for the reading of the Last Will and Testament of

Kathy Delacroy, also known as Ekaterina Palutova. For the record, please state your names and home addresses."

They went around the room, and as Peter sat and listened, he shifted in his seat and thought things should go quickly. Kathy had few possessions, and most were of little value. Even the home she had lived in since 1948 had questionable value. Except for a few sporadic, well-kept lots—including Kathy's, Maggie's, and Deborah's—the once peaceful and attractive neighborhood was now best described as *urban blight.*

As Peter daydreamed about what could be in Kathy's Will, Al touched his arm, and Peter realized it was his turn to identify himself. He responded slowly but with a firm voice in the old country accent that had never left him.

"I am Dmitri Vaselyvich, also called Peter Vasel. I live at 548 Garden Valley Road, Paia, Hawaii."

"Thank you, Mr. Vaselyvich. Well, we're all here then," announced Mr. King, and he began to read. "Per legal and tax obligations, the Delacroy house will be sold to pay medical and other bills incurred during the past few years of Kathy's care at Lakeside Manor."

Next up was the 1963 Chevrolet Corvair. One of the old rear engine jobs. She left it to Harry Collins, Jr. He and his father had taken care of it since Charles's passing. With only 17,643 original miles, it was in pristine condition. As she had told young Harry, "Mr. Delacroy said that being able to buy a new car was a sure sign of being successful in America." And she knew her Charles had been a success.

Kathy also had a voluminous assortment of classical music records, which she bequeathed to Maggie Waycross. Kathy loved Maggie because Maggie, despite their age difference, would come and listen to music with her just to keep Kathy company. Maggie never told Kathy that her musical preference was more southern country or country rock, like Lynyrd Skynyrd, the Allman Brothers, Alabama, and Reba McEntire. Maggie's middle child, Katherine, was a high school junior and wanted a music career. She played violin in the school orchestra and sang at her church, where she also played religious rock and gospel. Al, as executor, with help from Jacob, eventually sold the collection on Maggie's behalf for $8,600. Maggie used the money to give Katherine private lessons at a local music conservatory. Peter, Al, and Reverend Stillman knew Kathy would have heartily approved.

Besides collecting classical music, Kathy loved her gowns. On their second wedding anniversary, she and Charles dined at the Algonquin Supper Club in New York, and Greta Garbo was in attendance. While looking at Garbo, Kathy remarked to Charles, "How do you think I would look in her gown?"

Charles said she would look spectacular, and, according to Kathy, Charles went across the room and asked Garbo where she got her dress. The actress was gracious and told him the name of an exclusive designer from Paris, but she also told Charles that many designer gowns were routinely donated to charity and put up for auction. Another option was to purchase a *copy*. So began Kathy's collection. From 1948 until 1963, Charles bought Kathy a new gown at auction every year until he died. In her will, she left her *fancy party dresses* to Deb Collins, who was *always talking about fashion* and who had told Kathy how much she liked to *dress up*. The entire collection was appraised at more than $62,000. As Peter listened, he wondered why the assembled group had expected that Kathy didn't have anything of value. Not bad so far, for an old woman with no resources.

Milt Stillman was next to hear his name. Kathy had always found it easy to talk to Reverend Stillman. She trusted him and valued his opinion above most everyone else. She believed he was one of those rare individuals who truly lived his faith. Because of that, she wrote, "I place my Bible and St. Michael icon in the care of the Reverend Colonel Milton Stillman."

Colonel Stillman viewed life as a special gift, especially after his D-Day indoctrination in combat. Content in the here-and-now, he had never pursued the so-called finer things in life. A greater obligation had beckoned him. Yet, when Aloysious handed him the appraiser's report on Kathy's 17th-century Russian Bible and St Michael icon, it was evident his heart skipped a beat. He never disclosed the amount but told Peter and Al that Christie's, Phillips, and Sotheby's each offered to auction the items. He deferred and donated the pieces to the Episcopal Church of St. Mary the Virgin in Sagada, the Philippines, instead. The act was exceedingly generous and exquisitely appropriate. Placing the Palutov family heirlooms in the small convent in the mountains of northern Luzon made sense. The people there had saved Kathy's life.

Age and travel had tired Peter out, and he lost focus for a few minutes on the proceedings. He thought about Al, dressed to entertain, and wondered what Kathy had thought about Al's wardrobe. He couldn't recall ever talking to her about Al's clothes. Then he thought how lucky Kathy had been to have Al. Al had served faithfully as Kathy's guardian, helper, and de facto son. She had been grateful for his help and presence but rarely thanked him. She thought her homemade baklava was thanks enough. In the same respect, she rarely *asked* for help—from anyone, even when she needed it. Fortunately, the people in the room cared deeply about her and had invested countless hours checking on Kathy the last few years before she moved to Lakeside Manor.

Peter also knew Kathy gradually began to forget who Al was despite his regular visits. Al checked her mail, talked to her doctors, and chatted with her, but there were times she called him Charles, Papa, or Peter. She called the male aides Kuni, Dmitri, and Marcel. As he waited on Mr. King's next words, Peter remembered how Kathy always seemed to have secrets. Things she never wanted to reveal. He recalled teasing Kathy about keeping secrets, and the first time he did, she chirped back at him.

"If you reveal your secrets to the wind, you should not blame the wind for revealing them to the trees."

He had recognized the words from Kahlil Gibran, but was stunned Kathy knew them, because she only read newspapers.

She had laughed and said, "The Filipino Convent had a library."

Peter's thoughts abruptly returned to Albert when Mr. King called Al's name and read Kathy's words. "And, for Charles's son, Albert, I leave all of Charles's military memorabilia, naturalization papers, his photo albums, pocket watch, hand-carved Australian aborigine boomerang, Japanese screens, carved ivory tusks, and books."

Peter saw a smile creep across Al's face. Al already had possession of most of what Mr. King read. Kathy had given it to him in 1963, shortly after Charles's death. She had told him, "Take this stuff. Seeing it around makes me cry."

King continued to read. "And to Jacob Rabinowitz, who helped me improve my English; who understood my need for privacy; who never asked me why I did things, and who never once judged me; I repeat what I told you all these years: thank you for being my friend. And, thank you in advance for what I know you will do once the reading of my Will is over."

Jacob's eyes were swimming, and he patted them with his handkerchief. He had introduced Peter to Kathy at a Russian expatriate meeting, but now Peter sat a little befuddled. He wasn't sure how to feel about Kathy's comments. *What did she mean by what he—Jacob—would do when the reading was over? Strange. Jacob's the wealthiest man in the room and can do whatever he wants.* Jacob saw Peter looking at him, smiled weakly, nodded, and looked equally baffled by Kathy's words.

Finally, Mr. King called Peter's name. Peter looked up after staring at his hands. *The hands of a very old man*, he thought. The collection of lawyers and friends focused on Peter and waited for Mr. King to end the morning's dispensation with a final announcement as Peter was the last one on the list.

It read: "And to Peter Vasel, my darling Dmitri Vaselevich, I leave you my bells and all the love I failed to give you during our years together. I hope you understand why I could never leave Atlanta, and I will keep my eye out for you next time we meet."

Along with her Bible and St Michael icon, Kathy's bells were the most prized of all her possessions. Peter knew their story and understood they were more than just decorative and informative. The bells were symbols of home. They were the core of who Ekaterina was. The thought of Kathy's bells in his house brought tears to Peter's eyes. Then Mr. King passed him a note. The words "Вы—мой герой. Я буду любить Вас через всю вечность" were written on it. In English, "You are my hero. I shall love you through all eternity." Peter felt the color rise in his cheeks. He was embarrassed but kept his thoughts to himself. *Hero! Ha! Not me. I've been afraid of many things since I was a little boy. What heroic things did I ever do? Lover, yes, hero—I don't think so.* Oooh, how she could frustrate him, even from the grave.

With all Kathy's assets distributed and everyone accounted for, the group stood to leave, but King's voice brought them back. "Now hold on, y'all," he bellowed. "I know you think we're through, but there's one more envelope."

The group shrugged and sat back down.

"Thank you," King said as he sliced open a yellowed envelope with an ivory-handled letter-opener sporting an intricately etched blade of the finest Toledo steel. They watched with growing anticipation, wondering what final thought Kathy had penned on the old linen paper.

Mr. King cleared his throat and read Kathy's words. "In the presence of everyone in the room, call the phone number listed below, ask for Mr. Richter, tell him I died, and give him the enclosed account number and password." King looked up in surprise. "Excuse me, ladies and gentlemen, this isn't something I knew about in advance. Please wait, and we'll hook up a speakerphone."

An assistant hustled and plugged a speaker and microphone assembly into a small, recessed outlet near the center of the boardroom table. Mr. King dialed, and all ears waited for an answer. In moments, the connection went through, and a voice spoke.

"Guten abend. Dies ist Credit Suisse. Wie kann ich Ihnen helfen?" a pleasant woman's voice answered.

Mr. King asked if she spoke English. She did, and he asked to speak to Herr Richter. When Richter came on the line King told him who he was and the reason for the call. Herr Richter asked for everyone's patience and said he would be back momentarily. When he came back on the line, he said Kathy had left his company specific, written instructions.

"First," he began, "As of her passing, Kathy Delacroy of Atlanta, Georgia, had a portfolio with our firm totaling $1,078,452."

There was an audible gasp in the room. It was a staggering number. Everyone knew Kathy's income was modest, and she lived frugally. Where did the money come from? Herr Richter explained that Kathy had invested much of Charles's insurance and pension money from Georgia Tech and the Army into companies like Microsoft, Coca-Cola, and Delta Airlines. One of the Russian expatriates she met after Charles died had suggested she invest in blue chips like IBM, GE, and Disney back in the late 1960s and secure her funds in a Swiss firm. She did, reinvesting the returns year after year.

Herr Richter explained Kathy's instructions about how she wanted her investment portfolio disbursed; one-third to the American Heart Association, one-third to the Organization for International Adoption; and one-third to a granddaughter in Siberia.

Everyone in the room had shaken their heads in surprise at the amount of her estate, but learning Kathy had a granddaughter put them all in shock. It was stunning news and left them talking over one another in disbelief.

Ultimately, they calmed and wanted to know more about the granddaughter Kathy had kept secret most of her life, none more so than Al and Peter. Before they went their separate ways, Al asked Peter to spend a few minutes with him so they could compare notes.

They found a coffee shop not far from the law office and sat talking the rest of the day. They couldn't believe what they'd heard. As they swapped tales about Ekaterina Palutova, Al's eyes suddenly lit up, and he suggested Peter write Kathy's life story.

Peter balked. "At my age?" he responded.

"But you knew her best," Al insisted.

They looked at each other, and Peter hesitantly agreed. He only hoped he had enough time left.

17   SUMMER 2001
Khabarovsk, Russia

Al's voice was distorted and occasionally broken up as he joyously shouted to Peter from Siberia. It was a call Al had been hoping to make for nearly eighteen months. Both men were thrilled beyond belief. After running down lead after lead for months on end, and piling up enormous phone and internet bills, Al had found Kathy's granddaughter in Russia. with assistance from Jacob Rabinowitz and Aloysius King, he had secured a travel visa and special permits to travel to Russia. He was exhausted from the long journey, but energized by adrenaline.

"I plan to meet them tomorrow. I can't wait," Al said.

"Make sure you send me photos," Peter reminded him.

"Of course. Talk to you again tomorrow."

"Great. Thanks for the call. Bye Al."

"Bye."

* * *

Stepan and Isabel Danilov had received a phone call two days earlier from a representative of a Swiss bank, telling them to expect a visit from an American who had some business to discuss with them.

The agent provided no other information, but the Danilovs were excited by the prospect of meeting a real American. They couldn't wait to find out the reason behind the call and for the visit.

The visitor who arrived as scheduled was a man in his early seventies. He was thin, of average height, but seemed full of energy. He stood with a large trunk at his feet, an envelope in his hand, and an interpreter.

"Hello, Mr. Danilov. My name is Albert Delacroy. Thank you for agreeing to meet with me," the visitor said in poor Russian when Stepan opened the door. He switched to English, and the translator took over. "It took me a long time to find you, over a year, and…I'm so relieved my search is over."

"Welcome, Mr. Delacroy. We're curious about why you're here. Please, come in and have a seat," Stepan answered. He was a tall, rail-thin man in his early fifties, with visible acne scars but a pleasant and welcoming voice. After fifteen years as a welder, Stepan had recently received a promotion to supervisor at the local shipyard. Also in the room were his wife, Isabel, their son, Konstantin, who was nine, and Sasha, fourteen.

"I have a story to tell you, and then a gift to leave with you," Al said without preamble. "Well, two gifts to leave with you."

"One minute, Mr. Delacroy," Mrs. Danilova interrupted. "Let me get some tea."

Al gave a little chuckle at the offer.

Isabel turned around. "Is tea funny, Mr. Delacroy?"

"Ha! No. Not at all, Mrs. Danilova. You will understand better when I tell you my story. And thank you, I look forward to the tea."

The tea *was* excellent, and the Danilovs listened quietly as Al told them Ekaterina's story. Kathy's story. Specifically, he focused on a baby born to Ekaterina in Harbin, China, in 1932 and given up for adoption—to a family who ultimately moved back to Russia. To Vladivostok.

"When Ekaterina died," Al told the family, "She left a will which,

among other things, left money to a granddaughter—named Isabel."
Al turned and looked at Isabel. "That granddaughter is you, Isabel.
None of Ekaterina's neighbors, myself, or her longtime close friend,
Peter, knew she had a grandchild. So we had to find her. Find *you*."
Al took a sip of tea and continued. "It was letters that did it," Al told
them. "All the letters in this trunk." He opened the lid and showed
them hundreds of letters addressed to Katya from Grigor Korablin,
Mr. Korablin's cousins—the couple who adopted Katya's baby—and
Isabel's mother, Katya's daughter.

"It appears that Grigor Korablin had given Kathy the contact
information for his cousin and subsequently Kathy's daughter,
sometime after she became successful in Shanghai," Al told his hosts.
"Grigor's cousin, knowing Kathy couldn't safely return to Russia,
corresponded with her about the child's progress. Once the young
girl could write, she and Kathy began their own correspondence."

"My mother was killed in an accident when I was three, and
my father committed suicide when I was five," Isabel said. "I was
much older when I learned about my mother's adoption and my
father's history of alcoholism and mental health problems. I grew
up with my grandparents—my father's parents, the Egorovs, here in
Khabarovsk."

"I know," Al said quietly, "but instead of reliving sad times, I
hope I can bring you a little happiness today. We can only assume
Kathy felt ashamed about losing her child and that's the reason she
never told anyone, but we'll never know. We did discover she rented
post office boxes in New Jersey and Atlanta using the name Nadine
Bebchuk to preserve her anonymity."

Everyone stared at the neatly stacked piles of letters filled with
the stories of a little girl, a grown woman, and finally, a mother.
Firsthand epistles only Kathy had ever read. Isabel said she had no
knowledge of Ekaterina's correspondence and never saw any letters,
but she had been too young. However, she said she had an aunt who
had kept many of her parents' things. Or perhaps her grandfather,

who was still alive, might know the story and never bothered to tell her. She would check.

At last, Al got down to the most significant reason for his long voyage. "I have something else here for you, Isabel. I hope you use it wisely." Al handed her a check made out in United States currency for $312,479. The amount was equal to the value of one-third of Kathy's monetized stock portfolio, plus the accrued interest since the reading of her Will. When the translator told them how much that was in Russian rubles, Isabel nearly fainted. The Danilovs were suddenly rich. It was more money than Stepan could earn in five lifetimes.

Isabel smiled and said to Stepan, "Now Sasha can pursue her music, and we can send Konnie to a good school."

"And you, my wife," he added, "can stop doing laundry for the neighbors."

18   DECEMBER 23, 2003

New York City

After Peter hung up from talking to Al during his trip to Khabarovsk in the summer of 2001, he received digital photos. Isabel Danilova was, without question, Kathy's descendant, but it was Sasha, Kathy's great-granddaughter, that set Peter's eyes watering. Even in those electronic photos, he could see Kathy's grace, the curves of her body, the shape of her lips and eyes, and the color of her hair. In every way, Sasha was a young version of his beloved Kathy. And beyond every conceivable wish, Peter had been invited, along with his son's and Al's families, to attend Sasha's remarkable debut concert in New York. Noticeably frailer compared to two years earlier, but feeling strong, he decided he had to come east one more time. And in his seat at Carnegie Hall, Peter listened to Sasha sing.

And when he closed his eyes, he heard Kathy, his dear Ekaterina. And no doubt, he heard Anna, too.

After Sasha took her bows and left the stage, Peter remained seated. He told Al and his son, Ivan, he would be along shortly. Their families and the Danilovs were all going out to eat—The Russian Tea Room, of course. Peter had brought Kathy's Valday Bells to New York to give to Sasha at dinner. They belonged with her. He knew Kathy would approve. Peter sat there, alone, with the bells in his lap. The clean-up crew worked around him, sweeping and shuffling discarded programs. He was at peace and filled with happiness. As he gazed at the curtains drawn across the empty stage, he visualized Kathy, child of Valday, ringing her mother's bells, singing in the choir. With no doubt in his mind, he saw her performing on a grand stage for the hosts of Heaven. And when she stopped singing, the angelic multitude rose and gave her the standing ovation she always deserved.

THE END

AUTHOR'S NOTE

I knew *Ekaterina*. When I was old enough to understand, she told me stories about her life. Her anecdotes comprise numerous scenes in my tale. They range from cherishing her Russian heritage to loving classical music and fine clothes. She lived in Harbin and Shanghai in the 1930s, had an affair with a Japanese businessman resulting in an illegitimate child and survived by "doing what was necessary" in Shanghai. She was engaged to a man in the French Army, departed Shanghai shortly before December 7, 1941 and saw her best friend die in the bombing of Manila. Her stories included hiding underground in the mountains, marrying an Army officer in Manila not long after his wife died, and being shunned by his family. She was extorted by her husband's senior military officer, was fearful of J. Edgar Hoover's FBI, was highlighted in a major Atlanta newspaper, and witnessed the slow economic decline of her neighborhood. Significantly, she also had a long relationship with *Peter* after *Charles* died.

During my research, I learned *Ekaterina* could be aloof, stern, and set in her ways. But I also discovered she had always expressed love and thanks to *Charles*. She never remarried and never moved again until her dementia required full-time care. Her long-term neighbors said they liked her and never thought she was a communist. Upon her death, she bequeathed her car, dresses, music, and financial holdings as described—although the amount was somewhat less, it was substantial. The beneficiary granddaughter in Siberia indeed, surprised everyone.

As for *Ekaterina's* origins, I chose to have her come from Valday, setting the stage for the journey across the continent and adding a background to the lives of the thousands who were sent or who fled East. I used several sources for the trans-Siberian train ride, including *An Adventurous Journey: Russia-Siberia-China,* by Mrs. Alec-Tweedie, London, 1929, an enjoyable travelogue by a popular travel writer of the day. However, it may be likely the real *Ekaterina* was born in Harbin, but this remains a mystery. She never told me.

The exodus of Europeans and Americans from Shanghai in the years before December 1941 is well documented. Ship registries, such as Lloyds, also show which vessels were lost, where, and when. The *SS Tjipawan* never existed, but during the Pacific War, numerous commercial ships were lost with all hands, and incorrect reports were filed. The *SS Capillo,* owned by the United States Shipping Board, was bombed in Manila harbor on December 8, 1941, and others were destroyed off Corregidor on December 29.

The rise of communism precipitating the Red Scare of the 1950s, supported by Senator McCarthy, resulted in many people being sentenced to prison and ruined numerous other lives. The Berlin Wall, Soviet control of Eastern Europe, the assassinations of the 1960s—blamed to some extent, rightfully or wrongly, on communist influence—and the war in Vietnam compounded the concern of millions of Americans that far left-wing politics and philosophies needed to be held in check. One way to do so was "keeping watch" on potentially dangerous foreigners, a policy and practice common under J. Edgar Hoover's FBI, and ongoing since then. Similarly, many examples of police corruption continue to occur throughout the United States, allowing people such as the willfully ignorant *Elsa* and the greedy and uncaring *JJ Fuller* to live and thrive.

Lastly, the world is blessed by venues such as Carnegie Hall that serve as bastions of musical, operatic, and theatrical performances. More to the point, young voices, such as Laura Bretan of Chicago, Jordanian-American Emanne Beasha, and Jackie Evancho of Pittsburg offer aficionados and those less familiar with classical music their captivating talent, worthy of every significant stage. So why not *Ekaterina's* great-granddaughter, *Sasha Danilova?*

Thomas H. Brillat
January 13, 2023
Richmond, Rhode Island

ABOUT THE AUTHOR

 Thomas H. Brillat has been a naval officer, life insurance rep, coastal planner, commercial seaport harbormaster, Rainbow salesman (yes—Rainbows), square-rig sailor, oral storyteller, air-freight manager, non-profit executive, adult educator, and maritime museum professional. *Ekaterina* is his first novel.

Made in the USA
Middletown, DE
08 May 2023

30271121R00239